299

D0345577

LT. LEARY
COMMANDING

BOOKS IN THIS SERIES:
With the Lightnings
Lt. Leary, Commanding

BAEN BOOKS by DAVID DRAKE
Hammer's Slammers
The Tank Lords
Caught in the Crossfire
The Butcher's Bill
The Sharp End

Independent Novels and Collections
The Dragon Lord
Birds of Prey
Northworld Trilogy
Redliners
Starliner
Mark II: The Military Dimension
All the Way to the Gallows

The Belisarius Series: (with Eric Flint)
An Oblique Approach
In the Heart of Darkness
Destiny's Shield
Fortune's Stroke

The General Series: (with S.M. Stirling)
The Forge
The Hammer
The Anvil
The Steel
The Sword
The Chosen
The Reformer

The Undesired Princess and The Enchanted Bunny
(with L. Sprague de Camp)
Lest Darkness Fall and To Bring the Light
(with L. Sprague de Camp)
Enemy of My Enemy:
Terra Nova
(with Ben Ohlander)
Armageddon
(edited with Billie Sue Mosiman)

LT. LEARY
COMMANDING

DAVID DRAKE

Lt. Leary, Commanding

This is a work of fiction. All the characters and events portrayed in this book are fictional, and any resemblance to real people or incidents is purely coincidental.

Copyright © 2000 by David Drake

All rights reserved, including the right to reproduce this book or portions thereof in any form.

A Baen Books Original

Baen Publishing Enterprises
P.O. Box 1403
Riverdale, NY 10471
www.baen.com

ISBN: 0-671-57875-8

Cover art by Stephen Hickman

First printing, July 2000

Library of Congress Cataloging-in-Publication Data

Drake, David.
    Lt. Leary, commanding / by David Drake.
        p. cm.
    "A Baen Books original"—T.p. verso.
    ISBN 0-671-57875-8
    1. Interplanetary voyages—Fiction. I. Title: Lieutenant Leary, commanding. II. Title.

PS3554.R196 L78 2000
813'.54—dc21   00-031050

Distributed by Simon & Schuster
1230 Avenue of the Americas
New York, NY 10020

Production by Windhaven Press, Auburn, NH
Printed in the United States of America

10   9   8   7   6   5   4   3   2   1

DEDICATION

To my webmaster, cybrarian Karen Zimmerman,
who wasn't the model for Adele Mundy,
but might have been if I'd met her sooner.
(Of course, we'd have to work on her pistol shooting.)

ACKNOWLEDGMENTS

I guess one could say "the usual suspects" by this point.

Mark L. Van Name and Allyn Vogel took care of the series of computer events. (Did you know that files can become cross-linked on your hard drive? Well, at any rate, they could on mine.)

Dan Breen continues in curmudgeonly excellence as my first reader. There could be no better person for insights and scholarship.

When I'm working, I take up a lot of room and am frequently less than cheerful. I'm working most of the time. My wife, Jo, sticks with me; I really appreciate the fact.

AUTHOR'S NOTE

I'm using English and Metric weights and measures throughout *Lt. Leary, Commanding*, as I did in *With the Lightnings*. I wouldn't bother mentioning this, but the decision seems to concern some people. I'm doing it for the same reason that I'm writing the novel in English instead of inventing a language for the characters of future millennia to speak.

I'd like to note for those who're interested that the orders in Chapter Nine are a close paraphrase of those which sent the frigate USS *Congress* to Hawaii in 1845. Here as elsewhere, I prefer to borrow from reality rather than invent it.

David Drake
david-drake.com

When the skies are black above them,
and the decks ablaze beneath,
And the top-men clear the raffle with
their clasp-knives in their teeth.

—Rudyard Kipling

CHAPTER ONE

Lieutenant Daniel Leary rolled his uncle's wheelchair to the end of the catwalk and paused, gazing back at the corvette *Princess Cecile* nestled in the center of the graving dock. He turned the wheelchair. "Now that you've inspected her, Uncle Stacey," he said, "wouldn't you agree there's no finer ship in the RCN?"

The battleship *Aristotle* in the next bay lowered over them: seventy thousand tons empty, with a crew of two thousand and missile magazines sufficient for a day-long engagement. The eight-inch plasma cannon of the *Aristotle*'s defensive battery could not only divert incoming projectiles but also devour ships the corvette's size in rainbow cascades of stripped nuclei.

Daniel was as oblivious of the battleship as he was of the wisps of cirrus cloud in the high heavens. For him, the twelve-hundred ton *Princess Cecile* was the only ship in Harbor Three. He'd commanded her, after all. Commanded her and fought her and—by the grace of God and the best crew ever to come a captain's way—destroyed an Alliance cruiser of many times the corvette's strength.

"Didn't we, Adele?" Daniel said, forgetting how little of his previous thoughts had made it to his lips. He grinned over his shoulder at the severe-looking woman of thirty-one who'd joined him and Uncle Stacey on their excursion.

Adele Mundy smiled in response—it was hard not to smile when Daniel was full of happy enthusiasm, as he was at most times—but her expression gave no sign that she knew what he was talking about. Like Daniel she wore a 2nd Class RCN dress uniform, gray

1

with black piping. Her collars bore the crossed lightning bolts of a signals officer, a senior warrant rank with pay and allowances equal to those of a bosun.

Adele's handheld data unit slipped into a fitted pocket on her right thigh. That modification to her uniform was absolutely nonstandard and the sort of thing that would send an inspecting officer ballistic if it were noticed.

Daniel didn't even bother to wince any more. Adele without her data unit would be like Adele without hands, personally miserable and of no value to the RCN. Whereas with the unit—and with the little pistol, also nonstandard, nestled in a side pocket—neither Daniel nor Cinnabar ever had a better bulwark.

Adele Mundy was an RCN officer by grace of the Republic's warrant. By training and inclination she was an archival librarian, a task she'd performed with skill amounting to genius before circumstances required her to accept other duties. By birth, she was a Mundy of Chatsworth, one of the wealthiest and most politically powerful houses in the Republic before the Three Circles Conspiracy had forfeited the money and cost the head of every adult Mundy but one.

Adele had been at school off Cinnabar when the cycle of treason and proscriptions played itself out in blood. Distance had preserved her life; not her fortune, but she wasn't the sort to whom money meant much one way or the other.

For that matter, Daniel sometimes suspected that life didn't mean much to Adele either; but duty did, and craftsmanship. Daniel didn't try to remake his friends.

"She's a trim craft," Uncle Stacey said, assessing the corvette with a mind no less sharp for being confined to a wheelchair-bound body. Commander Stacey Bergen, the finest astrogator of his day, had opened or resurveyed half the routes in the *Sailing Directions for Ships of the Republic.* "I've never seen a Kostroman-built ship that wasn't as pretty as anything of her class, though some of them use lighter scantlings than I'd have chosen for anything coming out of my yard."

The old man cocked his head over his shoulder to catch his nephew's eye with the implied question.

"The frames and hull plating are at RCN specifications, Uncle Stacey," Daniel said quickly. "The only problem we've had in the conversion was that all the astrogational equipment is calibrated in Kostroman AUs instead of Sol standard like us and the Alliance. Granted of course that the *Sissie*'s a fighting corvette, not a dedicated survey ship built to accept stresses that'd turn a battleship inside out."

The *Princess Cecile*'s hull was a rough cylinder two hundred and thirty feet long and fifty-five feet wide, with bluntly rounded ends. Here in the graving dock she was clamped bow and stern by collars like the chucks of a gigantic lathe. They could rotate her into any attitude, so that the antennas that lined her hull in four rows of six each could be extended and canted throughout their range of motion.

Two twin four-inch plasma cannon provided the corvette's defensive armament in turrets offset toward the starboard bow and sternwards to port. Their bolts of charged particles could deflect incoming missiles by vaporizing portions of the projectile and converting that mass into slewing thrust. Offensively, a practiced crew in the *Princess Cecile* could launch her twenty missiles in pairs at one minute intervals. The crew which Daniel had brought from Kostroma was trained very well in that and every other aspect of war.

As a boy, Daniel had listened to Uncle Stacey and the naval friends who came to chat with him in the shipyard he ran after retirement. They'd talked of shifts in the Matrix, of sheared antennas, torqued hulls; of days at a time spent in the glare of Casimir radiation, picking a course where none was known before.

It was those tales, told by master astrogators to other masters of the art, that had led Daniel to join the RCN at age sixteen after the flaming row he'd had with his father, Corder. The Learys weren't a naval family: they were politicians, movers and shakers of the Republic, and never a one of them had risen higher than Corder Leary, Speaker Leary, himself.

Daniel laughed, surprising Adele and his uncle both. Grinning apologetically at their surprise he explained, "I was just thinking that six years on, there's no decision I'm more glad of than that I joined the RCN, but it could be that my reasons for making that decision had more to do with spiting my father than they did with making a name for myself."

"I've never noticed that the reasons people do things have much connection with how well or badly matters turn out," Adele said. "For example, I'm confident that my parents entered the Three Circles Conspiracy with the full intention of saving the Republic from men who couldn't be trusted with power."

She smiled. Adele gave the impression of being dispassionate about everything except knowledge, and then only knowledge in the form of marks on paper or electronic potentials. That wasn't true—the passion was there, Daniel knew, as surely as it was in his own explosive outbursts—but Adele's analysis would always be as cold and clean as the blade of a scalpel.

That was true even at times like this one, when Adele was analyzing the factors that led to the severed heads of every member of her family, including her ten-year-old sister, being displayed from Speaker's Rock.

"Your Lieutenant Mon's a good man," Stacey said. "Who did the yard assign for a supervisor? Archbolt, I suppose? Or did they give you Berol?"

"Yes, Archbolt," said Daniel, watching members of the *Princess Cecile*'s crew—the Sissies—clambering over the antennas with tool belts.

Harbor Three had a regular dockyard staff, but the strain of fitting out the fleet in anticipation of full-scale war with the Alliance had overstrained their capacity. There would have been jobs for three times the number of workmen, and there were no trained personnel to hire into the new slots.

One way around the problem was to use a vessel's own crewmen to perform all but the specialist yard work. Normally crews were paid off when their ship docked in its home port; now, a third of the *Princess Cecile*'s crew was at work refitting the vessel under the command of a ship's officer who also was kept on full pay.

Daniel, as the corvette's captain, would normally have been that officer. He'd passed the posting down to his first lieutenant, Lt. Mon, who would otherwise have been trying to support his family on half pay and no other resources. Mon had been a prisoner during the capture of the *Princess Cecile*; therefore he had no share of the prize money which the Navy Office would eventually adjudge for the ship.

Daniel had two eighths of the prize money coming to him.

That would be months or years in the future, but his bank was more than happy to advance him funds against the event. Daniel didn't have the expense of a wife, and he did have a great personal interest in meeting young women who might be impressed by a dashing naval officer. Leaving the full-time duties to Mon gave both officers what was best suited to their circumstances; an idyllic situation so far as Daniel was concerned.

"A trim ship," Uncle Stacey repeated, "and very well found."

In his present state of health, Stacey hadn't been able to walk the telescoping antennas and yards, so now he locked a pair of naval goggles down over his eyes to use their electronic enhancement to view them. They determined the position, attitude, and expanse of sails of charged dielectric fabric which created imbalances in Casimir radiation and drove the vessel through the Matrix.

Raising the goggles, the old man looked up at his nephew again. "Are they going to give you command again after she's commissioned, lad?" he asked.

Daniel shrugged. Civilians assumed the answer was obvious: of course the Hero of Kostroma would be returned to command. An RCN officer, however, knew there was much more to the question.

"I don't know," he said. "I performed well, but there're many skilled officers senior to me."

He smiled at a sudden thought. "Lieutenant Mon among them."

It was a grim joke, of course, because Mon would *never* have a command of his own. He didn't have the interest of a senior officer nor the sort of family money that would allow him to cut a figure socially and call attention to his undoubted abilities.

Worst of all, Mon had bad luck: he'd always been at the wrong place when there were prizes or honors to be won nearby. And there he differed from Daniel Leary, who'd been sent to Kostroma with no interest and no money, but whose good fortune had handsomely made up for those lacks.

"Short of Admiral Anston," Adele said dryly, "there's no better-known officer in the RCN today. You won't be the wonder of Cinnabar forever, but I think you still have some of your nine days left."

Daniel grinned, but he said, "That's not an unmixed blessing, you know, Adele. There'll be some who think I've carried myself a little higher since my return than an officer so junior ought to do. And they may be right."

Uncle Stacey nodded, his lips pursed. "You're young, Daniel, you're young, and they'll understand that. But still . . ."

"You carried yourself here with the same well-justified confidence that you showed on Kostroma," Adele said, raising her voice slightly. Her words had the precision of the teeth of a saw cutting timber to the proper fit. "The reason we're not in an Alliance prison—or dead—is that you never let any of us doubt that you were going to get us free. I have far too much respect for the organization of which I'm now an officer—"

She touched a fingertip to the rank flash on her collar with a thin smile.

"—to doubt that those in charge can also see the merit of a more extroverted personality than mine when the task involves leading others into battle."

A plume of steam expanded from a berth halfway across the port. The ground trembled for several seconds before the roar of a ship lifting off reached Daniel's party through the air. He slipped his goggles down to protect his eyes—the optics blocked UV completely and filtered white light to a safe intensity—and looked toward the event.

In truth, Daniel was glad to have an excuse not to respond. He was comfortable with the praise of his peers and generally amused by the compliments of civilians who hadn't the least notion of what they were talking about. Adele's words were disconcerting, though. He couldn't equate her cold analysis with the confused bumbling he remembered going through; to ultimate success, agreed, but that was due less to Daniel's own efforts than to luck and the expert assistance which Adele and so many others provided.

The ship lifted high enough that its plasma motors no longer licked a shroud of steam from the pool on which the vessel had floated. The plume of ions flaring from the thrusters was a rainbow beauty over which a long steel cigar continued to lift. She was an Archaeologist-class heavy cruiser, an old ship with a greater length-to-beam ratio than more modern vessels of the type. If

Daniel had wanted to, his goggles would have let him read the pennant number to identify her.

The plasma motors stripped atoms and voided them as ions to provide thrust. Any reaction mass would do, but water was ideal as well as being available generally on human-habitable worlds. Permanent harbor facilities were usually on seas or lakes which absorbed the plasma roaring from the thrusters at stellar heat and made refueling a matter of extending a hose.

When the vessel was well above the surface of the planet, she would switch to her High Drive, which used matter-antimatter conversion to provide sufficient inertial velocity to enter the Matrix. The High Drive was efficient but not perfect. If exhausted into an atmosphere, atoms of antimatter would flare and eat away the vessel itself.

The trio let the throb of the cruiser's liftoff drop back from its plateau before any of them tried to talk over it. Harbor Three was a huge installation with frequent movements, but the sound of a heavy ship taking off or landing made it impossible to speak in a normal voice anywhere within the perimeter.

Uncle Stacey took out his hundred-florin touchpiece—part of an issue struck twenty-two years before to mark the birth of Speaker Leary's son Daniel. He spun it so that the internal diffraction grating caught the light.

"People talk about how pretty Cinnabar coins are," he said as they watched the cruiser rise. "There's nothing as lovely as a well-tuned plasma motor, nothing. Unless maybe it's the way the universe shines on you as you drop into the Matrix."

"That reminds me," Adele said with a faint smile. "I need to talk to my banker again. It's time to make another draft on my prize account."

Uncle Stacey snorted. "Bankers!" he said. "The worst risk one of that lot faces is that the wine he orders with dinner won't be properly chilled."

He twisted his head one way, then the other to look back at Adele; she politely stepped out to the side and nodded to him.

"My brother-in-law interests himself in banking," Stacey said. "That's Daniel's father, you know. Though the lad's turned out an honor to his Bergen blood, *I* say."

His tone wasn't usually so sharp. Daniel would have been

surprised, but he knew that Uncle Stacey was in Xenos to render on behalf of Bergen and Associates, Shipfitters his quarterly accounts to the company's financial backer . . . who was Corder Leary.

Speaker Leary's financial interests were widespread. The only thing unusual about his share in Bergen and Associates was that the involvement was direct instead of being filtered through one or more holding companies. Daniel knew his father wasn't a cruel man, but he was extremely punctilious about power relationships, especially when kinship was involved. You always knew where you stood with Corder Leary; or, more precisely, where at his feet you were to kneel.

An open four-wheeled jitney was leaving the *Aristotle*, probably to pick up Daniel and his party. Aircars weren't permitted within Harbor Three for safety reasons: the risk of starships maneuvering in close proximity was great enough without adding aircraft to the mix. Heavy machinery and laborers at shift changes used the slow-moving overhead rail system circling the whole installation; branches led off the central line and snaked through sectors of six to ten bays, with shunts where carloads could wait until required.

The jitneys carried light cargo and small groups of people along the roadway beneath the rails. One had dropped Daniel and his party here at Dock 37, then whined off to make a delivery to the *Aristotle* in Dock 36 before returning. The driver claimed he was carrying urgent medical supplies in the hampers, but Daniel strongly suspected that liquor was arriving in trade for some item of the battleship's furnishings.

That was the way of the world, and Lt. Daniel Leary had no desire to complain. The *Princess Cecile*'s fire control system had been converted to RCN standard by means of similar off-book transactions.

A pair of limousines and a van with the pennon of the Harbor Administrator's office pulled up in front of Dock 37. Brass of some sort, obviously, but civilian brass by the look of the vehicles. Perhaps a Treasury delegation, checking on the way the Navy Office spent its appropriations? Though they wouldn't run to limousines, surely.

"Let's get you safely aboard the tram to home, Uncle Stacey,"

Daniel said. "As shorthanded as the RCN is with the number of ships going into service, there's a risk that some bosun'll snatch you up for a rigger and you'll be off-planet before you can catch your breath."

Uncle Stacey couldn't walk thirty feet unaided any more, though he seemed more resigned to his weakness than Daniel himself was. Some of Daniel's earliest memories were of being carried in his uncle's arms along the yards of a ship being refitted, hopping from spar to spar over what seemed like chasms—and probably were six feet or more. It had been a good upbringing for a boy who was to enter the RCN, not that anybody had imagined that at the time.

Daniel pushed the wheelchair down the concrete apron, glad to be off the catwalk which crossed the open dock to the corvette's main hatch. It was a steel grating and not much wider than the chair, though that didn't concern either Daniel or his uncle.

What had concerned Daniel was Adele. His signals officer— his friend—had many skills beyond those to be expected from one trained as a librarian, but a sense of balance was noticeably *not* one of those.

"Leary!" called one of the new arrivals. "By God, that's Daniel Leary, isn't it?"

Daniel turned, rotating the wheelchair to the side with one hand. That gave Uncle Stacey a clear view also instead of him trying to look over his shoulder in desperate isolation.

Mixed groups of civilians and senior officers in 1st Class uniforms were getting out of the limousines, but the speaker was the lieutenant in charge of the detachment of ratings from the van. He was of middling height with a florid face and a few extra pounds—like Daniel himself. Daniel found him half-recognizable but not really familiar.

"Tom Ireland, Leary," the fellow called, striding down the apron with his hand out to clasp Daniel's. "Two years ahead of you at the Academy, but in South Battalion while you were in North."

Good God, Ireland claiming his acquaintance! To the junior cadets upperclassmen at the Academy were generally aloof strangers, sometimes slavering monsters. Ireland had been in the former category, a vague presence to Cadet Daniel Leary; and Daniel Leary would have been less than the paving stones of the Quad to Ireland. Suddenly they'd become fellow schoolmates. . . .

"I heard about your little affair on Kostroma," Ireland said, seizing Daniel's hand and pumping it. Behind him the passengers from the limousines were drifting toward them with the sort of meaningful aimlessness of goats grazing across a field. "Well handled, I'll tell the world! Though you had a bit of luck come your way, it seems to me. Not so?"

"Very definitely so," Daniel said, feeling his lips form a smile hard enough to cut glass. "Permit me to introduce you to a great part of that luck, my signals officer, Mistress Mundy."

Ireland blinked with mild confusion; his little mustache twitched. If he'd noticed Adele at all it was as a signalman; a specialist, a *technician*, a category necessary for the proper functioning of the RCN but which operated on a different plane from commissioned officers like himself and Daniel.

"That's Mundy of Chatsworth, of course," Daniel added. "Death masks in the front hall from ancestors back to before the Hiatus, isn't that right, Adele?"

He was surprised at the anger which he hoped he covered with his bantering tone. Ireland had never harmed him at the Academy, and if he wanted to scrape acquaintance now with the Hero of Kostroma, well, that wasn't a terrible crime. Though flattery *had* begun to pall on Daniel from its constant repetition.

It was the comment about luck that had tripped a switch in Daniel's mind. Luck there'd been in plenty, and Daniel Leary would be the first to say that; but when the words came from a stranger who hadn't seen men die to make that luck a reality . . .

"*Those* Mundys?" Ireland said. The name would be familiar, though unless he were more politically attuned than the RCN encouraged its junior officers to be, he wouldn't remember the names and details of the Three Circles Conspiracy. "Ah, I see!"

Which of course he didn't; he just saw that he'd misjudged the status of Lt. Leary's companion.

Ireland started to extend his hand to Adele. Before the gesture was more than a hint, she crossed her arms behind her back and gave him an icily polite nod of greeting. "Pleased to meet you, Mr. Ireland," she said. "You're a tour guide for the Harbor Administrator, I gather?"

"I, ah . . . " Ireland said. He looked over his shoulder. The mixture of dress uniforms and still-more-splendid civilian garb had almost reached him. "Yes, I'm in charge of the escort for some officials from the Foreign Ministry and their liaison with the Navy Office. I, ah . . . they, that is, are showing the son of the President of Strymon around."

The dignitaries were on them. Ireland opened his mouth again, perhaps to introduce Daniel to the rank of dress uniforms, but the squat, jowly captain in front said, "Well, by my hope of a flag! Commander Bergen, isn't it? Mr. Vaughn, let me introduce you to the man who mapped a route to Strymon that cut three weeks sailing off the previous time!"

Uncle Stacey squeezed the arms of his chair. Daniel—and Adele to the other side, as smoothly as if they'd rehearsed the maneuver—each slid a forearm under the old man's hands and lifted him to his feet as soon as he'd transferred his grip.

"Young Wenslow, isn't it?" Stacey said with close to the old fullness in his voice. "You served under me on the *Queensland*."

"Senior midshipman and fourth lieutenant after Broker got his own command on Tuttel's World," agreed Wenslow—no longer young, and as Daniel knew, secretary of the RCN's planning council. He drew forward the slim young man at his side. "Delos Vaughn, allow me to introduce you to Commander Stacey Bergen. Commander Bergen has forgotten more about astrogation than anyone else in the RCN ever knew!"

Vaughn extended his right hand and shook Uncle Stacey's, showing a care for the old man's frailty that Daniel approved with a minuscule nod. Vaughn wore a severely tailored suit, but the cloth from which it was cut formed a series of chevrons which changed from red to gold alternately depending on the angle of the light. He was as hard to focus on as the flare of a plasma exhaust.

Apart from that he had a handsome, thirty-year-old face and an engaging smile. Three of the other civilians wore clothes of similar style and flamboyant materials; the rest, like the naval officers, were Cinnabar nationals.

"I'm honored to meet you, Commander," Vaughn said, speaking Universal with a better Xenos accent than Daniel—who'd been raised on the Learys' country estate of Bantry—could've managed. "You must have known my father. Your skilled explorations truly made the Sack a part of the greater universe for the first time since the Hiatus."

"President Leland Vaughn," Uncle Stacey said. He was standing without support, now, gaining strength from his memories; though Daniel and Adele kept close to either side in case of sudden weakness. "I sat at his right hand at the banquet on our arrival. Quite clear on the value of exploration for the trade that makes Strymon great. He's keeping well, I hope?"

"My late father, I'm afraid I should have said," Vaughn said with a deprecating rotation of his left hand. "My uncle, Callert Vaughn, succeeded him within a year of my arrival on Xenos, and now that Callert too has passed on, the presidency is in the hands of his daughter, Pleyna."

Momentarily Vaughn's tone became more sardonic than whimsical as he added, "Formally, that is. One assumes that a twelve-year-old is largely guided by her tutor, Friderik Nunes. I recall Nunes from when I last was on Strymon, fifteen years ago. He wasn't of much account . . . then, at any rate."

The hardness left Vaughn's expression, though now that Daniel had seen it once, he knew that it remained a part of the man himself. Delos Vaughn was more than a young foreigner living high in the fleshpots of Cinnabar—though he was probably that as well. Daniel would be the last man to suggest that a taste for liquor and amiable women precluded a man from taking a serious attitude toward his profession.

And what *was* the profession of Mr. Delos Vaughn?

Strymon had risen to prominence in the Sack, its region of space, following the thousand-year Hiatus from interstellar travel at the end of mankind's first flush of colonization. Strymon had regained links with Earth itself more quickly than most worlds; but, as the intricacies of sailing through the Matrix were laboriously rediscovered, the Sack became a backwater.

Cinnabar expanded its sphere of influence and that influence hardened into something not so very different from an empire; Strymon tried to compete. Twice the competition was military; the RCN had crushed Strymon's forces both times.

Distance from Cinnabar—two months of travel for a merchant ship and half that even for well-found naval vessels—preserved a degree of independence for Strymon, but by treaty her navy was now limited to light craft suitable for suppressing the endemic piracy of the three-star Selma Cluster nearby.

In halving the travel time between Strymon and Cinnabar, Uncle Stacey had done the Vaughns and their subjects a doubtful favor. Still, by forcing Strymon to realize Cinnabar's hegemony, it no doubt prevented the weaker power from wasting its substance in a third hopeless war. Certainly Delos Vaughn seemed friendly enough to the man who'd brought the threat of an RCN punitive expedition weeks closer to his planet.

"If it's not presumptuous of me, Commander," Vaughn continued, "may I ask if this is the Daniel Leary of whom we've begun to hear so much?"

"Mr. Vaughn," Uncle Stacey said, "may I present my nephew, Lieutenant Daniel Leary. He's a credit to the Bergens, though he doesn't bear our name."

Vaughn's handshake was firm, pausing just short of the pressure that would have meant he'd seriously tried to crush Daniel's hand. Daniel's eyes narrowed slightly. Vaughn was testing something more subtle than strength: he was determining whether Daniel was *willing* to try conclusions with a wealthy, well-connected foreign noble.

Daniel grinned faintly. When he was sixteen, he'd broken with his father in a shouting match that rattled the windows of the Leary townhouse. After that, neither Delos Vaughn nor Hell itself had any terrors for Daniel. He squeezed back till Vaughn released his hand.

"And I believe I heard you identify this officer as Ms. Mundy," Vaughn went on, offering his hand demurely, fingertips only, to make it clear that he wasn't going to attempt to bully the slightly built woman. "Allow me to say how pleased I am to see members of two of the noblest houses in the Republic standing together in the uniform of the Republic's staunchest defense."

There was no doubt from Vaughn's phrasing that he knew Speaker Leary had pushed through the proscriptions which crushed the Three Circles Conspiracy and with it the Mundys of Chatsworth. That wasn't knowledge to be expected of a foreigner.

"Delos, your schedule for this evening . . . " said one of his aides, a dark-haired man older than Vaughn who'd been fidgeting in the background ever since the conversation started. "If we're to inspect the . . . ?"

Delos Vaughn displayed the same imperturbable gloss as the throat of a plasma thruster fresh from the shipping crate. People like that seemed to make the folks around them worry double-time.

Now Vaughn shrugged easily. He gave Daniel and his companions a "you-know-how-it-is" grin and said, "Yes, Tredegar, I'm not forgetting that the caterer and the Gardens' representative will be coming by for final approval tonight."

Returning his attention to Daniel he went on, "I wonder, Lieutenant Leary, if you'd care to guide us through your command here. I wouldn't have thought of imposing, but since you're present . . . ?"

Daniel wouldn't claim to be a politician, but Corder Leary's son couldn't help but have learned that no matter is simple when there are human beings on both sides of the equation. It was an awareness which had proved useful in his dealings with women, also.

"Why, under other circumstances I'd be delighted to show you about the *Princess Cecile*," Daniel said with a smile of regret. "I'm afraid I have other commitments, however."

Uncle Stacey was trembling with fatigue; Adele, thank goodness, was easing him down into the wheelchair. The officers in Vaughn's own party didn't look pleased at the notion of being upstaged by a junior lieutenant. And as a matter of RCN regulation, not to mention fairness, the officer commanding the *Princess Cecile* was—

"Lieutenant Mon, the present captain, will be more than happy to do the job, though," Daniel continued, gesturing toward the corvette. "As for myself, I'm on half pay at the pleasure of the Navy Board for now."

Vaughn chuckled, then bowed to put a period to the discussion. "Perhaps I can hear about your adventures at some other time, Lieutenant," he said, allowing Captain Wenslow's slow movement to ease him toward the catwalk. "It'll have to be soon, though, I'm sure. The chiefs of your navy will never permit an officer of your demonstrated abilities to remain unemployed for long."

Adele started the wheelchair briskly toward the waiting jitney; it looked rather forlorn among its larger, flashier fellows. Daniel glanced over his shoulder as he took the wheelchair's handles himself a little farther down the apron. Vaughn was negotiating the catwalk with aplomb, but one of his aides and two Foreign Ministry officials had frozen at the edge of the dock like a trio of statues.

"The poor devil's an exile, I suppose," Uncle Stacey said as they neared the jitney. "Brought here as a hostage for his father's good behavior. Strymon isn't as bad the Selma Cluster next door to it—the Pirate Cluster, you know—but his life still wouldn't be worth a zinc florin if he tried to go home now."

"He seems a personable fellow," Daniel offered as he paused for Adele to open the door. He might have to hand his uncle into the vehicle; meeting the delegation had been as much of a strain on Stacey as the whole rest of the outing. "I wonder why he wanted to see the *Princess Cecile*, though?"

"Mr. Vaughn didn't strike me as a man who's often bored," Adele said without emphasis as she walked around to the other side where she could help if needed, "or one who gathers information without a good reason. Which is a good reason for me . . ."

Uncle Stacey lurched onto the bench seat without touching the arm Adele crooked for him to grip. Daniel began folding the wheelchair to set in the roof cargo rack.

" . . . to learn what I can about Mr. Vaughn, I think," Adele concluded.

Chapter Two

A monorail car stopped within moments to carry Daniel and his uncle in the direction of Xenos West, but Adele Mundy would have thirty minutes on the platform before a car arrived for her. City Center wasn't a popular destination for those leaving Harbor Three by public transportation. Laborers and ships' crewmen stayed either in barracks near the port or in tenements ranged on the city's outskirts. Senior officers, let alone dignitaries like Delos Vaughn's party, arrived and left the harbor in personally owned monorail cars if they even used the system rather than aircars.

The wait wasn't a hardship. As soon as her companions had departed on the rising whine of an electric motor, Adele drew out her personal data unit and started to learn what could be known about Delos Vaughn.

Until very recently the only parts of Adele's life she would've called happy were those she'd spent finding and organizing information . . . which to be sure was more time than she devoted to any other pursuit. The place Adele's body slept had never been of much concern to her, and since the Proscriptions she hadn't had a home outside her head.

A heavy starship lifted from the pool in the center of the harbor, shaking everything for miles around as its thousands of tons rose from a plume first of steam, then the flaring iridescence of hydrogen ions when the plasma motors no longer licked the water's surface. Adele was barely conscious of the event, adjusting her control wands in the precise patterns that guided her search.

16

The personal data unit was a featureless rectangle, four inches by ten inches, and half an inch thick. Its display was holographic, cued to the focus of the user's eyes. Though the unit had a virtual keyboard or could respond to voice commands, Adele preferred the speed and flexibility of the slim wands. She held them at the balance between the thumb and first two fingers of either hand. An expert in their use—and Adele was that if ever there was one—could access information almost as fast as her brain could frame the questions.

Delos Vaughn of Strymon, age twenty-nine Earth years; sole offspring of Leland Vaughn, former President of Strymon. Strymon presidency, a lifetime elective office with candidacy and franchise limited to members of the Shipowning class. Shipowning class: a group of originally thirty-seven, but now expanded to over a hundred, families; actually owning a starship is neither a necessary nor a sufficient criterion for membership in the Shipowning class. . . .

Adele's little unit had a considerable storage capacity, but its real value on a developed world was to give her access to other databases. Here on Cinnabar she was linked—through the monorail control circuit—to the central records computer in the Navy Office, which she used as her base unit.

It had occurred to Adele as she set up the connection on her first day back on Cinnabar that she probably could've gotten authorization to use the system if she'd gone through some of the channels available to her. She'd decided it was simpler to circumvent the electronic barriers to what she was doing than it would've been to plow through bureaucratic inertia. Besides, it amused Adele to break rules when she'd spent all her previous life obeying them.

In the past month Adele had gained Daniel Leary for a friend and the whole Republic of Cinnabar Navy for home and family. Between them they gave her a remarkable feeling of security.

She grinned as she shifted back to another aspect of the problem she'd set herself. *Delos Vaughn, arrived on Cinnabar aboard the RCS* Tashkent *as a guest of the Republic. . . .*

A car stopped in front of her with a clatter and squeal. She ignored it as she had the arrival of a party of laborers on the platform, shuffling heavy boots and talking about a ball game.

"Hey, Chief?" a laborer called.

Primary residence on Holroyd Square, Xenos, with secondary residences—

A different voice bellowed, "Lady, ain't this one yours?"

Adele's mind rose shatteringly from depths of pure knowledge where she preferred to live; it reformed in the present. An empty car stood in front of her. The lighted banner over the open door read ITY ENTER. Fifty yards down the rail, slowing as it approached the platform, was the Manine Village car that would haul home the laborers, crammed in as tightly as books in dead storage.

"Thank you," she called, stowing her data unit in its pocket with the ease of long habit and a precise mind. She stepped aboard the car just before the door closed; touched the destination plate over the Pentacrest—the map's clear cover was smeared almost illegible by the fingers of previous users, so Adele had to peer in doubt before she made her choice; and then sat back on one of the pair of facing benches as the car rocked into motion.

She was alone in a car in which twelve could sit and thirty ride in some degree of comfort. She might have taken out her data unit again, but she decided to experience the trip instead. She wasn't going to enjoy the ride, but there were things she could usefully learn about Xenos after her fifteen years of exile.

Besides, she was punishing herself for not noticing the car's arrival. She could've spent all afternoon there on the platform, lost in personal researches when she had business for others to accomplish. Adele had never been one to shirk her responsibilities, but the very degree of focus that made her effective sometimes got in the way of carrying out social obligations.

Not that this meeting was social except in the general sense of being part of Adele's involvement in human society.

The car swerved and squealed along the serpentine track serving a section of three docks. The *Aristotle* dominated the whole area, an outward-curving wall of steel as viewed from the car's grimy windows. Even if Adele craned her neck, she couldn't have seen the midpoint where the curve of the battleship's cylindrical hull reversed.

In some places the shipfitters had removed plates, giving glimpses of tubing, vast machinery, and once an open space the size of the Senate Chamber. It would be daunting to a civilian and was impressive even to Adele, who was beginning to look at the world with the eyes of a naval officer.

A warship was a community. The *Aristotle* was a town of some size, with a complex street system and rituals shared only with similar towns. Its population would be standoffish with strangers, even strangers who wore the same uniform.

But the same was true of the *Princess Cecile* despite the corvette's lesser volume and crew. People went to and from their bunks and their duty stations in a certain way, the same way every time, because there was no physical room for individualism and in a crisis there would be no time for confusion.

Crises were common on a warship. Action against enemy forces was rare, but the universe was a constant opponent before which Alliance fleets paled to insignificance. Naval architects crammed as much heavy, powerful equipment as they could into each hull. The machinery was dangerous even when it worked properly, and when it malfunctioned—which it did as regularly as any other human contrivance—those in the cramped spaces nearby had to react precisely if they and their fellows were to survive.

Adele smiled, remembering the times during the voyage from Kostroma when a spacer had slung her down a passageway in zero gee or even wrapped her in flexible netting to keep her safe—and out of the way. If Adele put her mind to it, she could probably learn the various calls and responses expected of an RCN spacer. She doubted that she'd ever be able to transfer that intellectual knowledge into motor skills, however.

Nor did she need to, so long as she was part of an experienced crew who'd take care of her. One spacer, come to the RCN from a farm on North Cape, had remarked that she was clumsy as a hog on ice as he snatched Adele away from the mechanism of a rotating gun turret.

Adele knew she amused her fellow crewmen, but they didn't laugh at her. They'd all seen the way she danced through the maze of a communications screen; and the ones who'd seen her shoot told the others about that, too. No, they didn't laugh at Officer Mundy.

The car bumped and chattered over joints in the track. The vehicle had been steamed with disinfectant in the recent past—the odor clung to the benches' dimpled surfaces—but it was still scratched and grimy.

Adele had never thought about public transportation in her youth. The Mundys had private cars to be hooked onto rails, for Mistress Adele and the servants who accompanied her to the Library of Celsus or wherever else her studies took her. Less wealthy nobles summoned public cars. Their servants and retainers then emptied ordinary citizens out of the vehicle so that the master could ride surrounded only by those who owed him allegiance.

Displaced passengers could wait for another car to arrive, irritated but not particularly angry. The citizens of Cinnabar expected their leaders to be proud folk. However else would they be able to properly represent the Republic to the folk of lesser worlds?

Adele's car jolted sideways onto a shunt serving a rank of modern apartment blocks with brick facings and swags molded to look like carved limestone. On Kostroma carving had still been done by hand.

Three housewives got on, carrying rolled shopping baskets and wearing hats with long, soft brims. One of them touched the destination plate as they continued a conversation begun on the platform. The car accelerated slowly up the shunt, paused for a gap in the line of vehicles now using the rail, then groaned as the drive motors exerted maximum effort to get back into traffic.

They settled into place, thirty yards behind one car, thirty yards ahead of another. Adele tried to guess where the women came from. Not Cinnabar, certainly. They were speaking a language that was neither a Cinnabar dialect nor Universal, and their fluidly attractive costume wasn't native to Cinnabar either.

Xenos had become a microcosm of the whole Cinnabar empire. Adele could access a rental list from the apartment building where the women boarded. She could then match the frequency of names with those of various worlds protected by the Republic, giving her a high probability of identifying the women's planet of origin.

Or of course she could ask them; and watch their faces freeze, and wait for one of them to answer in a voice either dead with fear or shrill, trying with anger to cover that fear—*She's in uniform. Why does she want to know? What does it mean?* But they would answer.

Adele smiled faintly; at life, at herself. They wouldn't believe it was merely curiosity, useless information being gathered by a person to whom nothing had use except information.

Half a mile from the apartments the car pulled into another shunt. The ground floors of the nearby buildings were given over to expensive shops, while the windows of the floor above were stenciled with business logos.

The housewives got off and were replaced by a score of officeworkers dressed in styles as stratified as those of the RCN. The one senior clerk wore a jacket with wide fur cuffs, showing that she didn't need to use her hands. The clothes of her underlings grew brighter with each step down in status; the trio of messenger boys chattered together like warblers in yellow and green and azure tawdriness.

The car staggered into motion again, sluggish with its load though not quite full. Close to the city center the cars ran slower than in the suburbs, so they bounced back onto the main line directly despite the traffic.

A woman sat next to Adele, talking with animation to the companion on her other side. The man standing in front of them joined in the conversation, his calf brushing Adele's knees as the vehicle swayed.

When Adele was last on Cinnabar, she couldn't have imagined being a part of this scene. Literally: she wouldn't have had the data to visualize being jostled and crowded on a public conveyance. How matters had changed. . . .

Not necessarily for the worse. She'd learned many things through disgrace and poverty that she never would have known in the ordinary course of things. She smiled. And she'd gained a family and a friend more trustworthy than those at the apex of power—people like her own parents and Corder Leary—would ever know.

The car groaned to a halt again. They'd reached the district ringing the Pentacrest, where the lesser nobility owned houses and rented ground-floor space to expensive shops. A group—a gang— of servants pushed their way into the car. Several of them held the doors open as their fellows chivied those already aboard out onto the platform.

Their garments were gray and bright green in horizontal stripes. That would make them Tanisards, a minor house which hadn't had a member in the Senate until the last century. All of them were in the full livery of underlings. Senior servants like the majordomo and his/her section heads would wear business suits with only collar flashes to announce their affiliation.

Adele squirmed to look out the window at her back. More servants waited to board, but no member of the house was present: these *servants* were clearing the car for their personal whim.

A husky youth—they were all young, not surprisingly—stood squarely in front of Adele with two of his fellows at his elbows. He grinned in an attempt to look threatening, but there was a degree of caution in his expression. Adele was alone, but the RCN was a very large organization.

Adele remained seated with her left hand in her pocket. "If you touch me, scum," she said in a clear voice, "your master will answer for your presumption on the field of honor!"

"What?" said the Tanisard. He'd expected *something* when the woman didn't scuttle away from his advance but not that particular threat, delivered with such absolute conviction in an upper-class accent.

"And while that's happening," Adele continued, feeling the tremble of barely controlled rage in her voice, "a detachment from my ship will be leveling Tanisard House. That won't concern you, because you'll have died here as you stand."

The Tanisard glanced to his friends—and found they'd backed away. He lowered his eyes and did the same, snarling at the fellow servant who jostled him when the car rocked into motion again.

There was only one more shunt before the City Center terminus. The car whirred past it without slowing. Adele rode in a clear portion of a vehicle otherwise crowded; the Tanisards kept their backs to her. Her lips smiled, but her eyes were empty and a red rage filled her mind. She visualized Bosun Ellie Woetjans leading every member of the *Princess Cecile*'s crew who was still on Cinnabar; with hammers and come-alongs, and very likely a section of mast to batter down the door.

Tanisards! How dare they?

The car reached the great roundabout of Pentacrest Vale, paused, and pulled into a shunt as the car that had just loaded there reentered the main line. A score of those waiting tried to board before the present passengers had disembarked, but the furious Tanisards rammed them back like the jet from a spillway. Well-justified fear had kept them from trying conclusions with the lone warrant officer, but they were too young to accept what had happened with philosophical resignation.

Adele followed closely in the Tanisards' wake, using the anger she'd engendered to shield her from the worst of the crowd's buffeting. She smiled faintly: this was almost like having servants again.

She'd never thought much about the servants when she was a girl on Cinnabar. Between Chatsworth Major and the townhouse there must have been a staff of a hundred or more, but they had less conscious impact on Adele than her bedroom furniture did.

Still, they'd existed. Even on public transit Adele would never have been faced with anything like this, because the Mundy retainers escorting her would have cleared the Tanisards out with the same ruthless unconcern as they'd have ousted dogs who'd somehow gotten into the car.

Tanisards block the path of a Mundy? Not till the sky falls!

The sky *had* fallen on the Mundys; fallen within days of when Adele boarded the packet that carried her to Blythe to continue her education in the Academic Collections there. Blythe was a core world of the Alliance of Free Stars, but what did that matter to Adele? She was a librarian, a member of that higher aristocracy of knowledge which cared nothing for mere politics.

As it turned out, politics had mattered a great deal.

The Speaker's Rock was a granite outcrop whose naturally level top had been improved by the first settlers; it stood at the west end of Pentacrest Vale. Adele edged out of the ruck around the transport terminus and eyed the Rock critically. Fifteen years ago the heads of her father, her mother, and her ten-year-old sister, Agatha, had hung from it in mesh bags to be viewed by all those who chose to do so.

There were many other heads as well, most of whom had as little to do with a conspiracy as Agatha did. Adele herself would have been there, save for the whim of sailing schedules. Political realities don't care whether their victims feel superior to them.

Because she'd found herself looking at the Rock with new eyes,

Adele paused to survey the whole setting for what was in a way the first time. Even before she reached age ten, she'd spent more of her waking hours on the Pentacrest than she had in the Mundy townhouse; but she'd never looked at it the way a stranger would, taking in its magnificence instead of simply accepting it the way fishes do the sea through which they swim.

The buildings on the five hills framing the Vale shone with marble, polished granite, and bronze. The only exception was the Old Senate House which had burned three centuries before during the Succession Riots. The shell of concrete with brick accents remained as a relic of Xenos—and Cinnabar—before the Hiatus.

The present Senate House embraced and towered above the original. The business of a planet had been conducted in the older building; the new one served an empire. As Adele watched, builders were working on an additional fourth floor in place of the Senate Roof Garden.

Before the Succession Riots, the palaces of wealthy families had covered the slopes of Dobbins Hill and a part of the Divan, on the south and southeast margins of the Vale. Most of those structures, that of the Mundys included, had burned with the Senate House. Rebuilding had taken place at a safer distance from the Vale, where political protest generally took form.

Now, even the palaces surviving from the time of the Riots had been converted to government use. The entire Pentacrest was given over to structures which either carried out the work of the Republic or vaunted the Republic's power.

Adele made her way through the crowd, around the statues and other monuments studding the Vale like tucks in upholstery. A juggler performed with burning torches while an animal resembling a bipedal armadillo paced a circle about him, holding up a hat for donations. A woman with the flying hair of a Maenad shouted the truths of her revelation—amusingly to Adele, from the shade of a stele commemorating Admiral Duclon. Duclon, a hero of the First Alliance War, was reputedly the most profane man ever to wear an RCN uniform.

The Church of the Redeeming Spirit stood on Progress Hill. Students filled both bays of the domed portico sheltering the foot of the stairs serving it, declaiming under the eyes of their rival rhetoric professors. As Adele passed between the groups, the girl to her left trilled, " . . . nor could the Republic long survive!" while the boy to the left boomed hoarsely, " . . . nor can the Republic long survive!"

Adele wondered whether they'd been set the same proposition or if chance had merely doubled an oratorical commonplace. She wasn't curious enough to listen for more; and anyway, time was short. Briskly she climbed the broad treads. They were hewn from hard sandstone, but nonetheless the feet of a millennium of passersby had polished them.

How would the Pentacrest look to a visitor from Rodalpa, say, or an even more rural world like Kerrace? Would he be impressed, or would it seem the mad chaos of an overturned ants' nest?

To Adele, sophisticated and dispassionate but not even now a stranger, the Pentacrest was the most amazing sight of her personal experience. It made her—unwillingly and amused by her own sentimental weakness—proud to be a citizen of Cinnabar.

The stairs mounted the face of Progress Hill steeply. Every generation or so, some politician moved to put in an elevator. The proposal was always defeated on the twin grounds of tradition and fear of defacing the Pentacrest. Retainers carried members of most wealthy families, and citizens in more moderate circumstances could hire a chair and two husky laborers to bear it.

Adele's mouth quirked a wry smile. The Mundys had courted the popular vote by walking on their own feet so long as health permitted them to. Her father would have said he supported the people as a matter of principle; and no doubt he did. But in the end principle boiled down to personal power, as surely for Lucius Mundy as it did for Corder Leary; and it was the Mundys whose associates—not Lucius himself, of that Adele was certain—took Alliance money to further their plans.

The open staircase ended in a terrace eighty feet above the Vale. Several of the city government offices were located here, their facades set back enough that they couldn't be seen from below. An archway enclosing more stairs zigzagged across the face of the hill, leading to the nave of the church and the wings flanking the main courtyard.

Adele stepped into the tunnel, ignoring the beggars around the entrance. Church ushers—guards—prevented mendicants from climbing farther into the complex, so they clustered here on the lower parterre. Adele knew what it was to be poor, but she wasn't wealthy now; and the sympathy for the poor that the political members of her family had shown as a matter of policy had died with them during the Proscriptions.

Electroluminescent strips along the axis of the tunnel's roof cast a cool glow over the interior. Mosaics made from glass chips, sometimes with foil backing, lined the walls. The images portrayed the settlement of Cinnabar in the third wave of human expansion.

The first colonists built with slabs of stabilized dirt extruded by vast machines carried in the bellies of four starships. In the artist's rendering, bladed tractors crawled across a forested landscape, leaving behind them fields green with human crops.

But the tractors and the furnaces forming construction material wore out. Later buildings were of wood, stone, and concrete, because Cinnabar's industry was incapable of repairing the equipment which had come from Earth. Cattle imported for meat and milk drew the plows.

Because the colony was less than a generation old when the Population Wars began, Cinnabar wasn't dragged into the fighting as a participant. The complete collapse of interstellar transport threw the planet onto her own weak resources, but she escaped the rain of redirected asteroids which wreaked cataclysmic destruction on the more developed worlds—Earth herself foremost among the victims.

There were perhaps more humans alive in the universe today than there had been at the start of the Population Wars, but the most populous single planet had only a fraction of the numbers which had caused the Earth government to pursue a policy of forcing its excess on daughter worlds because sending out further organized colonies would have been too expensive.

The population of the few remaining habitable portions of Earth was modest. In a manner of speaking, Adele thought with a cold smile, Earth's policy had achieved its stated objective.

The final panels at the tunnel's upper end showed the rebirth of space travel on Cinnabar. To the left, a multistage rocket rose on a plume of chemical flame; to the right, a starship using rediscovered principles spread its sails, slipping from the sidereal universe in a haze of Casimir radiation.

Adele stepped into daylight again. The church rose before her in polished splendor; if she turned, she would look out over the length of Pentacrest Vale to the notch between Dobbins Hill and the Castle, with the western suburbs of Xenos visible as far as the eye could see.

A starship was rising from Harbor Three. It was huge, though despite wearing the uniform of the RCN Adele didn't pretend to be able to identify vessels.

She sighed and walked across the marble pavers to the cantilevered gateway of the Library of Thomas Celsus, which filled both levels of the church's west portico. On the pediment was a statue of the founder—business agent to Speaker Ramsey, the unchallenged ruler of the Republic two centuries in the past—offering a scroll to the People, represented as a woman in flowing robes.

The Celsus served as the national collection and was the greatest library on Cinnabar. When Adele was nine, her tutor had told her that the Celsus was the foremost repository of knowledge in the human universe. Adele had immediately used the resources of the library to check his statement—and learned there were several collections on the older worlds of the Alliance which could put the Celsus to shame.

Adele had immediately ordered the man out of her sight with a fury that shocked her parents and frightened him—rightly, because at that age she might well have shot him if he'd attempted to justify his falsehood. He'd lied to her out of patriotism; error has no right to exist!

The usher inside the bronze doors nodded warmly to Adele. She blinked in surprise. "Fandler, isn't it? Good to see you still here."

The usher stepped out from his kiosk so that he could bow properly to her. "Good to see *you*, Ms. Mundy. All of us here at the Celsus were afraid something had happened to you during the late unpleasantness."

"Nothing worth mentioning, Fandler," Adele said. That was true enough, in absolute terms—what human activity *is* really worth mentioning?—and true also relative to those whose heads had decorated the Speaker's Rock.

She strode on through the cool rotunda, her steps echoing. It really was like coming home.

Banks of data consoles, separated from one another by panels of soundproofing foam for modest privacy, lined the tables of the wings on either side of the rotunda. There were three hundred and twelve consoles; there had been when Adele last entered the Celsus, at any rate, and it all appeared the same. Forty or so were occupied at the moment.

She walked to the desk across from the entrance, glancing down at the pavement tessellated in bands of soft grays and blues. It hadn't changed since the day Adele Mundy left Cinnabar.

She herself had changed, though.

Clerks sat behind the counter, working at consoles of their own. A page sorted volumes from a large table onto a cart, looking up at the sound of Adele's footsteps.

The official at the desk flanking the passage to the stacks of hard copy within the building was only a few years older than Adele; she'd never met him. His eyes glanced from the naval uniform to her face as she approached, his expression giving nothing away.

Adele handed him the access chip instead of inserting it into the reader herself. It was the one she'd carried with her to Blythe; she had no idea whether it would still work.

The official glanced at the number engraved on the flat. His eyebrows raised. He set the chip on his desk and stood.

"Ms. Adele Mundy?" he said, offering her his right hand. "I'm Lees Klopfer, Third Assistant Administrator. I've followed your work at the Academic Collections. We're honored to have you here."

Adele shook Klopfer's hand firmly, feeling a little disconcerted. So far as she could tell, the man was quite genuine. Only a guilty conscience made her wonder if he'd been told to greet her in that fashion—and if so, by whom?

The words "guilty conscience" raised another image in Adele's mind: a boy lurching backward, his duelling pistol flying from his hand; his brains a fluid splash in the air behind him.

Something of that image must have shown in her eyes, because Klopfer straightened with surprise and with perhaps a touch of fear. "Ms. Mundy?" he said. "If I gave offense, I assure you I—"

"No, no, not at all," Adele said, doing her best to force a smile. She probably looked as if she were being crucified! "Just a touch of an old pain."

Quite true: the pain of remembering the first person she'd killed. No longer the only person, not by a considerable number. Oh, yes, Adele Mundy had changed—and not even she was cynical enough to believe that she'd changed for the better.

Klopfer returned the chip to her. "You have complete access, of course, Ms. Mundy," he said. "If there's anything I or the staff can do to help, of course let us know."

"Thank you," she said as she entered the passage to the stacks, "I certainly will."

Klopfer's enthusiasm *had* to be genuine. It was odd to be honored again as a librarian, though that was the profession to which she'd devoted her whole life until the past few months. More recently compliments she'd received were for her ability to decrypt coded files, to explore and reroute communications pathways—and to fire a pistol with a skill unmatched by any of those who had faced her.

In another life Adele Mundy might have spent her whole existence in this library or a greater one, surrounded by knowledge and oblivious of her lack of friends. Well, service with the RCN didn't keep her from gaining and organizing knowledge. As for the other, she'd now rather die than lose the awareness that Daniel Leary trusted her implicitly with his life and honor, because they were friends.

She climbed the slotted steel stairs to the fourth level of the stacks, then turned left through art history . . . physics and cosmology . . . engineering. Pages wandered by, glancing at her with mild interest. Naval uniforms are never common in the heart of great libraries.

At the end of the aisle were rooms looking out through the upper colonnade to the main courtyard of the church. Cataloguing had the bank to the east; the five doors there were open, and the sound of chatting clerks drifted into the collection. On the west were a score of smaller rooms reserved for scholars visiting the stacks.

A pair of men stood facing the stacks while their eyes searched every other direction. They were making a half-hearted effort at pretending to be pages. As well dress Adele in a tutu and claim she was a ballet dancer!

The older of the pair nodded to her. She ignored them—she didn't need a guard's permission to do as she pleased in what

had been her second home—and tapped on the door with a stencilled 6. A poster was taped over the inside of the little window.

Bernis Sand, a stocky woman of sixty, dressed in plain but
very expensive good taste, opened the thin door. There was a
second chair inside along with the spartan desk and worksta-
tion, cramping the cubicle even more than usually would have
been the case.

Adele felt a surge of nostalgia. She'd spent years closeted with
a tutor in this cubicle and the others in the rank, learning the
most important part of an education: *how* to learn.

Now she was getting further lessons; this time from the head
of the Republic's intelligence service.

"You're looking fit, mistress," Mistress Sand said, stepping back
and gesturing to the nearer chair. "Was your voyage comfortable?"

Adele closed the door and seated herself, scraping the chair an
inch back to give her knees and those of the older woman more
room. "Lieutenant Leary assures me that almost everyone gets used
to the experience of entering the Matrix," she said. "I have no
evidence as yet that I'm among that fortunate majority. Apart from
that, yes. The *Princess Cecile* and her crew performed in accordance with the traditions of the RCN."

She permitted herself a smile to show that she wasn't trying
to sell Mistress Sand on the virtues of Daniel and his temporary command. Nonetheless, what she said was literally true. Insofar as possible, everything Adele said was the literal truth.

Sand chuckled, appreciating the subtlety of Adele's pre-
sentation. She took a conical ivory container from her sleeve
and poured a dose of snuff into the cup between her clenched
thumb and the back of her left hand. She didn't bother offering
what Adele had refused in the past; Mistress Sand didn't waste
motion—or anything else that Adele had noticed in their short
acquaintance.

"What do you know about Strymon, mistress?" Sand asked as
she lifted the snuff, blocking her right nostril with that index finger.

"I made a cursory search yesterday, before you called me to
this meeting," Adele said. Her face remained calm, but her brain
was racing to correlate Sand's question with Delos Vaughn's visit
to the *Princess Cecile*. "Not a great deal."

"There's rumors on Pleasaunce that Councillor Nunes is

intriguing with the Alliance," Sand said. "Nothing from Strymon itself, though."

She snorted the dose of snuff, grimaced, and sneezed explosively into a lacy handkerchief from the same sleeve as the snuffbox.

"There's rarely fewer than a dozen Cinnabar-registered vessels on Strymon at any time," Adele said, ignoring Sand's satisfied dabbing at her nose. "Cursory search" in Adele's terminology was more inclusive than many people's "full briefing" would be. "Generally twenty or more. Word would get out."

"You'd think so, wouldn't you?" Sand said, looking up again. Her eyes were mottled brown, as hard as chips of agate. "What about the rumors on Pleasaunce?"

"The Fifth Bureau—" Guarantor Porra's personal security service "—spreads lies," Adele said. "Bureaucrats lie to make themselves look effective without anyone else's encouragement."

"All true, all true," Sand said; her tone didn't imply agreement. "Regardless, I have a bad feeling about Strymon."

Adele said nothing. She hadn't been asked a question, and she didn't require amplification of what she'd just been told. Mistress Sand had remained in her position too long for her intuitions to be safely disregarded.

"The Navy's sent a squadron to Strymon to show the flag," Sand said. She eyed the snuffbox judiciously, then set it back within the sleeve of her frock coat. "Two destroyers and an old cruiser. They left Cinnabar a week ago Thursday."

Adele smiled faintly to hear Sand, an outsider for all her rank and knowledge, speak of what Warrant Officer Adele Mundy would have referred to as "the RCN." Her smile faded. If the squadron had already set out, why had Sand called her to this meeting?

"There was a bit of a communications failure between the Navy Office and my staff," Sand said, answering Adele's unspoken question. "It won't be repeated, at any rate not by the same people; and it's nothing that can't be remedied. A fast vessel can join the squadron en route."

Adele had never met any member of Sand's organization except the spymaster herself. Adele couldn't imagine that Sand personally controlled all her agents, but neither did she have evidence to the contrary.

"I'd like you to be on that vessel," Sand concluded, raising her eyebrow minutely to elicit a response.

"The *Princess Cecile*, you mean?" Adele asked; a genuine question because she didn't care to assume Sand's intentions. "Under Lieutenant Leary?"

"Both would be eminently suitable choices," Sand said mildly, her eyes on Adele's. There was nothing threatening in Sand's tone or appearance, but both commanded respect. "Cruises of this sort normally involve ships no longer fit for frontline use, but a foreign-built vessel like the *Princess Cecile* should fit in admirably."

Sand coughed into her hand without lowering her eyes. "Lieutenant Leary would accept the posting, you think?"

Daniel would turn nude cartwheels down Mission Boulevard if that were required to get the posting. Aloud Adele said, "I believe he will. I, ah, have in the past found working with Lieutenant Leary to be . . ."

She smiled; humor was only a part of the expression.

" . . . as much of a pleasure as the circumstances allowed. And I of course would be pleased to serve aboard the *Princess Cecile*."

Sand nodded. "I try to make the lives of agents doing difficult jobs as comfortable as possible," she said. "I want to know whether or not the government of Strymon is intriguing with the Alliance. It's possible that you'll be able to determine this without ever leaving your vessel. On the other hand . . ."

She turned her left hand palm down. The ring on her middle finger was set with a blue-and-white sphinx cameo which looked extremely old.

" . . . the Republic requires an accurate assessment of the situation, regardless of the risk to those gathering the information."

Adele ran through a mental checklist of what would be required to carry out the assignment. The corvette had a full RCN communications suite which, coupled to Adele's own equipment, would see to the hardware needs. Much of the remaining background Adele could gather herself more easily than by having Sand retail it. One aspect, though—

"Will the arrival of an RCN squadron alert the plotters?" she asked. "Perhaps even precipitate events? If there is a plot, of course."

"It shouldn't," Sand said. "Strymon is a loyal Cinnabar ally—

so long as it's watched. A naval visit every six months or so is normal. The present one is actually a little overdue because of the rush to refit the fighting squadrons."

Sand's left arm rested on the pad of the information console. When the machine was switched on it would become a virtual keyboard; the alternative control wands waited in a slot at the edge of the pad. It was an old system, though considerably updated since Adele's youthful visits to the Celsus.

"They'll expect Commodore Pettin's squadron," Sand continued. "They will not, I think, expect an information specialist of your abilities to accompany the ordinary naval personnel."

That raised another question. The RCN had its own channels and hierarchies; neither Adele nor Mistress Sand herself could give Daniel an order that he would obey. "I, ah, assume Lieutenant Leary will receive his assignment in the normal course of business?" she said.

Sand laughed, rising to her feet with the help of her hand against the desktop. "I'm afraid I rather anticipated your acceptance," she said to Adele. "I believe Lieutenant Leary is getting his orders even as we speak. Though I don't know about—"

She grinned, the satisfied expression of a person who does good work and knows it.

"—'the normal course of business.' Still, the orders will be coming from an acknowledged superior."

Still smiling, she waved Adele to the door ahead of her.

CHAPTER THREE

Daniel Leary sat in the General Waiting Room of the Navy Office, eyeing the ceiling thirty feet above him. The afternoon sun slanted through the skylights. It caught the whorls of webbing which clung to the corners of the coffers and turned them into so many jeweled accents.

There were three hundred officers in the waiting room at the moment, most of them senior to Daniel. Some talked quietly; some read or pretended to read professional works or the *Gazette*; most sat with their eyes forward and the grim expression of people who expect to hear the worst and are determined to take it like officers of the RCN.

Daniel was reasonably certain that he was the only person present who realized the webs hadn't been woven by a native Cinnabar species—nor Terran spiders, for that matter—but rather by the winged snails of Florissant. The flicker of movement in the shadows beneath the opposite row of benches was a Quatie Hopper, thumb-sized and warm-blooded, patrolling for dropped crumbs on the tiles with fans of hair-fine filaments sprouting from its forelegs. The faint but rhythmic *thumm*, barely audible over the susurrus of shoes and voices, was an amphibian common to all three of the Halapa Stars . . . and the Navy Office.

Over the centuries the RCN had touched most human-inhabited worlds; the natives of those worlds in many cases had touched the RCN as well. Daniel smiled: *You could write a history of Cinnabar expansion based on the natural history of the Navy Office.*

A wooden railing, darkened by age and polished by the thighs of centuries of petitioners, separated the waiting area from the administrative section of seven civilians. A junior lieutenant who must be nearly forty spoke urgently to the receiving clerk; the latter continued to type on her keyboard. If she heard the lieutenant's pleas, she gave no sign of it.

The chief clerk, wearing a dull green coat and an expression of cold superiority, oversaw proceedings from a desk at the back of the section with his fingers tented before him. His desktop was a sheet of black opal with neither paper nor a data console to mar its polished perfection. A small printer perched on the outer edge, as if contemplating suicide in remorse at intruding on so august a personage.

The staff was civilian to underscore the fact it was outside the authority of even the highest-ranking RCN officer. Several of those waiting for appointments were full captains; occasionally there might even be an admiral in the hall. The decisions about who passed and when they passed the bar to the offices within would be made without regard for how those waiting felt about it.

A printer hummed on a desk; the clerk there rose and handed the slip of hard copy to the annunciator at the podium.

"Number seventy-three!" the annunciator bawled.

Daniel's ivroid chit bore number 219. There wasn't any precedence, of course. It was just a matter of when the underclerk responsible for temporary staffing would come to Daniel's request: sixty additional personnel for twelve hours, so that he could lift the *Princess Cecile* and wring her out before turning her over to the Director of Forces as ready for assignment.

The overaged lieutenant arguing with—arguing at—the receiving clerk glanced down at his chit in delighted surmise. He started forward, then paused. Another lieutenant, a trim female in a uniform as crisp as that on a tailor's dummy, was already striding through the gate after handing her chit to the usher.

The older man looked again at his own bit of ivroid, then hurled it to clack on the floor. Others in the waiting room ostentatiously looked toward the walls, toward the ceiling. Daniel watched a pair of snails swathe a beetle in a shimmering arabesque of death. He alone looking *at* something rather than away from an embarrassment.

The officers gathered here weren't afraid of what they would be told. They were afraid that they wouldn't be told anything, that they would sit on these hard benches today and tomorrow and for all the future till they finally surrendered to despair, and that the RCN would never call them.

"Number fourteen!" called the annunciator. "Number one-hundred-and-fifty-five!"

Daniel wouldn't be ignored, not this time, though he might spend the rest of today and longer cooling his heels. Spacers were in short supply: there simply weren't enough trained personnel to serve both the merchant fleet and the RCN on a war footing. A temporary draft could be borrowed from the ships in port, however, to test a badly needed corvette.

When he'd handed over the *Princess Cecile*, Daniel would return to this waiting room to request his own assignment. That might mean a very long wait indeed. Enlisted personnel were hard to find, but there were more qualified officers than there were slots for them even in the expanded fleet.

Places went to people with interest: the support of a senior officer either because of personal contact or the recommendation of a civilian whose wealth or political influence might be of use to that senior officer. Daniel had neither of those things. He'd distinguished himself when he fell into command on Kostroma, but the swashbuckling manner of his success might itself give pause to an officer considering "young Leary" for an appointment.

The printer's hum was too faint for those beyond the bar to notice, but all six of the junior officials turned slowly and stared at their chief like rabbits facing a snake. Their motion drew the eyes of the waiting officers, Daniel's among them.

The chief clerk's printer had extruded a slip of hard copy. It was a moment before the fact registered on the man. He had to stand to lean over the broad, bare expanse and pluck the document from the output slot. He read it with disbelief, then walked to the annunciator as all eyes in the huge hall followed him.

The annunciator filled his lungs, aware that he had the greatest audience of his career. "Number two-hundred-and-nineteen!" he called.

Good God!

Daniel stood, knowing that his 2nd Class uniform had suffered in guiding and supporting his uncle during the tour of the *Princess Cecile*. The trousers had rucked up slightly and were sticking to the backs of his thighs; normally he'd have tugged them down unobtrusively as he walked, but now!

He strode forward, his face composed. Corder Leary's son knew what it was to be on display, certainly. Particularly when Daniel smiled, which was more of the time than not, he looked even younger than his twenty-two years. That didn't normally disturb him—indeed, a number of women seemed to find it intriguing. Right at the moment, however, he wished he could manage the gravity of a judge.

And he also wished he'd managed to lose the fifteen pounds he'd sworn he was going to scrub off this long time past!

The annunciator took chit 219 and dropped it into a drum on the receiving clerk's desk. He gave Daniel the slip of hard copy as the usher raised the gate to pass him through the bar.

Daniel stepped through immediately, just in case the usher changed his mind, then paused to read the slip. It was headed with his rank, serial number, and request as offered to the receiving clerk. In the destination block below was the legend:

GROUND FLOOR, ROOM 14

Daniel walked across the administrative section, past the desk of the chief clerk—still standing, watching Daniel with the expression of a man who's stumbled over a disemboweled corpse—and through the door of polished hardwood at the back. Only when he'd closed that door behind him did he let himself relax with a sigh of relief.

He tugged his pants legs straight. The female usher stationed in the long hallway watched him with cool interest.

"Room Fourteen," Daniel said, gesturing with the slip of hard copy.

"That's the Chief's office," the usher said imperturbably. "All the way down, right to the end." She nodded.

Daniel acknowledged the information with a nod of his own and strode down the hallway. There were six doors to his right, all unmarked and closed; the seventh had DIRECTOR OF PERSONNEL stencilled on the frosted glass and was open. Daniel paused, about to step into the small reception room where an assistant communications officer glanced up from behind his desk—

But this door wasn't all the way down the hall; and the numeral above the stencilled words was 10.

Daniel gave the clerk a smile of apology and continued on. Behind him a group of officers entered from the reception hall and turned in the opposite direction, headed for the stairs to the upper floors.

The usher had said "the Chief's office." Daniel had assumed "Chief of Personnel." He straightened his back and strode onward, completely puzzled and more than a little apprehensive. Well, the RCN expected her officers to handle whatever events they encountered in the course of their duties.

The remaining doors to the right were marked PURCHASING I, PURCHASING II, and PURCHASING III. A pair of civilians came out of the middle door as Daniel passed, calling cheerful farewells to someone inside. Daniel paused, but the taller one bumped him anyway—and bounced back.

"Oh, sorry, Lieutenant, very sorry!" the fellow said, patting Daniel's shoulder with a calloused hand. "If you're down at the Harborside Tavern this evening, come on over and have a drink on me!"

Daniel grinned and walked on. Apparently somebody's business with the Navy Office had gone to his liking.

Room 14 faced the end of the hallway. The door—closed—read CHIEF OF THE NAVY BOARD.

Daniel could hear voices through the glass. He paused again, completely at a loss, and then tapped on the door.

"Enter," someone called. Daniel turned the knob and stepped into another waiting room, though this one was paneled in lustrous black hardwood. There were three cushioned chairs for visitors and, behind a desk that matched the paneling, a wholly colorless middle-aged man.

"Admiral Anston brought the ensemble back after his capture of High Meyne," the man said. "The decor of the governor's private office there took his fancy."

"Ah," said Daniel, nodding to show that he'd heard what the clerk said. He offered the slip in his hand. "I'm afraid there's been a mistake. Can you direct me to the correct office, sir?"

The clerk glanced at Daniel's routing slip. "There's no mistake,

Lieutenant Leary," he said. "But if you'll have a seat, please? The admiral is still engaged."

The door to the inner office was open. A captain wearing a 1st Class uniform sat on the visitor's side of the desk, leaning forward intently. From where Daniel seated himself, *very* carefully not staring into the office, Admiral Anston on the other side of the desk was merely two neat hands holding a sheaf of documents.

"All right, Palovec, so much for the extrusions," the admiral said. It was his voice Daniel had heard through the outer door. "Now, tell me why you're recommending thruster nozzles from Kodiak Forges? Why is Kodiak even being permitted to tender?"

The hands slapped the papers down on the desktop of petrified wood. Another trophy of the admiral's active service?

"I believe they've sorted out their quality control problems, Admiral," the captain said with a bubbling good humor that didn't ring true in Daniel's ears. "I've made a personal inspection of their plant, you know. And the quote was very attractive, as you see."

The outer door opened without the formality of a knock. Daniel turned. A servant closed the door behind himself. He was far too senior to wear livery, but at his throat was a cravat in Anston's black-and-maroon colors.

"I'm here to collect the admiral, Klemsch," the servant said. His eyes flicked over Daniel the way light glances from a mud puddle. "Will you inform him, or shall I?"

Daniel's smile froze. He could take orders without hesitation or complaint; the RCN was no place for anyone who had a problem with hierarchies. But Daniel didn't expect ever to meet the *house servant* he considered his superior in any pecking order.

"Hold them for now, Palovec," the admiral said, shoving the papers across the figured stone surface. "I'll get back to you tomorrow."

"I'll inform the admiral that you're here, Whately," the clerk said. "This is the Navy Office, you'll recall, not Stamhead Square."

Captain Palovec rose and straightened his documents with a pensive expression. "I'll do what I can to convince them to hold the price, Admiral . . . " he said.

There might have been more to follow, but Admiral Anston stood and, with a hand on his elbow, ushered Palovec to the door.

Anston was a short man with trim features even now, but either he'd gained twenty pounds since the last picture Daniel had seen of him or he wore a corset during formal appearances.

Daniel jumped to his feet, barely restraining himself from saluting. By tradition born of necessity, no salutes were offered within the Navy Office; otherwise nobody'd be able to walk down the hallway without stopping in the middle of each stride to exchange salutes.

And as heaven and his Academy tutors knew, saluting wasn't a skill Daniel could ever claim to have mastered.

"Come along, Admiral," Whately said as soon as Anston appeared. "Your wife sent me to fetch you. You're an hour late as it is."

Anston looked at Daniel, then to Klemsch with a raised eyebrow. Captain Palovec opened his mouth to speak, then changed his mind and strode out of the office, clicking the outer door behind him.

"This is Lieutenant Leary, Admiral," Klemsch said.

"Admiral, your wife has been waiting at the gallery," the servant said sharply.

"Then she'll damned well have to wait longer, won't she?" the admiral boomed. "Come on in here, lad. I can spare you a minute without all the statues melting off their stands!"

With the exception of the splendid desk, Anston's inner office was relentlessly utilitarian. The walls were off-white with no pictures or other decoration, and the furniture was as spartan as that of junior officers' quarters on a warship. Daniel sat because Anston directed him to a chair, but he perched on the edge of the cushion.

"Are you married, Leary?" the admiral asked.

"No sir!" Daniel said. Had there been a complaint about—

"Didn't think so!" Anston said, sitting in the similar chair across the deck. "But rumor has it you've met your share of women. Is that true?"

A number of possible answers to the question raced through Daniel's head. There *had* been complaints. Coming home as the Hero of Kostroma and with money in his pocket—well, Daniel had always been able to meet women looking for a good time, and with his present advantages it was like shooting fish in a barrel.

"Yes, sir, that's true," Daniel said. He'd never been any good at lying, and he wasn't going to start now with the Chief of the Navy Board.

Anston nodded again. "That's a good thing in a young man," he said in an approving tone. "That way you won't have to make a fool of yourself when you get to be my age. Now—what do you think about Kodiak thruster nozzles?"

Daniel felt as though he was being slapped on the back of the head with feather pillows. Every time he turned, *whap!* and another one hit him from behind.

"Sir, I don't have personal experience with Kodiak's products," he said, "but my uncle, that's Commander Bergen, has stopped using them in his shipyard. He says the internal polish is fine, but you have to magnaflux each one for weak spots or you can expect to have plasma leaking sideways before you've got ten hours of service. He says he rejected the whole shipment he received last quarter."

Anston banged his fist down. "Just what I told Palovec when I took them off the tender list last year!" he said. "I don't mind a purchasing officer making his five percent on a contract, but I will *not* have a man who lines his pockets by providing my people with shoddy goods! Klemsch, take a note of that."

"I have done so, Admiral," called the little man from the outer office. The servant, Whately, shifted from foot to foot in the doorway though he didn't choose to break in on Anston again.

"You're here about the corvette, the *Princess Cecile,*" Anston said, grimacing at the vessel's name. No Cinnabar vessel would've been christened anything like "*Princess Cecile,*" but Anston was one of the old-fashioned officers who felt that renaming a ship changed her luck. "What do you think of her? Your assessment as an RCN officer!"

"Sir," said Daniel, "I'd match her against any vessel of her class, regardless of where she was built."

Like everything else he'd said since he entered the office, that was the simple truth. He didn't understand enough about the situation to guess what Anston wanted to hear; and when in doubt, the truth was always the best option.

Anston bellowed a laugh so loud that it trailed off into coughing. He slapped his desk again and said, "As all Cinnabar knows, lad, you matched her against a cruiser that was miles beyond her class. Oh, I know, you had luck to pull it off. I didn't make it to this office without knowing what luck was, I assure you. But you had balls enough to try, and that's the first requirement for a good officer."

"Admiral, *please . . .* " Whately said. He'd breezed in initially with the authority of Lady Anston. If that wasn't sufficient, he was likely to be ground to dust between her and the admiral.

"Yes, yes," Anston said, rising from his chair again. "I just wanted to meet Leary here. Leary, Klemsch will take care of you while I go pretend I see more in a line of bronze statues than so many bearings gone bad."

He walked Daniel into the outer office. Whately already had the door open and was hovering by it, a wraith of the self-important fellow who'd bustled in minutes before.

Daniel didn't understand what had just happened—*any* of the things that had just happened—but there didn't seem to be any advantage in commenting on the fact to Mr. Klemsch. He therefore said as the door closed behind Anston, "I'm requesting a twelve-hour draft of sixty ratings while I test the *Princess Cecile* before turning her over as ready for service."

The forty Sissies—former Aggies from the communications vessel *Aglaia*, aboard to handle the refit—were all experienced spacers. With them as a core, the corvette would be able to function even if the rest of the crew were ten-thumbed landsmen . . . which would very probably be the case.

Klemsch typed at a sheet of boron monocrystal marked with symbols. Daniel didn't recall seeing a physical keyboard like that in service anywhere within the RCN: the volume within a warship was too short to dedicate any of it to uses that could be accomplished by holograms. Klemsch's eccentricity would subtly disquiet any spacer who dealt with him, Daniel included.

But Daniel's passion for natural history disposed him to view the mechanisms at work within and among living entities. He recognized why the keyboard bothered him—and grinned broadly. It wasn't as though anything so minor as *that* was going to affect him in the present circumstances.

"The admiral has passed the *Princess Cecile* for service," Klemsch said as he typed. "You're to work her up in the course of your service cruise."

The printer whirred, extruding and clipping off a sheet of flimsy. Klemsch handed the document to Daniel.

"This appoints you captain of the *Princess Cecile*," the clerk said. His expression was perfectly deadpan, but it covered a sardonic grin as surely as flesh did his cheekbones. "You'll have to pardon the informality, but the stress of events prevents me from having it done with the proper seals and ribbons. You're to arrange for a full crew on long-term recruitment."

He cleared his throat. "Your orders give you authority to accept volunteers from any RCN vessel on Cinnabar, whether or not the volunteer's present commander acquiesces."

"Good God!" Daniel said; the phrase was getting to be a habit today, and this time he'd blurted it aloud.

He wasn't an unduly boastful man, but he'd brought the *Aglaia*'s crew back from a disaster and filled their pockets with prize money. Spacers preferred to serve beneath lucky officers than able ones, though Daniel hoped the Aggies and everyone they talked to thought Lt. Leary was pretty damned able as well. If he was allowed to recruit under those terms, he'd get the pick of the RCN.

By God! He'd get back the crew that fought the *Princess Cecile* on Kostroma, barring those few spacers posted to vessels which had lifted during the corvette's refit!

"Ah," Daniel said. "I'm very grateful for these orders, Mr. Klemsch, very grateful. But can you tell me what the, ah, reason for them might be?"

The clerk looked up coldly. "Do I care to speculate as to Admiral Anston's motives, you mean, Lieutenant? No, I do not."

Daniel's heels clicked to a brace. "Good day, sir," he said. "Meeting you has been an unexpected pleasure."

He stepped out the door and began to whistle. What would Adele say about this?

CHAPTER FOUR

Adele sat on a bench in the huge forecourt and took out her personal data unit. The upper court with six banks of theater-style seating for a few hundred worshippers was to her right. Beyond it rose the gilded eighty-foot image of the Redeeming Spirit, framed rather than shielded by a conical roof supported by columns. Those structures on the very crown of the hill were the only portions of the complex really given over to religious uses; and that only rarely, when representatives of the Senate and the allied worlds gave formal thanks for the safety of the Republic.

Adele smiled, half in humor. In another way the whole Pentacrest was a religious edifice, dedicated to the faith that Cinnabar was meant to rule the human galaxy. Daniel certainly believed that, though he'd be embarrassed to say so in those blunt words.

And Adele Mundy? No, she didn't believe it and she didn't imagine she ever would. But not long ago she'd believed in nothing but the certainty she would die, and today she was convinced of the reality of human friendship as well. Perhaps someday Daniel would manage to convert her—by example; Daniel was no proselytizer—into a Cinnabar chauvinist as well.

Adele felt, as she always did when walking out of a library, that the sunlight was an intrusion. Still, she hadn't wanted to call up her messages within the Celsus; not after the meeting with Mistress Sand. Contact with intelligence personnel always made her feel both unclean and paranoid, uncomfortably aware of how easily she could be observed within the confines of a building.

Adele was an intelligence agent herself now. That made her feel more, not less, uncomfortable. Perhaps the paranoia would prove a survival trait, but she wasn't sure she wanted to live if she had to worry this way in order to do so.

Most of the messages she'd downloaded were of no consuming interest—RCN information, updating her status; or even less significant queries from people who wanted to sell her things. Adele had gained a great deal of attention from publication of the list of those entitled to a share in the proceeds of the *Princess Cecile* whenever the government of the Republic got around to paying. She found it quite amazing that so many people thought she wanted to buy real estate, an aircar, or companionship.

She permitted herself another smile. Companionship of the sort those folk offered had never interested her, even as a matter of scientific curiosity. Daniel was the naturalist, after all. Mind, Daniel's interest in companionship couldn't be called scientific, though the way he hooked and netted each night's quarry showed the same tactical acumen that had turned the tables on the Alliance at Kostroma.

A short block of information was encrypted. Adele entered the day's key; even with the wands, the hundred and twenty-eight characters took some time.

The message was from Tovera, Adele's servant insofar as that intelligent, highly trained sociopath could be said to serve anything except her own will. Tovera knew she wasn't fully human: that there were things which human beings felt that she would never feel. Her strategy for coping with her lack was to attach herself to a human who understood what she was, and who didn't care.

Every time Adele looked at Tovera, she thought of the boy she'd killed fifteen years before; and the others. How many more lives could Adele Mundy end with a four-ounce pressure of her trigger finger, before her eyes were just as empty as those of her servant?

The message was simple: Adele's bank had called regarding the drawing rights she had established against the award of prize money for the *Princess Cecile*. They would like her to meet with them at her earliest convenience, giving an address.

It wasn't the address of the office where Adele had set up the account, but that was only to be expected. It was on the north slope of Progress Hill, however; easier to walk to than to take a car.

It was also only to be expected that something was wrong with her account. Well, she'd known poverty before; she could learn to skip meals again.

She set off through the archway beneath the upper court. It was unadorned concrete, the lighting muted but functional. This passage wasn't meant for show but merely for the use of visitors coming from the north to the Celsus or to offices in the complex.

Ahead of her walked a noble with a small retinue. A group of minor bureaucrats passed from the other direction, one eating the last of a roll-up and others carrying part-filled mugs. They were talking about a construction project and speculating on how much the contractor would pay for permit approval.

Adele felt her senses focus down: locking faces in her memory without appear to stare, catching intonations and freezing the precise phrasing of the discussion. She caught herself and rubbed the impulse—though not the series of impressions—from her mind.

The Xenos municipal government wasn't paying her to root out graft. Still, Adele had spent her life learning to gather and integrate information. The past months with Daniel—and Mistress Sand—had led her to consider other forms of information to remain alive, but she couldn't let that get out of hand if she were to stay sane.

She grinned. Her sanity was perhaps an unwarranted assumption.

There was nothing in the call from the bank that required encryption. Besides, if someone did want to know about it, the original message had certainly been in clear. Tovera had relayed it in secure form because Tovera sent all messages to her mistress in code, so that data which was of crucial importance wouldn't stand out because it alone was encrypted.

Tovera did everything by plan because she lacked the instincts on which normal humans operated most of the time. Guarantor Porra's Fifth Bureau had trained her well . . . and now Tovera did as Adele directed her, just as the pistol in Adele's left jacket pocket would do: no scruples, no hesitation—only action when the trigger is pulled.

Adele stepped out of the tunnel. She'd checked the address against a map reference but hadn't bothered to call up an image of the building. It was of five stories and, though quite new, had a pillared facade which echoed the architecture of the complex on the hill's reverse slope.

The small brass plate beside the door read SHIPPERS' AND MERCHANTS' TREASURY; its air of understated elegance would have been anathema to the populist pretensions of Adele's parents. She stopped dead when she read it.

Adele hoped she had few pretensions, and she'd lived as an impecunious member of "the common people" for too long to find anything in the concept to be idealistic about. Nonetheless, she'd gone to the People's Trust to set up a drawing account. This wasn't her bank, and if somebody thought to play games of that sort with a Mundy of Chatsworth . . .

She didn't follow the thought through, because she could thus far only visualize a pinkish blur instead of a real face over the barrel of her duelling pistol.

A doorman bowed politely as he ushered her into the lobby, an unexpectedly small room. A tree with a fan of broad leaves at the top grew from an alcove, lighted by a shaft to the roof high above; beneath it was a receptionist at a desk of age-yellowed ivory.

The two teller's cages were unoccupied. Closed doors along the back wall gave onto rooms which provided greater privacy for clients.

"I was directed to Office E," Adele said to the receptionist, wondering if her face showed the anger she was trying to suppress till she was sure of her facts.

The receptionist touched an unobtrusive button and rose with a smile. "Yes, Mistress Mundy," he said. "Will you come this way, please? It won't be a moment."

He opened a door into a drawing room appointed in muted good taste. The only apparent exception was the desk, a dense plastic extrusion. In this context it was almost certainly an antique dating from the settlement.

The door in the opposite wall opened for a plumpish, severely dressed woman of Adele's age. The banker would never pass for beautiful, but if she showed more tendency to smile she might have been pretty. Not that Adele was the one to cast stones in that regard.

"Please sit down, mistress," the banker said. Instead of stepping behind the desk, she went to one of the pair of chairs in front of it.

"Thank you, I'll stand," Adele said. She'd never met the woman, but there was a tantalizing familiarity to her nonetheless. "My account is with the People's Trust. Why have you summoned me here?"

"We bought your account from the People's Trust this morning, Mistress Mundy," the woman said. "The new arrangements are among the things I'd like to discuss with you. I should begin by saying—"

They bought my account? How do you buy—

"—that my name is Deirdre Leary. I believe you know my younger brother."

Oh.

Adele remained stiffly erect, ignoring the hand Daniel's sister offered her. "Mistress Leary," she said, "I am leaving *now*. If you wish any further communication with me, it should be through our seconds arranging a meeting."

"*Please* Mistress Mundy," Deirdre said. She didn't withdraw the outstretched hand. "Please, this will be to your benefit and that of my brother. On my honor as a Leary!"

Adele remained frozen, trying to understand the situation. Daniel spoke of his sister with respect if not warmth. Deirdre had followed their father into business and perhaps soon into politics as well. She appeared to be a paragon of moral virtue besides; which Daniel was the first to admit he himself was not.

Adele didn't have enough information to analyze what was going on. She smiled like a sickle, though the grim humor was directed at herself rather than the woman in front of her. Obviously, she needed to gather more information.

"I've known your brother long enough to value the honor of a Leary," Adele said. She took Deirdre's hand and shook it; the banker's grip was firm though the flesh of her hand was soft.

Seating herself on the offered chair she continued, "Now, if you can give me an explanation of why I'm here, Mistress Leary, I'd be pleased to hear it."

"You're aware that my father and brother parted on very bad terms, I'm sure," Deirdre said, sitting as well. The chairs were side by side instead of facing, so that the two women looked over their shoulders at one another. "They've had no contact since."

"Daniel's mentioned that, yes," Adele said. It had frequently occurred to her that testosterone was responsible for more than a few of the world's troubles.

Deirdre's moue suggested her opinion of the matter was much the same as Adele's own. "I informed Father of my intention," she said, "but I wouldn't want you to think that this contact was at his suggestion, let alone behest. On the other hand, he didn't attempt to forbid me either."

"Perhaps you should tell me precisely what your intentions are," Adele said, keeping her tone emotionless. What it appeared to be was an attempt to get at Daniel through his friend; and if that was the case, Adele was going to be more angry than she'd ever been before in her life.

"My sole intention, already effected," the banker replied in a voice as dry as a fresh brick, "is to decrease the discount on the sums you draw from twenty percent to seven percent. Seven percent is a better rate than a stranger who walked in off the street might expect, but we at the S&M trust the government to pay its obligations."

Adele digested the information, what Deirdre implied as well as the explicitly stated. "The discount I've been charged by my parents' bank is excessive, then," she said.

They must have seen me coming!

"I won't speak for the management of another firm," Deirdre said with a cold smile that suggested she'd be perfectly willing to do that if she weren't sure Adele already understood. "If one of my subordinates were to offer that contract to a naval officer, however, he'd be looking for another job. Outside the banking sector, because I'd blackball him as well as terminating his employment."

Adele, as the only surviving member of her family, knew very well how ruthless Speaker Leary was. It appeared that his daughter had inherited some of that personality.

"Before you blame yourself for allowing yourself to be taken advantage of, mistress," Deirdre continued, "I should mention that my brother made an even worse deal for his share of the prize money. Banking involves as much specialized knowledge as astrogation or archival research do."

"You bought Daniel's account also, then?" Adele said; hoping against hope that the answer would be "No," because Daniel's reaction would be—

"Good God, no!" Deirdre said. "I won't claim to understand my brother, Mistress Mundy, but I can guess how he'd react to that sort of interference. The S&M cultivates a genteel atmosphere, and the presence of a young naval officer threatening to demolish it stone by stone wouldn't fit in with that at all."

Adele choked when an indrawing breath met a jolt of laughter going the other way. She'd just had an image of a detachment from the *Princess Cecile* arriving at the Shippers' and Merchants' Treasury with axes and pinch bars.

"Yes, I agree with your assessment, Mistress Leary," she said. She stood because she had work to do, absorbing information on Strymon. If the banker had more to say, it was time to say it.

Deirdre rose also. "Since you raise the matter, however," she said, "it *would* be to Daniel's financial advantage to transfer his account to the S&M."

Adele suddenly remembered the first time she'd heard the details of her sister Agatha's abuse and murder. "I won't pledge *my* honor to induce Daniel to take any action whatever regarding the Leary family, mistress," she said. Her voice was as thin as stressed piano wire.

"Nor would I expect you to, mistress," Deirdre said, as little moved by Adele's anger as granite is by the rain. "But I am pledging my personal honor to you that no ill would result to my brother as a result of any dealings he might have with the S&M."

This woman has as much stiff-necked pride as a Mundy! Which was no surprise, because the families had been poured from the same crucible of Cinnabar politics.

"I noted when I reviewed your file," Deirdre said, looking off at an angle, "the irregular way that a portion of your family properties were restored after the Edict of Reconciliation. I suspect there was collusion between the court and the cousin claiming to be the closest surviving relative. Such a miscarriage of justice could be righted even now."

Adele smiled faintly and extended her hand. "Good day, mistress," she said. "I believe that the past is often better forgotten, however I'll keep that information on hand against later need."

She walked out of the bank; beside the building was a stop for the east-west loop of a car line. She'd go back to her apartment and from that privacy assemble the information she'd need. The first sweep, that is, to enable her to focus more accurately for the next pass.

She wouldn't say anything to Daniel about her meeting today; either meeting. It would merely make him uncomfortable to know about Mistress Sand, and as for his sister—

Adele wasn't going to mention Deirdre until she herself had a better notion of what to think.

Daniel Leary sat at the civilian desk, furnished when he rented the apartment, and switched off the phone on which he'd called Lt. Mon. The view from his window looked down the hillside over three- and four-story apartment houses similar to his own. Because most of them had roof gardens, the effect was more similar to Bantry, the Leary country estate, than a major city.

Hogg came in with a flimsy in one hand and a bleak scowl on his face. "Your new Dress Whites aren't going to be ready inside a week unless I squeeze Sadlack harder than I've done so far," he said. "Have we got a week, do you figure?"

Hogg was shortish, plumpish, and balding, although he was only in his forties. He was neither a gentleman's valet nor the typical naval servant, an enlisted crewmen who looked after one of the officers for an additional stipend paid from the officer's purse.

"A week?" Daniel repeated. Ordinarily it might take a week or even longer for sailing orders to make their labyrinthine way through the Navy Office, but the brusque certainty of Daniel's own appointment suggested there was nothing ordinary about this business. "Not a chance, Hogg. I've just told Mon to have the *Sissie* ready for liftoff in six hours if possible. It'll take two days to gather a crew, but that's the only delay I expect. I suppose I'll have to make do with my grays."

Hogg had watched over Daniel while he was growing up on Bantry. Nurses and tutors had come and gone. Mother was a gentle presence in the background, and Corder Leary made flying visits from the city to dispense commands, punishment, and occasional praise before returning to the things he found important.

Hogg was always there, teaching what he knew: about wildlife and women and cards, about how to hold your liquor and when to hold your tongue; about loyalty and courage and the history of the Learys of Bantry. As much as anyone can teach another, Hogg had taught Daniel how to be a man.

"Naw, I'll just lean on the snooty bastard a little harder," Hogg said, sounding more pleased than not. He was a countryman who'd learned city ways well enough to profit by them—in Hell, Hogg would probably win all the pitchforks with the three-card trick—but who would never lose his distaste for tradesmen with polished accents. "You'll not be going out on your first permanent command without a dress uniform, Master Daniel."

Daniel wondered exactly what "lean harder" meant in this context. He decided he didn't want to know. He *needed* Dress Whites to replace the set he'd lost on Kostroma—and he too had found Sadlack, Gentleman's Outfitter, to be a snooty bastard. If the fellow was going to tailor 1st Class uniforms for officers of the RCN, then he could damned well work the way naval officers did: all the hours the clock had, until the task was accomplished.

Hogg went back to his own room whistling cheerfully. Daniel lifted the handset again and jumped down the address rota to Adele's personal number. He pressed SEND and waited, looking out the window at the greenery.

Daniel had a naval command helmet on which he could make calls more easily than with the civilian instrument which was now less familiar to him. He didn't because of the view out the window: it would be disconcerting to use the helmet but see verdure instead of a gray-surfaced bulkhead in front of him.

Hogg returned, checking the action of a folding skinning knife. He dropped it into his side pocket.

Daniel's call brought no response until it cycled automatically to Adele's apartment phone. There was a click of connection but the screen stayed blank. Naval phones didn't waste bandwidth on visuals; Mon had been only a voice when Daniel spoke to him a moment before. In the case of Adele, or rather her servant, the emptiness was a matter of choice.

"Yes?" said Tovera, her voice as flat as a machine's. It wasn't a receptionist's greeting, but Daniel wasn't the one to complain. Hogg was as apt as not to say, "And who's this that's calling, then?" when he answered the phone.

"Tovera, please let your mistress know that we'll be getting sailing orders very shortly," Daniel said. "That is, the *Princess Cecile* will shortly be sailing under my command. Also I'd like her help in putting together a crew. She'll be able to get me real discipline records on spacers I don't know personally, the information I won't learn from their present captains."

"Ms. Mundy is out, Lieutenant," Tovera said, "and I don't know her whereabouts. I'll give her your messages as soon as possible."

The second of those three parts was almost certainly a lie, but Daniel was equally certain that torture wouldn't get any more definite response from Tovera. She wasn't a servant who'd suit everybody, but Adele seemed happy with her. That was good enough for Daniel.

"Thank you, Tovera," he said and broke the connection. The sooner he got off the line, the sooner Tovera would be able to contact her mistress. Besides—and he'd never say it to Adele, not in a million years, because it was none of his business—the pale young woman made Daniel's skin crawl.

"Supper'll be late," Hogg said, reaching for the doorknob, "but first things first. If you're afraid you'll starve, then I guess you can find somewhere they'll feed you."

"I dare say I can," Daniel said, wondering what his father's valet would say if he'd heard that exchange. On the other hand, the valet hadn't—and wouldn't—put his life on the line for Corder Leary, and Hogg had done that and more for the son. Daniel didn't need mincing subservience; he did need Hogg.

The door chimed, making both men jump. Hogg glanced at Daniel. Daniel nodded, wondering what to do with his hands as he always did at times like these. Hogg opened the door for a servant in puce livery with feathers along the arm and leg seams and a ribbon-tied scroll in his hand.

Daniel realized he was more interested in the feathers—he'd bet the bird wasn't native to Cinnabar—than he was in the document. The latter, after all, would explain itself momentarily while in all likelihood neither the servant nor the tailor knew where the feathers had come from. They were just accents to most people.

"Lord Delos Vaughn sends greetings to Lieutenant the Honorable Daniel Leary!" the fellow said with an accent more cultured than you'd ordinarily hear at one of Deirdre's urbane soirees. "The favor of a reply is requested."

He handed the scroll to Hogg, then bowed to Daniel. Hogg bounced the document—it looked like real parchment—in the palm of his left hand, then grinned and drew the knife. He used the gut-hook on the back of the blade to pull the ribbon off.

"It says you're invited to a party at the Anadyomene Water Gardens tomorrow afternoon from two till six," Hogg read, spreading the parchment with his left thumb and forefinger so that he could keep the knife open for the servant to goggle at. "Says you can bring a guest, too. Interested?"

That was playacting for the servant's benefit; normally Hogg would merely have grunted after opening the invitation and tossed it to Daniel. The poor messenger's face was nearly the same shade as his livery.

Daniel ran through the sequence of business which needed to be done before the corvette could lift. He should have his portion complete by mid-morning. The crew would begin reporting as soon as officers of the day read the proclamation to their companies at morning formation. And it *would* be read, however little other captains liked it, because it had been issued in the name of Admiral Anston personally.

Former Sissies would be enrolled as a matter of course. Any of the warrant officers could handle that. The only question for Daniel would be the handful of positions still open when all the Sissies on Cinnabar had decided whether or not to rejoin; that wouldn't be determined till after six, anyway.

"Yes, all right," Daniel said. "My guest and I would be pleased to attend."

The servant bowed again and backed hurriedly out the doorway open behind him. His eyes didn't leave the point of the skinning knife until he turned to scuttle down the staircase.

"Well, this ought to be interesting," Daniel said, rubbing his hands together. Of course he'd take Adele, who was far too good a friend for Daniel ever to think of her as a girl. It was the sort of gathering sure to be stocked with friendly young things who loved a uniform. Adele would sheer off and give him clear running, while if he'd brought a real date he'd feel honor bound to go home with her.

"It'll be formal dress, is what it'll be," Hogg said. "I'll be back with your whites, but better not wait up for me."

Quite apart from the women, Delos Vaughn was interesting... and interested in Daniel, which meant Daniel had best learn more about him. Speaker Leary's son didn't have to be taught politics that basic.

CHAPTER FIVE

Tovera was buying Adele a suit for the party, freeing Adele to do something she was good at instead: absorb background about Delos Vaughn and the situation on Strymon. Not that she regretted the invitation and Daniel's assumption that she would join him. Quite the contrary: there should be at least as much to learn at the party as there was from the databases on Cinnabar.

Her wands twitched. The blurs of holographic color her data unit projected in the air before her fused, shifted, and fused into new images.

On the wall beyond, a pair of feathery feelers extended from a crack in the plaster. Judging there was no risk, first one and then a score of flat, leggy things raced across the wall in the direction of the kitchenette.

Adele supposed she could apply the lowered bank discount to better housing, but her standards had slipped a great deal in the past fifteen years. She didn't need much, after all: plain food, basic shelter, and access to information. The latter was as easily available from here, a room in the servants' quarters of a former mansion broken up into apartments, as it was in a suite like Daniel's in a now-fashionable district. Adele wasn't going to be entertaining, after all.

She read: after the Quetzal Dispute, sometimes called the Second Strymon War, Strymon had accepted the position of Friend and Ally to the Republic. That meant in practice that her navy was limited to light antipiracy vessels, all external treaties were sub-ject to approval by the Cinnabar Senate, and the Senate also took an interest in any change of government.

It was a light yoke—Strymon was too distant for tight con-trol to be economically beneficial to Cinnabar—but the locals chafed under it nonetheless. The ruling class did, at any rate: Cinnabar had always found oligarchies and autocrats easier to deal with than democracies, so the Republic hadn't tried to change the existing political system.

Someone began screaming in the street outside Adele's barred window. *Either a woman or a man being gelded, and in this dis-trict you couldn't be sure....*

Under other circumstances Adele would have worried about the security of her few belongings during the times she was out of her room, but Tovera had seen to that. The first day, Adele returned before Tovera got back from business of her own. She found the corpse of a man with a swollen purple face lying in the doorway, still holding the hammer with which he'd smashed the lock. Poison of one sort or another, probably gas.

The second day Tovera was the earlier home. Adele knew some-thing must have happened from the way neighbors looked side-long at her, angry and very frightened, but she didn't ask questions. It was almost chance that she found the mortality report and learned there'd been three of them, swinging down from the roof to enter through the window. The eldest had been fourteen.

There were no further incidents. That was good, because Adele couldn't convince herself that being young and arrogant was properly a capital crime ... but neither was she willing to be a victim simply because she existed. The Mundys had supplied their share of such victims during the Proscriptions.

Adele separated her own actions from those of Tovera and others: *she* didn't see the faces of those boys when she awoke at two in the morning. She had company enough of her own at that hour.

She read: as President of Strymon, Leland Vaughn had paid lip service toward recognizing Cinnabar hegemony, but the Sen-ate suspected that he had ambitions toward greater independence. It was suggested that the president send his son Delos to Cinnabar for his education. The word "hostage" was never used, but all parties were clear regarding the reality of the situation. Vaughn, with an RCN squadron led by a battleship in orbit above his planet, perforce agreed.

The educational record of young Delos was not a scholar's, but Adele could tell even from the bare bones of the scores that the potential was there. Education simply wasn't Vaughn's first priority—nor yet his third, very likely, though it was hard to be sure how important the partying really was to him.

What were important were first, learning the power structures of the Republic of Cinnabar; and second, ingratiating himself into those structures with the determination of a buck pursuing a doe. The officials guiding Vaughn around Harbor Three were highly placed, but the personages who might have directed them to the task were among the elite of the Republic.

Adele permitted herself a half-smile. Corder Leary appeared in the list of those who'd exchanged hospitality with Vaughn.

Three years after Delos arrived on Cinnabar, Leland Vaughn was murdered—by "persons unknown," but his half-brother, Callert Vaughn, was prepared to instantly step into the presidency. Delos, now eighteen, had applied to the Senate for permission to return home.

Permission was refused. Callert had made a prompt submission to Cinnabar . . . and had bribed the senatorial envoy sent to assess the situation, as files provided by Mistress Sand clearly indicated. Strymon remained as much an ally as she'd ever been; the Republic would gain no advantage from stirring matters up. As for Delos—he had a secure income that would buy him anything he could want except for the thing he *did* want: passage home.

The cooler in the kitchenette moaned as the current dropped beneath what its compressor required, then picked up again. This district was subject to frequent power cuts, and occasionally the tap water slowed to a rusty dribble. It didn't concern Adele; they used the cooler more to keep vermin from the cheese and crackers than to chill food anyway.

Callert Vaughn had ruled Strymon until eight months ago, when riots against Cinnabar influence had broken out in the capital. Mobs killed several Cinnabar merchants and burned the building used by the Cinnabar observer mission; the Observer and her husband had escaped on a freighter leaving the planet hastily, but the local staff had been massacred.

Then Callert was killed—"by a stray bullet" claimed Friderik Nunes, the former head of the Presidential Guard and now regent on behalf of Pleyna Vaughn, Callert's twelve-year-old daughter. The riots stopped as suddenly as if a switch had been turned off.

Delos Vaughn had again petitioned to return home. His request was pending, but Adele's sources expected another denial. Pleyna had offered reparations and the apologies of her government for damage to Cinnabar interests. The Senate would probably decide that letting Delos return would merely reinflame a situation that had just returned to stability.

So long as he lived, Delos Vaughn would remain a club with which the Senate could threaten whoever was in power in Strymon: be good or we'll send Vaughn back to raise a rebellion against you. But there was very little chance that Vaughn would ever be allowed to leave his gilded cage here on Cinnabar.

Adele sighed, then muted her display and stared at the wall across the table from her. It couldn't really be called blank: successive water-stains had left patterns in gradations of sepia on the wallpaper.

She'd met Delos Vaughn the day Mistress Sand ordered her to Strymon. That was either coincidence—a vanishingly low probability; or Vaughn had penetrated Sand's organization; or Sand herself was playing a double game.

There was no way to tell which was true. Adele grinned. Of course, she could ask Mistress Sand . . .

Tovera had attached an alarm light to the wall above the bed. It now pulsed three times in a deep yellow that wouldn't disrupt vision at night. Someone was coming to the door. Adele turned but didn't get up. She was confident it was Tovera, returning with the clothes for the party. Even so, Adele kept her left hand in her jacket pocket.

Tovera entered with a garment bag over her arm, aware of the pistol pointed at her and mildly amused. She didn't worry that her mistress would shoot her by accident. Actually, Tovera probably didn't worry about dying at all . . . any more than Adele did.

"Time to get cleaned up and dress, mistress," Tovera said, hanging the bag on a cord strung the width of the room. She'd been carrying a dagger concealed beneath the garment bag; she sheathed it in a sleeve. Anyone who'd tried to snatch the bag would have been surprised, for a very brief time.

"Yes, all right," Adele said, rising and shrugging off her jacket. The water tap was at waist height in the kitchenette, over a tile drain. It made an adequate shower if you squatted under it.

She'd learned all she could from documentary sources. Perhaps the party would give her some useful insight.

Aloud she said, "Delos Vaughn isn't just a playboy, so why does he go to so much effort to pretend otherwise?"

Tovera smiled without humor or emotion as she took the garments Adele handed her. She looked like a menial servant, too downtrodden to have a personality, let alone opinions.

And that of course was the answer: because she looked harmless, nobody noticed Tovera until she struck. So when did Delos Vaughn intend to strike?

And where would Adele Mundy be when the blow fell?

The service area was a hollow rectangle and all four walls of the wine bar were mirrored. When Daniel heard over the hubbub the call, "There you are, Leary! Good to see you!" he had no idea where the voice was coming from. He looked to his left, turned to his right; saw hundreds of well-dressed men and women, infinitely multiplied in reflection, and Wex Bending slid in behind him. He'd come from the left after all.

It had to be Bending, though the goatee and flaring sideburns Daniel's childhood friend now affected had changed his appearance almost beyond recognition. He hugged Daniel around the shoulders and went on, "How's the Speaker keeping, Daniel? A splendid man, splendid!"

Daniel blinked, wondering if there was some mistake after all. Surely Bending would know that he and his father were on bad terms—or rather, on no terms at all?

"I haven't seen my father in six years and more, Wex," Daniel said. "From what I see on the news, he's much the same as always. But I don't have much call to watch the news, even now that I'm back on Cinnabar."

One of the three liveried bartenders set a drink in a fluted glass in front of Bending without being asked. He'd obviously suggested the location because he was a regular here.

"Thank you, Torvaldo," he said. He glanced at Daniel meaningfully. "Ah . . . ?"

"On my tab, waiter," Daniel said, catching the drift quickly enough. A junior lieutenant's pay was well beneath whatever Bending must be making in the Ministry of External Affairs, but Bending's upkeep must be equally high. Certainly the mauve suit he wore was several times as expensive as Daniel's uniform.

Daniel wasn't the sort to object to buying someone a drink, even at the prices this place charged. He'd called Bending on a whim when he realized they'd have time to meet before Vaughn's party, but he'd wondered if he'd be conspicuous in his Dress Whites. In fact, the doorman might not have passed him if he'd worn anything less pretentious.

In Bending's lapel was a small silver pin, three stylized knifefish leaping: the crest of the Learys of Bantry. Bending's father had been a Leary retainer with a post in the Agriculture department through Speaker Leary's influence. The son had obviously followed the same route to preferment and had already done rather better from it.

Awareness of the pin made pieces click together in Daniel's mind. "I gather you called my father's office after I called you, Wex?" he said. "To see whether you were permitted to talk to me, that is."

Corder Leary's goatee and sideburns framed his thin, ascetic visage to form a portrait of devilish wisdom. The same style made a clown of the round-faced Bending.

"Well, not permitted, Daniel," Bending said with a hurt expression. "But despite a friendship as close as ours, I couldn't dishonor my name by acting against the wishes of my patron."

"I know exactly what you mean!" Daniel said, slapping the bureaucrat on the back with a broad grin. He did indeed realize that the friend who'd played hide-and-seek with him in the gardens of the Leary townhouse when he visited his father had become a poncing little courtier to whom position was everything. Daniel hoped his smile hid that knowledge, but it really didn't matter: Bending wouldn't have met Daniel if he didn't think that was Speaker Leary's desire. That being the case, he would have grinned and obeyed if Daniel ordered him to hop around like a gerbil.

Which left the question of why Father had approved the meeting, but that wasn't the matter that brought Daniel to this place. They charged a florin a glass for wine that didn't hold a buzz in a caskful. "So Wex," Daniel said. "What can you tell me about Delos Vaughn? I saw him at Harbor Three yesterday."

"Oh, he's mad for warships, they tell me," Bending burbled, sipping his own faintly violet concoction. "Strymon had quite a fleet in its day, you know. But they're held to a few dozen antipirate frigates by treaty—and anyway, he's never going to leave Cinnabar, no matter how many senators he bribes."

"Ah," Daniel said, nodding to show that he was listening. He took a sip of his wine and found he'd drained the glass. The stuff had no more body than seafoam! "Someone's spending money to keep him here, then?"

Bending turned so that he faced Daniel directly. His right hand was on the bar; the left held his glass at a calculated angle. Unless Daniel was badly mistaken, he was admiring his pose in the mirror beyond.

"Oh, there's a certain amount of that, sure, Daniel," he said, puffing his chest out slightly. "Being appointed Observer on Strymon is known to be quite a political plum. No senator's ever come back poor from there, and the staff does itself bloody well too, let me tell you."

Bending drank, then lifted his glass slightly and appeared to admire the remaining liquid as he swirled it. "But that's not the real reason, you see," he said. He leaned closer to Daniel and added in a conspiratorial whisper, "Our Delos is too bloody sharp, *that's* the problem. Better for the Republic that he never goes home, do you see?"

Daniel frowned. Claiming to be a babe in the woods of interstellar relations was the right way to draw confidences out of a man who obviously delighted in playing the learned insider. It was also God's truth in this instance.

"To tell the truth, I *don't* understand, Wex," he said. "Surely nobody's concerned that Vaughn would try to claim independence again? We've crushed Strymon twice, and that was before Uncle Stacey cut the travel time to a fraction of what it'd been for Admiral Perlot's squadron."

"Ah, that's right, you're a navy man," Bending said in what seemed to be genuine surprise. Daniel would've thought a 1st Class uniform made that about as obvious as you could wish, but apparently rising members of the Ministry of External Relations operated in a sphere which didn't involve using their own senses. "It's easy enough to talk about sending a squadron heaven knows how far, but quite another thing to pay for it."

"I can see that's true," Daniel lied. What he really saw was that Bending had no idea of what was involved in manning, arming, and equipping a fighting squadron. For that matter, Bending probably had no real idea of what the Treasury had to go through either: those were just words to show that he was knowledgeable about government. "But we'd still send a squadron, despite the cost, and it seems to me that if Vaughn's as smart as he's well connected here on Cinnabar, he knows we'd break him as sure as we broke his predecessors."

Bending drained his glass and set it on the bar, looking obviously uncomfortable. Daniel set his own glass beside the bureaucrat's and signalled the bartender. God knew how much this afternoon was going to cost, but it was better to go ahead rather than waste the money already invested.

"Well, the truth is, Daniel . . . " Bending said. He seemed to have sunk in from his posturing frog manner of a moment before. "It's all very well to say that the Republic wants its allies to prosper—and we do, of course. But under Leland Vaughn, the Strymon fleet kept down piracy and regional traffic was almost entirely in Strymon freighters. Nowadays the pirates get a subsidy from shipping firms, a transit tax you could call it . . . and Cinnabar firms have deeper pockets than the locals do. More than half the trade's in Cinnabar hulls now."

"Ah," said Daniel again. He drank in order to hide what otherwise would have been a disgusted expression. "I see. And Delos is of the same mettle as his father, is that it?"

"Delos is twice anything his father dreamed of being, we think in the ministry," Bending said, showing the decency to be a little embarrassed. "I know it may not seem proper to a navy man—" *He was right about that!* "—but it really is the best option for the Republic."

For Cinnabar shippers to lick the boots of pirates? No, I don't think so.

Aloud Daniel said, "What do you suppose Vaughn was doing at Harbor Three yesterday, Wex?"

Bending laughed and drained his own glass. He set it upside down on the bar to indicate he was through with his liquid lunch.

"I suspect it's the reason a prisoner looks at the sky, Daniel," he said. "To remind himself of what he doesn't have."

He slapped Daniel on the shoulder again and pushed off through the crowd. "Remember me to the Speaker, Daniel," he called back.

"The very next time I see him!" Daniel replied cheerfully. He looked at the chit the bartender set between the empty glasses and raised an eyebrow, then rooted through his purse for a ten-florin coin.

And if I do ever see Father, we'll probably have another flaming row when I tell him what despicable toadies he has wearing the Leary collar flash.

CHAPTER SIX

The lane for aircars approaching Anadyomene Gardens was at four hundred feet over the road for ground transport, too low to gain a full panorama of the site. Nonetheless what Adele could see out the side window was impressive enough.

"Good heavens, do they have a pike tree?" said Daniel, peering through the window on the other side of the car. He had his naval goggles down over his eyes either for magnification or to view the scene in something other than the normal optical spectrum. "I believe they do. Adele, they've got a pike tree from Rouge and it must be over a century old! However do you suppose they transported it?"

A tree with branches fluting up from only the last ten feet of a trunk nearly two hundred feet tall grew from one of the Gardens' scores of artificial islands. Adele had seen it as the car followed the curve of the road below, though it meant no more to her than any of the other types of vegetation separated by the narrow waterways.

Still, with Daniel's identification of the imported tree to go by, it shouldn't be too hard to answer the question. Obediently she drew the personal data unit from her purse—the garments Tovera bought her for the party weren't fitted to carry it, and Adele certainly wasn't going to leave it behind—and set it on her knees.

A professional chauffeur drove the hired aircar. Hogg sat with Tovera on the rear-facing seat behind the driver's compartment, looking glum. He'd rented the limousine and had been looking forward to driving it himself, only to have his hopes dashed when the firm checked his professional credentials—Hogg had none— and put in their own driver as a condition of the lease.

Adele suppressed a smile lest Hogg realize what had amused her. He could have driven the aircar, true enough, but Adele would've been holding on with both hands, let alone expecting her data unit to stay on her knees.

"Oh, heavens, I didn't mean you should do that, Adele," Daniel said, sliding his goggles onto his forehead again. He looked apologetic. "I just meant, well, the Gardens were only built five years ago and I was surprised to see an adult specimen of so large a tree."

"But I *can* learn how they transported it, Daniel," Adele said. "I'm sure there's a record, in the construction files if nowhere else. It probably won't take more than ten minutes."

Daniel laughed and patted her hand. "I know you could, Adele," he said, "and at leisure I'd appreciate you doing that. Right now we have a party to attend."

He leaned back in his seat and looked at her appraisingly, though in the past few months he must have seen her thousands of times. "You know, I keep forgetting that you're always *on*," he said. "I ought to be used to that by now."

Adele put the data unit away, a trifle awkward because she wasn't used to keeping it in this purse. "I've been accused of being overly literal," she said dryly. "It appears to me that that wouldn't be a problem if fewer people were underprecise."

The car dropped to ground level to enter a parking lot covered by a marquee of frothy plastic. Scores of vehicles were already within, both aircars and ground transportation. Many of the former bore the flashes of houses of importance in the Republic; even the rental cars were, like this one, of a high class. Other guests wearing either civilian finery or dress uniforms were walking through the seashell-shaped entrance. Each was accompanied by a servant.

Despite its name and the marquee's decor, the Gardens arose not from seafoam but from channels cut across a bend of the Pearl River thirty miles from Xenos. The coast had been in sight as the aircar neared the location, but there was no actual connection.

Adele thought of checking a topographical display on her data unit, but after the business of the pike tree she was vaguely embarrassed to take it out again. Instead she said, "Wouldn't it have been better to join it to the sea? Surely the developers could afford coastal frontage."

Daniel paused in the door Hogg was holding open for him and looked surprised. "Well, the salt would kill the vegetation, Adele," he said. He didn't sound condescending, just puzzled. "Certainly most native and Terran species, and that of almost any plant that comes from a world that humans could live on."

"Oh," Adele said, suppressing an irrational desire to check what Daniel said on a natural-history database. The chance that he'd be wrong was beneath computation, but she still didn't in her heart of hearts believe anything she hadn't looked up for herself.

Tovera held the door for her mistress with one hand; her slim attaché case was in the other. Adele hadn't asked what Tovera had in the case, in part because her "servant" was likely to say, "Equipment," and refuse to amplify the statement. Barely aloud, Adele muttered, "Then they really ought to change the name of the place to something less confusing, you know."

Though that was probably another instance of her being overly literal.

The hired car slid off in the direction of long-term parking, leaving Daniel's group to walk through the gateway. The breeze from its fans was barely noticeable. Adele imagined the plume of dust and flying debris that Hogg would have raised. He was behind her and Daniel, so she allowed herself to smile as broadly as she ever did.

An unctuous man—short, dark, and topped with a head of luxurious chestnut hair that certainly hadn't appeared without the aid of science—greeted guests as they entered, shaking their hands with his right and gesturing with his left toward a hallway with a very prominent sign:

NO WEAPONS OF ANY SORT ARE PERMITTED
WITHIN ANADYOMENE GARDENS.
PLEASE USE THE SECURE LOCKERS IN OUR DRESSING
ROOMS TO STORE VALUABLES UNTIL YOUR RETURN.

The main entrance beyond the greeter was framed by the cage of a sophisticated detector screen. It could easily have been concealed within the molded wall coverings, but its very prominence was part of the message. Two immaculately dressed but burly attendants stood beside the apparatus.

Of course, Adele thought with a grimace. The Gardens would otherwise be a choice site for duels, which would drive away the ordinary visitors come to spend the day in a variety of exotic settings.

She sighed and stepped down the hallway to an unoccupied dressing room. Daniel made a small finger gesture to show that he understood. He waited, whistling a rigadoon softly while later guests passed by.

Adele closed the door behind her and examined the bank of lockers with thumbprint latches in the sidewall. Only two of the twenty were closed, that is, in use.

It was very unusual for people of the status of Vaughn's guests to carry weapons themselves: they had servants for their protection. Adele's parents, however, had believed in an ideal of equality—which meant that a Mundy should be able to do anything a servant could, only better.

Besides that, the Mundys' progressive political views meant they might at any time be challenged to a duel—*if* the affronted party thought he or she might survive the encounter. In her youth Adele had spent almost as many hours on a virtual target range as she had with a data unit, and her skill with a pistol was comparable to what she could achieve with her wands.

She took the small electromagnetic pistol from her side pocket and set it inside a locker, which she closed with her thumb over the plate. In theory, at least, only her thumb could release the latch. She hoped the lockers were as secure as the management claimed, because that gun had been a friend to her in difficult times.

Adele returned to Daniel and the servants. She glanced at Tovera's attache case and raised an eyebrow, a gesture that only someone with a great deal of knowledge of what Tovera was could interpret.

Tovera smiled blandly and walked through the detector without incident. Hogg sauntered after her, his hands in his pockets. His whistling was a discordant echo of his master's.

"That's odd," Daniel murmured to Adele, indicating that they'd been thinking along the same lines.

"Isn't it?" she said, taking his offered arm and stepping though the screen beside him. Ahead of them Hogg and Tovera stood back to back, their hands at their sides, taking in their human and material surroundings with perfectly feigned nonchalance.

When she'd first accepted Tovera's allegiance, Adele had wondered how she was going to get along with Hogg. In fact the two . . . "servants" was the wrong word; they were retainers in the full sense of the term—the two retainers showed mutual respect and a spirit of emulation which didn't spread to direct competition. Open rivalry between them would have been unpleasant and very brief: Tovera had been born missing a conscience, and Hogg was ruthless the way only a countryman can be.

On the other side of the detector arch, the Gardens opened out into a broad park with benches and, beyond the grass, a canal. A dozen awning-covered boats, ranging from a four-seater to a barge that would hold at least forty, were drawn up along the canal bank. Scores of guests stood in loose groupings; the servants formed a semicircle at a distance around their betters.

A man in silver-slashed magenta stepped from the largest group and waved. "Lieutenant Leary!" he called. Adele recognized the voice as Vaughn's; the facial makeup repeated the motifs of his garments and had completely concealed his identity so far as Adele was concerned. "Come over here and let me introduce you to a friend from Strymon before we get under weigh."

Why is he so interested in Daniel?

"I wonder why he's so interested in me?" Daniel murmured under his breath. He straightened his shoulders and added, "Well, perhaps we'll learn," as he sauntered with Adele toward their host.

Vaughn clasped Daniel's hand warmly. "Honored to have such an exceptional member of the RCN with us here, Leary," he said. "Given the way your career's started, I expect some day to be telling my grandchildren, 'Yes, darlings, I knew Admiral Leary when he was merely a dashing young lieutenant.'"

"I didn't know you even had children, Delos," said a spare woman of forty-odd, well dressed in a fashion much flashier than Cinnabar tastes. What she wore was obviously a business suit, but instead of a muted progression from black through silver gray—like Adele's—it was scarlet with gold accents up the right side.

Vaughn laughed. The aide behind him, the Tredegar whom Adele remembered meeting in the group visiting the *Princess Cecile*, scowled as though the sound had tripped a switch in his face muscles.

"No, Thea," Vaughn said, "the Vaughn bloodline is far too valuable to Strymon for me to waste it where it wouldn't be appreciated, don't you think? And I've been away from Strymon for what sometimes seems rather a long while."

He turned to Daniel, completely ignoring Adele. His attitude didn't disturb her; it was to be expected from one of Vaughn's status to one of her own. What was interesting was the fact that according to the same logic, Vaughn should be ignoring Daniel as well.

"Lieutenant Daniel Leary, the Hero of Kostroma," he said, "allow me to introduce Mistress Thea Zane. Mistress Zane was one of my father's dearest friends and has acted as a friend to me on Strymon during my absence."

"When someone's a long way away, Delos," Tredegar remarked harshly, "it's difficult to be sure that they *are* really friends and not secretly plotting to trap you!"

"I'm sorry that being out of touch with home for so long has so warped your perceptions, Tredegar," Zane said with a condescending smile. "In any case, I'm not at a distance any more, am I?"

Vaughn laughed easily and put a hand on the shoulder of both his partisans. "Come, let's board the boats, shall we? After all, there's no point in renting the whole Gardens if we're going to spend the afternoon on the entrance canal. Especially when the food—and the drink, Lieutenant, I know you navy men—is inside."

His eye caught that of a man wearing the uniform of the Land Forces of the Republic. "Colonel?" he said. "Would you and your lady care to join me in the lead boat? Tredegar will be driving. He made the arrangements, so he knows where things are placed."

"Yes, we'll stop at Rakoscy Island for refreshments," Tredegar said, walking toward the smallest of the craft with a gesture to bring those closest with him. "Then we can spread ourselves as taste determines."

In a louder voice directed at the entire gathering he added, "There's a barge for the servants. I thought the rest of us could choose our own seating."

Daniel looked at Adele. He gestured with a twist of his lips toward a craft with gilded seats for ten. The ends of a three-seat bench were being claimed by a pair of blond women who might have been twins and were certainly equally stunning. Adele smiled faintly and followed Daniel, shifting her line slightly to block a young Cinnabar aristocrat who'd been aiming for the same place as Daniel was—the one between the blondes.

Even if this outing taught them nothing about Vaughn's plans, Daniel should have no reason to protest the expenditure of time.

Smiling at the girls in turn, Daniel said, "Are both you ladies from around here?"

"Oh no," said Shawna, the one on his left. "I'm from Welter Heights."

The boat moved away from the canal side, rocking in the wake of the three craft ahead of them. Each vessel was piloted by a member of Vaughn's retinue rather than a servant or a professional from the Gardens' staff. The woman at the controls of this one was in her twenties and not at all bad looking. Under other circumstances Daniel might have chosen a seat in the bow beside her.

"And I'm from Welter Heights too," said Elinor, trying—with some success—to give the words a sultry air.

Welter Heights was the district of Xenos where Daniel was now renting an apartment. He'd meant, "Are you from off-planet?" but in fairness to the girls, he hadn't said that. Mind, if he had, they might have asked him what a planet was.

"You must have been a lot of places since you're a navy man, isn't that so, Danny?" Elinor said, shifting slightly and bringing her knee in contact with Daniel's. She lifted her hands to frame her hair, which swirled into a peak like a pale blond meringue.

The canal curved slowly between walls of stone covered with a Terran variety of moss. Daniel doubted that many of the Gardens' visitors recognized that the entranceway was a display in its own right, but he at least appreciated the attention to hidden detail.

"Why, I've seen some of the universe, yes," Daniel said with a broad smile to imply an exaggeration he would've choked before putting into words. In fact his two months on Kostroma were the only time he'd spent on a planet besides Cinnabar.

The boat's powerful electric drive set up a hum in the fabric of the hull, easily distinguished from the slap of wakes from the preceding craft. The tiny trolling motor on the transom must be intended to move them between the islets, named for the planets whose transplanted vegetation adorned them.

"Then tell me the truth," Elinor said. Her friend leaned toward Daniel from the other side, putting the fingertips of her left hand on his shoulder as if for balance. "Do the girls on Pleasaunce really wear their hair this way?"

Daniel blinked. "I can truthfully say," he said truthfully, "that I never saw a woman on Pleasaunce—" the capital of the Alliance of Free Stars, and a planet Daniel could only have visited as a prisoner during the past five years of open war between Cinnabar and the Alliance "—who was anywhere near as beautiful as you—"

He put his left hand over the fingers on his shoulder. Shawna responded by massaging his trapezius.

"—or Shawna."

Well, after all, he hadn't chosen this seat because he expected brilliant conversation during the trip. Adele, placed beside Mistress Zane on a bench forward, seemed to be having that. She caught Daniel's eye past Zane and gave him a sardonic grin— almost as if she could hear the girls.

The boat slowed, then turned sharply to enter the Gardens proper. Around the edge of the islet to the right grew amber trees from Albirus. Sap dripping from their horizontal branches down to the surface of the water had hardened into a curtain of translucent gold. There was a small dock and a passage through the wall, but the trees were planted to form a reentrant that screened the islet's interior even from that direction. An orgy there would have been only shadows and laughter to those elsewhere in the Gardens.

Daniel laughed, exchanging pats and flattery with Shawna and Elinor. Conditioned reflex and his tongue muscles were sufficient for the task, letting his eyes and brain get on with cataloguing the minihabitats which the boat crawled past on the thrust of the trolling motor.

He didn't recognize all the originals, though usually one plant or another was so distinctive that he could identify the source planet by that alone. The scarlet rippers from Swetna surprised him until he noticed that each leaf had a small cut at the base. The motive spines must have been removed, explaining how a plant which slashed animals' throats for fertilizer could be grown in a pleasure garden. The flowers' heavenly perfume floated over the water, stopping the girls in mid-sentence. Their faces took on a rapt, almost feral, look that was honest in a fashion no previous expression of theirs had been.

In the lead, Vaughn's boat nosed up a ramp which was long enough to berth the whole miniature fleet. Rakoscy Islet was equipped for large parties. There were no grasses on it, but short-stemmed plants whose leaves were the size of five-florin pieces covered the ground with soft resilience. In the center of the islet were refrigerated containers on serving tables. Bowers of larger, soft-bodied shrubbery around the circumference sheltered couches and eating tables.

Vaughn shook hands with the colonel who'd accompanied him in the boat, then walked over to where Daniel's vessel grounded softly. The aide at the controls lowered a gangplank, though that seemed scarcely necessary for a craft with less than six inches of freeboard.

"Lieutenant Leary," he called, "would you and Mistress Zane care to join me for a glass of wine before we adjourn to individual explorations? I'll pledge my honor as a Shipowner of Strymon that your lovely companions will be waiting for you when we finish."

He turned his smile toward Elinor and Shawna. Shawna made a face as though she'd bitten something sour and said, "He doesn't have to give me orders, Danny. I'd wait for you anyway."

"And me too!" said Elinor, rising on her tiptoes to kiss Daniel's cheek.

Daniel patted both girls on the shoulder and stepped past them. The aristocrat who'd lost out in the race for seating moved in; Shawna ostentatiously turned her back and began talking to Elinor in her normal affected voice.

Daniel pretended to ignore the byplay. He doubted that the girls were professionals, or at least fully professional. No question that they took whatever orders Vaughn chose to give them, however. Perhaps they just wanted to stay on the A-list for his parties.

Tredegar had turned when Vaughn spoke to Daniel. He came over with quick steps and said, "Delos, perhaps you should—"

"Tredegar," Vaughn said as though he hadn't heard the other man speak, "would you go organize the service for me? You know where everything is, you see."

Tredegar paused with his mouth open. He closed it, took on a blank expression, and strode off silently.

"Thea, Lieutenant, let's go over here," Vaughn said, leading the way to a bower whose curved couch had room for four. The barge with the servants was only now grounding, but an aide from the second boat was already setting a tray with a chilled bottle and three glasses on the half-round table facing the couch.

This invitation wasn't spur of the moment. *I doubt Delos Vaughn does things on the spur of the moment any more often than my father does,* Daniel thought with a flash of realization.

The aide poured the wine, then stepped back and set a screen of woven feathers across the open side of the alcove. Vaughn handed glasses to his guests, then took a sip himself. "Do you like the vintage, Lieutenant?" he asked.

Daniel tried his glass, remembering Hogg drilling him in company manners and not slurping it down all at once. It had a fruity taste with a tingle underneath. Besides that, the color was a nice blend of gold and pale raspberry.

"Yes, I like it well enough," he said, "but I'm not a connoisseur, I'd have to say. I'd probably be as well satisfied with any old thing from a jug as I would with what is, I'm sure, an exceptional wine."

He raised his glass for punctuation.

Vaughn laughed at the candor. "It's from my own planet, Strymon," he said. "Thea brought it with her to remind me of home, not that there was any likelihood of me forgetting."

"Are you familiar with Strymon, Lieutenant Leary?" Zane said, watching him over the rim of her glass. She wore a ring whose bezel was two serpent heads facing one another; the eyes of one were ruby chips, the other diamonds.

"After we met Mr. Vaughn at Harbor Three," Daniel said, nodding to his host, "I went over my Uncle Stacey's logs of his visit to Strymon twenty-seven years ago. Of course, that was a long time past, and ships' logs aren't heavy on local color."

But Daniel Leary, using the official logs and Uncle Stacey's annotations, would be able to take the *Princess Cecile* from Cinnabar to Strymon with an efficiency no other ship of her class could equal. Piloting a ship through the Matrix was an art. There'd never been a greater master of it than Commander Bergen, but his nephew had enough talent to gain full profit from his teachings.

"I haven't been back to Strymon in many years," Vaughn said. "As no doubt you know. Your father is Corder Leary, the former Speaker of the Senate, I understand?"

"That's correct, so far as it goes," Daniel said. He wasn't precisely angry at being interrogated under the fig leaf of polite conversation, but viscerally he reacted to it as a challenge. He knew that was affecting his choice of words, but even so he added, "You should be aware, however, that over the past six years I've seen no more of my father than you have of yours."

He drained his glass. Mistress Zane looked startled, but Vaughn merely laughed and offered Daniel the decanter. "I didn't have a warm relationship with my father either, Lieutenant," he said. "It might well have come to a similar pass if I'd stayed on Strymon . . . which of course I did not. And I don't mean that Leland should've been shot in the back, though that's neither here nor there."

"On Strymon . . . " Zane said. Her eyes were like agates, layered brown and green and blue. " . . . it's usual for a young man with political interests to serve in the navy for a few years first as a preparation for public life. Is that the case here on Cinnabar?"

"It is not," Daniel said, a little surprised at his own vehemence. He set down the glass he'd just refilled, afraid he'd otherwise spill it. The woman had—innocently, beyond question—spoken what was virtually blasphemy to an officer of the RCN.

He cleared his throat. "Mistress, the RCN is nonpolitical. Above politics, if you will. The RCN defends the Republic against her external enemies but has nothing to do with internal policies."

"I don't mean to contradict you, Lieutenant," Vaughn said, "but a number of senators *are* former naval officers, a background they frequently mention during debates on naval appropriations."

"Yes, sir," Daniel said, nodding forcefully, "yes indeed. But I think you'll find that when Admiral Marks or Pereira of Amadore speak in the Senate, they're representing the RCN as a whole, not aligning the RCN with one or another of the civil factions. As for myself—"

He took a deep breath, then grinned with a return of good humor. "Mistress Zane, my father—and I gather now my sister—are very much a part of the political establishment of the Republic. I'm not, by temperament. If my father and I hadn't had words, I'd probably be managing Bantry now. Doing an adequate job, I'm sure, but spending most of my time hunting and fishing as I did when I was a boy."

And meeting girls in the evening; which was easy for the young master to do on Bantry, but not so difficult for an engaging youth in a naval uniform either.

"But what I've found now in the RCN is not only a career but a life, sir and madam," he concluded, raising the glass again. "Any suggestion to the contrary is ill-founded."

Smiling to take the sting out of a statement of faith, Daniel drank. He forgot he was in urbane society until the full contents had slid down his throat; the sensation was like peppercorns in ice cream.

"I wouldn't dream of doubting the word of a Leary of Bantry," Vaughn said easily. "You're a lucky man to have found your vocation and been permitted to practice it, Lieutenant."

Daniel looked at him, wondering how much of the statement was sincere and how much was Vaughn's attempt to curry sympathy for his own plight. He snorted more with irony than humor. As with Speaker Leary, *everything* Vaughn said was for effect. The statement's truth or otherwise came a bad second in the decision tree.

"Yes, sir," Daniel said. "I am very lucky. "

He coughed lightly, to clear his throat and punctuate the thought. "I wonder, sir," he continued, "since we're answering questions for one another—"

Daniel had been answering questions for the Strymon citizens; it was time to remind them of that.

"—if you'd tell me why you were visiting the *Princess Cecile* yesterday when we met? She's a lovely ship, as I'd be the first to tell you, but not one of the more impressive sights in Harbor Three at present."

"The *Princess Cecile* is the corvette Lieutenant Leary captured almost single-handed," Vaughn said to Mistress Zane. He turned to Daniel and continued, "You're thinking I should have been interested in the battleship in the next dock, I suppose? Strymon didn't have battleships when I lived there; we hadn't had anything so large in a generation."

"By treaty," Zane said. Her tone wasn't bitter, but there was a hint of something harsher than resignation in her voice.

"By treaty, of course," Vaughn said. "A treaty my father supported and I fully support, because it prevents Strymon from wasting resources by trying to compete where we cannot compete successfully."

He lifted the decanter and gestured toward Daniel; Daniel shook his head minutely in refusal. Vaughn poured for himself and continued, watching the sparkling liquid swirl into the glass, "Strymon does have frigates, though, very similar to your ship. I think with those frigates, properly commanded and supported as they should be by the government, we could sweep the Sack clear of pirates as we did under my father. Don't you?"

He met Daniel's eyes. Daniel nodded and said, "Well, sir, if the opinion of a junior lieutenant is of any importance—yes, I think you're right."

And I hope it happens soon, he thought; but while Daniel was no politician, he was too much his father's son to blurt that while stone sober. Which he wouldn't be much longer if he didn't watch himself.

"I think I've monopolized the company of my host for long enough, sir," he said, offering Vaughn his hand. "Mistress Zane, a pleasure to meet you. I hope your stay on Cinnabar is profitable."

The Strymon aide slid the screen away as soon as Daniel's hand touched it. He stepped out of the bower and saw Hogg waiting for him with a glass of something clear that wasn't likely to be water. That looked even better than Shawna and Elinor, but by heaven they were waiting too!

Whistling a tune he'd learned on Bantry as "The Farmer's Daughter," Daniel walked toward the trio. The rest of the afternoon was for pleasure, or he'd know the reason why.

CHAPTER SEVEN

The barge nosed back up on Rakoscy Islet with the last load of the guests who'd dispersed throughout the Gardens during the course of the party. The leaves on the shrubs and the islet's ground cover were canted to catch the late afternoon sun, giving the shore a subtly different appearance from the one Daniel and his companions had left two hours before.

Shawna and Elinor pressed close to Daniel from either side, cooing things that probably wouldn't have made sense even if he'd bothered to listen to them. The young noble he'd cut out was sitting under a bower, drinking straight from a bottle and glaring at Daniel with undisguised hatred. His nervous-looking servant was close by; a balked noble was likely to be a dangerous master.

You're welcome to them now, buddy, Daniel thought. *I haven't been so tired out since I climbed Hessian Hill when I was six and then realized I had to get down again before nightfall.* In a few days this afternoon would be one to remember fondly. At the moment, Daniel just wanted to be shut of the girls and to have a chance to sleep.

Adele had been sitting primly alone in a bower with the personal data unit deployed on her lap. She didn't look out of place; from her smile, she was having at least as good a time as anyone else at the party. When the barge tooted twice to announce its return, she'd shut down the data unit and walked toward the shore.

Tovera wasn't at first visible, but Daniel suddenly spotted her at the serving tables where she could see the interiors of the bowers. Hogg waited where the barge had grounded, standing stiffly with his hands crossed behind his back. He was probably very drunk. It was hard to imagine a circumstance in which Hogg, surrounded by free liquor, wouldn't become very drunk.

"Girls," Daniel said, holding a hand of each girl and then joining them to one another as he stepped away, "I have to speak privately with my servant at once. I'll never forget having met you!"

"Oh, Danny!" they said in dismayed unison. They'd have clasped him again but he managed to make his escape.

Adele reached where Hogg stood at the same time Daniel did. "Quick!" Daniel whispered. "Come up with a reason I can't ride back with those girls."

"Lieutenant Leary," Adele said without missing a beat, "I need your input immediately to make up the crew list." She tapped the purse where she'd just placed her data unit.

"Very good, Mundy," Daniel said in a similarly carrying voice. "We'll go over it on the way back."

"Looks to me like you had a pretty good time," Hogg said, flicking a shower of dust from beneath Daniel's collar. It glittered in the air, then vanished. When disturbed, the trees of Joart sprayed great silver fountains of pollen which sublimed in sunlight unless it touched receptive stamens within a few moments. Daniel's collar had shielded a portion of the gouts loosed while the trio thrashed in a glade on Joart Islet.

"Besides which," Hogg added judiciously, "you're missing both epaulettes." He patted the denuded shoulders for emphasis.

"Ah," said Daniel. He'd almost forgotten that. "Ah, yes. Shawna wanted one to, ah, remember—"

Though he'd have thought the memories would be clear enough without a trinket; heaven knew his own would be.

"—and of course when she said that, Elinor too . . . It just seemed simpler. And I figured they could be replaced?"

The last sentence, though phrased as a statement, was really a question and not much short of a prayer. Daniel knew what effort Hogg had gone to so that his master would have a 1st Class uniform, and now on first wearing Daniel had gone and damaged it.

"And so they can," said Hogg with the formality of a priest giving absolution. "I will waylay an admiral this very night and remove his epaulettes, young master."

"No, Hogg," Daniel said firmly. "I personally will visit Sadlack and buy a pair of epaulettes. I regard the task as proper punishment for having mutilated my uniform in this fashion."

Which was true in a way, but it was also a lot easier than dealing with the consequences if Hogg hadn't been joking. Hogg had a sense of humor: a bawdy, raucous one that had rubbed off on Daniel. On the other hand, there was almost nothing that Hogg *might* not do, especially if he was drunk. There were many things that Daniel wouldn't do; though now that he thought about it, forcibly borrowing an admiral's epaulettes probably wasn't beyond the realm of possibility.

"As you say, young master," Hogg muttered. "A Hogg would never be able to live with himself if he disobeyed his master's order."

"Daniel," Adele said to break into Hogg's maunderings—and whatever the truth of the threat to an admiral, the notion that Hogg would never disobey Daniel was *not* to be taken seriously, "Tovera placed an eavesdropping device at Vaughn's table. I've heard the conversations."

She tapped the data unit in her purse. Daniel controlled his reflex to glance at Tovera. Adele continued, "During the afternoon Vaughn's agreed with three people here to rent a new townhouse for the next year. That's three *separate* townhouses, giving each owner the same story about wanting larger quarters. He must be lying to two of them, but I can't imagine why he'd do that. He's bound to be caught in a few weeks."

"Ah!" said Daniel, because Adele's words gave him a vivid recollection of some of the things he'd recently been murmuring to Shawna and Elinor. "Only if he's here, you see."

It wasn't the same, well, *quite* the same, because Daniel had used words like, " . . . for all the time I'm on Cinnabar. . . ." But he knew the girls thought the phrase meant, "for the future," while Daniel knew he'd be off-planet in a week at the latest.

"I think," he amplified, "that Vaughn expects to leave Cinnabar very shortly. I don't know of any reason he should expect that . . . but it seems he's confident enough that he's making sure as many movers and shakers as possible 'know' that he's planning to stay."

Guests were moving toward the boats under the gentle urging of the aides from Strymon. Many were under the weather, and a few were being supported or even carried by servants: Vaughn's hospitality had been lavish and of high alcoholic content.

"Lieutenant Leary?" Vaughn called. He stood with Tredegar beside the four-seat craft which had led the flotilla to Rakoscy Islet. "I'd appreciate it if you and your guest would ride back with me. I'd like to hear from your own lips how you captured the *Princess Cecile*."

Daniel hid his frown, but he darted a quick glance at Adele. She smiled thinly—her back was to their host—and said in a soft voice, "Yes, of course he's lying, but we may as well go along with it."

"Delighted, sir," Daniel said cheerfully as he strode over to the nobleman. "And I should say at the outset that Officer Mundy here had more to do with the success of the operation than any other person."

They got into the small vessel, Daniel and Adele sitting behind Vaughn and Tredegar respectively. Two well-dressed Cinnabar nobles and a woman whom Daniel recognized as a senator's widow had been standing close by. They looked vaguely put out as they moved off in search of other seating for the trip back to the entrance.

Mistress Zane had returned to the larger boat which she'd ridden on the way in. Unlike the trio, she seemed quite at ease to be separated from her host.

"I really would be delighted to hear about your exploits, Lieutenant," Vaughn said in an undertone. "And yours as well, Officer Mundy. But I have to admit to a small subterfuge—I've just short of promised three of your fellow guests that I'd rent a house from each of them, and in truth I don't intend to go through with any of the deals. If I were alone with one of them I'd have to descend to flat lies, and if I rode in a larger craft with all three together, my entire imposture would be exposed."

Tredegar reached past the steering column to touch the joystick on the dashboard; the trolling motor whined and the boat started to back away from the shore. Vaughn put his hand over the aide's and said, "Wait for the others to board, Cornelius. We're not in a hurry, after all."

Tredegar turned to look at Vaughn. His expression was empty, his eyes glazed in a taut face. He didn't seem to be taking in the words, but at last he glanced down at the control and lifted his hand away.

"Are you all right, Tredegar?" Daniel said sharply. "You don't look well, if you don't mind my saying."

Or if you do. The aide looked as if he'd been poisoned; that, or he was utterly terrified.

"Sun," Tredegar said. "Just a touch of sun. I'm all right now."

The blood had indeed returned to his cheeks, but as he spoke he engaged the motor again as if he'd forgotten the exchange of a few seconds earlier. Vaughn looked puzzled, but the other vessels were loaded by now so there was no further reason to delay.

The boat eased into the channel. Tredegar centered the joystick, then clicked it upward to send them toward the entrance. In the clear water beneath, fish like strands of gilded tinsel schooled in the waterweed. They reminded Daniel of lightning flashing among the clouds.

"If you'll permit a question, Mr. Vaughn," Adele said coolly, "why *did* you suggest you were going to rent a house if you didn't intend to do so?"

"Am I simply a pathological liar, you mean, mistress?" Vaughn translated with a laugh. "No, or at any rate I don't see it that way. But you see, if my enemies—Friderik Nunes and his friends from the Alliance of Free Stars—learn that the Republic is sending me home, they'll try to eliminate me before I leave. I'm practicing a mild deception to encourage spies here on Cinnabar to believe that I expect to remain on your planet for the foreseeable future."

"It's not safe for you to go back," Tredegar said. He kept his face straight ahead so that he didn't have to meet his superior's eyes. "You trust Zane but she'll be your death. Death, Delos!"

"Cinnabar is a wonderful planet, Lieutenant," Vaughn said, seeming to have ignored Tredegar's words. "She isn't my planet, however. I'm looking forward to returning to a home I haven't seen in fifteen years."

To the left was an islet whose trees seemed swathed in cobwebs instead of having ordinary foliage. Daniel couldn't place their origin and suddenly regretted not having made more of an exploration of the Gardens. Even though the habitats were selective and thus artificial, the vegetation and the few permitted animal species were real so far as they went.

"Why are you telling Daniel and me the truth if you're lying to others?" Adele said, pressing the point with a lack of tact that made Daniel smile. They were very different people, he and Adele, but they both had a capacity for directness that startled others. "Our social superiors, many would say."

Vaughn smiled at her. His expression was perfectly open and natural—and false. Daniel was convinced of that, though he had no more evidence to go on than he did about the state of the universe before time began.

"Well, Officer Mundy," he said. "I don't believe you're going to help my enemies, knowing that you would thereby help the Alliance. And if you'll forgive a foreigner a bit of romance—I don't care to lie to officers of the Cinnabar fleet. We on Strymon have had ample reason to respect you and the ships you crew."

You know Adele's been listening to your conversations, Daniel realized. *You're telling us a story that fits what we already know, but that doesn't make it true.*

"I see," Adele said. "I wish your endeavors well, Mr. Vaughn."

Albirus Islet with its wall of amber trees was coming up on the left. Tredegar had gone rigid again, except that he kept sucking his lower lip in and out over his teeth. He kept pressing the joystick but the trolling motor's throttle was already full-open.

"Is Mistress Zane here to make arrangements for your return, then?" Adele asked. Daniel saw her fingers twitch and almost smiled: Adele desperately wanted to enter the data somewhere to make it real to her.

"Well, Thea is a friend," Vaughn said. "I don't think I should—"

There was a fresh hole in the sheets of hardened sap, a saucer-sized window from the interior of Albirus Islet that hadn't been there when the party entered. It could've been casual vandalism, but that wasn't the first explanation that went through Daniel's mind.

"Watch out!" Daniel said, pointing to the opening. The boat was coming parallel to it. "There's a—"

Only shadows showed through the amber curtain, but metal glinted on the other side of the hole. Vaughn was looking at Daniel in surprise; Adele groped in her left pocket for the pistol she'd been forced to leave behind. Tredegar, his face set and tears streaming down his cheeks, gripped the joystick as if it were his last hope of life.

There was no time for thought, only instinct. Daniel seized the aide's throat with both hands, lifted him bodily from the seat, and threw him into the crystal water.

The boat pitched wildly, but craft in the Gardens were broad-beamed with the expectation that many passengers would be clumsy and no few of them drunk besides. Daniel stepped into the pilot's seat, jerked the separate steering wheel to the left, and stamped on the foot throttle which controlled the main motor. The boat surged toward the islet, the bow lifting to a thirty-degree angle as the powerful waterjet torqued the vessel around its center of mass before accelerating it.

"*Are you*—" Vaughn said, grabbing Daniel around the shoulders. Adele threw herself over the Strymonian's face. She wasn't strong enough to break the grip of a well-built man, but suddenly being blindfolded made Vaughn jerk away.

The world exploded in heat and the flash of a sun going nova. What was left of the boat flew over on its back, flinging its three remaining passengers into the canal not far from Tredegar.

Air, fiercely hot and compressed by a thunderclap to the density of tons of sand, enveloped Adele. She thought she'd let go of Vaughn, but she couldn't be sure. She felt nothing—not even the pull of gravity—until she slammed into the canal.

She rose spluttering. The canal's knee-high water was clean and sweet; it must be filtered with the same care that the proprietors showed with every other aspect of the Gardens. Except that occasionally they failed to prevent assassins from bringing heavy weapons into their emasculated precincts. . . .

The weight of the motor held the boat's stern down, so the remainder of the plastic hull stuck up in the air. The dashboard had survived but the lower portion of the bow had been converted into a stench of resin matrix. Only a few tatters of fiberglass reinforcement were still attached to the undamaged mid-hull.

A gray fog hung above the wreckage, and a few wisps of ionized air were dissipating like yesterday's rainbow. A plasma bolt, then, from a weapon concealed behind the wall of amber sap. The light-speed particles liberated their energy on the first solid object they encountered. They'd destroyed the boat, but they hadn't been able to penetrate even the thin hull when Daniel lifted it with the throttle.

Daniel sloshed toward the islet, staying to the left of a direct line with the gunport. He should have looked silly, unarmed and dressed in a dripping uniform. Adele doubted that he looked silly to the gunmen, though. As the commendation for his activities on Kostroma had put it, "*Faced with a superior enemy, Lt. Leary chose to attack in accordance with the finest traditions of the Republic of Cinnabar Navy.*"

Feeling extremely foolish, Adele also started toward the islet, keeping to the right of the opening. If she'd had her pistol she might have done some good. So far as she could tell, this was no better than suicide. Still, she was acting out of cold analysis, not passion: she knew she'd rather be killed than live to remember that she'd let her only real friend die alone.

It occurred to Adele to wonder what had happened to her purse with the personal data unit, dropped when she tried to get Vaughn out of the way. She hadn't the least notion of what Daniel was doing, but she knew *him* well enough to support him regardless.

The boat's hull had reflected some of the bolt's energy back toward the weapon, eating away a fan of hardened sap and fracturing the smooth amber wall for ten feet in either direction. A man wearing a poncho of light-scattering cloth ran past the enlarged opening, holding a handgun. *Why didn't I insist on keeping my—*

A bow wave washed Adele to the side as the barge carrying the servants surged between her and Daniel. She had to splash forward clumsily to keep from being pushed onto her face.

The craft had a small cockpit in the rear. The aide who'd been at the controls floundered in the water thirty feet back while Hogg drove the vessel at a slant toward the islet. Several of the servants had jumped overboard; all but one of the remainder had ducked behind the gunwales.

The exception, Tovera, stood in the bow. Her left arm was locked at an angle before her; across the crooked elbow rested her right hand holding a pistol.

The ship slid onto the islet, pushing over the amber trees and shattering the hardened sap. The louder crash was the vessel's lower hull breaking on the concrete retaining wall. Three men wearing camouflage capes were running across ground covered with flowers like a carpet of tiny flags. The assassins' primary weapon, a bipod-mounted plasma cannon, rested on the ground behind them. They couldn't fire it again till the white-hot barrel had cooled from the previous discharge, and they showed no signs of planning to use the pistols each waved in his hand.

Tovera shot—with a very compact submachine gun, not a pistol, and how *had* she gotten it through the detection screen at the entrance? Despite the light-scattering garments and the fact that the boat was breaking up beneath her, Tovera's first burst sent the most distant assassin onto his face with his arms flapping.

Tovera stepped to the islet just before the impact. The posts supporting the vessel's canopy flexed till they cracked, slamming her in the middle of the back with the whole structure, frame and fabric together. She fell under a pile of debris.

The remaining assassins reached a skiff nestled onto the shore across the islet; on that side, the branches of the amber trees hadn't been pleached together to form a continuous wall. One of the men settled behind the controls while the other turned, aiming toward the pursuit just as Daniel and Adele squelched onto the islet.

Tovera's weapon crackled from the tangled wreckage. Its electromotive coils accelerated pellets up the short barrel at several times the speed of sound. The gunman fell backward, dropping his pistol. The driver slumped on his face, half out of the skiff as it rose on the balanced static charges induced in the ground and its own hull. The pilot's weight dragged the little craft into a slow circle like a horse guided by a lunge line.

Daniel ran toward the fallen assassins. Adele instead waded back into the water. The rest of the flotilla clogged the channel, some vessels halting on reversed thrust while others chose to ground on the fern-covered islet to the right.

Delos Vaughn hunched below the retaining wall where undamaged sap still provided a curtain from sight. Tredegar stood in the middle of the canal, his eyes wild and his mouth open though speechless.

There's my purse. Despite the violence, the water remained clear except for swirls of weed and air bubbles. The channel was concrete colored to give it the appearance of mud.

Adele raised the purse and took the data unit from it. *Pray whatever Gods there were that its seals are as good as they're supposed to be.*

Tredegar came to his senses from watching Adele's organized action. He sloshed toward the nearest of the undamaged boats, the ten-seater which had brought Daniel and Adele into the Gardens. Shawna and Elinor stood in the bow, watching events with perfect aplomb while everyone else on the craft lay flat on the deck.

"Hogg, don't let Tredegar get away!" Adele cried. It wasn't an order. She didn't have authority to order Daniel's servant to do anything, as Hogg would be the first to tell her if provoked.

He wasn't the man to ignore a warning, though. Hogg turned in the cockpit and judged his distance as the aide splashed past him. Ten feet of weighted line shimmered from Hogg's hand and wrapped around Tredegar's arm and throat. The aide fell backward into the water.

Adele stamped ashore again, clumsy from the weight of water trapped in her pant legs. The suit Tovera picked for her had gathered cuffs, a matter that Adele hadn't paused to consider when she put the garment on. Clothes were something she wore as a social or environmental necessity, not out of any intrinsic interest they had for her.

If she had to do it again, she'd specify drain holes at wrist and ankles. Though how the *damned* fabric could let water in so easily and then hold it there like a set of fluid leg irons was beyond her.

An alarm had been given—many alarms, judging from the number of sirens she could hear at varying distances. Ignoring them, ignoring also the shouts and bustle of people around her, Adele walked over to the nearest of the dead men.

There were three holes in the back of his neck, so close together that she could have covered them with her thumb. Tovera was already there, going through the man's pockets. Daniel had switched off the skiff's power, bringing it down to the ground again. He was searching the other two assassins.

Adele took the pistol from the dead man's hand and thrust it through her waist sash. Tovera looked at her. "He doesn't have any identification, but he's carrying a thousand florins."

"They're probably just local thugs," Adele said. She took one of the peacock-hued hundred-florin coins Tovera had fanned on the ground beside the man's purse. "Anyway, I don't need identification if the money's there."

Adele had brought up her personal data unit as she spoke. Her wands flickered, entering the coin's serial number into the records of the Central Bank of the Republic.

The database was supposed to be restricted, of course. Because Adele was using the Ministry of Defense computer for access, she was probably getting the information faster than one of the bank directors could have done after entering a series of codes and passwords. Even so, a search so enormous took some time.

She looked at the submachine gun in Tovera's hand. The barrel was only four inches long and the few pounds the weapon weighed weren't enough to stabilize it when fired full automatic—Adele would have thought, barring the evidence of the corpse before her.

"How did you get that through the screening at the gate?" she demanded.

Tovera's expression became guarded. "My case projects the image of a data unit and other ordinary office equipment," she said. "There are ways to defeat it, but none that these *civilians* would have available."

Carefully, her eyes never leaving Adele's, she added, "I'm sorry, mistress. I should have carried your weapon through the screen with me."

Adele thought about the mindset that was always prepared in case of an assassination attempt at an innocent party. She could learn to live that way, she supposed, but it seemed to her that the alternative to life was preferable if such paranoia were necessary.

She smiled. "Not at all, Tovera," she said. "I think I'm better off delegating those concerns to you."

A number of the party guests were standing around the plasma cannon, discussing it in amazed tones. The bolt had shrivelled a broadening wedge of vegetation from beneath the muzzle to the edge of the islet. The iridium barrel was no longer glowing, but any of the spectators who decided to touch the metal were going to cook their flesh to the bones.

Adele smiled grimly. Not so very long ago she wouldn't have had any more experience of a plasma cannon than did any other Academic Collections staff member. Being caught in the Kostroma rebellion had certainly broadened her horizons.

Adele's display shifted into the answer she'd expected. She looked up, hoping to catch Daniel's eye. He held two pistols by the barrel in his left hand and was talking to a young man in the beige uniform of the Militia, the national police. Despite the flashing lights and the downdraft, Adele hadn't noticed the Militia aircar landing beside the assassins' skiff.

Delos Vaughn walked up on shore, surrounded by servants and several aides. One of the latter had taken off her taffeta cape and was toweling Vaughn's legs with it. Adele watched her for a moment, blinked, and went back to the display feeling queasy. The Mundys hadn't encouraged that sort of abasement from their retainers; though when she let herself remember, there had been times . . .

She shook herself. She didn't want to think about the night her father won the race for Treasurer of the Republic and a dozen women, wives and daughters of his retainers, had buffed the gilded body of his aircar with their long hair. That was what they did for him in public. For herself, she didn't want anybody to offer her honors that she would never grant to another living person.

"You there!" Vaughn said. "What in heaven are you doing with Cornelius? Let him go at once!"

Everybody turned at the shout. Hogg was holding Tredegar upright, trussed by the neck and—behind his back—his wrists. An aide stepped forward.

"*No, Tovera!*" Adele shouted.

Hogg's hands were occupied with a prisoner who was conscious but noosed too tightly to be able to stand without help. He kicked the aide squarely in the crotch, doubling her up with a scream that a man in a similar situation couldn't have bettered.

It could have been worse. Tovera had turned also. Adele wasn't absolutely sure that her shout would've been enough to keep the pale woman from killing Vaughn's aide with the same wasplike skill that had eliminated the three assassins.

"But this is Cornelius Tredegar," Vaughn said, no longer speaking with an implicit threat in his voice. "He's one of my oldest associates. He came into exile with me, for God's sake!"

"He knew about the ambush," Daniel said, walking over and drawing the policeman with him. The fellow's partner was still in the aircar, calling for additional help. Another Militia aircar had landed, but its personnel were fending off the crush of velvet-clad Gardens employees gabbling about the damage to the settings. "If he didn't plan it, then he was helping whoever did."

"Tredegar was the paymaster," Adele said, drawing everyone's eyes from Daniel to her. They were quite a pair, dripping wet and muddy besides. "He withdrew six thousand florins from his account at the Divan branch of Stevenage Trust ten days ago. He must have paid the assassins the second half of the money just this morning, because they're still carrying it."

"Mistress?" the policeman said, glancing at the coins beside the dead man's purse. "How do you know that?"

An enclosed twelve-place aircar with Militia markings wallowed to a landing at the edge of the islet, smashing another section of the amber wall. Daniel winced though he didn't say anything. Almost half the carefully formed circuit of trees had been snapped off or uprooted.

Adele visualized a similar battle—quite small, as battles go—taking place within the precincts of the Academic Collections on Blythe. Her lips tightened. She knew how Daniel felt.

"Large coins are all registered with the central bank," Adele said. "Every time they pass through a bank, the transaction is recorded. The most recent movement of these—"

Well, at least the one she'd checked; this wasn't the time to be overprecise.

"—was to Tredegar here in a withdrawal he made personally."

Policemen wearing body armor and carrying carbines spilled out of the van in a hectoring wave, pushing through the guests in evident disregard for military uniforms and indicia of wealth. "What's going on here?" said the officer in charge, bellowing at the patrolman standing between Adele and Daniel.

The officer noticed Tredegar. Though his face was hidden behind the visor, there was no doubt of the angry exasperation in his voice as he snapped, "What's this? What the *hell* is this?"

"Sir, he's a prisoner," the regular patrolman said, standing up to a faceless bully who was doubtless also his superior in rank. "He appears to be behind the attack that—"

"Cut him loose!" the officer said. "Secure him with legal restraints." One of his subordinates drew a knife whose blade extended as the hilt came free of the clip.

There was a flicker in the air. The knife hand jerked upward, bound to the policeman's shoulder by a loop of the same weighted cord as had caught and held Tredegar. The line had two ends, after all.

Hogg grinned with absolutely no humor at all. "What the—" the officer repeated, his tone an amalgam of anger and amazement.

Daniel stepped close to Hogg, his back to the Militia officer. "Hogg," he said, "release the prisoner immediately into the custody of the civil authorities! You know how Speaker Leary will complain if he has to use his influence again to get his son's servant out of jail!"

Daniel would never have used his father's name that way for anything less serious than this incident was rapidly becoming. If the officer had acted as he might have tried in the full arrogance of his power—

Adele was again struck by the way Tovera vanished into the background under any circumstances. You would have thought that at least one member of the riot squad would have noticed the pale blonde holding a submachine gun down beside her thigh.

—then anything might have happened.

"Sure, Master Leary," Hogg said, releasing Tredegar and giving him a gentle push in the direction of the policeman who'd planned to cut him loose. "What's twenty piastres worth of fishing line and a couple pebbles?"

"I don't mind you cutting the cord," Daniel said to the officer in an innocently helpful tone, "but do be aware that it's *sea* fishing line which we use in the ocean off Bantry. It's boron monocrystal, and the tug of your man's knife blade on a thin strand would very likely have strangled the prisoner if Hogg hadn't stopped him."

Daniel's instinct made him step between Hogg and the chance of lethal danger. That's not how Tovera would have saved her colleague. And it's not what Adele would have done either, if she'd still had her pistol.

Three riot policemen began unwrapping Tredegar and their fellow. After a moment, they all flipped up their visors.

"I still can't believe . . ." Vaughn said, though the way his voice trailed off indicated that actually he was indeed beginning to believe. "Cornelius, you wouldn't betray me?"

"He wasn't planning to have you killed, Delos," Mistress Zane said scornfully. "You're his golden goose—so long as you ignore your heritage and stay here on Cinnabar! The little wretch planned to kill *me* and blame it on your niece and Nunes."

Almost everybody was looking at Zane. Adele saw Hogg grin broadly as he glanced at the prisoner he'd just surrendered. Tredegar's right wrist was now attached to a policeman's harness by a flexible restraint. He took a handkerchief from his breast pocket with his left hand and put it to his mouth.

It's probably the best result.

"Casdessus, get this one into the van," said the officer, raising his own shield. His face was surprisingly delicate; much of his apparent bulk must have been the armor. "We'll hold here till the investigative squad arrives, then—"

Tredegar's cheeks flushed bright red. Blood spurted from his nose and ears; his limbs went slack and he fell, all but the arm still tethered to the policeman's harness. The Militia officer jumped back, but blood still splashed his trouser legs and his right boot.

"I figured he'd do that, so I kept him tied up," Hogg said to the officer in a conversational voice. "It's a real education to watch a city professional like you work, Captain."

More sirens were approaching. Adele sat on the ground and brought up her data unit again. She didn't want to waste more time here, and Daniel almost certainly had things he should be doing instead of discussing with a series of officious bureaucrats a matter that was already closed. The message she was sending to Admiral Anston's office might bring a quick end to the irritation.

And if it didn't, the copy to a site Mistress Sand used for confidential dispatches certainly would.

CHAPTER EIGHT

Lt. Daniel Leary sat at the command console in the middle of the *Princess Cecile*'s bridge. In Kostroman service the console had been fixed facing the bow; now it would rotate 360 degrees in accordance with the most modern RCN practice, so that the captain could watch what was happening down the axis of C Level by dimming his holographic display to a fifty-percent mask.

Pasternak, the chief engineer—new to the corvette but a man with an excellent record both on paper and in the opinion of Sissies who'd served under him on other hulls—came up from A Level. The smile he wore on the companionway faded as he turned toward the bridge, facing Daniel at last with an expression of gray concern.

"Captain," he called across the bustle of the bridge, "I've a full crew and the stores are catalogued, but I don't vouch for the quality of either till we've had time to work up properly."

"Very good, Mr. Pasternak," Daniel said. "As it chances, all but three of your crew have served with me before so I think I with honesty can vouch for them to you. As for the sealed stores, we'll trust the warehouse inspection system till we have reason to doubt it—and we'll raise holy Hell if there *is* reason, right?"

Pasternak grinned. "They're a prime lot, sir," he said. "I'm honored you wanted me aboard to run things hull-side. But I didn't want to sound, you know, too confident before you'd seen me in action."

"Understood, Pasternak," Daniel said. "I expect we'll both be pleased with the relationship when the *Sissie* pays off the next time."

Daniel's display was running a crew list, an equipment status report, and a schematic of the *Princess Cecile* which highlighted mechanical changes in a red that faded through shades of orange with time. This last showed that a dorsal airlock had just cycled. Through the hologram Daniel could see Ellie Woetjans, timing the return from topside of a section of the port watch wearing rigger's suits.

"Lamsoe!" the bosun bellowed. "Lock that Goddamned helmet down or you can see how you like being derated for the tour!"

"I'm going to check the alignment of Number Three thruster, sir," Pasternak said, already backing toward the companionway. "We may have to readjust it after the shakedown run, though."

Betts, the chief missileer, was new to the *Princess Cecile* also. He turned from the attack console and said, "As ordered, sir, we're carrying the tubes loaded and a full twenty reloads. There's no guarantees short of launching them, of course, but I'd bet my life that all twenty-two'll function clean as a simulation."

"It's quite possible we'll all be betting our lives on that, Mr. Betts," Daniel said, with a smile to draw the sting from the reminder. "I'll expect to test your readiness with some target practice if luck doesn't send us real targets on this voyage."

The *Princess Cecile* was carrying two more missiles than her Table of Equipment. They would be expended before she returned to Harbor Three, of that Daniel was determined.

He'd noticed in the past that missileers tended not to think of their charges as being weapons for real use. Missiles were expensive and so big that relatively few could be carried on even a large warship. Missile practice was rarely carried out live, and even during wartime the chance of a missile engagement with a hostile vessel was slight.

Chief Baylor, who'd been the *Aglaia*'s missileer, had retired after the ship—including the missiles that had been the children of his heart and mind—had died in the harbor serving Kostroma City. Daniel regretted losing Baylor: the missiles launched in the *Aglaia*'s final moments had functioned perfectly, putting paid to most of an Alliance invasion fleet. Still, Betts was an experienced man and far more senior than a corvette would normally rate.

The *Princess Cecile* had been on Kostroma during a major war and revolution. Many items of value had been saved from destruction by members of the corvette's crew, with Daniel's personal servant Hogg chief among the list of rescuers.

Daniel couldn't have stopped the practice—it would be wrong to call it looting; mostly wrong, at any rate—if he'd tried, and he was too well aware of the risks his crew had run to feel they didn't deserve anything they could make off with. He wasn't comfortable with accepting the half share Hogg insisted was his, however—as a moral question, not from fear of being caught. Theoretically Hogg could fall foul of the Republic's customs authorities, but the chance was too vanishingly small to affect Daniel's decision on the matter.

Then it occurred to Daniel that any doubtful money could be spent on raising the *Princess Cecile*'s fighting readiness. No one wearing an RCN uniform would find anything morally reprehensible in *that*, even if the money came from brothel receipts. Daniel accepted his half, then spent it on missiles and extra rations for the crew.

Surely the money *didn't* come from brothel receipts, did it? Though knowing Hogg, it was probably better not to enquire too closely.

Adele stood up at the communications console. "My systems are in order, Captain," she said, remembering this time to be formal while in uniform. She was as likely as not to say "Daniel," which from her couldn't be considered a breach of discipline.

"Then I think we're ready to lift as soon as we have orders and port clearance," Daniel said, beaming with pleasure. "It might be as little as four hours."

His grin became rueful. "Or not, of course," he added. "We act at the pleasure of the Navy Office, which is rarely to be hastened."

"I, ah, wonder, Daniel," Adele said. "If we have some hours, might I . . . absent myself on some personal business?"

Daniel blinked. "Why of course," he said; just as he would have said to any of his officers, knowing that even the ones who had a tendency to drink were too excited about the planned voyage for them to risk missing liftoff. Daniel didn't imagine that the truth of the corvette's orders would be half as wonderful as the rumors circulating about them, but the stories had been enough to keep an already crack crew in a state of wire tautness.

Mind, the rumor that the *Princess Cecile* was being sent to capture a disabled Alliance treasure ship was one that had Daniel himself counting shares of dream wealth.

Adele looked down at her clothing as if in puzzlement, pinching a fold of the blouse between her thumb and forefinger. Like everybody else aboard she was wearing a utility uniform of mottled gray fabric. "I'll change and be off, then," she said. "I don't suppose I'll be very..."

She stepped toward the cabin off the bridge which she shared with Tovera. It was officially the captain's lounge, half of his tiny suite. Daniel preferred to have Adele bunking there in a crisis rather than in the Warrant Officers' Quarters. Those were at the other end of C Level, adjacent to the Battle Direction Center where Lt. Mon commanded the midshipmen and mates of the missile and gunnery officers on a set of duplicate controls.

"Ah..." Daniel said, but he couldn't think of a way to continue.

Adele's few personal belongings were already aboard. She had no friends or family in Xenos—no friends or family anywhere beyond the hull of the *Princess Cecile*, if it came to that—and she wasn't the sort to go out for one last hell-raising party before lifting ship.

Even in the midst of his concern, Daniel felt a smile start to crinkle the corners of his mouth. He'd tried to imagine Adele raising hell—and had collided with a brick wall.

But what in heaven's name *was* she planning to do?

"Wait a moment, Adele," Daniel said, rising from the command console. "I'll tag along if I may."

There wasn't a right answer to the situation. The *Princess Cecile's* captain had no business leaving her on the eve of departure; on the other hand, Daniel Leary wasn't going to let a friend go off alone wearing the expression he'd seen on Adele's face. Needs must, Mon could handle the corvette; probably handle her better than Daniel could.

Adele turned. "No," she said. "There's no need—"

"No, Mr. Leary," said Tovera from the hatch of the cabin. The pale woman's expression was, as always, unreadable, but this time it had an unfamiliar *depth* to it. "I'll accompany the mistress. It's my duty, after all."

"There's no need for anyone to come with me!" Adele said. "I'm just—looking over some real estate before I leave Xenos again."

Daniel looked from one woman to the other. "Yes, all right, Tovera," he said. "But you'll inform me if there's some way I or others can be of service, will you not?"

"Yes, Mr. Leary," Tovera said. "I'll be sure to do that."

Adele grimaced, but rather than argue she disappeared into the cabin. Tovera swung the hatch to, but remained on the bridge.

"With all respect, Mr. Leary," Tovera said softly. "I'm a member of the Mundy household. Accompanying her is my duty."

"I see," said Daniel, who suddenly *did* see. "Ah, I could send Woetjans with a detachment to, you know . . . provide visual evidence of Adele's high merit?"

"That won't be necessary, sir," Tovera said with a crooked smile. "And I think even the suggestion would embarrass the mistress."

Adele opened the hatch and stepped through, wearing civilian clothes of brown fabric with fine black stripes. Her expression would have been angry on another person; Adele being who she was, Daniel suspected it was merely a general comment on the unsatisfactory nature of human existence.

"Good luck in your endeavors," Daniel said. "I—the whole ship, Adele—look forward to your return."

Adele quirked an odd smile. "Yes," she said. "I'm rather looking forward to that also. But I think I have to go."

She stepped down the companionway awkwardly, still not fully comfortable with a warship's structure. Her servant followed without expression.

Tovera was carrying her attaché case.

The new front door was the same style as the one Adele had known, but the center of the solid lower section was the head of a barking dog in relief; worked into the grille protecting the glazed upper portion was the legend ROLFE HOUSE. The doorman playing solitaire on the doorstep gathered his cards into his hand and stood when he saw Adele and Tovera eyeing the dwelling as they approached.

"My mother's people were Rolfes," Adele murmured, feeling a touch of disdain that she supposed was undeserved. "Their crest's a pun on that: Rowf!"

She added, "I suppose they had to replace the door after the Proscriptions, but one could wish that they'd shown a little better taste."

Adele walked up to the doorman, smiling faintly as she considered what she'd just said. It wasn't true, though if she were a better person it might have been. The Adele Mundy who existed in *this* world was glad that the present owners of what had been Chatsworth Minor were people that she could look down on.

The Mundy townhouse was in the style of three centuries past: narrow and four stories high, with brick facings accented by stone transoms and tie courses. The ground floor openings were simple, save for the rose window decorating the pediment above the door. The central windows of the second and third stories were bays half the width of the building, and the facade of the level immediately beneath the peaked roof was fully glazed. At night it had frequently provided a lighted backdrop when Adele's father had stepped onto the balcony to address a crowd of his supporters in the street below.

The doorman looked at Adele with something between a sneer and a frown. His orange-and-black livery hadn't been cleaned in too long, and he didn't bother to slip the deck away into a pocket.

"I'd like to view the interior of Rolfe House," Adele said, offering the doorman her visiting card. "Please inform your master, or whoever's in charge in his absence."

The doorman took the card, read its face, and sniffed. "The master's not entertaining spacers, that I can tell you," he said. "I'll put it in the tray for him to see when he comes down if you like. You can come back another day for your answer."

He held the card back toward Adele. "Or you can just save your time."

Adele took her card and turned it over as she removed a stylus from her breast pocket. The face of the card read:

ADELE MUNDY
RCS *PRINCESS CECILE*

On its reverse she wrote *Mundy of Chatsworth*. She smiled at the servant. "Take this to your master," she said pleasantly, tucking the card between his lapel and shirt front. "Now. I will await him in the anteroom for a reasonable time, which I have set at two minutes. If he hasn't come to greet me by the end of that period, I will go looking for him."

"But—" the doorman began.

Tovera pinched the man's lips closed. "And I'll come looking for *you*, laddy," she said. "Let's not learn what'll happen when I find you, all right?"

The servant stumbled as he reached for the door because he was patting Adele's card to keep it safe as he moved. He started to close the panel behind him, then remembered the visitors were following. He was leaving the entrance hall on the way to the servants' stairs as Adele entered.

Adele glanced at the floor, then stared in horror and disbelief. What she'd expected was the beewood of her childhood, twenty-inch boards cut from trees on Chatsworth Major, the country estate, and set edgewise. Every generation or so the surface was planed flat, but even so the patterns of wear had an organic reality that bound the house inextricably into the fabric of Cinnabar.

"Good God," Adele said under her breath. She was standing on the cravat of the male half of a pair of mosaic portraits. Gold letters curving like a halo above the man's hair read LIGIER ROLFE. The woman facing him was Marina Casaubon Rolfe, if her caption was to be believed.

A housemaid carrying a laundry basket stepped into the hall from the door under the formal staircase. She called over her shoulder toward the basement, "Well you can tell her for me that—"

She saw the visitors, fell silent, and gave them a half-nod as she scurried out the back door. Adele caught a glimpse of doors at close intervals on both sides of the hall beyond: the servants' quarters here on the ground floor. That at least hadn't changed in the past fifteen years.

"Ligier is your cousin, mistress?" Tovera asked mildly. Her eyes danced across doorways and up the four levels of the staircase, covering angles from which someone might spy on them—or shoot.

"A second cousin of my mother's, I believe," Adele said. Her lips formed the words while her mind still tried to cope with the *desecration* beneath her feet. The mosaic was quite recent; the glazing of the chips in the center of the pattern showed no sign of wear from grit tracked in on the feet of visitors. "I never met him."

She smiled without humor. "If he'd been close to the family, of course," she added, "his head would have been on Speaker's Rock instead of here on the floor."

Two servants started down from the top of the formal staircase. One of them ducked into a room on the third floor and shouted a half-intelligible demand. Moments later he returned with two more footmen in tow, one of them adjusting his cummerbund.

At least the stairs were still honey-colored beewood; though the newel posts, once Mundy arrows, were now capped by barking dogs. It was an ugly—and worse, a silly—crest, but Adele grudgingly admitted that the woodcarver knew his business.

A man smoothing a hastily donned jacket came to the head of the stairs. The footmen arrayed on the third floor started down; he followed in their wake.

"*Just* inside the two minutes," said Tovera. She sounded regretful.

There was no doubt that this was Ligier Rolfe, but his hairline was a good deal higher than that of his mosaic portrait. He held Adele's card in his hand and his expression was troubled. He was in his mid-fifties; about the age Adele's mother would have been if she were still alive.

The servants parted at the bottom of the stairs. Their master, standing on the lowest step, said, "Mistress Mundy? I'm Ligier Rolfe ... of course, as you know. We weren't expecting ... that is, I had no idea you, ah ..."

"Had survived?" Adele suggested in a dry voice. She raised an eyebrow.

"Not that!" said Rolfe, increasingly flustered. "Of course I knew. . . . That is, but we didn't realize you'd returned to Cinnabar. Can I offer you refreshment? Ah, perhaps if you told me the purpose of your visit, I could . . . ?"

"I don't require refreshment," Adele said. She wasn't sure what she'd expected to find at Chatsworth Minor, but dithering panic on the part of the present owner hadn't been on her list of possibilities. She found it amusing in an unpleasant sort of way. "And my purpose is simple curiosity. I'd like to look over the house where I was born, before I leave Cinnabar again on my naval duties."

The footmen stood to either side of the staircase, eyeing her and less frequently Tovera. The doorman hadn't reappeared, Adele noticed.

"Naval duties?" Rolfe repeated. His eyes focused on Adele's visiting card; his face cleared. "Ah! Yes, of course, mistress. Anything you care to see. I only regret that my wife is still out, for I'm sure that she'd want to join me in guiding you. Though she should be back momentarily."

"The rooms on the third floor, then, if you please," Adele said, gesturing minutely with her right index finger. "Those were where my sister and I stayed while here at Minor."

You couldn't tell much from a mosaic portrait, but Adele didn't regret missing Marina Casaubon Rolfe. The Casaubons were a family whose money hadn't been able to buy them office by the time Adele left Cinnabar for Blythe. She suspected that Ligier's successful claim for Chatsworth Minor in the settlement which followed the Three Circles Conspiracy had earned him a wealthy wife.

"Would your servant care to wait in the kitchen, or . . . ?" Rolfe said, glancing at Tovera. Tovera's absence of personality made her virtually invisible.

Tovera raised an eyebrow minusculy in assent. "Yes, that will be fine," Adele said. Presumably Tovera wanted to look over the house on her own; in any case, no one could imagine Adele was in any danger from her host.

"Take care of it, Wormser," Rolfe said to one of the footmen, making a shooing motion with his hands. He noticed the card he still held. He dropped it into the salver beside the bust of a Rolfe who'd risen to the Speakership. "Mistress Mundy, if you'll follow me?"

Adele followed, noticing that Rolfe wore slippers with his name in cutwork on the gilded leather uppers. *Does his wife choose his wardrobe?*

The second floor had been mother's territory when Adele was

a child. It was Mistress Rolfe's as well, though the decor of the sitting room open off the staircase was froufrou in contrast to the severity Adele remembered.

Father had been the politician, but mother was the ideologue of the Mundy household. She practiced the same "simple life of the common people" that she preached at her salons and to her family.

Unlike her mother, Adele had personal experience of how common people live; she'd found their taste in furnishings to be very like that of the present Mistress Rolfe. Which was only to be expected, from a Casaubon.

The doors off the third floor were closed. Adele's apartments had been to the right, her sister's to the left. Rolfe paused. "Ah," he said, "if you'd informed us you were coming . . ."

"Actually, I wasn't sure until this afternoon that I *was* coming," Adele said. She opened the right-hand door herself.

The room beyond had been her library as soon as she stopped needing a nurse sleeping nearby. The bookshelves and the data console were gone. Furniture of several different styles filled all the space around the boundary of the room. A captain's chair with dog-headed armrests even blocked the door which once had led to Adele's bedroom.

The center of the room was filled by a large flat-topped desk. One of the drawers was missing and half the veneer had peeled away. The servants were using the room as a lounge. There were plates of fried potatoes, two mugs, and the remains of a pitcher of beer on the desk; stacks of dirty dishes on several of the chair seats showed how slackly the household was directed.

"I, ah . . ." Rolfe repeated. The reality of the room had obviously taken him aback, despite his previous low expectations.

"There were books here," Adele said, her voice expressionless. "I suppose they would have been sold before you took ownership of the real estate?"

"Yes, that's right," Rolfe said, glad to have something to focus on that didn't make him look like a pig. He stepped past Adele to the desk and dragged open one of the drawers. "But I recall we were given a copy of the receipts when we . . ."

Adele watched with cold amusement as her host pawed inexpertly through the drawer. She'd gone through many such agglomerations in her days as an archivist. She'd learned quite quickly that there was no document that was completely without value to *some* researcher, but there was a limit to what could be catalogued and thus become available for research.

She suspected she could trim the present mass by 99% without doing irreparable harm to posterity. And if it were limited to the Rolfe and Casaubon houses, the percentage saved could be even lower.

"Yes!" cried Rolfe. "Here they are, just as I remembered!"

Adele took the document, a four-foot continuous coil folded to fit into a drawer. It was a printout of the auction listing with numbers, presumably the amounts paid, written in holograph beside them.

"Yes, we had our bailiff, well, my wife's bailiff really, present at the auction," Rolfe said as Adele scanned the list. "Our claim was to the real estate alone, but Marina thought we needed to be careful that the auctioneers didn't try to sell fixtures as well as the personal property."

His voice was an empty background like the rustle of mating insects; not overtly unpleasant but not of any concern either. *Furniture, bedclothes, kitchen utensils. Paintings, electronic equipment, shop tools.* The last had probably belonged to Mick Hilmer, the chauffeur and mechanic. Had he survived the Proscriptions? Mick should have been exempt—he was no Mundy by blood or marriage, to be sure—but neither was he the sort to bow meekly when a gang of street toughs burst into his quarters.

"My wife has been responsible for redecorating," Rolfe burbled. He seemed to have forgotten he was standing in a junk room which once had been a private library equal to any in Xenos. "We have heirlooms from her family and mine both."

Assorted books/316 florins.

"I had laid out over five thousand florins for the books I'd purchased," Adele said. No one listening to her could have told from her voice how she felt. "Of course the more valuable items came to me as gifts. Friends of the family found it amusing that the older Mundy girl was a real antiquarian. Many of them had something on a shelf or in a trunk that even my allowance wouldn't have run to."

"Pardon, mistress?" Rolfe said. He hadn't heard the words, and he wouldn't have understood them anyway.

The Mundy children had been as much a part of the family's political entertainments as the images of ancestors in the entrance hall were. Agatha hadn't been any more outgoing than her elder sister, and unlike Adele she hadn't the taste and intellect to escape into scholarship. She'd buffered herself from the public stress with a parliament of stuffed animals, each of which had a distinct personality as well as a name.

Assorted stuffed toys/Five florins fifty.

Adele's hand began to tremble. She quickly dropped the auction list on the desktop. She wondered if she could ask to wash her hands.

"I wonder if you wouldn't be interested in some walnut pudding, Mistress Mundy?" Rolfe said. "My father-in-law has some marvelous trees on his country estate, that's Silver Oaks in the Varangian Hills."

Adele forced her mind up from the frozen horror of the past. Noises from downstairs penetrated her awareness. A woman was shouting—screaming—and feet were pounding up the stairs.

"Ah, that must be Marina," Rolfe said with false brightness. His eyes were glazing and his face looked as rigid as a mummy's. "I'll see if I can introduce—"

A woman whose garments were trimmed with off-planet furs burst into the room; the doorkeeper and several other servants followed in her wake. If the entryway mosaic had flattered Ligier Rolfe's hairline, it had excised at least fifty pounds from his wife. She tended to a naturally ruddy complexion; in her present anger she looked nearly purple.

"Darling," said Rolfe, "this is—"

Marina Rolfe flung Adele's card to the floor. "Ligier!" she said. "Get this woman out of here! She has no right to Rolfe House, none! Get her—"

She turned from her stunned-looking husband to Adele. "Get out!" she cried. "The time to protest our claim is past, past years and years ago. It's Rolfe House now and you have no right to be here!"

"Please, dear!" Rolfe said in obvious embarrassment. "She's just visiting before—"

"Shut up, you!" his wife said. "If you were any kind of man I wouldn't have to take care of this myself."

Her eyes, brown and hysterically wide, returned to Adele. "Now, are you going to get out or—"

"*Mister* Rolfe," Adele said. "If you don't restrain your dog, I will restrain her for you. Do you understand?"

Adele wasn't certain how Rolfe would react to the whiplash in her voice, though she didn't doubt what she would do if he reacted the wrong way. The anger leaping within her threatened to burst through her skin and consume everyone present.

Assorted stuffed toys/Five florins fifty.

It shouldn't have mattered, not against the greater horror of Agatha's ten-year-old head displayed on the Speaker's Rock; but it mattered.

"Marina, you're overwrought!" Rolfe said with a strength Adele hadn't credited to him. Either he'd understood what he saw in Adele's eyes or, more likely, he'd just been horrified by his wife's boorish behavior to a guest. The Rolfes were a noble house, as old as any in the Republic. "Go up and wait in my apartment while I see Mistress Mundy out."

He pointed at the doorman, perhaps blaming him for the outburst. "You! Escort your mistress to my room. Immediately!"

Mistress Rolfe stepped back, putting her hand to her cheek as though she'd been slapped. The shouted command had much the same effect on her hysteria as a slap might have done; her breathing steadied and the flush began to fade.

"See that you do, Ligier," she said in a controlled voice. She turned and marched up the stairs, her high-laced shoes whacking the treads in an attempt to sound dignified.

The doorman followed her, looking over his shoulder, but the footmen who'd escorted Rolfe remained on the landing. A step below them, smiling faintly as she watched events in the servants' lounge, stood Tovera.

Marina Rolfe had been afraid; afraid of the same thing as her husband, now that Adele had leisure to analyze it. The Rolfes thought that the real heir to the Mundy estate had returned to claim her property. How strange. Despite Deirdre Leary's offer to look into the matter, Adele hadn't imagined trying to overturn the settlement based on the Edict of Reconciliation twelve years previous.

Not until now.

Rolfe took a deep breath and looked warily at her. The left corner of Adele's mouth quirked into a smile of sorts. "You needn't worry, Mister Rolfe," she said. "I'll be leaving presently. But I'd appreciate the use of this desk—"

She gestured toward the wreck beside her. One of the legs had broken; that corner was supported by a metal document box.

"—to write a note. It's on a matter I hadn't given thought to previously, but I'd like my servant to deliver it before I leave Xenos. I'll only be a moment."

"Of course, mistress, of course," Rolfe said. "You can use my—"

He strangled the rest of the offer. He must suddenly have remembered he'd sent his wife upstairs to his suite, rather than down to her own where Adele would have to pass her on the way out.

"This is quite adequate," Adele said coolly. She drew out another visiting card and on the back wrote,

Mistress Deirdre Leary:
I would appreciate any support you could provide in the matter of my regaining title to Chatsworth Minor. I will be in touch with you on my next return to Cinnabar.
Mundy

She closed her stylus, then gave the card to Tovera while Rolfe waited with politely averted eyes. "I'll take my leave now, Mister Rolfe," Adele said aloud. "I appreciate your hospitality."

Rolfe looked embarrassed again, but at his quick gesture the footmen started down the stairs. Rolfe bowed his guest ahead of him, then followed. The doorman was still with his mistress, but Wormser pulled the outer door open in fine style, then closed it behind Adele and Tovera.

Adele's skin felt prickly. Her anger was a cold emotion, and it left her feeling like the dirty slush of a winter streetscape.

"I don't know where you'll find her," she said to her servant. "I'd try the office on—"

"I'll find her, mistress," the pale woman said. "And I'll be aboard the ship before it lifts."

"Yes, that too," Adele said. "I'll meet you there."

Tovera looked at Rolfe House. "It bothers you?" she said.

Adele's face tightened. Then she remembered who'd asked the question and said, "Yes. It bothers me very much."

"It leaves me empty," Tovera said softly. "But then, everything does."

She strode toward a monorail platform. She was quite unremarkable, an office worker heading home with a briefcase full of work.

Adele sighed and walked to her own stop on the opposite end of the street. The sky was threatening; there'd be rain before sunset, she supposed.

That would fit her mood quite well.

CHAPTER NINE

The drizzle gave way to a sheet of rain which thundered on the hull of the *Princess Cecile* and lashed the surface of Bay Ten, the ready slip to which the corvette had been transferred at the completion of her refit. Lightning pulsed continuously, backlighting the thunderheads without ever striking in the cone of Daniel's vision through the open main hatch.

"Like a cow pissing on a flat rock," Hogg muttered, though he didn't sound especially unhappy about it. The rain was blasting itself to mist on the canopy over the walkway from the edge of the pool to the corvette. Watching it, Daniel could imagine he was in one of the metal-roofed hunting cabins deep in the interior of Bantry—

Instead of waiting for the arrival of the courier whom the Navy Office had an hour ago alerted them to expect.

Apparently thinking in the same track, Ellie Woetjans said, "If the RCN don't teach you nothing else, it'll teach you to wait." There was a chorus of, "Amen!" and "Too right!" from the half dozen spacers in the the *Princess Cecile*'s entranceway.

Woetjans was a rangy, powerful woman who was taller than Daniel by six inches. As bosun she rapped helmets with a length of electrical cord to get the attention of landsmen she was turning into riggers. No need of that with the present crew, of course.

Woetjans was soaking wet, having just come in with the team which had changed out the main hinge of Dorsal 3. The antenna had stuck a few degrees short of closure twice during testing.

Daniel had been willing to lift with it—joints loosened in service, after all—but since there were a few minutes unexpectedly available, the bosun had taken five riggers out despite the rain. She hadn't bothered to change when she returned in case the courier with the *Princess Cecile*'s orders arrived during those few moments. The crew was even more excited about the corvette's next deployment than her captain was.

Well, make that *as* excited. Admiral Anston had called Daniel in personally, after all. He wouldn't have done that if he'd planned to send the *Princess Cecile* to the Home Squadron protecting Cinnabar against Alliance raiders—who had last attacked some seventeen years ago. There was every chance that Lt. Leary's first operational command would be an independent one.

"Daniel?" said Adele's voice through the earphones of the commo helmet Daniel was wearing along with his utility uniform. "A car and truck have just cleared the main gate with Bay Ten as their announced destination. Over."

He should have guessed that Adele would be monitoring not only ordinary communications traffic but also intercepting limited-distribution messages that she and her software thought might be of interest to the *Princess Cecile*. A truck, though? Why on earth would the courier have a truck with him?

"Adele," Daniel said, "we're only about three minutes from the gate here. Why don't you come join me for the courier's arrival? You can monitor the console through your helmet, you know. Over."

Adele sniffed. "Can I really?" she said, not angrily but with enough of an edge to remind Daniel who he'd been talking to. "Perhaps I'll print out the instruction manual for my equipment to read while I'm waiting with you. Signals out."

Smiling faintly but tense all the same, Daniel said, "He's on his way from the gate," loudly enough to be heard by those with him in the entrance. He lifted his equipment belt with his thumbs to settle it more comfortably over his hipbones.

The rain had slackened again, though that was hard to tell because of the water still dripping from the antennas through the flare of the area light above the *Princess Cecile*'s hatch. Headlights swept down the curving roadway toward Bay Ten in Vs of spray. The lead vehicle, illuminated by the following one, was one of the enclosed two-place scooters used by the Navy Office message service.

Adele came down the companionway from C Level and the bridge. Unconsciously her hand brushed the right cargo pocket where her personal data unit rode. She had no need for special tailoring when wearing a utility uniform.

The vehicles pulled up at the shelter for visitors to Bay Ten. A figure in a close-drawn rain cape got out of the scooter and started down the walkway toward the corvette's hatch, hunched over against the weather. The rain was coming down harder again. It wasn't the downpour of minutes earlier, but it still blew under the canopy.

"There's a driver in the car," Hogg noticed aloud. "Since when do couriers get drivers?"

Adele frowned, then flipped down the jump seat intended for a sentry at the airlock and took her data unit out. Daniel glanced at her, wondering what in the world she was doing.

The wands flickered. Without looking up Adele said, "I'm finding what department the truck is assigned to. Its vehicle number went into the records when it passed the gate."

Daniel opened his mouth to say, "Well, we'll know in a moment. . . ." But it wasn't certain that they *would* learn in a moment; and anyway, that probably didn't make any difference to Adele. She had more faith in data that she uncovered herself than she did in what somebody from the Navy Office told her; and thinking about it, Daniel too had more faith in what Adele learned in her own fashion. He swallowed his comment unspoken.

The courier reached the hatch and stepped into the entryway, out of the weather. The trousers of his 2nd Class uniform were darkened several shades from the original dove gray where the rain had soaked them.

"Orders for the officer commanding RCS *Princess Cecile*," the man said, his voice rough. He coughed to clear his throat.

Daniel stepped forward. "I'm Lieutenant Leary, commanding RCS *Princess Cecile*," he said.

The stiffened bill of the courier's cowl shadowed his face. He brought from beneath his cape a packet closed with the Republic's seal, a winged sandal, over an embossed RCN.

Daniel broke the seal with his index finger, watching the holographic wings flap three times. If the envelope had been opened before it reached him, the charge would have dissipated whether or not the seal itself were damaged. There was no reason to suspect forgery, but the Matrix makes people—those who survive—careful about details.

He drew out the document and read:

Navy Office, 16 xi 45
Lt. D. O. Leary,
Comdg. RCS *Princess Cecile*, Harbor Three.

Lieutenant: So soon as the Republic of Cinnabar corvette which you have been appointed to command shall be in all respects ready for space, you will proceed to the Strymon system, touching at such ports as you may think proper.

If possible you will meet at Sexburga the squadron under Commodore Pettin, already en route to Strymon, and place yourself under his command for the remainder of the cruise. If you do not join Commodore Pettin en route, you will report to him in the Strymon system.

During your presence at Strymon you will do all in your power to cherish, on the part of their government, good feelings toward the Republic of Cinnabar. In addition you will carry out such other duties as are placed on you by competent authorities. You will return to Cinnabar in accordance with the directions of Commodore Pettin.

The courier bearing these orders will provide additional oral instructions which you will carry out as a part of your duties.

You will communicate to all the officers under your command the orders of this Office that no one be concerned in a duel during the course of this cruise.

Commending you and your ship company to the protection of Divine Providence, and wishing you a pleasant cruise and a safe return to your planet and friends, I am,

Very respectfully,
Anston

Frowning slightly, Daniel handed the dispatch to Adele to read. To the courier he said, "You have oral instructions for me?"

The courier undid his cape's throat catch and shrugged the garment off. It fell on the deck behind him. He was Delos Vaughn. He said, "Indeed I do, Lieutenant."

Daniel's face didn't change. He said nothing while his mind shuffled through possibilities.

"And I have a reserve naval commission," Vaughn continued in the silence; sharply, a little nervous in the face of Daniel's lack of reaction. "I have a perfect right to wear this uniform."

The others present were taking their cue from Daniel. Apart from Adele, none of them saw anything remarkable in the situation.

"All right, Mr. Vaughn," Daniel said. "Come into my cabin and you can deliver your instructions."

He turned, catching Adele's eye. She'd risen to her feet when the courier arrived, but the data unit was still in her hand. She gave a minute shake of her head, her expression guarded.

"There's no need for privacy, Lieutenant," Vaughn said. "The further instructions are that you carry me to Strymon aboard your vessel, and that you provide me with such assistance as is commensurate with your duties as an officer of the Republic."

"Mr. Vaughn . . ." Daniel said. The storm had resumed in all its elemental fury. Its thunder and actinic glare were anchors for Daniel's mind, underscoring how trivial human concerns were against the majesty of nature. "An RCN corvette is not a pleasure yacht. Perhaps—"

"You have your orders, Mr. Leary," Vaughn said, momentarily the aristocrat to a servant. "They are clear, are they not?"

Daniel felt his face tighten and grow warm with the blood rising to the skin. "Quite clear, Mr. Vaughn," he said.

"As for the comfort of a yacht," Vaughn said, a gentleman to a peer again, "I don't require anything excessive for the few months the voyage will require. The van there—"

He twisted his head, sketching a gesture toward the vehicles waiting at the poolside.

"—holds my baggage. We can store it here in the entryway for the moment. As soon as we've reached orbit, you can expend a missile and then put the baggage in the emptied missile rack. And you'll need to find accommodation for my two servants, though they can sleep with the common spacers."

He beamed at Daniel in open-faced enthusiasm.

Daniel had a sudden vision of himself as a cog in a vast machine which stretched away in all directions. Parts whirring, trembling; wheels and pistons and slides in vibrant motion, and somewhere a control board at which a faceless figure sat. He thought, *I am Daniel Leary, officer by grace of God and the will of the Senate. I am not a cog in anyone's machine!*

"I see, Mr. Vaughn," he said aloud. "As you say, my orders are clear. You may board with the clothes you're standing in. We won't be making room for your traps by lessening our combat effectiveness in time of war; but as you say, the first leg of the cruise shouldn't be too long. And we haven't room to accommodate servants for supernumeraries, I'm afraid. This is a corvette, not a battleship."

The first leg would be no more than eighteen days or he'd know the reason why!

"We can find you utilities to wear, I'm sure, until you can buy civilian kit at our first planetfall."

He nodded to Adele. "Since Officer Mundy," he said, "has moved into the captain's lounge—"

One of the two small cabins of Daniel's suite off the bridge, intended for entertaining non-RCN guests where they wouldn't have access to a console tied into the corvette's data bank.

"—then we can put the passenger in that cabin." He smiled at Vaughn. "Which you will be sharing, sir, with the infirmary and Medic; if you're determined to take passage with us."

"You know I don't care where I sleep, Daniel," Adele said with a moue of irritation.

"Nor do I, Lieutenant Leary," Vaughn said, grinning—to Daniel's surprise—in satisfaction. "But if it hasn't become a point of honor with you, I have two small cases waiting in the car that brought me. In total they amount to the one and a half cubic feet permitted a midshipman under naval regulations. And I'll hire a spacer to do for me on board, as I believe is customary?"

Aren't you a clever devil? Daniel thought. *Trying me on to see if I'd let you have whatever you wanted. A Leary of Bantry kowtowing to a foreigner!*

"Yes," Daniel said aloud. "That should be workable."

He checked the time on the flat multifunction card he wore on a wrist clip while in utilities, then looked up again. "You have five minutes to get your two cases aboard, Mr. Vaughn."

He smiled and felt the thrill of the words as he added, "We're to lift ship as soon as we're ready, you see. And the *Princess Cecile* is ready for her first operational cruise now!"

As the *Princess Cecile* trembled, white rings became blue solids on the sidebar to Adele's communications display. One at a time, eight of them: the plasma thrusters switching from standby to live, expelling minute streams of white-hot ions into the pool. Very shortly Daniel would slide his linked throttles forward and the thrusters would lift the corvette to transatmospheric orbit.

Adele was detached, unaffected by the tense bustle of the bridge around her. She had duties at this moment, though they were of the negative variety: to block all incoming messages unless they directly concerned the vessel's liftoff. The operation was complex and potentially dangerous if botched, though there was more risk of the sun going dark in the next minutes. Between the time the liftoff sequence began until the *Princess Cecile* reached orbit, even Admiral Anston could wait.

Betts, the Chief Missileer, and Sun, the gunner's mate—a corvette was too small to rate a master gunner—were taut at their consoles to the left of Adele's, though neither of them had as much to do with the process of liftoff as the Signals Officer did. Woetjans and a team of riggers waited in the corridor. They would climb onto the hull after the *Princess Cecile* reached an altitude at which the antennas could be deployed. That would be at least ten minutes and might be thirty, but the riggers already wore their suits with the faceplates hinged open.

They were all spacers, feeling a responsibility to the ship and its performance. To Adele, the *Princess Cecile* was the metal box in which she happened to ride at the moment. She would do her job and whatever else Daniel or another asked of her, but she couldn't even pretend to care whether the ship rose to orbit—as it would, as surely as the sun would rise—or instead exploded here in Harbor Three.

The hatches were closed, the thrusters lighted; the fusion bottle that provided both plasma and auxiliary power was a green sphere in Adele's holographic display, and the High Drive a hollow green-edged bar indicating that the antimatter converter was on standby but fully functional. Adele didn't need to echo the ship's indicators on her screen; she did so merely from a desire to show solidarity with the rest of the crew to whom they were important.

A smile touched the corners of her lips. *If the ship blows up here, who will Mistress Sand get to replace me?* Not that the answer was of any real consequence to Adele. She just liked information.

Daniel spoke tersely, authoritatively. The console's dynamic suppressor cancelled the sound of the words even a few inches away. Adele could have listened to the conversation on a dedicated line to the power room, but there was no need to. Lt. Leary was receiving oral confirmation from Chief Pasternak of what the instruments showed: the *Princess Cecile* was ready to lift.

Daniel grinned through his holographic display which was only a haze of light except to the eyes of the person seated at the console. His hand touched a switch and an electronic alarm whistled three times on a rising note. Signal lights pulsed red to orange, warning the crew during times that sound wouldn't carry because the ship was depressurized.

Daniel brought the throttles forward in a smooth motion. The linkage was physical rather than virtual so that the captain had feedback through his own flesh instead of just a gauge to watch.

Adele flexed her fingers, imagining the control wands between them. The trained human body is capable of wonderful subtlety. Unexpected, unwanted, she remembered a boy's face bulging as the bullet from her pistol punched through the bridge of his nose. That had required only a few ounces' pressure, expertly applied by a trigger finger trained in the gallery in the basement of Chatsworth Minor.

The thrusters roared to full power, squeezing Adele down in her seat. It was a gentle pressure; even with the antennas folded at minimum length along the hull and the sails furled tightly to them, a starship wasn't stressed for high accelerations.

Ships covered interstellar distances by entering bubble universes where physical constants differed from those of the sidereal universe, but velocity was conserved during the passage. There was no need of high accelerations when you could leave the universe for one in which distances were logarithmically shorter and the pressure of Casimir radiation drove vessels across light-years in a matter of hours. The High Drive, though very efficient, was needed only for maneuvering over distances too short for the captain to trust her astrogation.

The *Princess Cecile* bucked and started to yaw. Daniel's hands danced on the throttles. Adele snapped her eyes to her own display. The indicator for the third thruster in the upper bank—starboard—was quivering. It dropped to a hollow gray circle at the same time as the indicator kitty-corner—Port Two—became a white standby circle.

The *Princess Cecile* steadied. Adele thought she felt a minuscule vibration that hadn't been present before, but she might be imagining a change because her mind knew *something* had happened.

Her fingers touched a key with the same precision as Daniel had shown in juggling the throttles. Through her helmet Chief Pasternak was shouting, "—*ing bloody bracket gave and the feed line started thrashing like half an earthworm! Henning's got a loop of cargo tape on the whore, and we'll have her welded in numbers three minutes. Over!*"

"*Carry on, chief,*" Daniel said calmly. She glanced at him again. His face wore an absent-minded smile as he tweaked a throttle—no longer linked to the other seven—and the vibration smoothed to glassy perfection. "*After all, this is a shakedown cruise. Needs must we can reach altitude on four thrusters. Bridge out.*"

"*Engineering out.*"

Instead of concentrating on his display as Adele expected, Daniel stabbed the public address switch as forcefully as if he were trying to dent the plate beneath his virtual keyboard. Adele smiled: a control was never in doubt when Daniel activated it. He left delicacy for others.

"*Captain to ship,*" speakers said, the words echoing themselves from the ceiling of every compartment. "*The waterline feeding Starboard Three came adrift. Engineering has it jury-rigged, and it'll be at a hundred percent in a few minutes. Bridge out.*"

As Daniel switched off, he saw Adele watching him from the other side of his display. He grinned and made an O from his right thumb and index finger, then went back to his controls.

Adele did the same. Of *course* Daniel wouldn't forget that the crew would worry—or at least wonder—because the *Princess Cecile*'s thrust had gone ragged. His duty was even more to the personnel than it was to the vessel's hardware.

Spacers shouted to one another. Under normal circumstances only the officers had communications helmets. When ordinary crewmen spoke to one another, they had to make themselves heard over the thrusters. The pulsing thunder muted as the corvette rose through ever-thinner layers of atmosphere, but even in hard vacuum the fabric of the ship shivered in a kind of low moan.

Two crewmen ran along the corridor carrying a rope-handled footlocker between them. They disappeared down the companionway, undeterred by the weight and awkwardness of their burden. Adele hadn't any idea what they were doing, whether it was a problem or simply personal belongings that somebody had forgotten to stow before liftoff.

The whistle called a two-note signal; the emergency lights glowed blue for a moment. Adele remembered the call from when the *Princess Cecile* left Kostroma: atmospheric density had fallen to the point that the captain could switch power to the High Drive at will.

Daniel engaged the PA system again. *"Engaging the High Drive,"* he announced in a tone so emotionless as to sound bored. He waited still-faced for five beats of the second hand, backed the throttles to quarter power, and with his right hand threw the toggle that shut off fuel to the plasma thrusters at the same time as it engaged the matter-antimatter power plant.

The *Princess Cecile* shuddered. A high-pitched keen replaced the tremble of the plasma motors. Any change in acceleration was too subtle for Adele to sense, but she did feel a slight queasiness, familiar from her previous experience.

The High Drive delivered its thrust from a multithroated central port rather than eight—six during most of this liftoff—widely separated plasma nozzles. It was as though the *Princess Cecile* were balancing her thirteen hundred tons on the point of a needle. The controls kept the corvette aligned by minute changes in the thrust vector. The direction of "down" changed many times a second.

Adele smiled wryly. In this case, the delicate measuring ability of her inner ear was a detriment to her well-being.

On a sudden whim, she filled her display with a holographic image of the planet beneath. The first time she'd left Cinnabar, she'd sat in the passenger lounge and watched her world shrink on the display. She hadn't found it particularly interesting. Being who she was, she'd watched a perfect simulation of the process as soon as she decided to continue her schooling on Blythe.

Fifteen years ago, Adele had expected to return home. More accurately, it had never crossed her mind that she wouldn't return home, much less that her home would cease to exist. Now . . .

Adele turned from the image of a planet, the lines of its continents softened by the blue haze of atmosphere, and looked at the spacers around her. They were intent, ready for an emergency but cheerful nonetheless. Betts and Sun slapped hands in acknowledgment of a successful liftoff, and the riggers joked in the corridor.

Adele laughed aloud. She didn't worry about coming home again this time either.

Because this time she was taking her home with her.

Daniel rose from his console and stretched, a full-bodied exercise that ended with him leaning backward and bracing his hands on the seatback with a deck sandal locked around the chairpost. Liftoffs—and landings, even more so—were so all-involving that tension drew his muscles up like drying rawhide until the job was complete.

Delos Vaughn walked onto the bridge, smiling pleasantly. He wore a set of fawn coveralls which were utilitarian in cut, though grease stains would show as they didn't against the gray-on-gray mottling of RCN utilities. Over his left breast pocket was a tape with his name in glowing gold letters.

"Allow me to be the first to congratulate you, Lieutenant," Vaughn said. "Your recovery was so quick that I scarcely noticed the systems failure."

You have no business on my bridge! Daniel thought. *A bracket snapping on liftoff is no more a systems failure than you're an RCN officer!*

"Thank you, Mr. Vaughn," Daniel said aloud, "but I'd appreciate it if you'd consider the bridge off-limits unless I inform you otherwise. This is a warship on active service."

Turning his attention immediately to his console so that the comment would appear trivial rather than an angry dressing-down, Daniel keyed the Battle Direction Center channel. "Mr. Mon?" he said. "Come to the bridge please and take the conn. I'm going topside."

"*On the way, Mr. Leary,*" Mon replied immediately. There was no need to go through full communications protocol on a dedicated line, any more than there was when dealing with one's fellows face-to-face.

Daniel straightened and again glanced around him. Vaughn had retreated into the corridor. He was watching with the bright interest of a bird but was careful not to interfere with the team of riggers preparing to go onto the hull. He must have felt Daniel's glance, for he waved an index finger in friendly greeting.

"Officer Mundy," Daniel said in a carrying voice, "we're preparing our initial entry into the Matrix. I'd appreciate it if you'd join me on the hull."

As he spoke, Daniel felt a flash of resentment, an uncommon emotion for him. Having a passenger like Vaughn was almost as bad as—indeed, perhaps worse than—carrying a senior officer. He couldn't feel that the *Princess Cecile* was really his, the way the officer commanding should be able to do. Although now that Daniel analyzed his feelings, he couldn't see why he *should* react that way to a foreign civilian.

"Why yes, thank you, Daniel," Adele said in pleasant, cultured impropriety. She rose from her console. "I suppose I should have that experience. Now that I'm an RCN officer, that is."

A valued member of the RCN, Daniel thought, letting the grin reach his lips. *RCN officer in the sense that instructors at the Academy would understand it, though . . . that would be going a little far.*

Woetjans gave Daniel a thumbs-up. He nodded. The bosun tongued a control in her helmet and the cheery, four-note Riggers Aloft call rang from the PA system as the signal lights pulsed yellow.

Lt. Mon—dark, wiry and professional—was striding down the corridor, dodging obstacles both human and inanimate, mostly equipment stored there for lack of a better place. Daniel nodded to him at the hatchway, said, "You have the conn," and slipped past with the ease of long practice.

Adele shifted left when she should have gone right and bounced off Mon's arm, then bumped Daniel from behind. It was amazing that a person with the physical dexterity Adele showed at a console— or with a pistol—could so consistently move in the wrong direction when she had to get from one point in a starship to another.

And of course when she was *on* a starship it was worse. Daniel reminded himself to attach her safety line personally.

The Bow Dorsal airlock was cycling, sending Woetjans and five riggers onto the hull. Six more crewmen waited to follow the first watch: the initial deployment of antennas and sails employed all the riggers rather than merely the port or starboard watch.

Burridge, one of the waiting riggers, tossed Daniel a suit from the open locker. He slid into it like a body stocking, then glanced at Adele to help her if she was having difficulty.

She wasn't: Dasi and Jonas held Adele by the arms while Burridge pulled the suit over her limbs and torso with as little ceremony or trouble as a cook has stuffing a sausage. From Adele's expression of mild disinterest, the process wasn't one that disturbed her. Vaughn, squeezed against the opposite bulkhead to keep out of the way, watched with a frown.

The light over the airlock glowed green, indicating the outer door was sealed. Dasi, the team's senior man, slammed the crash bar with a gloved hand and led his riggers into the lock. Daniel latched Adele's faceshield, drew her with him into the lock—it would hold a dozen in a pinch, times when speed was more important than comfort—and locked his own shield closed.

The world was silence except for Daniel's own breathing, heavy and echoing until he caught himself and consciously slowed it. He met Adele's eyes through the faceplates of optical-grade moissanite and grinned. She wouldn't be able to see his lips, but the muscles around her eyes crinkled in an answering grin.

The outer lock opened. The first result of air venting into space was that the light went flat: there was no longer a diffracting atmosphere to soften and spread the illumination.

The riggers surged out of the lock, each one going to a predetermined post. Daniel followed, shuffling forward so that one electromagnetic boot was always flat against the steel hull. He kept his right hand on Adele's equipment belt.

The *Princess Cecile* was spreading her antennas as quickly as the riggers could unlock them from their cradles along the hull. Hydraulic pressure extended and telescoped the masts and yards. Daniel noticed a dozen places where starlight blurred into iridescent fog. Some leakage was inevitable where new gaskets hadn't worked in or old gaskets had worn, and the vacuum of space emphasized the flaws. A trained eye—and Daniel's was—could tell the difference between a trivial seepage and a potential problem.

He leaned to touch his helmet to Adele's. "Look at Port Two," he said, pointing forward toward the second mast on the corvette's port side. "If that leak doesn't slow by tomorrow, we'll have to do something about it. The main joint is new, and the seal may have been pinched when it was being replaced."

Adele turned to follow the line of Daniel's fingers, taking her helmet out of contact with his. Riggers' suits weren't normally fitted with radios. An accidental transmission in the Matrix could have incalculable—literally—effects on a ship's velocity and location in regard to the sidereal universe.

The riggers didn't adjust the sails: hydraulics controlled from the bridge did that. But the pumps, the joints, the parrels—even the gossamer fabric—were machines and worked the way good machines do: most of the time.

The riggers patched and stretched and replaced. If an antenna was beyond quick repair they signaled the problem through the hull, using a hydromechanical semaphore with a keyboard for unusually complex problems. The captain and navigation computer could then choose another solution to the astrogation task.

It wasn't a handicap for a trained crew to operate by semaphore and hand signals even while the ship was in normal space. Riggers as experienced as those of the *Princess Cecile*'s present crew could put a ship through her paces with no direction at all. Stiction, leaks, breakage—all were as obvious to the crewmen as they were to Woetjans or Daniel, and they could do the repairs in their sleep.

The riggers didn't need to talk. Daniel needed to be on the hull *to* talk to Adele without risk of being overheard. For this too the lack of a radio was an advantage, so long as both parties remembered they had to keep their helmets touching to hear one another.

Which Adele now did, a moment late, clanking her head back against Daniel's. He winced, more at the thought than from the shock itself. Riggers' gear had to be able to take a hammering, but the very violence of the environment meant spacers learned to be as gentle as a nurse handling infants.

"Sorry, Daniel," she said contritely. Adele had the saving grace of knowing she was clumsy on shipboard. The dispatch vessel

Aglaia from which most of the *Princess Cecile*'s crew were drawn had often carried high-ranking civilians. Some of them insisted on coming out on the hull but because of pride refused to wear a safety line like the one which joined Adele to Daniel. Woetjans told of leaping between masts to snag a treasury official who was on his way toward Canopus if she hadn't caught him.

"Adele, I'd asked an acquaintance in Foreign Affairs about Delos Vaughn," Daniel said, holding his friend tight so that she wouldn't absentmindedly pull away. "I was told that for reasons of state Vaughn would never be allowed to leave Cinnabar. Ah, I don't want to be privy to any matters that aren't my business to know, but if there's anything you *can* in good conscience tell me . . . ?"

Adele turned to face him, then caught herself and brought her helmet back in contact temple to temple. "My information was much the same as yours, Daniel," she said. "Though I should emphasize that I wasn't specifically told anything about Vaughn."

There was a pause; Daniel knew his friend well enough to visualize her frowning as she chose words with her usual precision. "The thing is," she said, her voice robbed of all overtones by the method of transmission, "I would have expected that I *would* be told, especially if Vaughn were to be travelling on the same vessel as me. Even though his affairs have no direct connection with mine or those of the RCN."

Daniel didn't know what other duties Adele had to the Republic, but he knew there had to be a connection well above that of the Personnel Bureau in the Navy Office. Her skills made her a marvelous addition to the *Princess Cecile*'s crew, but there was no way in Hell that a faceless clerk would have approved a signals warrant for someone with Adele's deficiencies on paper.

Daniel had been prepared to use what influence he had. The "Hero of Kostroma" business didn't gain him much ground in the RCN directly, but there were admirals' wives to whom he might seem a romantic figure. All the more so, because young Leary was trying to get his *lady*friend aboard his ship in despite of a hard-hearted bureaucracy.

He might have succeeded, but he hadn't had to try. Adele's warrant whisked through the Navy Office like grass through a goose. It was delivered to the *Princess Cecile* before the port commander decided which bay the corvette would refit in.

Daniel grinned. Adele was his friend, and she was a lady in every sense of the word; but for romance, Daniel preferred something younger, rounder and, frankly, not so *smart*. Besides which, so far as Daniel had been able to tell, Adele had no interest in romance whatever.

The sails were stretching the length of the yards. The electrostatic fabric was so thin that bright stars were visible through it. For this initial deployment Mon was running everything out to its maximum extent. The antenna and sail mechanisms had been tested thoroughly on the ground, but vacuum and the vibration of liftoff could expose flaws that would only appear in real service.

"Aren't they beautiful?" Daniel said, speaking more to himself than his companion. A warship's enormous suit of sails spreading to shadow the universe was a sight to move a dead man.

"What is, Daniel?" Adele said. "Cinnabar from up here, you mean?"

A dead man, but not necessarily a librarian. "Ah," Daniel said aloud. "I was thinking of the arrangement of the sails fully set. Imposing their own order on the universe, so to speak."

Cinnabar was "rising" beneath them as the *Princess Cecile* rotated slowly on her axis, though that wasn't a sight Daniel would ever have called attention to. Planets were very interesting places—when you were on the ground. From low orbit, they were simply a difficult problem in shiphandling.

Before he left the bridge, Daniel had programmed a rotation to introduce a slight angular strain on the rig. The purpose of a shakedown cruise was to find anything that might have gone wrong during a refit. Daniel appreciated the compliment implied when Admiral Anston ordered the *Princess Cecile* into operational service immediately, but he still intended to wring out the corvette while he had the leisure of no one shooting at them.

"Ah," said Adele in turn. She shifted slightly in an obvious attempt to feel what Daniel felt.

The rig had reached its fullest extent; now its elements began to retract to the setting programmed for entry into the Matrix. Masts and yards telescoped, rotating on their axes and occasionally tilting to bring the sails into precise alignment.

"Daniel," Adele said. She'd lowered her voice reflexively so that Daniel could barely make out the words vibrating from her helmet to his. "Vaughn being sent back to Strymon means either that there are factions in the government working outside the knowledge of . . . the people who talk to me. Or that when they talk to me, they conceal as much as they tell. Unfortunately, both of those options are quite possible."

"Yes," Daniel said, pursing his lips in a look of frustration. He thought of his own interview with Admiral Anston: what he'd been told—virtually nothing—and what he hadn't. "The same's true within the RCN, of course. Well, we'll make do, won't we?"

The *Princess Cecile* was about to enter the Matrix: Daniel felt the charge building. He'd never been sure whether it was a real sensation or something his soul recognized. Engineers had sworn to him that a rigger's suit was completely insulated, even if the minute potentials being bled into the sails could be sensed at all.

It happened. The charged fabric of the sails formed a series of precisely calculated barriers against the Casimir radiation that flooded the cosmos. Pressures that could not be relieved in the sidereal universe built up, shifting the *Princess Cecile*—

Golden light suffused the corvette, throwing her rig and outside crew into silhouette as though against an angel's wing. Daniel shivered with anticipation.

Palpable energy flared. The *Princess Cecile* slipped from the universe of her creation into the greater glowing infinity that would take her to Strymon . . . under the command of Lt. Daniel Leary.

CHAPTER TEN

Dasi and Barnes had collapsed the wall between the two rooms of the captain's suite, then pegged it down as a central table. The bunks—Daniel's and the one from what had become Adele's cabin—became cushioned benches at the long sides of the table. The arrangement was tight, but not notably worse than any other portion of the corvette's interior.

Daniel beamed at his guests from behind the data console, now reversed at the head of the table. Adele knew that this was the first operational command group meeting Daniel had called as captain, and he was correspondingly proud. Not that Daniel ever did anything with less than enthusiasm.

There was no formal seating order, but Mon sat at the captain's right and the others had by silent consensus granted Adele the seat at Daniel's left. In the middle places were the other watch-standing officers: Pasternak, Woetjans, Betts and the ship's machinist, Taley.

The two midshipmen, Dorst and Vesey, sat in the end seats with big eyes and their lips clamped nervously shut. They were present to educate them, not by right, since they ranked only as petty officers. They'd reported aboard a few hours before the *Princess Cecile* lifted off: the grandson of an old shipmate of Stacey Bergen, and an intense young woman who'd brought Daniel a curtly phrased introduction from Klemsch, the Secretary to the Navy Board.

Adele had checked their backgrounds, of course. Chances were

Vesey was the bastard of Senator Dryer; her record at the Academy was far superior to that of Dorst in any case.

Tovera had put glasses at the places, and Hogg held a tray with a carafe of a respectable Cinnabar sherry. The wine was too fruity for Adele's taste, but she wouldn't have to drink much of it. Open bottles didn't last long, not in a company of naval officers.

"Pass the wine, Hogg," Daniel said. "Fellow officers, you know our orders are to join the squadron under Commodore Pettin en route to Strymon. As Pettin lifted from Cinnabar ten days ahead of us, that means we'll have to crack on a bit."

"Too true," said Taley, nodding solemnly—an expression that came naturally to her as she looked as cadaverous as a corpse buried three weeks. "And right after a refit, too. I'll be busy in the repair shop, I can see that now."

"I dare say we'll all be busy, Taley," Daniel said with a grin. "Because I propose to reach Sexburga with no intermediate planetfall. We'll only make dips back into sidereal space to take star sights."

"Holy Father of Grace!" Betts said. The missileer tossed off his sherry and would have retrieved the carafe if Hogg hadn't interposed his hip so that little Vesey could serve herself. "That's three weeks, Captain. They say that the devil himself walks the corridors if you're that long in the Matrix."

"If he does," said Pasternak tartly, "then we've the first proof of religion that *I've* ever heard. We'll be famous for bringing the comfort of faith to benighted skeptics of the sort I've been all these years."

Adele's eyes narrowed slightly. Both officers had gained their experience aboard large vessels operating as part of a fleet.

"The *Aggie* was under for twelve days, bringing the news of the Wroxter Fight back to Cinnabar," Woetjans said, knuckling her scarred jaw. "I saw my mother on the bridge, all tarted up like she was when we buried her."

"I think we can manage the leg in seventeen days, Betts," Daniel said. "I'm using Commander Bergen's logs, and I like the way the Matrix has been shaping thus far."

He smiled, then shrugged. "And Pasternak? I've never experienced Immersion Phantoms myself—"

He nodded to the bosun.

"—as Woetjans has, but I've heard my uncle and his fellows talk about them often enough. They're quite real and we'll have to bear with them, I'm afraid. On the credit side, I've never heard that phantoms do any sort of harm."

"There's been ships that didn't come back from the Matrix, though," Betts said, his eyes following the carafe.

"So there have," Daniel said with a sharpness that turned agreement into something just short of a rebuke. "But the *Princess Cecile* is going to reenter the sidereal universe, so that needn't concern us here."

Adele took her wine, and Hogg emptied the rest into Daniel's glass. Tovera was filling another carafe; the label was identical, but the fluid within had a mauve undertone that the first bottle hadn't. Daniel wouldn't think of cutting the quality of what his guests drank after they'd had a first glassful to numb their taste, but Hogg wasn't one to pour his master's money down a rathole if he saw other options.

"I served with Pettin at Wixallia Base," Mon said, frowning as though he'd just been told his legs had to be amputated. Mon had more experience than most with getting bad news, and he'd perfected a suitable expression. "Most Godforsaken place anybody thought to plant a Cinnabar flag. I started drinking."

The lieutenant glared down the length of the table as if daring anyone to contradict him. There was small chance of that: Mon drank on Kostroma, on Cinnabar, and on shipboard, though Adele had never seen him unable to carry out his duties.

Mon grinned sourly. "Pettin prayed. Believe me, I'd rather have served under a drunk than a pulpit-pounder. *And* it didn't help him with the Navy Office. He was promoted captain, all right, but he retired on half-pay four years ago. He'd still be retired if it wasn't the war's on again."

He raised his glass, just refilled by Hogg. "God bless the war!" he said.

"God bless!" echoed other officers, the midshipmen the loudest. Daniel quirked a smile but didn't drink *that* toast; Adele set the personal data unit before her on the table and picked up its wands.

"You say 'squadron,' " Taley said. "Being we're going to the back of beyond, all the way into the Sack, I suppose that means a couple crocks that should've been broken up thirty years back, does it?"

"The heavy cruiser *Winckelmann*," Daniel answered mildly. "The Archaeologist Class was an innovative design, though she's not new, of course. With the destroyers *Petty* and *Active*."

"The *Active*?" Betts said. "She *was* broken up, I heard. Two thrusters blew out while she was landing and she hit a pier with her bow."

"They cut the forward section off and mated her to what was left of the *Plump* when her Tokamak failed," Pasternak said. "They kept the *Active*'s name, I guess because she hadn't killed quite so many of her crew as the *Plump* did."

Daniel glanced at Adele. "Mundy, do you have information on the complements of Commodore Pettin's ships?" he said.

Adele hadn't been expecting the question, but she'd absently brought up data on the three vessels as Daniel spoke their names. She increased the display's saturation for easier reading, then said, "The destroyers are crewed at seventy percent of their organizational standard. The cruiser is at sixty-five percent."

There were seventeen messages from Captain Pettin—Commodore when the squadron lifted off, under his command as senior captain in lieu of an admiral—demanding that the Bureau of Personnel provide him with more spacers. The only response he'd gotten was the MESSAGE RECEIVED notation that the bureau's computer created without the intervention even of a junior clerk.

"Hide our complement records, Ms. Mundy," Woetjans said, looking across the table at Adele. "Pettin'll take forty of our people if he learns we're fully staffed, *and* with real spacers instead of the landsmen he'll have in half his berths."

"She can't," Mon said sadly. "The pay record can't be changed till we reach home port again and link to Navy Office database. When our system handshakes with the *Winckelmann*, it'll all be there for Pettin to see."

"Of course I can change it," Adele said. "Should I, or was that a joke, Woetjans?"

"Actually, that would be rather helpful," Daniel said, pursing his lips in careful consideration. "That is, if it can be done without risking the pay or widow's pension of any of the personnel, that is?"

"Of course," Adele repeated. She didn't see why the officers thought it was that complicated a procedure. Any navigational computer had sufficient power to defeat a payroll encryption, and the *Princess Cecile*—because of Adele's secret assignment—had specialized software besides.

Daniel smiled like the sun rising. "Woetjans and Pasternak, after the meeting please give Officer Mundy a list of the personnel you'd like formally off the record."

He put his left hand on Adele's right and added, "I have a warrant from the Navy Office authorizing me to accept volunteers from RCN vessels. That might very well cover the situation, but it isn't an argument a junior lieutenant cares to make to a senior captain."

"Captain?" Lt. Mon said. "You'll have us at weapons training throughout the cruise, we all know that who came from Kostroma with you. But is there a chance, do you think, of real action?"

There were murmurs of agreement around the table, and possibly an increased sharpness in Tovera's expression also as she decanted more sherry. She felt Adele's eyes and shrugged in embarrassment at showing interest.

Mon was Daniel's senior on the lieutenant's list by eight years, but Adele hadn't seen any sign of resentment toward his youthful commanding officer. She wondered if Mon was smart enough to believe his best route to promotion was to serve under a flashy, fortunate officer like Daniel Leary, or if it was something more basic: loyalty to a man who had treated him well.

"The pirates of the Selma Cluster are supposedly pacified," Daniel said. "And the Alliance has no bases in the Sack, so our chances of meeting a raider are limited."

He pursed his lips, then grinned engagingly. "On the other hand, *I* wouldn't trust a pirate's word that he'd reformed, and besides, they're always having a coup or a revolution on one planet or another there. The losers aren't going to be bound by treaties, so there's the chance we'll get in some hunting."

He frowned. "Depending on Commodore Pettin's notions of how the *Princess Cecile* would be best utilized, of course."

"Captain?" Woetjans said. Of the officers excepting Adele, the bosun had the most experience of Daniel and the least hesitation of asking a straight question. "Can you tell us why we've been sent to Pettin anyhow? You know and I know that a clean ship like the *Sissie*'s got no business farting around in the Sack when there's a war on."

"She's foreign built," said Pasternak. He spread his hands to fend off reaction to what sounded like an insult when it came out of his mouth. "I've never served aboard a tighter hull than this one, I don't mean that. But what I know and what some bean counter in the Navy Office knows, that's not the same thing."

"That don't explain the crew, Red," Woetjans said, rasping over the voices of three other officers who were probably about to make the same point. "A first-rate crew for the *Aglaia*, sure, she was a dispatch vessel and likely to be carrying anybody from admirals to a planetary observer. But we've got the pick of the *Aggie*'s crew aboard, and I *don't* think that's because some clerk fucked up."

"Is it Vaughn?" Betts asked. He sounded vaguely tense, as was to be expected from an ordinary space officer who fears he might be involved in high politics. "Vaughn carries himself like he's somebody, that's for sure!"

Everyone stared at Daniel. He nodded twice, his mechanism for getting time to organize his thoughts. He looked around the table, deliberately *not* letting his eyes fall on Adele.

"The appearance of Mr. Vaughn was a surprise to me," Daniel said, "and to all the other officers of the *Princess Cecile*. There may be wheels moving within wheels, but I don't have the impression that Admiral Anston decided we needed a crack crew to take some foreigner home."

Adele knew that Daniel had distanced the RCN from the passenger in order to keep the crew's morale up; it was a wonder he hadn't said "wog" instead of "foreigner." Even so it set her teeth on edge. It was a betrayal of her cherished belief that humans should be citizens of the universe rather than chauvinists for their particular planet or organization.

She grinned. Of course she was now an officer of the RCN, an organization that stood head and shoulders above every other group in the universe.

"As for why we've been sent to the Sack, Woetjans . . ." Daniel said, smiling at the bosun. "I don't know and I won't speculate."

Woetjans and Pasternak both glanced at Adele, drawing the gaze of the other officers. She said nothing, and Daniel kept his own gaze blandly off her. Woetjans lowered her eyes in embarrassment and muttered, "Well, it'll be all right."

Daniel's expression hardened slightly. "I will say," he said, "that if the Republic had a difficult task that was within the capacity of a corvette, there couldn't have been a better choice than the *Princess Cecile* and her present crew."

Lt. Mon rose to his feet. His glass was full because Hogg had just been by with the fourth carafe.

"To the *Princess Cecile* and her captain," Mon said. He didn't slur his words, but his voice boomed louder in the small cabin than it might have done a few bottles before. "Because they'll get us out of any Goddamned hole the politicians manage to stick us in!"

It was silly. It was the kind of emotional gesture that offended Adele's belief that the intellect should dominate in all human endeavors.

But she downed her sherry in a single gulp and cheered with the others.

"Ready to enter normal space," called Lt. Mon over the intercom from the Battle Direction Center. Daniel's display already echoed the BDC data, which was identical to that of the main computer. The chance of the systems being out of synch was vanishingly small, and even in that event the smaller BDC computer was more likely to be in error; but spacers lived to retirement age by making every calculation redundant.

"Ready to record data," Adele said, frowning slightly at her console. She accepted that standard operating procedure required her to verbalize each step of the process, however obvious it might seem to her—however obvious it *was*, given that Daniel was echoing her display also. She did it, but she was unlikely to ever come to like the process.

"Ready to return to normal space," Daniel said. He touched the alarm, sending whistle calls and green light across the *Princess Cecile*'s corridors and compartments. On the hull, the semaphore posts—four each at bow and stern, offset from the lines of antennas—flipped their arms out at 90 degrees and 270 degrees to warn the riggers still topside. Normally, but not now, they were already in the air locks.

Daniel pulled the astrogation module's main switch, cutting off the trickle of power that charged the sails. The corvette staggered. When the charge dropped, the bubble universe which the *Princess Cecile* was crossing squeezed the vessel out as incompatible with its natural order. The potential dropped at various points of the hull and rig at minutely different times. The discontinuity was noticeable, the way a sleeper can be aware of lightning.

Delos Vaughn watched intently from the corridor just outside the bridge. When Daniel called general quarters for a position check, Vaughn had as usual been playing cards in the wardroom with the off-duty officers. He lost money consistently, though never in large amounts.

A suspicious man might suspect that a fellow who was as knowledgeable about poker as Vaughn showed himself to be should at least break even. Daniel didn't like to be suspicious. Still, he'd spent his youth among the influences of his father's political maneuvering and the natural world he observed under Hogg's tutelage. In both environments only the strongest could survive without using deception.

"*Ready to enter the Matrix!*" Mon's voice reported, a half-tone higher than it had been a moment before. Vaughn's face looked like a skull, and even the RCN officers on the bridge were suddenly taut.

Humans adapted to the Matrix. They could live and work outside the sidereal universe for days at a time and not be fully conscious of the strain—until it stopped. It was wrenching to experience the relief of returning to sidereal space, only to bounce back in seconds to a bubble universe in which what humans thought of as the natural order was an intrusion.

Wrenching for the captain as well, but Daniel was determined to harden his crew and himself to the process. "Entering the Matrix!" he said. He hit the five-second warning. Then, as the whistle called and red light surged and subsided, he slid the navigation module live again.

Bony fingers clutched his heart; somewhere a man screamed in abject horror. The *Princess Cecile* rippled into another universe in a wave of golden light.

Nobody spoke for a while, though Daniel could hear heavy breathing over the whirr of electronics and groans as the hull worked. He got his own pulse under control. Impressions flickered in his brain like afterimages of something glimpsed in bright light. He didn't know what they were, but his subconscious insisted they were important.

"Daniel?" Adele said in a small voice. She swallowed as if she was trying to keep breakfast down. "Will I get used to this after a time?"

"If you do, mistress," Betts mumbled through fists clenched against his mouth, "you're the first one who ever did!"

He turned his gray face to Daniel and added, "These touch-and-goes, they tear a ship up and they do the same to the crew. It's not RCN practice!"

Daniel's face hardened, and a fresh jolt of adrenaline quelled the twitchiness of his stomach. The missileer's words were a challenge to his authority.

"It's the practice of the RCS *Princess Cecile*, Mr. Betts," Daniel said. "We're going to a region frequented by pirates. If we're to be effective against them, we must have the same skills as the pirates do. Since they hide in and strike from the Matrix by quick entries and exits, we will do the same."

Betts drew himself up into a proper military posture at his console. "Sorry, sir," he said. "I come from big ships, you know that. If this is the way we'll get a bite at a pirate or two, then by God I'm up for it."

"Of course you are, Betts," Daniel said warmly. "As for myself, I'd rather face a dressing-down by an admiral, but we're still going to practice quick insertions all the way to Sexburga, I'm afraid."

Adele was doing something involved at her console; Daniel wondered what. She didn't analyze the star sightings, though they were collected and processed by equipment in the signals officer's charge.

He had a thought and switched on the PA system. "Captain to ship," Daniel said. As he listened to the electronic echo of his voice, he thought he saw figures with too many legs walk across the corridor and through the wardroom bulkhead. "Fellow spacers, I'm proud to be part of a crew who can do its duty even while our guts are being turned inside out. We won't ever learn to like the experience, but any pirates we meet are going to like what *they* get from us even less! Captain out."

Airlocks cycled. Woetjans had put both watches on the hull in case of trouble during this first touch-and-go; riggers were as likely as anybody else to find the experience disorienting. Now the extra crewmen were reentering the hull, moving with unfamiliar clumsiness.

"The data regarding the effect insertions have on service life . . ." Adele said, speaking loudly enough to be heard clearly despite continuing to face her holographic display. "Indicate that there's no difference between entries and exits from the Matrix taking place in a short duration and those which are spaced out over a longer period of time. The absolute number of insertions is all that matters, not the rate of occurrence."

"There's records on this?" Sun said in amazement. The gunner's mate had recovered quicker than anyone else on the bridge, but there was a hint of tension in his cheek and jaw muscles too. "I've heard of ships doing it, but not often enough you could put it in a book."

Adele turned to face the others in the compartment; the display framed her face as though with a multicolored aura. "The data comes almost entirely from exploration vessels," she said with a dry smile that only those who knew her well would recognize. "As a matter of fact, the bulk of the data comes from vessels commanded by Stacey Bergen. The analysis indicates it should be valid for ships of all varieties, however."

"Uncle Stacey says you lose the flow of the Matrix if you stay in normal space for six, eight hours the way most captains do," Daniel said in a combination of pride and embarrassment. He didn't want it to sound as though he thought he was the equal of his uncle as an astrogator. "His crews were all volunteers, of course. But he never had better personnel than the *Princess Cecile* does today."

Daniel stood and forced himself to stretch; at the moment his body wanted to curl into a ball and hug itself. "Right now I'm going to compare his notes with the patterns *I* see."

He keyed the BDC channel and said, "Lieutenant Mon, please take the conn while I go onto the hull for an hour or so. There's no need to come forward unless you prefer to."

"I'll come along, if I may," Adele said, rising to her feet. She seemed to be fully herself: cool and detached, with her normal pale complexion in place of the green undertone of a few minutes before. Apparently searching out data had been as bracing for her as a month in the country.

"A pleasure to have you," Daniel said truthfully, though he was a little surprised.

Of course Adele had a way of surprising him. He hadn't known about the life-cycle analyses of Stacey's ships, and if asked he would've agreed with Betts that quick in-and-outs would wear a hull at a higher rate than the normal practice.

What he did know—and what Adele probably knew also, though he was glad she hadn't broadcast the information to the crew— was that despite his picked crews, Uncle Stacey's commands had abnormally high rates of psychological casualties. Much as Daniel regretted the fact that he was going to lose spacers in the performance of their duty, the *Princess Cecile* was a warship and they—like him—were members of the RCN.

Daniel offered Adele his arm and walked to the suit closet just off the bridge. The riggers of the port watch had stripped and were going below to their bunks. From the look of their faces, few would be able to sleep. The starboard watch, still on the hull with Woetjans, might well be the lucky ones. As Daniel had noted in Adele and himself, falling into one's duties seemed to lessen the effect of rapid transitions into and out of the Matrix.

Delos Vaughn lay half-conscious on the floor of the wardroom across from the suit locker. Daniel paused; he hadn't wanted to take Vaughn aboard, but nonetheless the fellow was his responsibility. Timmins, the power room crewman Vaughn had hired to look after him aboard, lifted the passenger's shoulders with one arm and brought a tumbler of clear fluid to his lips with the other.

"Mr. Vaughn, are you—" Daniel began.

Vaughn drank reflexively. His eyes flashed open and he spewed the rest of the glassful across the room. Apparently Timmins' idea of a restorative was neat alcohol from the power room hydraulics.

"Good *God*, Lieutenant Leary," Vaughn said. He didn't sound angry, merely amazed. "Is that sensation normal?"

"I'm afraid it's going to be normal for this cruise, sir," Daniel said. He crossed his hands behind his back, a way to keep from fidgeting while he waited for something distasteful.

Instead of the expected shouts and threats—vain, of course, but unpleasant regardless—Vaughn managed a weak smile. "I see how the Cinnabar navy wins its battles, Lieutenant," he said. "Well, I asked to travel with you."

Using Timmins as a brace, Vaughn got to his feet. "And Lieutenant?" he said. "I win my battles too."

CHAPTER ELEVEN

Adele sat primly in her place, taking her cue from Ellie Woetjans who presided at the head of the table. The senior warrant officers had invited Lt. Leary, Mr. Vaughn, and the two midshipmen to dinner. Adele was tense because she wasn't good at rituals, and this one was both new to her and important. A gaffe here—and formal dinners were always minefields—risked hurting the feelings of her family by adoption.

Balsley, classed as a Mechanic II but in practice the wardroom servant, stood at the hatchway. In a loud voice that made his brushy little mustache wobble he announced, "The guests have arrived."

"Rise for the captain and our honored guests!" the bosun said, suiting her action to her words.

Adele scrambled to her feet. She was so careful not to overset the chair behind her that she bumped the table with her thighs. As the table was bolted to the deck neither it nor the place settings were affected an iota, but Adele knew she'd have bruises in the morning.

And not for the first time. She was perfectly comfortable in tight spaces. What she didn't like—and couldn't seem to learn—was *moving* in tight spaces.

Daniel appeared at the door, wearing his dress grays just as his hosts were. "Please be seated, sir," Woetjans said. When she spoke formally, her words came out as though so many cuts of a buzz saw.

"My fellow officers, thank you for your hospitality," Daniel said as he entered. He took the seat to Woetjans' right. He winked at Adele beside him.

Vaughn was behind him, wearing a suit of vivid chartreuse and carrying a bottle. "Mistress President," he said, offering the bottle to Woetjans. "I thank you as well. I hope you'll accept this small addition to the festivities."

It was brandy, a distillation from Pleasaunce and expensive even within the Alliance. Betts, peering past Adele's shoulder, said, "God *damn*! The *Marat*'s wardroom got a case of that stuff at a souk on Rigoun. A shot of that'll put lead in your pencil, let me tell you!"

Adele saw Daniel frown slightly. "Then it'll make an excellent stirrup cup when we go on leave on Sexburga," he said. "In ten days, I expect, at the rate we've been shaping."

Woetjans nodded and handed the bottle to Hogg, who'd been drafted for the night along with Tovera and Timmins. She looked a trifle wistful, but she wasn't the person to question her captain's orders even when they were delicately phrased.

Adele knew perfectly well that alcohol impeded the physiology of mating, though no doubt a lot of the process was in the mind. It wasn't an area in which she could claim expertise, of course.

The midshipmen entered last, carefully groomed and as stiff as if they expected to be shot. They were both eighteen, just out of the Academy and on their first operational deployment. In a large vessel they would have had as many as a score of other midshipmen to provide fellowship and a degree of concealment. Instead they'd been placed in a small ship with a picked crew and a captain little more than their own age and already famous. Of course they were nervous!

Adele thought of her own entry into the Blythe Academy. Her smile was grim.

She'd been an outsider—of course; she'd been an outsider all her life and perfectly happy about it. Her skills even at age sixteen were beyond those not only of her fellow students but of her instructors and most of the staff of the Academic Collections. She couldn't imagine wanting to fit in with people whom she considered only a short intellectual step above lapdogs.

Dorst and Vesey couldn't tell themselves that. Besides, from what

Adele had seen, they were far too nice to consider doing so. For that matter, if Adele had been trained by instructors as able as the Sissies were at their different jobs, *she* wouldn't have been so sure of her superiority.

"Be seated!" Woetjans said. Adele started to sit, then noticed everyone else was waiting till Daniel's trousers touched the cushion. She grimaced. She *would* learn how to do this, because it mattered to people who mattered to her.

It was strange, and remarkably pleasant, to be around so many people who mattered.

Glasses of water were already at the places. Hogg was filling squat, four-ounce tumblers from the punch bowl on the sideboard. It looked like lemonade, but Adele knew to be cautious even before Tovera, handing the punch around, whispered, "From the hydraulics."

"The Republic!" Woetjans said, rising. Adele rose with the others and sipped.

There was a choking sound from the end of the table. Dorst's face was very red. He saw the others staring at him and quickly downed another gulp of the punch from the glass he'd half-emptied at the toast.

Daniel nodded approvingly at the lad. Adele supposed that displaying bravado in the face of adversity was a virtue the RCN wanted to inculcate in its young officers. Certainly it was behavior that Daniel himself could be expected to approve.

Hogg was refilling glasses. Tovera set a pitcher of water on the table to Adele's right; the other diners politely pretended not to notice, the way they'd have done if she'd lost both arms and had to eat using her toes. Throughout most of her life Adele had never imagined she'd feel embarrassment at not being able to down the equivalent of eight or ten ounces of absolute alcohol in the course of an evening; but then, she'd never imagined that she'd be an RCN officer, either.

As Balsley took the first course, a tureen of soup, from an undercook at the doorway—hatchway, she had to remember to call it a hatchway—Vaughn said to Daniel across the table, "I've heard you're a naturalist, Lieutenant. Are you familiar with the zoology of my Strymon? I think you'll find it quite interesting. Our major predators are descended from flying species, while the herbivores are all semiaquatic."

Hogg and Tovera continued to dispense punch, which kept them busier in this company than Balsley and Timmins were serving the food. Adele tasted the soup and found it thick and rather good, albeit bland.

Apart from being overcooked and underseasoned to her taste, formed as it was in sophisticated circles, Adele had been surprised at how good RCN rations were. At the start of a cruise, a vessel's first lieutenant drew and inspected stores from a naval warehouse. The chief of ship and chief of rig—engineer and bosun—then had to give their approval to the lieutenant's assessment.

If the officers protested the quality of the offering, the agent could either provide replacements (which had to be approved in turn) or convene a Navy Office tribunal to decide the matter. Given that two of the tribunal members were by regulation former or serving space officers, very rarely did the warehouse personnel choose to argue the point.

The warehousemen were allowed five percent "shrinkage" for their profit. Any more than that, however, required the collusion of a vessel's senior officers. Given the number of ways a fatal accident could occur in space, even the most venal officers would think twice about starving the spacers who might be standing behind them at a steam line, or a hundred and fifty feet above them with a wrench.

"No, I haven't had the opportunity to study your biota, I'm afraid," Daniel said. From him the statement was no conventional excuse: Adele had first-hand experience of her friend's interest in the whims of nature on various planets. "Our sailing orders came so abruptly that my concerns were limited to the ship herself. I didn't have time to prepare for relaxation after we arrived on Strymon."

He paused to wash a mouthful of soup down with a hefty swig of punch, then turned to Adele and said, "We'll have loaded natural history files with the regional briefing data, won't we, Adele?"

Adele paused to remove with as much delicacy as possible something that hadn't responded well to chewing. A glance into her napkin suggested that it was a piece of plastic container that had been opened with a sharp knife.

"Yes," she said. *It couldn't very well have been poisonous, after all.* "Though I didn't request a natural history database for

Strymon proper, and I'm afraid that the data in the regional overview may be skimpy. Because Terra is in the same files, that is."

Adele had loaded specialist political and economic data, but . . . She felt her face tighten with cold anger. It was directed at herself, of course, as her anger generally was; but Vaughn, who didn't know her the way Daniel did, flinched back in surprise.

"I should have gotten specialist files, Daniel," she said. "I know your interests. I apologize."

"Well, that needn't be a difficulty," Vaughn said. "I have quite an extensive library aboard. If you'd care to use it, Lieutenant, I'd be delighted to share. I'm something of a booster for my homeland, you see."

What Adele saw was that Vaughn had managed to bring most or all of his truckload of luggage aboard the *Princess Cecile*. A chip library needn't take up much volume, even with a reader, but Vaughn's wardrobe and personal rations hadn't been packed into one and a half cubic feet.

Presumably he'd bribed crewmen to slip his baggage aboard in the rain and conceal it. That couldn't be said to degrade naval discipline—Adele had learned quickly that all spacers were smugglers, as surely as all good librarians were obsessives—nor was the corvette's fighting efficiency degraded if some of her crew members shared their narrow bunks with cases of off-planet finery.

In the initial interview with Vaughn, Daniel had made the point that he'd decide the *Princess Cecile*'s activities without regard for his passenger's wealth or influence. Vaughn had bowed to the captain's authority and achieved his end in a time-honored fashion that put money in the crew's pocket for leave on Sexburga.

Politics in action, as Adele's father might have said. Backdoor compromises, indirection; face-saving gestures. The social lubricants for which Adele Mundy had no taste or aptitude. Data in files were so much easier to deal with.

"I appreciate your offer, Mr. Vaughn," Daniel said, spooning the last of the soup into his mouth. "I would indeed like to borrow your library, then. We can copy it into the ship's database and return the chips immediately."

"I regret that my library is in a specialized Strymon format, Lieutenant," Vaughn said with a deprecatory lift of his hands.

"We're an insular people, I'm afraid. But it shouldn't matter, since you're welcome to borrow my chip reader during the voyage as well."

Daniel glanced at Adele and raised an eyebrow. She started to say that, given the ship's communications suite and her own skill, there was no format in the human universe that she wouldn't venture to read. She caught herself an instant before the first syllable left her tongue.

"And when we reach Strymon, Daniel," Adele said blandly, "you'll be able to buy a suitable reader of your own, I'm sure."

Intellectual pride had always been her besetting sin; it had become a danger to her life and work since she accepted Mistress Sand's duties. Vaughn obviously had no idea of how completely open to Adele's perusal any documents he had would be. That ignorance was probably to the benefit of Adele's mission and to the officers and crew of the *Princess Cecile*.

"Yes, that's a good idea," Daniel said, momentarily surprised but concealing the fact beneath commonplaces. "I wouldn't have had time to view them before, but now the cruise has started to settle down to a routine, so I can—"

"A damned hard routine," Taley said. She hadn't eaten much of her soup, but she was matching Mon mug and mug with the punch. "*Damned* hard."

"Aye, that's so," said Pasternak without raising his eyes from the table. "But the fittings're solid, just like Signals said—"

He gave Adele a sidelong glance of acknowledgment.

"—and by God, the crew's solid too, most of them!"

"I got a couple I don't have on the hull when we're making in-and-outs," Woetjans said, staring into her mug with a bleak frown. "They're going to scream and flail around the compartment if they're inboard, but that's better than . . ."

She swallowed down the contents of her mug, then waggled the fingers of her free hand in the air.

Adele had a bleak vision of a rigger drifting in a bubble universe that had nothing human in it but him—forever. She shivered. Death didn't frighten her, but the thought of that eternal loneliness had a terror for even her gray soul.

They were all looking at Daniel. Adele was suddenly aware of how pale the officers' faces were, how deep-sunk their eyes. The spacers gathered here in the wardroom were among the most experienced in the RCN, but even they were being ground down by Daniel's daily regimen of the Matrix punctuated by heart-freezingly brief returns to the normal universe.

"It is a hard routine," he said softly. "A very hard routine. When we reach Sexburga, I'll give every person in the crew the opportunity to transfer to another vessel of the squadron. It's no disgrace to be unable to withstand an environment that isn't meant for humans."

"Aye, we know that, sir," Pasternak said. His voice was steady, but his hands trembled until he laced them around his mug. "We're spacers of the RCN. We'll stick it."

"And there won't be any of our people who go off to a clapped-out cruiser, sir," Woetjans said, gripping her glass as if trying to strangle it. "They'll stick with the *Sissie*. They'll stick with the *Sissie* if it kills them!"

Adele felt herself trembling. Without glancing toward her, Daniel covered her right hand with his left and said in a measured voice, "The purpose of practicing touch-and-goes is so that we and our friends *won't* be the ones who're killed, of course. That's the only justification I would accept for the cost."

He lifted his tumbler to call attention to it. "A very dry atmosphere here in your wardroom, Mistress President," he said. "All the punch appears to have evaporated from my glass!"

The general laughter as Tovera filled the mug dissolved the mood of a moment before; but though Adele smiled at the humor and the skill with which Daniel used humor for a tool, there was a cold weight in her guts. She thought of the insertions of the next day and the nine days after that—if they lived so long.

And unlike Daniel, she couldn't convince herself that avoiding death was really that valuable a benefit.

Daniel watched a trio of strangers enter the bridge through the exterior bulkhead, talking in silent animation. They looked perfectly normal—an older man, a boy, and a woman Daniel wouldn't have minded getting to know better—except that they had downy feathers instead of hair.

"*Five minutes to return to normal space,*" said Lt. Mon from the BDC. His voice sounded shaky, but that could be a flaw in the communications system . . . or in Daniel's ears. The voyage had been hard, very hard.

"Acknowledged," Daniel replied, then switched to intercom and said, "Captain to ship. We're five minutes from entry to the Sexburga system, spacers. If God favors us and I've done my calculations correctly, there'll be liberty for all but an anchor watch inside of twelve hours. Captain out."

He could hear faint cheering from other compartments. After seventeen days of discomfort punctuated by agony, nobody had much energy even for that.

Adele stared transfixed at the three phantoms, looking horrified. The remaining bridge personnel kept their attention on their displays.

"Ah, you see them too, Mundy?" Daniel said. The older male was making wide, oratorical sweeps of his right arm while his left remained cocked over his chest.

It was all automatic from here on in unless there were an emergency. Betts was setting up missile launches. That had drawn Sun to simulate gunfire targets on his display. Daniel was all for training, but plotting for immediate attack on entry into a major Cinnabar naval base couldn't be called realistic preparation. So far as Daniel was concerned, calming a friend who looked uncomfortable was at least as good a use for his time.

Adele let her breath out slowly and looked at him. "You mean they're real?" she said. "Daniel, I thought I was going mad!"

"I don't think they're real—well, not part of the sidereal universe, at any rate," he said. "But to be sure, I see them too."

"I knew three fish couldn't really swim through the wall," Adele said. "I'd forgotten what you'd said about phantoms."

She looked at the men on the battle consoles and said, "Sun, Betts? What do you see over there?"

The gunner's mate turned and smiled shyly at her. "I don't see anything right now, mistress," he said. "But I know what you mean, sure. They've been walking the corridors since the third day, I know."

Betts said nothing, utterly engrossed in plotting courses for his missiles. The muscles in Daniel's jaw bunched, then relaxed. The missileer was reacting to the stress of the voyage in his own way.

He was no more to be censured than Daniel and Adele were for seeing feather-haired strangers on the bridge.

Adele shook her head in wonder. "But why do we see fish standing upright, Daniel?" she asked.

"Ah!" said Daniel. Apparently the range of options was wider than merely seeing a phantom or not.

"Uncle Stacey and his friends had no idea what caused the visions," he said. "Stacey claimed to think they were random synapses firing in the watcher's brain, but I don't think he really believed that. You know as much as I do. Ah, I see people, more or less; not fish."

"*Three minutes,*" Mon said, verbalizing the countdown that Daniel's screen showed as a sidebar.

His main display was a navigational tank in three dimensions, the portion of the sidereal universe analogous to the *Princess Cecile*'s location in a wholly separate bubble of the cosmos. A bead of pure cyan drifted across the star map in tiny caracoles like a leaf blowing in the wind. If Daniel were to cut the charge of the sails *now*, the bead would be the corvette's location; if the astrogational computer was correct.

Abruptly, almost angrily—the voyage had been just as hard on the captain as it had on the rest of the complement—Daniel switched his display to the *Princess Cecile*'s sail plan. Instead of the icons that provided information in the most concentrated form, he rolled the controller up to give him a simulated real-time view of the corvette hanging in space, lighted by a sun like Cinnabar's at a distance of 107 million miles.

Color codings on the icons would have told Daniel that the port sails were all set at 37 degrees; that ventral and starboard courses were at 63 degrees; and that the mainsail on Dorsal Three was spread straight fore and aft to serve as a rudder.

Daniel needed a reminder of the reality of the ship about him, the ship he commanded. This image provided it. He didn't care about the precise details, though his trained eye could have called the settings to within a hair's breadth if he'd been out on the hull.

Which is where he wanted to be. Duty kept him aboard.

"Every day we've been out of normal space . . ." he said, aloud but not really concerned whether anyone else on the bridge heard him.

"It's seemed that the hull was getting thinner. Subliming like a block of dry ice. I wasn't sure there'd be anything left in another day."

"God help us!" Betts said, bent over his console; plotting solutions that were as imaginary as the holographic sails on Daniel's display. His missiles were, like Daniel's sails, the anchor that held his mind to—if not sanity, then to the memory of sanity.

"*One minute!*" said Mon. Again Daniel failed to acknowledge. All that mattered was that the spacers aboard the *Princess Cecile* each find a way to create reality. Create: because such long immersion in the Matrix proved to every soul aboard that reality wasn't an absolute, that it was no more than the whim of an individual mind for as long as the mind could stay sane.

The time column on the sidebar was shrinking to zero. If Daniel switched back to the navigational display, he would find the cyan bead approaching the pinpoint that was Sexburga. Toward ze—

"*Now!*" a voice screamed; maybe Mon's, maybe Daniel's own as his left hand drained the sails' charge and the *Princess Cecile* shuddered back into normal space, this time to stay.

Nothing changed within the hull, but the light was richer, the fittings had palpable density instead of being gassy umbras, and the air filled Daniel's lungs with the smells of weeks of being lived in. The stench was indescribably wonderful, like the rough texture of a log in the grasp of a man who had been drowning.

The cheers were rough, bestial. The relief the spacers felt came from far below the conscious levels of their minds.

His fingers moving by reflex, Daniel switched his display to a Plot Position Indicator. The icon that stood for the corvette was less than 150,000 miles out from the planet Sexburga, almost too close for a proper approach.

"Power room, light the High Drive!" Daniel said to his console. His fingers moved on the semaphore controls, directing the riggers to unpin the antennas.

Then through the intercom Daniel added, "Captain to ship. We've arrived, spacers. And by God, every one of you is going to have a drink on your captain when we're on the ground!"

CHAPTER TWELVE

Adele—Signals Officer Mundy—was busy for the first time since
the *Princess Cecile* entered the Matrix outbound from Cinnabar. Since the events on Kostroma, really. She'd studied the
corvette's electronics on the voyage to Harbor Three, and during the past seventeen hellish days she'd been learning all she could
about Strymon and the adjacent planetary systems.

That had been work at her own speed—which didn't mean it
was done in a leisurely fashion by most people's standards, but
there was no outside pressure involved. Now—

"*Condor Control to Gee Are one-seven-five-one*—" GR1751 was
the *Princess Cecile*'s pennant number, which her transponder sent
automatically when interrogated "—*you are cleared to land at Flood
Harbor in numbers nine-five, I repeat nine-five, minutes. There will
be no liftoffs or landings from Flood Harbor for half an hour either
way of your slot, but be aware that there may be traffic from the
Cove or Drylands. Hold to your filed descent. Condor out.*"

Adele had reconfigured the communications console to use wand
control as its default. This wasn't ideal, as a computer capable
of missile launches and astrogation had a much broader range
of options than a civilian database. Adele preferred to layer command sets within her wands' existing software rather than use
the virtual keyboard created for the console. It was still much
faster, and for her there was less risk of an error.

Her hands moved, sending the core of the message from Condor
Control—the station that handled starship traffic for all

Sexburga—to Daniel's display in visual form. The course plot, the time parameters, and the two smaller harbors with their approach cones were instantly visible; if Daniel for some reason wanted the audio message as well, he had only to key an icon to get it.

That was the open part of Adele's duties. At the same time she'd entered the Condor database covertly and copied from it the complete records of landings and departures from the planet in the past thirty days. Her real concern—Daniel's real concern— was to see when and whether Commodore Pettin had arrived, but for safety's sake Adele had given her search broader parameters.

RCS *Tampico*, arrived four days previous. From . . . Adele's wands moved . . . Holtsmark, berthed at Slip Thirty-two, Flood Harbor. She accessed another file, this one internal RCN records held in the *Princess Cecile*'s database. RCS *Tampico*, communications vessel, 1700 tons empty; defensive armament only.

"*Condor Control to Gee Are one-seven-five-one,*" the controller on Sexburga said. "*You're to put down in slip thirty. I'm transmitting a plot of Flood Harbor. Condor over.*"

The speaker was male, probably in his forties, and sounded alertly professional. He hissed his esses and more generally spoke with a soft lilt; Adele decided to class the peculiarities as a Sexburga accent until she learned otherwise.

A schematic appeared in gold light on the left side of Adele's display. It was offset from but identical to the harbor plan from the *Princess Cecile*'s database. The local transmission also showed cigar-shaped vessels settled in roughly half the fifty-seven slips. Sexburga was clearly a major port, though most of the ships berthed here were of moderate size.

Adele framed the plan and retransmitted it to a suspense file serving the command console while Daniel set up his final approach. It was received, becoming a sidebar on the upper left corner of a screen almost completely filled by numerical data.

"Gee-Are one-seven-five-one acknowledges receipt of the Flood Harbor berthing plan," Adele said. "Gee-Are one-seven-five-one out."

Nothing went to the command console until it had been cleared through Adele's filters and then requested by the captain. The captain could set up categories for immediate update—this harbor schematic, for example—but even so the data didn't appear on Daniel's display until he called for it. The priorities were determined by a human being.

Adele returned her attention to the right half of her display, another RCN internal file: current deployment orders for RCN vessels. The *Tampico* was on a triangular run from Sexburga to the Cinnabar outpost at Fort Hill Station and finally to Langerhut, an allied system with a Resident Commissioner but almost no direct contact with Cinnabar. The *Tampico* carried dispatches, supplies, and personnel who were being transferred. The vessel wasn't connected with Commodore Pettin's squadron.

The *Princess Cecile* braked under one-gee acceleration. Even to the naked eye, the image of Sexburga swelled on the real-time display at the margin of Adele's screen. Speaking loudly to be heard over the whine of antimatter annihilation, Sun said to Betts, "Did you see that? Mr. Leary didn't quite kill our momentum with the last shift in the Matrix. He was so sure he'd drop us just short of the planet that he left us with a way on to save time. Ain't he a wonder?"

Betts nodded solemnly. He was clearing his display of the targeting fantasies that had preserved him in the Matrix, moving methodically through a checklist. "A wonder . . ." he breathed.

A wonder indeed.

There were no other RCN vessels on Sexburga or in the PCT-3301 system of which Sexburga was the fourth planet. Adele moved to checking grouped arrivals.

Three ships had arrived in hailing range of Condor Control within minutes of one another a week ago, but they were freighters from three separate systems linked only by chance. Adele called up visuals from the Flood Harbor security cameras and proved beyond doubt that the ships weren't warships, let alone Commodore Pettin's squadron with disguised identities.

She thought a smile that eventually touched her lips. She was obviously being obsessive. In that, at least, she'd make a good spacer.

Adele had tapped into the automated stream of Sexburgan meteorological data as soon as the *Princess Cecile* emerged from the Matrix. The first and last twenty thousand feet of a voyage were statistically the most dangerous, because starships weren't streamlined for operations in an atmosphere.

The corvette's hull was a cylinder with rounded ends, a stable enough shape initially. The antennas and rigging on the exterior, however, created turbulence as well as twisting the vessel off-line when they caught gusts of wind. Even though ships in an atmosphere moved with the deliberation of belles making their entrances, they were fitted with sensor suites to make their own observations from space to be compared with whatever the planetary controller supplied.

Daniel let out his breath in a long sigh and flopped back in his seat. Almost at once he straightened and resumed keying commands, now with a look of eager attention. He caught Adele's glance and grinned at her through the haze of his new task. Moments before, as he'd been setting up the approach, he'd had the rapt focus of a cat watching potential prey.

Adele echoed the navigation display in a corner of her own screen, just to see what Daniel was working on now. It was a plan of the *Princess Cecile*'s antennas and sails, which were being collapsed for storage. Daniel would be able to understand the process by a glance at the schematic, but to Adele it was merely bumps and lines.

She would have cut away, but a red arrow suddenly careted a point on the white outline. Daniel's voice said through her communications helmet, "*See here? Port Three hasn't fully retracted. These three hollow triangles—*"

It was hard to see details of the sail plan when it was shrunk down to a sidebar; Adele raised the schematic to three quarters of the display. She looked up to meet Daniel's eyes; he was grinning as he moved a light pen to mark the image she was importing to her console.

"—*are the riggers working on it. They've shut off the hydraulics so they can crank the mast down manually. Now here—*"

The caret jumped. Adele gave Daniel's explanation half her attention while she sorted the shipping log for vessels which had lifted from Cinnabar within thirty days of their arrival on Sexburga. No ship but the *Princess Cecile* herself would have made the voyage direct.

"—*you see the dorsal mainsail we've been using for a rudder during our last leg of the Matrix,*" Daniel continued. "*It kinked on its track, so these riggers and the topside officer—*"

Who appeared to be a solid pink triangle close to the six hollow ones.

"—*that's Woetjans on this watch, they just finished furling it by hand.*"

On the right of Adele's display, itself now a sidebar, a single name appeared: the *Achilles*, a private yacht of three hundred tons. It had landed on Sexburga six hours ahead of the *Princess Cecile*.

"*The other problem's here on Ventral Five,*" Daniel continued, moving his pointer. "*There's a jammed yard—see how she sticks out like a broken finger instead of lying along the mast. Woetjans has a rigger on that, using a wrench if he can and a cutting torch if the wrench doesn't work. We can't have that if we're going to land on our belly.*"

"Ah," said Adele, but she was frowning at the data on the right of her screen. The *Achilles* was fleet-footed indeed to have reached Sexburga only twenty-three days out from Cinnabar.

An attention signal whistled as the track lights pulsed green. "*Hull reports the antennas are stowed and locked,*" a voice from the BDC reported. Dorst was speaking rather than Mon; the lieutenant was giving the midshipmen actual experience as officers, albeit in small ways.

"*Acknowledged,*" said Daniel, captain of the *Princess Cecile* again instead of a friend explaining details of his expertise. He touched the command bar on the separate semaphore panel to his left, then keyed the intercom.

"*Captain to ship!*" Daniel announced, his voice in Adele's helmet preceding by a hair's breadth its analogue through the ceiling speakers. His fingers continued to type commands as he spoke. "*The riggers are coming aboard. All hands prepare for entry into the atmosphere. Captain out.*"

Icons on the far left of Adele's display shifted. The whine of the High Drive ceased, and the braking thrust Adele's body perceived as gravity lessened for a heartbeat or so before the plasma thrusters roared to full life. Adele must have looked startled, because Sun glanced over at her and shouted, "We can't chance double thrust, mistress. The masts wouldn't take it, even brought in and locked."

Adele nodded understanding. She'd known that, of course. This wasn't the first time she'd landed in a starship, for heaven's sake, nor even the first time she'd done so as an officer on the bridge with full access to the details of what was going on.

But—her *intellect* had known what to expect. The lizard brain deep within Adele had known only that it had suddenly dropped into nothingness.

The riggers were coming through the airlock, unlatching their helmets and congratulating themselves with enthusiasm. Riggers even more than other spacers loved the void, but this had been a hard run. In the future the crew would brag to others about how Mr. Leary had brought the *Princess Cecile* from Cinnabar to Sexburga in seventeen days . . . but for the moment, they were glad to know they'd be walking on solid ground in an hour.

Daniel switched his display to the harbor plot. Adele, still watching her echo of the navigational console, saw pennant numbers blink into life beside each cylindrical hull. She smiled wryly. That was a much simpler route into the problem than those she'd taken.

"*Commodore Pettin isn't on Sexburga now,*" Daniel said through her helmet. "*Has the squadron already landed and lifted for Strymon?*"

"We're the only RCN vessel to arrive from Cinnabar in the past thirty days, Daniel," Adele said. "Pettin had a ten days start and you've beaten him."

The upper atmosphere began to buffet the corvette. Over the windroar came a *bang* and a momentary fluttering rattle outside the hull. Woetjans snatched the handset from beside the suit locker and shouted into it.

Daniel focused on his screen, then looked unperturbedly through the hologram toward Adele again. "*A furling clamp on the Starboard Three topsail gave way,*" he said. "*Rule of thumb is you'll lose a sail on every leg of a cruise. If we'd made five or six intermediate landings as the squadron probably did, we'd have a much higher damage bill than this one.*"

He frowned. "*Commodore Pettin had no reason to push the way we were doing,*" he continued in a careful tone. "*I couldn't be more proud of the ship, the crew, and the—and my astrogation that brought us to Sexburga in a record run. But I do hope the commodore doesn't feel, ah, challenged. That would add complexity to a situation that's already less simple than it could be.*"

Woetjans and the riggers still wore their suits as they waited in the corridor. Delos Vaughn stood in the doorway of the wardroom, looking into the bridge past them. The hard voyage had worn him as badly as it had anybody else aboard the *Princess Cecile*; his face looked like a mummy's skull.

But he was smiling.

The echoes of the corvette's landing had stopped reverberating around the high cliffs of Flood Harbor, but when Daniel switched to a panoramic view he saw that a vast doughnut of steam still hung in the sky. The Harbormaster's office was a blockhouse built out from the natural rock wall at the base of the broad embayment. A vehicle pulled away from it and turned up the quay that would bring it to the *Princess Cecile*. That was greater efficiency than Daniel had expected on so distant a world.

He keyed the intercom and said, "Captain to crew. After the ship has been opened, spacers, there's a twenty-four hour liberty for everybody but the designated anchor watch. I'll remain aboard as officer of the watch."

He paused, then added, "Good work, Sissies. God grant this won't be the only record you and I will set! Captain out."

Daniel sighed and stretched his arms back, then forward to where they muddied portions of the display. The panorama provided a holographic image of what he would see were he standing on the *Princess Cecile*'s spine *and* if the rigging weren't in the way. Like quite a lot of things—Daniel's fingers idly called up a file; women's faces, little mementos, cascaded across his display—the image was more attractive than the reality.

He grinned. Adele got up shakily from her console and said, "Daniel? I'd have thought you'd want to go ashore yourself."

"And so I do," he said, grinning even wider. "In fact I was just thinking that I'd always take the living, breathing reality over however pretty an image."

Daniel got up also. Riggers opened both doors of the forward dorsal airlock, letting in a gulp of air with touches of steam and ozone. Down the length of the ship clanks and squeals announced the undogging of hatches, both ordinary ports and the access panels used for major overhauls. Some of them would be closed again after the corvette had aired out, but for the moment everyone wanted the maximum ventilation.

The makeup of Sexburga's atmosphere differed by a few percentage points from Cinnabar's or Earth's. All that mattered just now was that it hadn't been lived in for seventeen days by over a hundred and twenty people, plus a wide variety of machinery and electronics. The corvette's filters scrubbed the carbon dioxide down to safe levels and removed actual toxins, while hydrolyzed reaction mass kept the oxygen constant; the stench was a permanent companion regardless.

After a time you no longer noticed the smell at a conscious level, but it still did damage to morale and efficiency. Like a mild toothache, the omnipresent discomfort of bad air robbed spacers of those top few points of intellect which could mean life or death in a dangerous environment. Flushing the ship's atmosphere was the first and most longed-for reward of landing after a long voyage.

"On the other hand," Daniel continued, quirking Adele his grin, "I'm going to be just as glad to be ashore come tomorrow, and I can relax better if I've already taken care of the ship's administrative business."

Feeling a little embarrassed, he added, "Besides, though it isn't exactly traditional for the captain to take the first shore-side watch, it's . . . traditional among the captains that I'd choose to serve under myself. So in a way I don't really have a choice, you see."

"I see," said Adele, with a smile that looked suspiciously like a smirk. "Well, I wasn't in a hurry to go ashore myself. I have a new series of databases to pry into, after all. I can do that best from my console here as soon as I've linked us to the local net."

The corridor was filling with spacers who'd changed into their shoregoing clothes. For Betts, Taley, and the midshipmen, that meant dress grays. The same was probably true of Pasternak, though Daniel didn't see him. The chief bunked in the office attached to the power room on A Level rather than in the warrant-officer accommodations here on C.

The lower-ranking crewmen and the officers who'd first shipped as common spacers wore liberty dress. These had started out as sets of utilities, but the owners had decorated them during off-duty periods in space.

Woetjans's liberty suit was the highest state of the art Daniel had seen. What with appliques, cutwork, embroidery, studs, and the ribbons fluttering from the seams, there wasn't a thread of the wave-pattern fatigues visible.

"Actually, Adele, you could do me a favor," Daniel said, feeling a touch of embarrassment. He should have broached this sooner. It was going to sound like he wanted to be shut of her company on the ground, which was far from the truth. "The midshipmen will be going ashore, as you know. Now, as you know, I'm not a moralist—"

"Actually, I believe you are a moralist, Daniel," Adele said. She grinned, reminding him that she must have been a child once upon a time. "But not in the fashion you mean, no."

On B Level, the accommodations deck, at least a dozen spacers were singing, "*When I was a young girl I used to seek pleasure . . .*"

Daniel cleared his throat. "As I say . . ." he said. "Dorst and Vesey *are* young, though, and this is the first landfall of their first cruise. Normally the first lieutenant would shepherd them about, but Lieutenant Mon won't get farther than the first tavern beyond the docks."

He shrugged. "Not that I'm complaining," he added. "Mon does his job a hundred and twenty percent; it wouldn't be fair to deny him downtime he's so richly earned. But I was wondering . . . ?"

"You want me to chaperone the midshipmen?" Adele said carefully. She didn't seem hostile to the idea, though "cool" would be a fair description of her attitude. Well, "cool" would generally describe Adele's attitude.

"Not that, not *controlling* their behavior," Daniel said, trying to explain a concept that was more subtle than words could really express. His words, at any rate. "Dorst and Vesey are adults with the rights and responsibilities of officers of the RCN. And God knows, when I was their age . . ."

His voice trailed off. He wasn't much beyond their age now, not in years. Had his first commanding officer, Commander Gray, felt this way about him?

"Anyway . . ." Daniel continued, feeling his face warm as he looked at himself with the eyes of Midshipman Daniel Leary, age eighteen. "I don't want you to keep them on leashes, Adele, but

I'm afraid that if they go off with any of the other senior warrant officers, they'll . . . well, the only question would be whether they spent their liberty in bars, brothels, or a gambling house."

A smile drove the self-conscious embarrassment from Daniel's face. Voicing the thought he said, "Of course, Sexburga's a major port. I'm sure there are a number of establishments providing all three entertainments under the same roof."

Sobering he went on, "And I don't care if my midshipmen *do* spend their liberty in one. I don't want to force them into that choice, though, as sending them off with Woetjans would guarantee. I can't order you to do this—"

Actually, he could: he was captain of the *Princess Cecile*, and if he ordered his crew to spend their whole liberty in church, regulations permitted him to do so. His chance of having anybody report aboard for the next leg of the cruise was a great deal more problematic, however.

"—but it would be a favor to me and to the RCN."

Adele nodded. "All right," she said. "I didn't have anything more exciting planned than sightseeing in what seems from the description in the *Sailing Directions* to be quite an interesting city. If Dorst and Vesey would care to join me, I'd be pleased to have their company."

She looked down at her rumpled utilities. "I suppose I should change? I see the others are."

"Dress grays are traditional for officers on liberty," Daniel said. "If you'd prefer civilian clothes, that's perfectly acceptable also. That is, on my ship it is."

"I sincerely hope I'll never travel on anybody else's ship, Daniel," Adele said with a faint smile. "Certainly not as a member of the RCN."

She stepped toward the suite she shared with him. "I'll put on my uniform. It's perfectly comfortable and I'm—"

Adele paused, looking back over her shoulder. "Actually, I'm rather proud to wear the uniform. Although I'm still surprised to feel that way."

Grinning broadly, Daniel keyed first the attention signal and then the PA system. "Midshipmen to the bridge," he ordered.

Hogg stepped onto the bridge, wearing his version of liberty dress—high boots, red beret, orange pantaloons, and a canary yellow shirt with flaring sleeves. He'd been waiting politely in the passage for his master and Adele to finish their conversation. "If you won't be requiring me, sir," he said, "I thought I'd go ashore and pick up a few things we'll need for the voyage."

"Certainly, Hogg," Daniel said. "I only hope that you don't pick up anything that you don't mean to."

Hogg drew himself up, which still left him a hand's breadth short of Daniel's own modest height. "Loose women," he said in a tone of injured innocence, "are not a problem of mine, young master."

He cleared his throat and added, "Though I'll be fair and say that I never noticed you to have problems finding them neither. Quite the contrary."

"We'll trust that they don't have anything on Sexburga that the sick-bay computer can't solve," Daniel said. "But of course you're free to go, Hogg. Have fun."

Daniel watched the vivid form of his servant disappear down the companionway. Hogg had grown grayer day by day during the long, brutal voyage. It wasn't so much a physical change as a lowering of the intense spirit that usually animated his pudgy form. He'd never flinched, let alone complained, but Daniel wasn't sure how much reserve there'd been remaining.

Perhaps very little—but Hogg had always rebounded swiftly.

Delos Vaughn came out of his berth, dressed in a flowing blend of blues and greens. His servant, Timmins, watched him head for the bridge. When he was sure of Vaughn's intention, Timmins ducked down the companionway. He was still wearing fatigues, having waited to change into liberty dress until he'd attended to the passenger.

Daniel's eyes narrowed slightly. To get that sort of service from a spacer after a voyage like the one just ended, Vaughn must be paying quite well. Which shouldn't have been a surprise, of course.

Vaughn paused at the bridge hatchway. "Lieutenant Leary?" he asked. "May I speak with you?"

"Yes, of course," Daniel said. "Welcome to the bridge, Mr. Vaughn."

It didn't bother Daniel, but he'd noticed that Vaughn always called him by his rank, lieutenant, rather than his position as captain of the *Princess Cecile*. If the choice was a political game,

Daniel didn't understand it. But perhaps Vaughn was just ignorant, the niceties of shipboard usage having passed him by.

It didn't *exactly* bother Daniel.

"I have friends here on Sexburga, Lieutenant," Vaughn said as
he stepped over the hatch coaming a trifle shakily. He spoke
normally, but his cheeks had sunk noticeably in the past seventeen days. "I believe they're waiting for me on the dock now. I
wonder if you might be able to join us for dinner tonight? I'd
like to show my appreciation for the skill as well as the hospitality you demonstrated on this voyage."

Daniel reached over to Bett's console—his own keyboard was
out of reach from where he stood—and brought up the panoramic
view with quick keystrokes. He hoped he wasn't frowning at
Vaughn, though he wouldn't pretend that he really cared that
much.

"Your friends waiting for you, Mr. Vaughn?" he said, adjusting the display to expand the quay to which a team of riggers
was extending the corvette's gangplank.

"Why yes, Lieutenant," Vaughn said. "I believe you met Mistress Zane at my party? Though of course you might not remember her with all the excitement that day."

"I remember her," Daniel said in a quiet voice. Indeed, that
was Zane standing ramrod straight beside the open door of the
ground car now waiting on the quay. Daniel had thought the
vehicle was bringing harbor officials to handle the administrative details of the *Princess Cecile*'s stay on Sexburga. "She must
have made good time to arrive before we did."

Vaughn shrugged. "There's quite a lot going on, Lieutenant,"
he said. "As no doubt you realize."

Adele had come out of her cabin; Tovera straightened an everted
pleat of her mistress's jacket with fingers as thin and white as if
they were merely the bones. The midshipmen waited stiffly in the
passage, their faces scrubbed and saucer hats in their hands. Vesey
was squinching forward, apparently in an attempt to minimize
the grease stain she'd somehow managed to get between her first
and second jacket buttons.

"I appreciate your invitation, Mr. Vaughn," Daniel said, changing
the subject back to one he felt comfortable with, "but I'm afraid
tonight is impossible. I'll remain aboard the *Princess Cecile* until

the liberty parties return tomorrow and Mr. Pasternak takes charge."

"I see," said Vaughn. A flash of anger suggested that at heart he didn't see any reason *ever* that his will should be thwarted, but the emotion was gone as quickly as it appeared. "Well, can we say tomorrow, then? I really feel a duty as a citizen of Strymon to thank you before a gathering of my compatriots. Quite a number of the chief residents here are natives of Strymon, you realize."

What Daniel realized was that Vaughn was making the invitation a matter of planet-to-planet protocol. Why he'd want to do that was puzzling, though a simple desire to get his own way would be a believable explanation; but Vaughn certainly had the power to make trouble for Daniel on the grounds of a political snub if the invitation was refused.

"I'd be pleased to attend you, yes, Mr. Vaughn," Daniel said. "With the proviso that I'll call on the Cinnabar Commissioner as soon as I go ashore; and whenever Commodore Pettin arrives, I'll be entirely at his disposal."

Daniel wasn't under any illusions about Vaughn's instinct to dominate, but it wasn't something that put the man outside the pale in the mind of an RCN officer. More important was the fact that the young nobleman controlled his impulses. Whatever Vaughn might have been at the core, his intellect made him a civilized man who operated within the norms he found around him; and it was intellect, after all, that divided men from beasts.

"Let's say tomorrow evening then, Lieutenant," Vaughn said with a smile, bowing as crisply as a punch notching a ticket. "The twelfth hour, as they calculate things here on Sexburga; and at the Captal da Lund's residence outside Spires. I *will* expect you."

He turned and strode to the companionway, nodding in friendly acknowledgment to the midshipmen. The interchange with Daniel had restored Vaughn's poise: he walked with none of the stiffness and doubtful balance that had hampered him when he entered the bridge.

Adele stepped to Daniel's side. In a low voice she commented, "The hormones that emotions release do wonderful things for a person's physical condition, don't they? I wonder if I've been wrong all my life in thinking people would be better off without emotion?"

Daniel looked at his friend sharply, not quite certain that she was joking. Deciding he didn't want to ask a question that might have the wrong answer, he said, "Yes, it seemed to me as well that more was going on than a party invitation. But I wonder why?"

He glanced sidelong at Adele and raised an eyebrow. She shrugged and said, "I truly don't know, Daniel. It's no affair connected with . . . me or mine, to the best of my knowledge."

In the glum pause that followed, Tovera turned her palm up. The slight movement called attention to her. Daniel started: it was like a magician's illusion. *Poof!* and Adele's servant stood where his mind hadn't registered anything a moment before.

"I wonder, mistress?" Tovera said. "Will I be going with you today?"

In place of the coveralls she'd worn during the voyage, she'd donned baggy gray slacks and a beige shirt that would have hung to her knees if it hadn't been belted at her waist. The loosely bloused fabric could conceal any number of weapons or other devices—and probably did.

"I don't believe I'll need you, no," Adele said, her words as careful as the taps of a gem-cutter. "You're welcome to come, but if you'd rather be off on your own . . . ?"

"Spires gets all sorts of people," Tovera said. She smiled; the expression belonged on a bird of prey. "Some of them may enjoy the same things I do."

She took a ring of dark hematite with a simple gold inlay from a purse hidden under the drape of her blouse, then slid it on her left little finger. "I'll see you tomorrow, then. At this hour?"

"Yes, that will be fine," Adele said. "If I need you sooner, I'll . . ."

She tapped the personal data unit that she used for communication. Tovera might have a mastoid implant for all Daniel knew, though a simple pager the size of a pea would be sufficient.

"Thank you, mistress," Tovera said as she walked away. Daniel shook his head in wonderment. It was like seeing the shadow of death thrown on the corridor bulkhead.

"And before you ask," Adele said in a bleak voice, "I don't have the faintest notion of what she means."

Daniel hadn't had the least intention of asking. He put his hand on Adele's shoulder and squeezed it, reassuring both of them that their truths remained.

Adele looked at the image Daniel had called up on the attack console. The gangplank was an internally braced structure that could unfold an entire twenty yards if necessary, though Daniel had brought the corvette much closer than that to the concrete slip. The *Princess Cecile*'s crew, bright and fluttering in their liberty dress, crossed in loose formation. The crew from the anchor watch who'd just extended the gangplank watched their singing, laughing, fellows without expression.

Daniel sighed. Well, that was why he was aboard himself. A captain had to be willing to carry out unpleasant duties occasionally, if he expected his crew to obey when he ordered them to do things they'd rather not. Which, after all, covered most of the activities aboard a warship.

"That's Thea Zane, the woman who visited Vaughn on Cinnabar!" Adele said. She sat at the console, apparently oblivious of her surroundings, and began switching between screens without bothering to explain what she was doing. The view of the dock shrank to a corner of the display.

"Yes it is," Daniel said. Dorst and Vesey remained at the hatchway, teetering with nervous anticipation. He crooked his finger to bring them to him. "And I can't imagine how she reached Sexburga ahead of us, even if she left immediately after Vaughn's party."

"She came aboard the yacht *Achilles*," Adele said with satisfaction, leaning her head aside. "Twenty-three days out of Cinnabar."

Daniel stooped to bring his head into position to read the personnel manifest the yacht had filed with the Harbormaster. Fifty-three crew—a large complement for a 300-ton vessel, but she was carrying the sails of a much larger hull—and one passenger: Mistress Thea Zane.

"I see," he said, straightening. His smile had a degree of calculation in it. "I suppose we should be glad that they didn't have Uncle Stacey's logs, or our run from Cinnabar might not have been a record after all."

He straightened and gestured to Adele. She switched the console back to a full-sized image of the dock and stood, nodding to the midshipmen to show that she was aware of them. On the display Vaughn gripped arms with Mistress Zane, then got into the closed car with her help. Obviously, he wasn't fully recovered from the voyage.

Well, neither was Daniel, though he was getting there. He forced his face into a serious expression and said, "Dorst, Vesey, I have a favor to ask of you. I realize you have plans for your liberty—"

He was fairly confident that the midshipmen had no real plans, just concern sparked by the tall tales they were bound to have heard. They'd be afraid that they wouldn't measure up to what was expected of an RCN officer.

"—but I'm going to ask you to put them on hold for our first day here." Daniel cleared his throat. "Normally I'd escort Officer Mundy myself, but I have anchor watch for the next twenty-four hours. I don't want her to stumble around Spires alone, so I'd appreciate it if you'd accompany her. I won't make this an order, but—"

"Sir, we'd be happy—" Vesey said. Her tongue caught and she glanced at Dorst. "Ah, I'd be—"

"We'd be honored to join Officer Mundy!" Dorst said with relieved enthusiasm. "We'll keep her, ah . . ."

He wanted to say "safe," but he suddenly doubted that was the right word. Wisely, Daniel thought, he let his voice trail off.

Adele seemed to be on the verge of open laughter; which, if not a first, certainly wasn't something she had great experience with. Still working to keep his face straight, Daniel said, "This meets with your approval, Officer Mundy?"

You had to know what you were looking for to see the flat bulge in the side pocket of Adele's jacket. If the midshipmen had heard the stories about what Adele could and had done with her pistol, they probably classed them with the stories about the night Barnes serviced all thirty of the girls in a brothel on LaGrange, having reached the madam just as dawn broke.

"Yes it does," she said solemnly. "I'm afraid my taste in amusement is staid by any standards, but we can at least get the flavor of the city together. In future days you'll be free to indulge yourself."

"Oh, that'll be fine, ma'am," Dorst assured her. "To tell the truth, I was sort of looking forward to . . . I've never been out of the

Cinnabar system, you know, and I'd like really to see some things besides—"

He broke off and pointedly didn't look at Vesey.

"We don't have to leave the *Sissie* to get drunk," Vesey said primly, her eyes fixed on the far bulkhead also. "Anyway, we're glad to join you, mistress."

"Then you'd best learn to call me Mundy," Adele said as she shepherded her charges toward the corridor. "I have the *Sailing Directions*—"

She tapped the pocket with her data unit.

"—and a map of Spires, so we should be all right if we stay together."

She nodded to Daniel as she followed the midshipmen down the companionway; a thin, stiff-looking woman in dress grays. He winked in reply. Yes, they'd be all right; no question about that.

The people telling about Barnes' exploit exaggerated: there'd only been fifteen women in the house, not thirty-one. And they exaggerated about Adele as well. She hadn't really killed a hundred Alliance soldiers on Kostroma with single shots to the head, snapping the rounds off every time a target offered.

But it probably wasn't as much of an exaggeration as the story about Barnes.

CHAPTER THIRTEEN

Nine funicular railways climbed from Flood Harbor to the city of Spires on beyond the cliffs. Three were for personnel, leaving at fifteen-minute intervals according to the scarred metal plate in the shelter where Adele stood with the midshipmen. The others were much larger, with cogged rails to give positive traction to heavy loads. They hauled cargo to and from the freighters berthed in slips formed from golden limestone quarried from the cliffs themselves.

"How does the harbor flood?" Dorst said, looking back at the rounded hulls of starships which showed over the slips like so many oxen in their stalls. "It looks to me that the locks keep the water level pretty constant whatever the tide's doing."

"Captain Ludifica Flood refounded the colony from Earth after the Hiatus," Adele said, restraining the urge to bring out her personal data unit and *show* the boy the reference. "The harbor's named after her."

The funicular lines carried two cars in balance, going up and down simultaneously on a single set of tracks with a double-tracked shunt in the middle where they passed. The lower set of pulleys squealed loudly as the cars above reached midpoint.

Adele eyed them without pleasure. The cables were no thicker than her thumb, which seemed modest when they had to support forty-odd passengers and the vehicle against a thousand-foot fall. Deliberately she said, "I wonder, Dorst; are these—"

She gestured.

"—going to be thick enough to hold us?"

"Oh, yes, ma'am!" Dorst said, forgetting he was supposed to treat her as a peer. "This is beryllium monocrystal felted in an elastomer— single-strand, you see, not woven, to limit the stress. You could haul the *Princess Cecile* to the top if your motor was up to it."

"The strands are continuously tested for current path, Mundy," Vesey said. "The operator, well, the system itself I suppose, knows if there's any breakage. It'd shut down long before there was danger."

They both reacted to Adele with a sort of frightened deference. It wasn't her rank: though they were classed as petty officers for the time being, Dorst and Vesey were in line for commissions which would make them the titular superiors of any warrant officer, let alone a specialist like Adele who knew virtually nothing about the running of a starship.

Her question, crafted to emphasize that ignorance, must have relaxed them somewhat, though. Vesey, her eyes on the approaching car, added, "How long have you known Captain Leary, Mundy, if you don't mind...?"

Good God, *they* thought she was Daniel's mistress.

"I met Mr. Leary on Kostroma, where I was working for the Elector," Adele said calmly, suppressing the urge to shout, "You idiots!" in anger at the obtuseness of people. "And Woetjans and most of the rest of the present crew, as a matter of fact. Our families had had dealings in our youth—"

That was an honest if incomplete way of describing the Three Circles Conspiracy and the Proscriptions that followed it.

"—but we didn't know of one another's existence until a few hours before the Alliance invasion."

She was tempted to add that they were doing Daniel a disservice in believing he was the sort of man whose penis made all his decisions. She didn't say that because it wasn't her place to; and in fairness to the midshipmen, Daniel's off-duty behavior could lead one to that conclusion.

The pulleys divided the waiting area. There was a mounting platform on either side of the tracks, though Adele could see that the descending car had a single bay. She and the midshipmen had walked to the right side because a dozen or so Sexburgan traders were already waiting on the left.

The locals, males and females both, wore loose blouses gathered at the openings, and drab-colored pantaloons with heavy sandals. One of the younger men carried two racks of candy trays, mostly emptied, on a yoke. He noticed Vesey—quite an attractive girl, now that Adele thought about it—and postured for her, arms akimbo.

Vesey deliberately turned her back on him and said, "I knew that Sexburga was a naval base, but I didn't realize there was so much civilian trade. What do they produce here?"

The question—the words couldn't be heard on the other side of the shrieking cable—was simply to remove the local man from her society. After a moment the fellow fluffed his full mustache and also turned away, though he was still puffed out like a rooster displaying.

Adele found it hard not to provide information even if it wasn't really expected. "Very little, actually," she said. "There's some small-scale manufacturing, mostly to rebuild systems for the ships that land here. Local agriculture's barely above subsistence level. But almost all the traffic into or out of the Sack touches on Sexburga so there's quite a lot of transshipment as well as resupply, even though almost everything but the reaction mass has to be imported."

The car shuddered to a halt. It was full, or nearly so, of spacers returning from liberty, and it looked to Adele as if there were as many planetary backgrounds represented as there were people.

That didn't necessarily mean they were from different ships. A dark-skinned woman whose rough-out leathers were embroidered in eye patterns helped a male shipmate who was thin, blond, and wore only a silk shift and a beret. They were both drunk, but the woman could at least walk; her companion, hopping up and down, babbled in accented Universal that his feet had been cut off.

The peddlers got on, nodding in tired acknowledgment as Adele and the midshipmen boarded the car from the other side. The locals had finished their day, going from ship to ship to serve the spacers still on duty.

Adele noticed from the way the returning panniers and satchels swung, they weren't always empty. Almost the first thing she'd learned when she began associating with spacers was that no matter how open a society might look from the outside, there was always *some*thing it considered contraband; and there were always smugglers ready to supply that contraband to whoever could afford it.

She smiled coldly. Since that seemed to be a universal trait, she supposed it was the way things were supposed to be. Adele had never been one to argue against observed reality.

Though that did leave the question of who or what had set up the system in the first place. Adele didn't believe in a supreme being; but occasionally it seemed that things couldn't possibly be so *damnably* absurd unless someone, Someone, was deliberately making them that way.

"My grandfather was on Sexburga with Admiral Perlot's squadron in '21," Dorst said, craning his neck to peer up the cableway. "He said it was a really wild port, but of course it would be with twenty thousand spacers based here before the Strymon fleet surrendered. It won't be like that now."

It was hard to tell from the midshipman's voice whether he was disappointed or relieved. Probably a little of both.

The top cable grew taut. Adele braced herself on one of the vertical poles that doubled as support for the canopy, and the car started upward with a jerk.

"I'm sure there'll be plenty of ways to get into trouble in Spires," Adele said dryly. "Whether they'll be much different from the entertainments of the Strip outside Harbor Three is another matter."

"What are the local animals like?" Vesey said; an apparent non sequitur until she added, "I saw a dog once in the New World Lounge."

Dorst gasped and turned away, coughing or laughing. Vesey's face lost all expression as she reviewed what she'd just blurted. She had a naturally dark complexion, so the blush took some moments to show on her cheeks.

"There's no proven native life above the invertebrate level," Adele said. She hid her smile, though perhaps Vesey would have felt better if she let it show. "With the flow of traffic through the port, I'm sure that the entertainment industry has as wide a range of options as the restauranteurs."

She frowned, looking back at the harbor now hundreds of feet below. The question reminded her that she wanted to find Daniel data on the natural history of all the planets in the region. That should be possible on Sexburga.

"The *Sailing Directions* mention rumors of large animals on South Land," she went on. "Sexburga has two continents, North and South, but South isn't settled and isn't often visited."

The young peddler with the candy trays leaned forward. "South Land is haunted, lady," he said with polite earnestness. "Nobody lives there, nobody goes there except foreigners."

"The Tombs of the Ancients are there," added a local woman, a substantial person holding a basket woven in slant patterns in varicolored straw. "The Ancients still live in them, but they only come out when nobody's looking."

The other peddlers nodded, all those who could hear over the sounds of the car rising. A more distant man held a whispered conversation with the woman with the basket, then nodded enthusiastic agreement.

"My grandfather heard about the ghosts," Dorst said. "I don't think he ever went there. What do the *Directions* say, mistress?"

"There are regular rock formations that look like the foundations of buildings," Adele said, speaking carefully. She was repeating what she'd read, and she didn't want to give the impression that she had an opinion beyond the words in the *Sailing Directions*. "Some people have conjectured that they're the remains of the first settlement, but judging by wind erosion they're far too old for that. The official explanation is that they're natural."

"There's nothing natural about the ghosts, lady," the man with the candy trays said fiercely. "You keep away from South Land. There's plenty of fun for rich spacers here in Spires, you bet!"

That was indeed a safe bet. This funicular rose very steeply, but the one halfway around the bowl to the left followed a notch at no more than 45 degrees. Spaced along the tracks were three taverns that had been cut into the cliff face. Bunting fluttered from their railings, and at the uppermost a naked girl danced on a barreltop to lure custom. There were mounting platforms set where the slow-moving cars would just clear them, but Adele couldn't imagine people as drunk as the spacers who'd descended in this car managing to board on the move.

"They must cater to riggers," said Dorst, who seemed to have been thinking along the same lines.

"And they're not thinking very hard about anything except the first drink," Vesey added. "If I had to spend all my duty hours out on the hull, I might feel the same way."

The car was nearing the upper terminus; brakes within the take-up drum began to groan as they slowed the rig. Down in the harbor a bell chimed faintly, calling watch changes within a ship which had been opened to the world around it.

"M-Mundy?" Dorst said. "They say . . . that is, I've heard that Captain Leary can read the Matrix. Is that true?"

"What?" Adele said. Why were they asking her about ship-handling? That was *their* business! "Well, yes, I suppose so. I believe I've heard him say as much."

"But *how*, mistress?" Vesey said. Her face was screwed up with the tension of someone who knows there's a secret key to the universe and that someone else has it. "I can memorize the sail plan, but then Captain Leary goes topside and takes a reef here, changes an angle there. And I don't see any reason for it, but when we next check our position we've gained six hours!"

"I calculated the time from Cinnabar to Sexburga," Dorst said. "Without allowing anything for position checks and using the course plotted by Commander Bergen, the best time mathematically *possible* was twenty-one days, ten hours and fifty-one minutes. But Commander Bergen himself made the distance in twelve hours less than that, and Captain Leary cut cut off three and a half more days."

The car shuddered to what Adele thought was a halt. She would have stepped—up a handsbreadth—to the platform, but she noticed that the peddlers were waiting. She waited also; thus the final jolt upward didn't throw her onto her face.

"I'm really not sure what Daniel does," Adele said. "When I look at the Matrix when I'm on the hull, I just see swirls of light. But then, I can't tell much from clouds—"

She stepped onto the platform, then gestured at the pale blue sky streaked by horsetails of vapor.

"—either. Unless they're raining on me. Don't they teach you whatever it is you need to know at the Academy?"

"Mistress," Vesey said, "the patterns of the Matrix show energy levels between universes. Go here, go there, and your velocity relative to the sidereal universe increases or decreases. We understand the theory—that's what astrogation *is*, after all. But you can't take a computer out on the hull, and I don't see how anybody can read the Matrix with his eyes alone."

The upper platform was crowded with hawkers, touts, and pimps. The peddlers passed through them as water does a screen, but they were around Adele and her companions like goldfish feeding. The voices babbled in Universal—

"*Never food like it in your lives!*"

"*Sheets clean this morning, on my soul as a woman!*"

"*The delicacy of the carving by Blind Master Shen!*"

—but it was spoken in a singsong that had nothing to do with the normal accent and ictus of the lines. After a moment it was perfectly understandable, like a document printed in an unfamiliar typeface. The pack wasn't saying anything Adele *wanted* to understand, of course.

Dorst's broad shoulders led the trio through without real difficulty. Adele, last in line, saw an old fellow with a waxed mustache try to grope Vesey. She slapped him away with a practiced reflex. Nobody offered Adele indignities.

A wide roadway paralleled the line of the cliffs. Traffic was heavy, but it was almost entirely of pedestrians or slow-moving vehicles with four large wheels. They were geared for the steep slopes on all the city's other streets.

Adele nodded and the three of them started across. On the other side were five- and six-story buildings. The windows of the lower floors advertised business premises, but the railed balconies higher up had flower boxes and lounging spectators.

"Any of the riggers can tell me things that I can't see," Dorst said glumly as the trio waited in mid-street for an electric-powered dray to crawl past on tracks instead of wheels. "They all think Captain Leary's a wizard, though. Except for Old Hagar who served with Commander Bergen; she says the captain's a babe in arms compared to his uncle."

"Daniel says the same," Adele agreed, "though I gather there's more to promotion in the RCN than skill at astrogation. Daniel may have things to teach you that his uncle couldn't."

"Oh, heavens yes!" Vesey said. "Oh, we're so lucky to serve under him!"

Dorst leaned forward to see past the dray. "Now!" he shouted.

They sprinted to the overlook. Traffic direction wasn't controlled by which side of the street it was on, but the midshipmen seemed to have the spacers' ability to look all ways at once. Adele didn't and by now had determined that she never would, but by staying between her companions she managed to make it across with no worse problem than tripping on a crack between paving blocks. Vesey caught her.

The view was breathtaking. Though not nearly as steep as the cliffs they'd just climbed, the ground to the east sloped down for as far as Adele could see. Beyond the buildings of Spires stretched fields separated by drystone walls. The crops were planted so thinly that the predominant color was that of the russet soil, not green leaves.

"It's impressive," Adele said, "but with so many worlds available I don't know why this place was colonized. And recolonized after the Hiatus."

"Why, for its location," Vesey said in surprise. "Twenty days from Earth, forty days from Cinnabar even before Commander Bergen's survey."

"Even from Pleasaunce it's only sixty days," Dorst added. "And I'm sure you could cut that by a third with a proper survey, which *isn't* going to happen while the RCN controls the region."

"And there's plenty of water for reaction mass," Vesey said. "It's really an ideal location."

Adele nodded slowly as she viewed her surroundings. Plenty of reaction mass, even if it didn't fall as rain. She was a spacer now, so she had to remind herself to think like one.

"The pirates track ships by the disturbance they leave across the Matrix," Dorst said, reverting to the earlier subject. "They follow ships there, then drop into normal space with them and strip their sails with plasma cannon. Strymon's patrol ships do the same thing to take pirates."

Scattered across the landscape were buttes standing a hundred feet above the plain around them. One was topped by a man-made wall; a dusty road led to it from the city proper.

"Daniel's talked about that," Adele said, bringing her data unit out and—after a moment of trepidation—setting it on the stone railing instead of sitting crosslegged on the pavement to use it.

The rail was flat and six inches wide, so there was no real danger that she'd bump the unit down the other side. "Woetjans and some of the other riggers say it's quite true, that you can see wakes."

She scrolled across a street plan of Spires till she found what she was looking for, then compared it with her own location according to the data unit's inertial navigation system. Sexburga didn't have positioning satellites, just a handful of ground beacons for the rare traveller who went any distance from Spires.

"There's a pre-Hiatus church that's been converted to a museum and library," she said, nodding toward her display. She couldn't point because she held a wand in either hand. "I'd like to see that. But first, shall we try a local meal? The tomato-stuffed potatoes are supposed to be the local specialty."

"Granddad said the potato lager's something, too," Dorst said with enthusiasm.

"We'll try that as well," Adele said. She put her data unit away and started toward the nearest of the streets leading down into the city proper.

"Mundy, do you think we'll ever learn how to see wakes?" Vesey asked in a tiny voice.

"If it's something about starships that can be taught," Adele said in a tone of confidence that surprised her, "Captain Leary is the best person I know to teach you. And Dorst?"

"Ma'am?"

"He's equally skilled at picking up company when he's off-duty," Adele went on in the same crisp voice. "But if you study his technique, I do hope you'll use it on women of better quality than he does."

Dorst and Vesey both hesitated a half step, then burst out laughing. Adele allowed herself a smile as well.

She found the presence of the midshipmen oddly pleasant, rather like having a pair of intelligent dogs along to share her interests without imposing their own. This layover on Sexburga promised to be quite relaxing.

"Well, this *is* a bloody fort, ain't it?" Hogg said as he hauled hard on the steering wheel to bring them around the final switchback. Hogg had rented the car to bring them to Vaughn's party, but Daniel was half wishing he'd simply paid for a cabman to drive instead. "That or a bloody prison!"

The vehicle couldn't manage more than twenty miles an hour with the throttle flat against the firewall, but steering required a lot less effort than Hogg put into it since the wheel adjusted power to the hub-center electric motors, speeding or slowing them as the turn required.

That offended Hogg. He needed to hear chirps and moans from a vehicle to be sure it was really under his control.

"It's a fortress," Daniel said, looking into the compound past the attendant at the open gate. The walls were seven feet thick. "That's the cap of a vertical-launch missile system in the middle of the courtyard. They're ready to fight off an attack by starships."

Hogg stopped smoothly beside the attendant despite his effort to get the regenerative brakes to jerk them to a halt. "Bloody foreign crap!" he muttered. The comment seemed intended to inform the car that no matter how well it had been designed, it was still crap because it hadn't been made on Cinnabar.

The attendant wore boots to mid calf, checked trousers, and a red frock coat with a gold dicky. He wasn't dressed like a Sexburgan or like anybody else Daniel remembered seeing, though some clowns came close. Mind, the Dress Whites Daniel was wearing weren't the most practical garments either.

"State your business with the Captal da Lund so that I can admit you," the fellow said. "Please."

Daniel frowned. There was no question of his having gotten the address wrong: this walled compound on a hill ten miles east of Spires was the only possible structure that matched Vaughn's directions. Besides, from the dozen vehicles—two of them aircars—already in the courtyard, there was a party going on.

"He's Lieutenant Daniel Leary, commanding the *Princess Cecile!*" Hogg said, sounding more disgusted than angry. "Delos Vaughn invited him, if you know who that is."

"You're expected, Lieutenant," the attendant said, waving to the guard watching from the tower above the gate. The tower windows were beveled sharply so that the automatic impeller mounted there could fire down onto the access road. "Nothing personal. You see, the Captal's got to be careful."

He waved to the courtyard. "Park where you please. Ferde will take you to the third floor where the party is."

Another attendant waved from the door of the narrow three-story building directly across the courtyard. He was dressed like the gate man, but his coat was azure blue instead of scarlet. Apparently it was a national style rather than livery.

Hogg engaged the motors. Over their whine he muttered, "They look like bloody clowns!"

"We're guests in their master's house, Hogg," Daniel said. He cleared his throat. "And after all, their liquor should be perfectly good even if it comes in a funny-shaped bottle."

Weeks in the Matrix had roughened Hogg's personality beyond its normal degree of abrasiveness. Daniel understood his servant's xenophobia, but it couldn't be allowed to get out of hand.

Daniel didn't share Hogg's attitude. So far as he was concerned, foreigners were perfectly all right. Some of them were almost the equal of Cinnabar citizens.

The building's top story was completely glazed; from there figures with drinks in their hands looked down. Most of them wore flashy Strymon costumes, though one was in garb cut like that of the attendants. His coat was black over a white cummerbund rather than of bright colors.

"Yeah, I'll be better for a drink," Hogg muttered as he pulled in at the end of a row of similar though more ornate vehicles. "And I guess you'll be doing some drinking too, young master, because none of the women upstairs looked worth even *my* time."

Before Daniel had managed the car door—it hinged at the back edge, not the front as he was used to—Delos Vaughn himself brushed past the attendant and called, "Lieutenant! Very pleased to see you. Come up and meet my friends and our host."

Besides the residence, the compound held a power room—the blow-off roof on a squat, thick-walled structure pointed to a fusion bottle inside—and a utility building holding shops, a kitchen, and a laundry. The long, one-story building along the back wall was a barracks if Daniel had ever seen one. Fortress indeed!

Daniel let Vaughn take his arm because the other choice was to slap the fellow's hand away. No point in coming at all if he was going to do that.

"I'd thought you were the host, actually, Vaughn," he said as they entered the building. The walls were decorated with a mural of lush meadows, an incongruous contrast to Sexburga's sere landscape. An open elevator waited across the tiled foyer.

"Well, I don't have a suitable place of my own on Sexburga," Vaughn said with a chuckle. The elevator door closed behind them without any command that Daniel noticed. "The Captal is an old friend of my father, you see. He was Lord Protector of the Berengian Stars until he decided to retire a few years ago. Mistress Zane contacted him, and he was glad to lend his premises."

The Berengians were five—or occasionally seven—stars in loose confederation. The little Daniel knew of their political history reminded him of watching piglets squirming against a sow with two more offspring than teats.

The elevator started with a gentle hum. There weren't any controls inside the circular cage. The curved mirror of the walls gave Daniel a view of himself looking uncomfortable in the white-and-gold of his 1st Class uniform.

"Retired?" Daniel said. "Not that I want to pry, but . . ."

Of course he wanted to pry. This place was defended like an outpost on the edge of Alliance territory.

"Well, yes, the Captal had some help deciding," Vaughn said. "But his support on his home world, Lusoes, was still strong. The new government voted him a hefty pension on condition that he . . . stay retired. It was the most cost-effective alternative."

Daniel nodded. The pension was cost effective if it wasn't practical to assassinate the pensioner. That explained the compound's defenses.

The elevator door rotated open, a section of the gleaming metal vanishing into itself like an oil film. The guests already within the large room stared at Daniel appraisingly; the servants paused.

"Ladies and gentlemen," said Vaughn, "our guest of honor, Lieutenant Daniel Leary who brought me here from Cinnabar!"

There was a dusting of applause. Those who held drinks tapped the fingertips of their free hand on the wrist of the other.

Servants began to circulate again with trays of drinks and finger food. It was obvious that Daniel had been given an arrival time—which he'd met within thirty seconds—later than that of the other guests.

He stepped out of the cage, his face stiff in his determination not to give anything away. He didn't have enough information to know what was going on, but he was in no doubt that *something* was happening beyond Vaughn proving he could crack the whip over Daniel on land as surely as Daniel had done to him on Cinnabar. He'd learned *that* much about politics by being Speaker Leary's son.

"Though the lieutenant wears the uniform of the Cinnabar navy," Vaughn continued as though he were reading Daniel's mind, "he is of course the only son of Speaker Corder Leary."

"There's no 'though' about my uniform, Mr. Vaughn," Daniel said, controlling his irritation as well as he could. "I'm a serving officer in the RCN and much more proud of that fact than I am in being a Leary."

He heard what he'd said and frowned. At any rate, he hoped that was true. Pride was a funny thing, especially when you were in the middle of a lot of foreigners.

"This is our host, the Captal da Lund," Vaughn said, gesturing Daniel toward the tall man in the black coat. He was in his sixties, with short hair, gray eyes, and a face whose fleshy lips were the only hint of softness. "An old friend of my family."

The Captal and Daniel gripped elbows, forearm to forearm. Daniel was surprised to note that so ascetic-looking a man wore perfume.

"Mistress Zane you already know," Vaughn went on, nodding to the woman Daniel had met on Cinnabar. "This is Mr. Angele, who's in transit trade out of Cove Harbor. He was one of my godfathers...."

Vaughn went around the gathering, introducing Daniel to one Strymon national after another. Some, like Angele—a heavy-bodied, hard-eyed fellow who spoke mainly in grunts—were expatriates with businesses on Sexburga, but Zane and most of the others present were normally resident on Strymon itself.

This was obviously a gathering of conspirators. The Captal was involved either through family friendship as Vaughn claimed, or simply the desire of a born intriguer to keep his hand in, even if that meant meddling in others' affairs for lack of his own.

The question remaining as Daniel embraced his way around the room was why *he* was present.

The last guest was equally anomalous, a man of thirty-odd

in clothes of closely tailored Cinnabar cut. "And finally, Mr. Gerson," Vaughn said, "who's on the staff of the Cinnabar commissioner here, Admiral Torgis. Were you able to see the admiral, Lieutenant?"

"He was occupied when I called," Daniel said, clasping Gerson and stepping thankfully away. "He was kind enough to send a courier to the *Princess Cecile* before I left for this party, inviting the officers to a gathering at his residence tomorrow, however."

Gerson looked healthy enough, but his muscles felt doughy and his breathing was fast and shallow. Was Gerson a Cinnabar spy? Supposedly the Office of External Relations always had someone on a resident's staff, and a strategic port like Sexburga might attract other organizations as well.

That line of consideration brought Daniel's mind uncomfortably back to Adele. He wished again she was here; or, even better, that he himself wasn't.

"I'm not surprised, Leary," Gerson said. "You're quite the celebrity since the Kostroma business. Certified heroes rarely appear on Sexburga during peacetime."

And just how peaceful is this gathering? Daniel thought, though all he said aloud was, "I was particularly pleased that the admiral is giving a separate party for the crew, using a depot ship docked in the slip beside ours so that even the anchor watch can get a taste of it."

"Oh, Admiral Torgis is an old space rover, all right," Gerson said. "You two should get along swimmingly, Leary."

If Gerson was trying to hide his bitterness, he was doing a very poor job. Was the man drunk?

"I certainly hope I will," Daniel said, turning slightly as he spoke as though he was being drawn by the view out the windows. The Strymonian guests had formed a group beside a statue that looked like tall hands reaching up from the floor. They spoke in low voices, their eyes on Daniel instead of on one another.

Gerson affected Daniel like a bad smell: bearable if necessary, but something to be avoided whenever possible. Daniel said, "I wonder if I could find a—yes, thank you!" to the servant who came by with a tray of drinks. He snatched one that turned out to be pink and frothy; sweet as well, but when it hit the back of his throat he had to admit it was sufficiently potent.

Delos Vaughn had noticed the awkwardness. His brow furrowed, then cleared in an ingenuous smile as he said, "Captal, the lieutenant here is a naturalist of note. Why don't you tell him of your explorations on South Land?"

"Why yes, I'd heard that mentioned, Mr. Leary," the Captal said as he turned toward Daniel. "A man could make himself famous by exploring the ruins of South Land properly. They are beyond question the remains of a prehuman civilization!"

He picked up a slender, arm's-length rod from a display of knickknacks and sliced it absently in a figure eight. It took Daniel a moment to realize that other items on the table included thumbscrews and manacles with spiked protrusions on the inside.

"Really, sir?" Daniel said. "I hadn't heard about that. Have they been studied?"

The Captal tapped the table with his rod. Daniel had taken it for translucent plastic at first; now he realized it was the penis bone of a carnivorous mammal or mammaloid that must weigh tons. Or be hung like a horse, of course.

"Not at all, sir!" the Captal said. "This is a crime, and I believe you are the man to right it. Would you care to see for yourself? I'll provide you with an aircar and a guide."

Daniel sipped, careful not to drain the bit of his drink remaining. He held his liquor as befitted an officer of the RCN, but this pink fluff was deceptively strong. He didn't know how long the party was going to go on, and he was *quite* sure that he didn't want to blurt something in an uncontrolled moment.

Blurt *what*, he had no idea. All he knew for certain was that these people had an agenda of their own, and that Lt. Daniel Leary was a pawn they were maneuvering for purposes that weren't his own.

"I appreciate the offer, sir," Daniel said, "but I don't believe that'll be possible. I need to stay in Spires until the arrival of the squadron to which the *Princess Cecile* has been attached. After that time my whereabouts will be at the disposition of the squadron commander, Commodore Pettin. I very much doubt he'll wish me to go—"

He almost said, "haring off," but caught himself in time.

"—exploring on Sexburga, however much I might like to do so."

The Captal's face became a mask of cold fury. He lashed the table with the penis bone, a *snap!* like nearby lightning.

"I wholly agree with you that there should be proper examination, sir," Daniel continued. "I'm sure you'll be able to carry it out yourself more ably than a transient RCN officer could do."

If the exiled ruler cut at *him* with the penis bone, Daniel was going to take it away and worry about the consequences later. Cinnabar nobles had never lacked for arrogance, but theirs was the pride of oligarchs who knew that even the greatest of them was merely first among equals. Autocrats, even fallen autocrats like the Captal, were a wholly different breed.

The Captal dropped the rod disdainfully. "A real leader knows how to delegate, Lieutenant," he said. "Point to the task and reward the laborers suitably when they've executed his will. No doubt your father understands this principle, though you do not."

"Very possibly he does, sir," Daniel said, trying to keep a straight face. Imagine this Berengian *rube* implying similarity between himself and Speaker Leary! "To be honest, I'm rather surprised that a planet that's been continuously settled from before the Hiatus has any major unexplored regions."

"It wouldn't surprise you if you'd spent any length of time on Sexburga, Lieutenant," said Mistress Keeton, a Strymonian who'd been introduced as "a factor with interests in Spires and elsewhere." Her clothes were of Sexburgan cut but colored in vivid vertical stripes like nothing Daniel had seen on local citizens. "They're a very conservative people here, the families who trace their lineage back to the original settlement even more so than those from Captain Flood's refoundation. South Land has a bad reputation, so why go there?"

"It's not as though there's population pressure, after all," a Mr. Cherry said. The gathering under the bronze hands had broken up, and the conspirators were drifting closer to Daniel. "There's an astrogation beacon on the north cape of the continent. And foreigners visit it occasionally. I've been there myself."

He grinned at Daniel, then to the Captal. "None of my party saw ghosts, and I've never heard of anyone who has. But I had to hire spacers to do for us on the trip, because none of the locals would go to South Land."

A servant took Daniel's glass and substituted a full one. He'd noticed many times in the past that the drinks he held seemed to vanish as if by osmosis through the sides of his glass. Still, a few drinks, however strong, weren't going to be a problem.

"I'm not an archaeologist, I'm afraid," Daniel said with a lift of his hand. "I'm sure that, with the traffic coming through Sexburga, there'll be a suitable person for the task if you keep your eyes open."

The Captal da Lund stood with his back to the window, his hands on his hips. Behind him russet fields stretched away to the horizon. He looked as though he ought to have been on a dais.

"There are no men of vision any more," the Captal announced in a sepulchral voice. "Mankind has devolved to a race of pigmies who cannot see and fear to act."

"Oh, I don't know that I'd agree with you there, Captal," Delos Vaughn said with an easy smile. "I think it's still possible to find men of vision. Wouldn't you say so, Lieutenant?"

"Yes, I would," Daniel said, a little more forcefully than he might have done if he hadn't first slugged down his fresh drink.

Vaughn meant himself, of course, and he was probably correct in his self-assessment. But Lt. Daniel Leary could see and could act also . . . and *his* vision didn't include a Leary of Bantry digging around on South Land at the whim of an exiled wog.

Daniel took a full glass from the servant headed toward him and raised it. "A toast!" he said. "To the Republic of Cinnabar and all her loyal allies!"

Everybody drank, but an appraising glint came into the eyes of Delos Vaughn. It remained there until the gathering broke up at the end of the hour.

CHAPTER FOURTEEN

"Good afternoon, mistress," said the man behind Adele in the buffet line. "Or 'officer,' I suppose I should say. You're one of young Leary's crew, I take it?"

"*He's named Cherry,*" said Tovera, speaking through the bead placed deep in Adele's right ear canal. It dulled her normal hearing on that side of her head, but it was the only alternative to a surgical implant in her mastoid bone if she wanted commentary from her servant. "*He was at the gathering for Captain Leary yesterday.*"

"I'm Signals Officer Mundy of the *Princess Cecile*, yes," Adele said. She smiled, though she'd learned that didn't help put others at their ease with her. Some called her smile wintry, while others were less charitable. "And you're a Sexburgan, sir?"

"Ardis Cherry," the fellow said with a deprecating laugh. "And not a Sexburgan, no, just an expatriate like yourself. My business is here on Sexburga, but I'm a citizen of Strymon. Quite a little party here, wouldn't you say?"

Adele reached the head of the table. She took a plate and began plumping food onto it. Although normally abstemious, she'd been extremely poor for fifteen years. The habit of eating everything she could get at formal gatherings of this sort, common in Academe, was so deeply ingrained in her that it could be described as a conditioned response.

"I'm certainly impressed," Adele said truthfully. The next dish looked like candied beetles. She took one; poverty was even better than travel for making one open to new experiences. "There must be three hundred people here." According to Tovera, there were three hundred and forty-seven guests in addition to fifty-odd staff members and the guests' two hundred servants. "Most of Sexburgan society, I would guess."

"Sexburgan and expatriate," Cherry agreed. He seemed somewhat surprised at the food piling up on Adele's plate, then looked quickly away to avoid commenting on it. "Our two communities don't interact a great deal, except for Residency functions like this. We expats have no share in the local government, but our off-planet connections are frequently advantageous in matters of business and the attendant profit. There's rivalry but not hostility, thanks to the Resident Commissioners."

The Residency and its several outbuildings stood on the cliff south of Flood Harbor. If you looked past the buffet tables through the fourth-floor windows—small with thick glazing against the frequent winter storms—you could watch the ocean tossing sullenly all the way to the horizon. The complex was much older than Sexburga's agreement to become an Ally and Protectorate of the Republic early in the past century.

The stack on Adele's plate had risen beyond the practical possibility of adding to it. With a longing glance at a tray of unfamiliar sliced meats, she stepped back—then paused to snatch a roll.

Tovera was outside in the van which had brought Adele to the party, watching a bank of images transmitted by tiny cameras secreted in every room of the Residence. Their fish-eye lenses distorted the views to the point Adele would have found them useless, but Tovera seemed to have no difficulty.

Adele didn't see any reason for such paranoia; but then, she wouldn't have suggested her servant bring a submachine gun to Delos Vaughn's party on Cinnabar. She could certainly appreciate Tovera's fastidious attention to the details of her profession.

Large though the Residency was, the present number of guests comfortably filled it. Most were well-fed and all but the Cinnabar nationals from the RCN and the Commissioner's staff wore bright costumes, though they differed widely in style. Perhaps half the number were Sexburgans; the others came from at least a dozen other worlds within the Republic's sphere of influence.

Lt. Mon got up with three locals who'd been crushed against him at a tiny table, apparently a father, mother, and their strikingly attractive daughter. Mon tossed off another tumbler of tawny liquor. He looked stunned by the attention. Adele was virtually certain that he'd never imagined he'd ever be part of a gathering like this. The daughter took his arm as the parents beamed.

Cherry and Adele moved to the just-vacated table as Mon and his new friends walked toward the stairs to the roof garden. "How often does the Resident have parties of this sort?" Adele asked as they waited for a servant to clear the table of litter.

"Admiral Torgis gave a similar do on Republic Day both years that he's been here as Resident," Cherry said, settling down opposite her. He was in his forties and well-fed, if not exactly fat. "This is obviously because of Mr. Leary's presence."

"Because of Kostroma, you mean?" Adele said. She started with the candied bug since it seemed to watch her sadly from its perch at the edge of her dish. "Because surely a great deal of RCN traffic passes through Sexburga in the course of a year? Vessels more prepossessing than a corvette, that is."

Cherry tapped the side of his nose. "Oh, the admiral's given out that it's because of the business on Kostroma," he said, "and I suppose most of the guests believe that. But some of us know the *real* reason Speaker Leary's son has been sent on this mission. I understand you're an intimate of Mr. Leary yourself?"

Adele swallowed, hoping that her shocked expression would be put down to the mouthful she'd just consumed. The bug had been pickled before being coated with honey; the combination of flavors would take a great deal of getting used to.

"In a manner of speaking," she said. "We're on duty for the full period of the cruise, of course."

Adele had bitten back a retort along the lines of, "And what do you mean by 'intimate,' sir?" when she recalled that she had duties to Mistress Sand. If this fat civilian was ready to blurt secrets to Mr. Leary's light-o'-love, then it wasn't the business of Mistress Sand's agent to disabuse him.

"Yes, yes, of course," Cherry agreed through a nibble of bread. "The deception has worked excellently, you'll be pleased to know. Why, the common folk here are falling over all of you on the say-so of Admiral Torgis. And you'll notice that the admiral pretends he doesn't even know that the President-to-be has arrived on Sexburga."

"*Delos Vaughn isn't here,*" Tovera agreed. "*Nor is Mistress Zane. All the other persons who met Captain Leary at the Captal da Lund's dwelling are here.*"

"Yes," Adele said mildly as she speared a sausage from her plate. Another result of her earlier privations was that she tended to the foods of the highest calory and protein content; starches and greens were relatively cheap. "Quite a clever ploy for a man who appears to be a bluff old spacer, isn't it?"

"Between us . . ." Cherry said. *Surely no one could be so great a fool as to believe that anything shared among conspirators as amateurish as Cherry and his friends wouldn't also be common knowledge with anyone else who cared?* "I think the idea came from young Gerson. He's the one who's been appointed as our liaison with the Republic."

"I see," said Adele. "I'd noticed that Mr. Gerson spends rather more money than his position on the admiral's staff would run to. That explains it."

Which it did. Adele had examined Admiral Torgis's record, both the public version and the one Mistress Sand had provided. The admiral was exactly what he seemed, a well-born, reasonably competent RCN officer who'd been put in place on Sexburga because of its value as a fleet base if trouble broke out again in the Sack.

Giving a gala reception for a naval hero was perfectly in character for him. Involvement in subtle diplomatic and intelligence activity was as unlikely as Torgis defecting to the Alliance.

And to corrupt a man like Gerson, who borrowed large sums of money and spent it in the form of cash, would be no more difficult than persuading a bitch in heat to couple. Adele didn't know what Gerson's unpleasant vice was, but it was obvious that he had one.

On the third floor guests danced to the accompaniment of a percussion band which played castanets, tambourines, and a glockenspiel. The effect was melodious and, though penetrating, didn't overwhelm speech even on the outskirts of the dancers. When the stairwell door opened, however, chiming music poured out over the refreshment room. It drew the attention of all the diners.

Admiral Torgis, imposing in Dress Whites instead of civilian attire, strode out of the stairwell looking even more red-faced than he had when Adele met him in the reception line. Behind him, his right hand gripping her left and pulling her along, was a woman who could pass for his twin sister but was in fact his wife. Lady Torgis wore a white dress with gold braid in the form of panels and hussar knots: not a uniform, but close enough to one to make her Tweedledee to the admiral's Tweedledum.

"Damned elevators in this place take forever!" Torgis boomed. "Who needs them, eh, Lieutenant? A companionway was always good enough for me during forty years of service!"

Daniel Leary emerged from the stairwell at a polite distance behind Lady Torgis. Instead of dragging his companion, a striking redheaded woman, the way Torgis did his wife, Daniel supported her in the crook of his right arm. Adele would've said that the redhead looked healthy enough to climb stairs by herself, but no doubt Daniel knew his business. Climbing stairs probably wasn't the—person's—preferred form of exercise.

Daniel caught Adele's eye and waved his free hand to her. She smiled back, causing Cherry's face to brighten with speculation, then go studiously blank.

Behind Daniel and his tramp came a stream of other guests, panting and distressed. The line was long enough to keep the door to the third floor open; thus the dance music flooding out to announce Admiral Torgis's arrival.

"*Holodi of Zampt and her husband, they're factors for Zampt and the Learoyd Cluster,*" Tovera said as the first couple came into view. Her running commentary continued, identifying those following Torgis as among the leading residents of Sexburga.

They were divided equally between natives and expatriates, just as Cherry had suggested. When the Resident Commissioner had decided not to wait for the elevator, all his chief guests had to follow suit.

Adele felt a faint smile play at the corners of her mouth. There were extensive floral arrangements on the buffet tables. If Admiral Torgis picked an iris and began chewing on its stem, his guests would strip the displays of iris... though Adele believed they were poisonous. She withstood the urge to pull out her personal data unit and get a certain answer to the question.

"Let's get some more tables here for me and the lieutenant!" Admiral Torgis said. Harassed servants held a quick conclave, then shunted food from one of the serving tables to the others and brought the emptied one out to join the smaller eating tables.

"Adele," Daniel said, stepping over to her while the admiral's orders were being obeyed, "allow me to present Mistress Kira . . ."

He looked suddenly stricken.

"*Lully*," Tovera said in Adele's ear as the two of them rose.

"I believe you're Mistress Lully," Adele repeated in straight-faced amusement, touching fingertips with the redhead. She'd already noticed that women didn't clasp one another on Sexburga—any more than they did on the Alliance worlds. "Very glad to meet you. I'm Signals Officer Mundy of the *Princess Cecile*."

"Leary, bring your Mundy over to join us," Torgis boomed. "Who's that, Cherry? You come over here too, Cherry, if you like. Anyone good enough for the company of an RCN officer is good enough to eat with me!"

Servants were rustling chairs from around the room. One of them had started to snatch Adele's when she stood up, then froze in horror as he realized the junior officer had become one of the admiral's pets. Working for a master whose whims were as strong and (from a diplomatic perspective) unconventional as those of Admiral Torgis must be a nervous business at best.

"You had luck, Leary," the admiral said in a voice that could probably be heard on the floor below over the orchestra. "You know it and I know it. But all the luck in the world wouldn't have saved Kostroma if you hadn't been a man and a damned fine officer. By God, I'm glad the RCN still makes men the way she did when I was a cadet!"

"Hear, hear!" cried the members of his entourage, locals and expatriates evidently trying to outclap one another. They'd have been cheering just as loudly if the Resident Commissioner had called for infanticide and immediate submission to the Alliance of Free Stars. In Sexburga's social hierarchy, the Cinnabar representative was the sun and everyone else seemed desperate to become the planet in the nearest orbit.

Daniel leaned close to Adele's ear and whispered, "I know, it's all nonsense . . . but I'd be a liar if I didn't admit it feels good."

Adele patted him lightly below his gold-encrusted right epaulette.

That raised eyebrows from not only Cherry but Mistress Lully as well.

"Quite all right, my dear," Adele said to the local woman in an accent redolent of the highest strata of Xenos society . . . to which she had, after all, belonged. "Our association is purely professional."

Good God, I *am* jealous! Adele realized in shock. Not of Daniel's body, of course; but the outrage on this red-haired trollop's face at a hint of intimacy between her and Daniel had lit an unexpected fuse in Adele's mind as well.

"Actually, Daniel," Adele said, uncertain whether or not he could hear over the bustle, "it's not nonsense. The admiral is quite correct about what happened on Kostroma."

The buffet was for ordinary guests; Admiral Torgis and those about him would have a sit-down dinner. The servants were now handing the expanded entourage into chairs, trying to judge status and fearful of their master's anger if they mistook his preferences.

Daniel went into the chair at Lady Torgis's right hand. After a moment's hesitation, the stick-thin, gray-haired female major-domo put Adele herself on the admiral's right and Mr. Cherry, of course, beside her. The Strymonian businessman looked as amazed as Mon had at the preference.

There were service stairs or at least a dumbwaiter, because three servants hustled in through the side door bearing place settings. The china was blue-and-gold with the RCN insignia, but instead of metal the flatware was made of plastic or—

"Scaleware from the Cassiterides, Admiral?" Daniel said in unfeigned enthusiasm. "I don't believe I've ever seen a set so fine."

Adele had her personal data unit half out of its pocket before she caught herself. *Cosmographical directory, initial sort* CASSITERIDES, *sub-sort* SCALEWARE . . .

Not her job, not necessary, and *very* much not the right time to call attention to herself. Daniel was bonding with the former admiral. In a thoroughly innocent fashion, of course; simply by being his own engaging self.

"You're not likely to see a better set ever, Leary," the admiral said. "I haven't and I've got a few years on you. A few decades, by God! But I wasn't more than your age when a grateful prince from Cassis gave them to me for saving his son and heir from the Alliance privateer who'd captured his ship. In the knickers of time, if you catch my drift. The privateersman was as queer as old Jaunty Teillor who commanded the Home Squadron when I was a boy."

Torgis, his wife, and Daniel all bellowed with laughter. Mistress Lully looked puzzled, and the member of the admiral's staff hovering in the background winced with psychic pain.

A servant set Adele's place; she picked up the outermost spoon and examined it more closely. The material weighed amazingly little. She'd thought the color was gray, but in fact there was a lambent fire—gold to green to a black that was total absence of hue—at the core of the piece. It was so clear that she could read the whorls of her finger pads through it.

"Cassis III is a sea world, Adele," Daniel said, leaning toward her over the table as the fingers of his right hand caressed Ms. Lully's bare shoulders. "The top of the food chain is the saberfish that grows to forty feet long. During the Hiatus only princely houses were permitted to have flatware made from saberfish scales, and even now very few sets of the real thing ever leave the planet."

"Right, right," Torgis said, bobbing his head with the animation of a man who believes he's met his soul mate. "They fob off muck made from the gill-rakers of filter-feeding worms on foreigners! This is the real thing. You can tell by the axial pinctatus, see?"

He held a fork up to the light, apparently trying to display the internal color that Adele had already noticed. Other guests peered at their host's waving utensil instead of looking at their own.

The expressions of Daniel and Admiral Torgis suddenly shifted. The humor was gone, replaced by an eager intentness. Around them the party continued to swirl.

Daniel's hand lay on Ms. Lully's back, but he had become still. A servant offered Torgis an urn of consomme she'd plucked from the serving table; another servant held the ladle ready to fill his bowl. The admiral ignored them.

Adele felt the rumble, though she wouldn't have noticed it for another minute or more had not the spacers' attitude shown her there was something *to* notice. Almost simultaneously the voice of Woetjans, the duty officer tonight, said through a roar of static in Adele's ear, "*Bridge to Signals. The* Winckelmann's *on her way down with two destroyers waiting in orbit to follow. Warn the captain that Pettin's arrived, mistress. Bridge out.*"

"The thrusters are set to pulse in triple sequence," Admiral Torgis said, "and they're just as far out of phase as they always were on the *Maspero* when I was her third lieutenant. That was the sort of idea that only a naval constructor who'd never tuned a thruster himself would've come up with."

"She's Archaeologist class, all right," said Daniel, rising to his feet. The poor servant barely avoided sloshing herself with an urn of soup. "That means Commodore Pettin's here in the *Winckelmann*, and *that* means, Admiral, that my officers and I need to return to the *Princess Cecile* at once."

"Of course you do, Lieutenant," Admiral Torgis said, also rising. "The service of the Republic is a hard life, I'll tell the world—but by God, I wish I had a real command myself instead of being a damned chair-bound politician like they've made me!"

"But Danny...?" Ms. Lully said with a stricken pout. "You were going to come out in the desert with me tonight to watch the moons rise."

Daniel bent down and kissed her forehead, right at the part from which the red hair flared to either side like a boat's bow wave. "Sorry, child, and you can't imagine how sorry I am, but I need to get back to my ship ASAP or sooner yet."

"We can get there fastest if I fly you," the woman said. "Remember, I have my aircar here."

Just possibly she wasn't the bubble-brain Adele had assumed. At any rate, Lully had grasped the salient point of the situation and responded to it with impeccable logic.

"Yes!" Daniel said. "How many seats does it have, dear one?"

"Well, four," Lully said through a recurrence of the pout. "But I thought you and I could—"

"Right!" said Daniel. "Lieutenant Mon! Front and center! We've got to be aboard the *Princess Cecile* before the commodore opens his ports."

Mon had already pushed in through the double doors from the balcony. He walked with the studied earnestness of a man who was sure that his head would fall off if he didn't keep it centered squarely over his spine.

Daniel grimaced and turned to Adele. "And you as well, Officer Mundy," he said. "If we get back in time, you'll take over as duty officer from Woetjans. I'm certain that the commodore will expect the duty officer to be sober, and I'm equally certain that Woetjans is even less likely to meet that standard that I am myself."

Lifting Ms. Kira Lully, now chauffeur, in much the same fashion that he'd carried her up the stairs earlier, Daniel said to the room, "Good citizens, duty calls! May my every landing find people half so generous as you!"

He strode to the stairwell, the redhead clutched against him like pirate's booty. Though unburdened, Adele struggled to catch up. Even so Lt. Mon was treading on her heels as she reached the door. Real spacers were amazingly surefooted when moving through clutter.

"By God, we'll all go greet the squadron!" Admiral Torgis cried behind them. "Gerson, get my car ready!"

Kira Lully held her trim red-and-gold aircar in ground effect just above the pavement until a roar of steam drowned the snarl of the *Winckelmann*'s plasma thrusters. Only then did she drop the vehicle's nose over the cliff edge and plunge toward the *Princess Cecile* in spirals so tight that centrifugal force pressed the occupants outward.

Daniel had thought of suggesting he take the controls himself, but he'd kept his mouth shut for fear that the redhead would order them all out of the vehicle in a fit of pique. As it turned out, Kira was a much better driver than he was.

Also his fear that she'd blind herself by looking into the heavy cruiser's exhaust was remarkably silly when he used his head—which wasn't the part of Daniel Oliver Leary most often to the fore when he was dealing with pretty girls. Obviously, nobody living adjacent to Flood Harbor could be ignorant of the dangers of starships landing and lifting off.

"She's been running on eighty percent of her masts, and four of her thrusters are out of service too," Lt. Mon remarked from the rear seat beside Adele. "Christ, I'd forgotten what a bucket the *Winckelmann* was."

"How do you tell?" Adele asked over the echoes still hammering around the cliffs. "About the masts, I mean, since they're all withdrawn for landing."

Mon liked and respected Adele, but he had an abrasive manner at the best of times . . . which didn't include times he was as drunk as he was tonight. Before he could snap, "Use your bloody eyes, woman!" or the like, Daniel said, "Antennas five, six, ten, and twelve in each row haven't been unbound at least since the *Winckelmann* lifted off from Cinnabar, Adele. You can see the pitting from micrometeorites is uniform over the hinges and locking pins."

Kira dived into the warm salty fog which the *Winckelmann*'s thrusters lifted from the harbor. The big cruiser was indeed a sad sight to anyone who knew ships: a clumsy design, now overage and poorly maintained in the long interval of peace. Commodore Pettin could see that as well as any other officer of his seniority, and it would gall him like a boil on the butt.

"I'm going to miss you tonight, Danny," Kira said plaintively as she fluffed them to a featherlight landing on the dock where the *Princess Cecile*'s gangplank terminated. The harbor's surface was twitching from the nearby arrival of 13,000 tons of heavy cruiser, but the concrete slips kept other vessels from bouncing around unduly.

Adjacent to the corvette was the depot ship Admiral Torgis had moved there this morning. It was a freighter, now nameless save for its pennant number: SDN 3391. All but four antennas had been removed, and its High Drive had probably been cannibalized in the distant past to equip some warship that had limped down to Flood Harbor.

Under normal circumstances the depot ship provided stores, power for vessels whose fusion bottles were deadlined, and a repair shop. Tonight her cavernous bays were decked out with bunting, food, and liquor for the *Princess Cecile*'s crew.

"Not half so much as I'll miss you, sweet thing," Daniel said, knowing as he framed the words that the truth was a little more complex. True, he'd been looking forward to the night and morning—and who wouldn't, after the run the *Princess Cecile* had just made? But it was even more true that Daniel would willingly forego the redhead's charms if there was just some way he could avoid the interview with Commodore Pettin he knew was coming.

Why in the name of all that's holy did the pulpit-pounding commodore have to land in the middle of the Resident Commissioner's party for the crew?

Daniel hopped over the side of the aircar without bothering to open the door. "Mon," he said, "roust the crew as best you can—they'll understand it's an emergency. Adele, get onto the bridge soonest and take over. With luck we'll have the anchor watch sorted before—"

"Christ on a crutch!" Mon snarled. "The sanctimonious old bastard's making a hot exit!"

The *Winckelmann* was opening up in the usual fashion of airing ship on arrival. Hatches were lifting, the turrets for the secondary battery of plasma weapons were being cranked out to provide more room within the hull, and crewmen double-timed onto the outriggers to unlock access plates that couldn't easily be reached from inside.

Normally no one would disembark until the process was complete. This time, as soon as the hatches serving the water-level stern hold had clamshelled wide enough open, the twelve-place aircar assigned to heavy cruisers as a utility vehicle—the *Princess Cecile* had a jeep that could carry four if they were good friends—roared out.

Mon, not sober but used to functioning with a heavy load aboard, swung his legs over the side of Lully's car and ran for the depot ship with a rolling gait. The *Winckelmann*'s arrival had called a good half the crew out already. Those who were vaguely sober were mustering less-steady comrades and helping them to the quay.

Adele tried to jump out of the aircar. She tripped, which was so likely a result that Daniel had already turned to grab her when he realized what she intended. He swung her to her feet, then tucked her into the crook of his arm and trotted for the corvette. It was much the way he'd carried the redhead, Kira, in what now seemed the dim past.

"But *Danny* . . ." the girl called. He heard the words and instantly discarded them as being of no importance under the present circumstances.

Daniel's reason for carrying his signals officer was quite simple. Adele *had* to be on the bridge when Commodore Pettin came aboard. Woetjans wasn't going to pass Pettin's standards of Ready for Duty, though the bosun would have the liquor bottles hidden and other evidence of good-fellowship out of the way.

Woetjans's taste ran to men who could make her look frail, though like most spacers she'd make do with what was available after a voyage like the past one. Daniel fleetingly wondered how lucky she'd been here on Sexburga.

Though, by the living God! absolutely nothing harmful to the good order of the RCN was going on here. The problem was that Commodore Pettin wouldn't see it that way; and thank God—thank Admiral Anston—for an experienced crew which could react to changed circumstances without the captain's orders.

Barnes and Inescu were on guard at the main hatchway. They'd managed to get to their feet and lift the stocked impellers they'd been issued for the duty. "Here comes the captain!" Inescu called cheerfully as Daniel pounded over the narrow gangplank with Adele in his arms.

It was a tossup in Daniel's mind whether Pettin would be more infuriated by a drunken officer of the watch or by one who was soaking wet from falling into the harbor in her haste to board. Adele was a solid weight, tall and not as slender as she looked from a distance. She didn't speak and held herself as stiff as a balance pole. Daniel suspected she didn't understand what was going on, but early in her contact with the RCN she'd learned how to keep from getting in the way in a crisis.

Daniel saw three earthenware jugs floating between the corvette's hull and the starboard outrigger. Barnes also noticed them and leaned over the hatchway, pointing his impeller.

"No!" Daniel shouted over the howl of the *Winckelmann*'s car landing on the quay beside the redhead's. Barnes was too drunkenly focused to hear anything. He squeezed the trigger—

WhackWHOCK

—and the weapon spat a fifty-grain pellet of osmium into the water at five times the speed of sound.

Daniel half-turned, trying to shield Adele, but the waterspout was thirty feet high and drenched both of them. There were bits of shattered pottery in with the froth and flotsam. Daniel couldn't say much for Barnes's judgment, but he shot straight despite being pie-eyed drunk.

Daniel set Adele onto the *Princess Cecile*'s entryway. Barnes blinked in horror at what he'd done. "Sorry, sir," he mumbled. He lowered the impeller's muzzle so that it pointed at Daniel's feet instead of in line with his belt buckle.

Adele headed for the bridge without further direction. The soles of all RCN footgear, even the shiny half-boots Daniel wore with his whites, were of high-hysteresis rubber that gripped wet or dry. Adele squelched with each step, but she didn't fall down.

Daniel took the impeller from Barnes, switched the power off so that the coils couldn't accelerate another slug—into the harbor, into Daniel himself, or into God knew where—and returned it to the spacer. He could hear shouts echoing through the corvette as crewmen faced the sudden emergency.

"Steady on, Barnes," Daniel said quietly. "Try not to shoot the commodore."

Though that possibility had a degree of attraction just at this moment.

Daniel turned and braced himself to attention, facing the three RCN officers and the sergeant of marines tramping down the gangplank. Captain, acting Commodore, Josip Pettin was in the lead. He was a lean, white-haired man, fifty but looking older. Normally his face would merely have been pale, but at this moment Pettin was so angry that his expression could have been carved from sun-dried bone.

Daniel saluted. He'd never managed anything so crisp during his years at the Academy. He might as well have mooned the commodore for all the good it seemed to do.

"Sir!" Daniel said. "Welcome aboard RCS *Princess Cecile*! I'm Lieutenant Leary, reporting to you in accordance with my orders."

"Leary . . ." Commodore Pettin said, his nostrils flaring as though he detected a horrible stench. Maybe he did: even Daniel noticed Barnes's breath, and it wasn't that there was no alcohol on his own. "I queried Condor Control from orbit when I saw a corvette in the harbor. The controller told how it came there. Furthermore, they very kindly added that your splendidly handled ship left Cinnabar ten days behind my squadron and still arrived on Sexburga well ahead of me!"

Oh, God, that *had* torn it. No wonder Pettin looked mad enough to gnaw a junior lieutenant down to his boots.

The officers with Pettin were a plump, worried-looking commander—probably the *Winckelmann*'s executive officer—and a lugubrious young woman with the single collar flash of a midshipman detailed as an aide with the rank of acting lieutenant. The sergeant of marines was just that—and it was instructive that Pettin hadn't brought a marine *officer* instead. This was a burly fellow whose nightstick had gotten real use in the past.

"Sir, the Navy Office directed me to spare no effort to join the squadron at Sexburga despite our late start," Daniel said, his eyes unblinkingly focused on the center of the hatch instead of meeting the commodore's glaring fury. It wasn't much of a lie, and it seemed for a moment that it might just calm Pettin's anger. Then—

Oh *God*. Kira whatever-her-name-is was trotting primly down the gangplank. The skintight skirt didn't hobble her in the least.

"Danny, sweetheart?" she called in a voice so clear that nobody within fifty feet could mistake the words. "You didn't kiss me goodbye, darling."

The quartet from the *Winckelmann* turned. The marine's face showed momentary appreciation, then went professionally blank. Commodore Pettin looked at Daniel again.

"Lieutenant Leary," he said. "I was concerned when I detected signs of obvious inebriation in the tones of the duty officer when I queried your vessel from orbit."

His voice started gently enough but it quickly rose to be heard over the howl of another aircar landing. The vehicle was ornate, with enamel escutcheons on the doors and a fringed canopy.

"But I never, never in my worst nightmares, could have imagined the sort of debauchery that I saw taking place as we landed! I will not ask for your explanation, because there cannot possibly be an explanation!"

"Danny . . . ?" Kira peeped. Even she seemed to have come to the realization that something was wrong.

The *Princess Cecile*'s crew—the bulk of the spacers who hadn't had time to scramble aboard before the commodore's aircar arrived—had formed in ranks on the quay as though for an inspection. Through them, moving with the stumping precision of a man who'd spent his time in a starship's rigging, came Admiral Torgis with civilian aides in his train.

"Do you have anything to say before I remove you from command and order your confinement for court-martial?" the commodore shouted.

"Sir!" said Daniel. It was reflex, drilled into him at the Academy and absolutely the only thing *to* say under these circumstances. "No excuse, *sir*."

"Who's that?" boomed Admiral Torgis. "Pettin, isn't it? I'm glad you finally got here, Captain. You can have a drink with me in honor of Lieutenant Leary, who's been posted to your command."

"Admiral?" Commodore Pettin said, half turning and forcing his face in the direction of a smile; not very far in that direction. "The condition of the crew... Have you noticed...?"

He gestured toward the depot ship, a little flick of his hand as though trying to brush away a fly. His subordinates had stepped aside and stood at parade rest, studiously *not* looking at either the commodore or the admiral.

Kira vacillated on the gangplank. Torgis took the girl by the waist in both hands and swung her behind him, showing skill and balance that a rigger could appreciate.

"Quite a little party, isn't it?" he said with a chuckle. Daniel noted a hard glint in the admiral's eyes, though: he knew exactly what had been going on when he arrived here and what would have happened if he'd been a few minutes later. "Thought it was the least I could do. Paid for it myself, that is. Though I think I could've justified Commission funds for the crew that saved Kostroma from the Alliance."

"But Admiral," Pettin said, swaying slightly with the tension he held himself under. "The condition of the officers as well as the crew—"

"Well, for God's sake, Pettin," Torgis said. He stepped into the *Princess Cecile*'s entryway, pressing the *Winckelmann*'s personnel back by sheer force of personality. "What do you expect their condition to be after a run like they made? Seventeen days from Cinnabar to here. *I* never knew of a crew who pushed so hard. They'll be fit to fight as soon as yours are, though, I warrant."

A second ship was descending; one of the squadron's destroyers, Daniel assumed, though he couldn't see from where he stood within the corvette. The thruster pulses were audible, though it would be some minutes before the sound smothered normal conversation.

Though "normal conversation" didn't describe what was going on here.

"Sir, the duty officer was obviously drunk!" Pettin said.

"With respect, sir!" said Adele Mundy in a hard voice without a hint of respect in it. "I believe I was eating dinner at the time the *Winckelmann* announced its arrival, but I most certainly am not drunk."

Daniel blinked in surprise, then choked back a laugh when he realized that Adele's statement was literally true. She stood ramrod straight on the companionway from C Level. She'd changed into her utility uniform, and he knew without question that the ship's log now would indicate she'd been on duty all night.

Pettin looked as though he'd been sandbagged. Admiral Torgis proved he understood as well as Woetjans did that the first rule of brawling is that you *always* kick your opponent when he's down.

"And if she isn't, that's a violation of my instructions to Lieutenant Leary, Captain," the admiral said. "I made it as clear as I knew how that *every* member of his crew should have a good time at my expense tonight. I may be retired, but there's still people in the Navy Office who'd listen if I told them the RCN doesn't need Goody Two-shoes for commanding officers. There'll be no Alliance attack here with the satellite defenses in place."

"Thank you, Admiral," Adele said in ringingly aristocratic tones, "but my sobriety is entirely a personal choice. I would be unsuitable as a commanding officer for other reasons as well."

"I see," said Commodore Pettin. He shuddered like a man lifted from freezing water. His tongue touched his lips. "Lieutenant Leary, report to me at ten hundred hours tomorrow."

He looked at Torgis and added in a voice that would have been venomous if it had more life, "If that meets with your approval, Admiral?"

The destroyer was within three thousand feet, slowing to a near hover as the captain steadied her for landing. Admiral Torgis, raising his voice to be heard over the throb of plasma, said, "I'm retired, remember, Captain. In any case, I wouldn't interfere with another officer giving proper commands to his subordinates."

Daniel had been standing at attention from the moment of the commodore's arrival. "Sir!" he said, throwing another salute. It wasn't nearly as crisp as the first; maybe despair was what he needed to perform drill and ceremony properly. "Ten hundred hours tomorrow, *sir!*"

Commodore Pettin turned and stalked off across the gangplank without returning the salute or further acknowledging the Resident Commissioner. His subordinates followed, each with a surreptitious salute to the former admiral.

The *Princess Cecile*'s crew must have heard the entire exchange; now they began to cheer. They were so loud that Daniel could hear them until the destroyer licked the harbor into a roar of steam.

The cheering wasn't going to help matters tomorrow morning; but even before there hadn't been much doubt about how Daniel's formal interview would go.

CHAPTER FIFTEEN

"Enter!" Commodore Pettin called through the open hatchway to his office.

Daniel took two strides and halted before Pettin's desk. He was well aware of the three clerks in the outer office, staring at his back, but Pettin continued working at the holographic display between him and the lieutenant he'd summoned.

Daniel took an Academy brace and saluted. "Lieutenant Leary, reporting as ordered, sir!" he said.

Pettin thumbed the display to lower intensity and looked through it sourly. He touched his forehead in a perfunctory salute and said, "At ease, Leary. Pretending you were an honor graduate isn't going to fool me. The only respect you're owed is for your uniform, however much you may disgrace it."

Daniel stepped sideways to parade rest, keeping his eye on the corner of the holoprint of a vaulted cloister behind the commodore. It was the only portion of the compartment's furnishings that wasn't RCN issue. Granting that Pettin wasn't a wealthy man, this was still an unusual degree of asceticism in an officer of his seniority.

"I've met your sort before, Leary," the commodore continued. "Well-born wastrels whose political connections put them on a fast track to honors despite their manifest incapacity for command. Professional officers soon learn to work around them."

Pettin was wearing a utility uniform, technically acceptable since he was aboard a warship on active duty but a studied insult when welcoming the captain of a vessel recently posted to his command. Daniel had finally settled on his grays for the interview, knowing that whatever choice he made would be grounds to damn him—for a popinjay in a dress uniform or because his utilities lacked respect for his superior officer—if Pettin chose to take it that way.

As Pettin certainly was going to do.

"Any comment to make, Lieutenant?" Pettin asked, raising an eyebrow.

"No, sir," Daniel said to the cloisters.

With the exception of astrogation—and there because of his skill in practice rather than on theory—Daniel's Academy scores had been toward the lower limit of adequate. Even that degree of success probably owed less to Daniel's efforts than to the fact that a naval career didn't appeal to many grinding intellectuals. Still, there *was* more to being an RCN officer than your academic record.

But to protest to Pettin now? Daniel Leary had made a fool out of himself many times, and not always over a woman; but he'd never been so great a fool as that.

Pettin continued, looking vaguely displeased at Daniel's lack of reaction, "The portion of the squadron that accompanied me from Cinnabar will require three days to refit. No doubt the *Princess Cecile* will be ready long before that since you'll have taken advantage of your early arrival."

Pettin raised his eyebrow again. It was hard to distinguish the expression from a scowl, but Daniel decided a response was the better choice. "Yes, sir," he said.

He'd wrung the *Princess Cecile* out, no question about that, but she'd come through the test with flying colors. Parts of the rigging needed replacement, and one of the triply-redundant pumps feeding the antimatter converters had lost its impeller in spectacular fashion, but all this would be classed as normal wear and tear for a run of such length.

With the exception of a turnbuckle that wasn't in store on Sexburga, the repairs were already complete. Tally and her assistant were machining that last part out of bar stock; they'd have it in place by mid-afternoon.

"Fine," Pettin said with heavy irony. "Then that frees you to undertake a survey of ruins on the south continent here. I understand they've never been properly catalogued. A local resident, the Captal da Lund, has kindly offered the use of his aircar and a guide. They'll be ready by ten hours thirty local time, and I expect you and your support personnel to be ready also."

He paused with an expectant smirk.

"Yes, sir," Daniel said. The aircar he'd seen in the Captal's compound would hold twenty people, but there'd be gear to carry as well. He'd take ten crewmen plus Hogg—a worthy scion of generations of poachers and outsdoorsmen—and Adele if she wanted to go.

Disappointed again, Pettin continued, "You'll turn over command of the *Princess Cecile* to your first lieutenant and report back in seventy-two hours for liftoff with the rest of the squadron. Is that clear?"

"Yes, sir," Daniel said. In the RCN, carrying out a superior's order always took precedence to wondering why the sanctimonious jackass had chosen to give the order in the first place.

"Leary . . ." the commodore said, leaning back in his chair as his fingers writhed on the desk before him. "I don't imagine that removing you from the high life of Spires is going to make an RCN officer of you—I doubt anything could do that—but it's as much as I can do at present. Do you have any comment to make?"

"Yes sir," Daniel said to the hologram. "Am I dismissed to prepare for the expedition, sir?"

"Dismissed!" Commodore Pettin said.

Daniel saluted, turned, and strode out of the office as smartly as he could manage. To his back Pettin shouted, "And I only wish I could dismiss you from the service as well!"

He could have saved his breath. Daniel hadn't been in the least doubt about the commodore's opinion.

The bustle around Adele on the *Princess Cecile*'s bridge hadn't penetrated her concentration, but when Daniel appeared, still shouting orders back down the companionway, she looked up from her console. Daniel already had the jacket of his 2nd Class uniform off and was unsealing the fly of his trousers to drop them also.

"Adele!" he said. "Are you interested in seeing South Land? Frankly, I'd just as soon have you here to handle communications, but you're welcome to come if you'd like. I've told Woetjans that I've got Hogg to shepherd me so she's not going to tag along. Mon may need a bosun in the event the good commodore gets another harebrained idea."

A sidebar showed that Lt. Mon was in the Battle Direction Center, alerting the crewmen who'd be accompanying Daniel to the middle of nowhere. A few of them might start out with a hangover, but they were all present and accounted for. Daniel hadn't known what was going to happen when he formally reported to Commodore Pettin, but he'd made sure he and his whole complement would be prepared for it.

"I'd go if you wanted me," Adele said. "I've slept many a night on a cot in the Academic Collections. A tent in a rocky desert isn't going to be worse. But if you really want me here, there are ways I can be more useful."

With Tovera's help, Hogg had finished packing duffle bags for himself and Daniel. Unasked he traded Daniel a utility jacket for the grays. As he did so, the kneeling Tovera slid Daniel's trousers down and tapped his ankle for him to raise his right foot. She gave Adele a sidelong smile.

"I'll tell you one way right now," Daniel said. "See if you can find out how Pettin decided to send me off to the South Land. I'm surprised he even knows about the ruins. He certainly doesn't have the reputation of being an archaeologist!"

"I've already determined that, I believe," Adele said, half smug and half peeved at being told to do something that had been obvious to her from the moment Daniel called in as he left the *Winckelmann.* "I don't know if you have time . . . ?"

"Yes," he said, now lifting his left foot as directed to step out of his trousers. "Everything's obviously under control here. I'd like to know what's going on before the arrival of the Captal's guide—and spy, I presume."

At the open arms locker down the corridor, Sun handed impellers or submachine guns to the spacers told off for the expedition. His assistant, Gansevoort, ran the recipients' ID chips through a reader that paired them with the weapon serial numbers.

Adele's wands refocused her holographic display so that Daniel could view it from where he stood. Tovera was pulling the leg of his utility trousers over his right boot.

"It'll be quicker if you explain it, I believe," Daniel said with an austerity that was not quite a rebuke. He switched legs while his hands did up the buttons—more rugged, weather resistant, and silent than any other closure system—of his jacket.

Adele considered what had just happened. Daniel thought her gesture was a way of saying, "You can't match my skill even if I show you what you ought to be looking for." He was quite possibly correct. Both he and the situation demanded better performance from her.

"Sorry," Adele said, readjusting the display. "I checked Commodore Pettin's message log."

"His secure log?" Daniel asked with a frown of puzzlement. Tovera was buttoning his trousers.

"It's not *that* secure," Adele said. "If there's anything else you'd like to know from the *Winckelmann*'s records, just ask me."

Daniel grinned and shook his head. Hogg, who already wore a stocked impeller slung muzzle-down over his right shoulder, handed Daniel an equipment belt complete with a holstered pistol.

"Mr. Gerson from the Commission staff called for an appointment yesterday at twenty forty-seven hours Cinnabar time," Adele resumed. The Sexburgan day, slightly longer than that of Cinnabar, was brought into alignment by adding an intercalary eighty-one minutes to the ship's clock at midnight. "I think he was with Admiral Torgis when he—"

She wasn't sure how to describe the admiral's intervention, so she gave a shrug that didn't affect the angle at which she held her wands.

"When he saved my ass," Daniel said as he buckled the equipment belt around him. "Saved the *Sissie*'s collective ass, very possibly. And yes, Gerson did accompany the admiral."

"The message said that—" Adele said. She paused, then instead of paraphrasing quoted, "Gerson said, 'I have information for your ears only, regarding the workings of the Commission and their bearing on your command. It is imperative that we speak before ten hundred hours tomorrow.' Pettin called him. Gerson refused to say anything further even though the line was encrypted."

She was quite certain that Gerson was simply being paranoid

rather than that he really believed anyone could hear the message. This was a case where paranoia had paid off.

"They met three hours later—" Two hours and fifty-one minutes later, but Adele had learned overprecision tended to bother those she spoke to. "—according to Pettin's appointment record. Gerson stayed forty-five—" forty-three "—minutes, during which time Commodore Pettin called up all the information about South Land in the *Winckelmann*'s data banks. That was limited to the *Sailing Directions*, of course. He then put through a call to the Captal da Lund, confirming that a car and guide would be here at ten-thirty hours local time today."

"I see," Daniel said quietly. Now dressed for action, he sat at his console and looked over the changes Lt. Mon had made in the watch roster to reflect the personnel going off to South Land for three days.

"All right, muster on the quay with your ground packs!" Sun said to the spacers he'd just armed. He'd be acting as Daniel's second in command so he had every right to order them out, but Adele knew that the shout—which had startled her—was meant to alert Daniel to the detachment's readiness.

The ten crewmen trotted toward the companionway, carrying in one hand the weapons they'd just been issued and the small pack holding toiletries and a change of clothes in the other. RCN crews were frequently used for detached security and fatigue duties on distant worlds where no other Cinnabar personnel were available, so there was a Standard Operating Procedure for it. Adele doubted whether "detached" often meant a dozen people being put in the middle of a desert over a thousand miles from their ship, though.

Daniel looked up to see Sun, the last in line, heading down toward the quay. Pasternak was coming up from the power room, using the other companionway. He looked worried, but Adele knew by now that was the engineer's normal expression.

"We'll be sleeping under tarps," Daniel said to Adele and to Banks, waiting silently at the attack console although he was technically off duty at the moment. "That shouldn't be too bad if rain's as rare as the data say."

"I've downloaded all the available information on Sexburga into your helmets," Adele said. "They have plenty of storage capacity, and it'll save time by you not having to go through the communications satellites to reach the ship's data bank."

"Ah," Daniel said. "I appreciate that."

His face twitched as if he were trying to suppress a smile. Then he said, "Adele, why do they want me to go to South Land? The Captal can't really care about the ruins. He'd go himself if he did."

Adele shrugged again. "There's nothing available electronically that even suggests a reason," she said. "There's a physical archive in the basement of Council Building, that's the local government. The midshipmen and I found it the other day. While you're roughing it, I intend to search there to see what I can find."

Pasternak entered the bridge; Lt. Mon was coming down the corridor from the Battle Direction Center. Betts got to his feet. Daniel rose from his console also, to take his leave of his officers before joining the detachment on the quay.

"There's worse forms of busy work that a captain can find for a junior lieutenant," he said, flashing Adele a boyish grin. "But I really wish I knew what Vaughn's friends are playing at."

"So do I," Adele said aloud. Her mind added, *And one way or another, I'm going to learn.*

CHAPTER SIXTEEN

The aircar's central compartment had luxury seating for eight. Sun, Vesey, and the eight ordinary crewmen found it uncomfortably roomy: spacers liked close quarters or they'd have found some other line of work. The rear compartment had jumpseats for servants as well as cargo tie-downs; the expedition's food and luggage rode there now.

Daniel and Hogg were on either end of the bench seat in front, sandwiching their driver/guide Dorotige, the attendant Daniel had met guarding the Captal's gate. Today he wore a gray jacket over loose khaki trousers instead of the clown suit he'd been in for the party.

"I wish to God that you'd packed those guns away in the back," Dorotige said, shouting over the sound of wind and the fans' vibration. The central compartment was slung in elastic to isolate the passengers from the noise of operation, but the driver had no such luxury. "Or left them back in Spires, better yet. There's nothing bigger than your thumbnail on South Land."

"You've been here before," Daniel said, looking down at a plain broken by ravines where russet vegetation found enough moisture to grow. In the forward distance rose sandstone hills which the wind had weathered out of the surrounding clay. "My crewmen haven't, and this isn't the sort of business they're trained for anyway. They're more comfortable being armed."

In truth, Daniel's only real concern about the expedition was the same one the Captal's man had voiced. The spacers weren't for the most part any more familiar with hand weapons than they were with camping in the middle of a barren desert. Even though he'd ordered them to leave the guns' power switches off, there was a real chance that somebody'd put a bullet through himself, a fellow, or the car's drive fans.

"They'll be all right, buddy," Hogg said. "Most of this lot know which end the slug comes out of. And I told 'em that if anybody looses off a round, it'd better kill me straight out, because I'm sure as shit going to cut his throat if it don't."

Hogg was quite capable of exaggeration. He was also capable of cutting somebody's throat. Daniel hoped the comment was in the former category, but he even more hoped that he'd never have to learn.

An intercom connected the vehicle's three compartments, but Sun used his helmet's unit channel to ask, "*Captain? What's the ETA now? We ought to be getting close, right?*"

"Hold one," Daniel said, flipping down his visor and cueing the geographical overlay. It didn't show what he expected it to. Frowning, he used the thumb dial under his left ear to increase the scale until the destination pip showed on the same screen as the point where the helmet's inertial navigation system placed the aircar. They were to the north of the plotted ruins and well inland of them as well.

"Dorotige," Daniel said without raising his voice more than the noise level required. Hogg must have heard something in the tone, because he reached into his pocket.

"Yeah?" Dorotige muttered.

There was a snick from Hogg's side of the compartment. "Look at the master when he's talking to you, fishbait," Hogg said. He didn't speak loudly either, but with the point of a seven-inch knife blade resting against Dorotige's throat, he didn't have to.

"What the hell!" Dorotige screamed. The aircar lurched sideways. If Hogg hadn't been very fast, the jolt would have done exactly what the driver was afraid of; but while you could fault Hogg's judgment occasionally, Daniel was pretty sure his servant would never kill anybody that he didn't mean to. He had the knife back and closed before Dorotige managed to spit himself on it.

Daniel steadied the control yoke with his left hand, bringing the car straight and level again. He said, "We aren't heading for the ruins like we're supposed to be, Dorotige. Why is that?"

"What do you mean not the ruins?" the driver shouted, angry and terrified at the same time. He pointed through the windscreen toward the ground five hundred feet below. "What the hell do you think that is down there? Look, right at the bottom of the hill, there! We're here, you—"

The sound of Hogg's knife reopening punctuated the driver's bluster. He choked the next word off in his throat.

Daniel grimaced. He could see a pattern of lines in the stone, but until he dialed up the magnification on his visor they looked like mere weathering. That still might be what they were, but at 40x magnification and with the helmet's optical stabilizer engaged, Daniel could tell they were straight or at least seemed straight.

"There's two sites!" Dorotige said, now in a tone of injured innocence that Daniel had to admit his right to. "This is where the Captal told me bring you. The water you can get at the place down south has a lot of sulfur in it."

"All right," Daniel said. "Set us down, please."

He glanced into the passenger compartment. The helmet communicator was still engaged so the crewmen had heard everything that was going on. Dasi had his impeller pointed at the back of the driver's head. The heavy slug would punch through the clear plastic without difficulty, true enough, but it'd also send fragments of the panel across the compartment like a grenade blast.

Daniel frowned and waved the weapon away. He said, "All personnel prepare for landing. We've reached our destination."

He felt uncomfortable, but that might be simply because he seemed to have made a fool of himself. Still, the Captal should have mentioned that he'd directed them to a site that wasn't . . .

Ah. The Captal might not even know what the RCN *Sailing Directions* said about South Land. Anyway, there was no way of telling what the Captal had said to Gerson or Gerson to Commodore Pettin during their interview.

"I'm very sorry, Dorotige," Daniel said, sitting formally upright. "I jumped to conclusions. It won't happen again."

"And if you watch your tongue when you're talking to the master," Hogg said, "I won't have to prick you to better manners again neither."

Dorotige brought the aircar to a hover, raising a huge dough-nut of red dust from the spiky vegetation. The cloud was inevitable, but he let the vehicle slip backward and landed expertly out of the worst of it.

Daniel opened his door; he'd studied the odd pull-lift motion of the latch before they left Spires. He'd learned as a child stuck in a narrowing cave that he didn't want to get into anything where he didn't know the way out.

Hogg stepped onto the deck on his side and surveyed the landscape: dark red rock with horizontal striations where the wind had dug deeper between layers; a sky so pale it was almost white; and cushions of reddish grass an inch or two high and about a foot in diameter. The vegetation vanished into the general rocky undersurface from any distance in the air, except in the ravines where greater moisture and protection from the wind let it grow higher.

Hogg spat. "Yessir," he said. "This is *just* where I was hoping to spend the next three days."

He turned to glare at Daniel over the cabin of the car. "And don't tell me I didn't have to come, young master," he added, "because you know damned good and well that I wasn't going to leave your ass swinging out here with nobody to look after you!"

"Yes, I did know that, Hogg," Daniel said, stepping to the ground. The contact jolted him all the way from his heel right up the spinal column. For some reason sandstone felt harder than other kinds of rock, even granite and basalt.

"Barnes and Keast, you're on guard till we know what we're dealing with," Sun ordered, lifting the gate of the cargo compartment. "The rest of you, stack arms and let's get the tarp up for shelter so we don't have to screw with it after the sunset. This wind's cold as ice up the ass already!"

That was true beyond doubt. Maybe it was a whim of the weather rather than a variation in climate, but the air here was ten degrees cooler than it had been on Spires when they left this morning. This site was far from the coast, which probably made a difference also. And speaking of the site—

"Hogg, let's look at the ruins," Daniel said. There was high-definition imaging equipment in the kit Adele's servant, Tovera, had packed for the expedition, but for Daniel's initial survey his helmet's recording capacity would be sufficient. "Dorotige, come along with us. You've been here before, and none of our records mention the location at all."

"There's not a hell of a lot to see," Dorotige muttered as he slid across the seat. "God but it's cold!"

Patterns that Daniel had taken for mineral deposits on the rock were actually the stems of woody plants. They crawled across the surface because the wind would shear them if they rose any distance in the air. Their purplish leaves were as tiny as grains of rice.

"Some're up this way," Dorotige said, waving toward the hillside. "But they're all over the place, for what they're worth. It's just ditches in the rock."

He started up the slope. His foot slipped on bare stone; from then on he stepped on the flat mounds of grass that gave him some traction. He was wearing soft-soled sandals better suited for a drawing room than a wilderness.

Daniel thought about how long it must take plants to grow in this windswept aridity but didn't say anything to Dorotige. Besides, only the outer rim of the cushions was still alive; the centers were coarse gray stems.

"Here's one," said Dorotige, pointing to his feet. "Not much to come a thousand miles for, it seems to me."

"You got that right," Hogg said. He spat again, grimacing as the wind blew the gobbet back just short of his boot.

Daniel squatted beside the indentation in the rock, hoping to find some reason to disagree. He couldn't come up with one immediately.

So: there was a trough in the sandstone. It was straight, true enough, but it never got deeper than his index finger and its margins were rounded. Eight feet up it crossed another trough, shallower yet, at right angles. When Daniel held his head low to the ground he could make out a whole network of the markings, just as Dorotige had said.

"They could be footings for walls," Daniel offered. The patterns had been easier to see from the air, because the shadows thrown by the indentations were more obvious than the grooves themselves.

"*Or* they could be cracks that the wind routed out with sand," Hogg said. His education had been practical rather than scholarly, but there was very little new about the countryside an academic would be able to tell Hogg. "And anyhow, it didn't happen any time in the last couple thousand years."

His boot pointed to—but didn't touch—a shrub growing where troughs joined, its four stems writhing up the intersecting lines. "If this wasn't about as big back when they settled the planet, I'll never touch liquor again."

"I'm getting a jacket," Dorotige said. He stalked off, rubbing his hands together. Daniel ignored him, so Hogg merely shrugged.

Sun had the aircar emptied; Vesey was leading a section with buckets and shovels into the nearest ravine, searching for the water that was supposed to be there. They'd brought three days' supply in jerricans, but it'd be nice to have extra so they could wash.

Daniel stood, feeling momentarily dizzy. Squatting had cut off the circulation in his legs, robbing his brain of blood when he rose too quickly.

"This is fine-grained rock," he said. "I don't see any reason why it should crack at right angles the way it has. And granted that the sand has worn it—"

The aircar's drive fans whined, spinning up from idle; Dorotige hadn't shut the motors down when he landed. Daniel turned, frowning slightly. Sun and the other spacers were nearer to the vehicle, but they were upwind and probably didn't notice.

"Officer Sun?" Daniel said, the name cueing his direct channel to the warrant officer. "Did you order the local to move the—"

Dorotige slammed full power to his fans, sending the aircar downslope in a spray of grit. He kept it sliding only a handsbreadth above the ground so that surface effect supported the vehicle and as much power as possible went to accelerating its mass. The spacers shouted angrily, shielding their eyes as the car passed.

Hogg rolled his impeller's butt to his shoulder. His left hand gripped the fore-end while his arm stressed the sling to provide two more contact points locking the weapon on target.

"Don't shoot!" Daniel said. He knocked the impeller up with the edge of his hand.

The weapon's *whack!* punctured only the empty sky. The hairs on Daniel's arm stood out straight; the pellet's aluminum driving skirt, ionized by the flux through the barrel's coil windings, quivered like a blob of rainbow in front of the muzzle.

When Hogg's shot crashed out, Barnes and Keast opened up with their submachine guns. If they'd heard Daniel's shout (which wasn't certain against the wind), they ignored it in favor of the direct appeal of somebody else shooting.

Daniel saw two sparkles from the vehicle's quarter panel where ten-grain pellets disintegrated against the dense structural plastic. A swatch of hillside fifty meters from the car erupted in miniature dust devils. If the guard—no way to tell which one—had missed the same distance to the left instead of right, he'd have laced his burst into fellow spacers scrambling for their stacked weapons.

Hogg, his face as dark and stiff as an old boot, lowered the weapon across his chest in a carry position. He didn't look at Daniel.

"Cease fire!" Daniel bellowed on the unit push. He spread his feet and stood arms akimbo, hoping to dominate the situation by example since he was too far from the others to interfere the way he had with Hogg.

The aircar dipped behind a knoll too low to notice in the ordinary course of events. Daniel could still track the vehicle by the line of dust rising in a dull red haze.

"I could've taken the bastard's head off," Hogg said in a tight voice, still refusing to look at his master. "Easy as nailing a tree-hopper back in Bantry."

"I know you could have, Hogg," Daniel said quietly. "Let's go down to the others. They don't know what's happened and it probably worries them."

"*I* don't know what's happened," Hogg snarled. "And I don't know about worried, but this ain't exactly the place I'd figured to spend my declining years."

They started toward Sun and the others. Vesey and her team appeared at the lip of the ravine. The midshipman's pistol, the only weapon among the four of them, was in her hand.

A mile from the site he'd marooned the Cinnabar spacers, Dorotige lifted the aircar from the nap of the earth. It was a black dot against the pale sky. Hogg paused.

"Bastard's going straight away so I wouldn't need to lead him," he said. "I could still . . . ?"

"Yes," said Daniel. "And if you brought him down, how are we better off? I don't imagine he intended to kill us or he wouldn't have waited for us to unload all our equipment and provisions."

"*I'd* be better off knowing the bastard was dead," Hogg muttered, but he knew it wasn't an argument he'd win with his master. He didn't push beyond the bare comment.

Daniel could be as ruthless as was necessary to safeguard his mission and his crew. If he didn't care to kill for no better reason than anger, though . . . well, that was his business. There was nobody on South Land to overrule him.

Sun already had the satellite radio out when Daniel and Hogg reached the intended campsite. It was part of the gear the Captal had supplied with the aircar and driver. Adele could have adapted one of the corvette's own units, but it was simpler to borrow a radio keyed to the planetary frequencies.

"I swear I tested it before we packed it aboard, sir," Sun said miserably. "It's dead as Todd the Founder, now."

"I'm sure you did, Sun," Daniel said. "It was my mistake not to expect sabotage."

A wry smile lighted his face. "And of course, there was a satellite communicator as part of the aircar's commo suite if we needed a backup."

He glanced around the semicircle of his subordinates. They straightened and tried to look unconcerned as they met his eyes, all but Barnes. The big man had turned his back shamefacedly as he reloaded the submachine gun he'd emptied without—or against—orders.

"All right, spacers," Daniel said. He saw his subordinates through the mask of the terrain display projected onto the inner surface of his visor. "We've been left here without communication. I assume the intention is to keep us—"

To keep Daniel himself; though he couldn't imagine why. The rest of the party were top spacers, but the *Princess Cecile* could certainly operate without them.

"—out of the way for reasons that aren't clear at present. Our food is RCN issue, so we'll have no difficulty there for at least a week. The water we've brought should last as long if we're careful.

According to the background Officer Mundy prepared for me, some of the vegetation here is edible."

Though Daniel for one would have to be damned hungry to get up an appetite for lichen soup.

"Vesey?" he said. "What's the situation for water locally?"

The midshipman looked down in horror at the pistol she still held. In squeaky embarrassment she said, "Sir! We found water a few inches below the pebble surface of the ravine's bottom and just started filling our containers with osmotic lifts. It, ah, tasted all right. Sir!"

"Very good, Vesey," Daniel said. He deliberately turned his head so that Vesey could holster her weapon out of his sight.

"Spacers," Daniel resumed, "we've been left some three hundred miles to the north of where Lieutenant Mon will expect us to be. That's my fault also. I think there's a fair likelihood that the people who marooned us here plan to pick us up again in the future."

Daniel felt a grin form at the corners of his mouth. That provided a good reason not to shoot down the Captal's aircar, though he knew his decision had nothing to do with reason.

"I don't know that's their plan," he continued, "and in any case, they aren't people we could trust."

He grinned more broadly. He didn't even know who they were with certainty.

"We could hike overland to where we were supposed to be," Daniel said, "but I believe there's a better option. A hundred and fifty miles to the north of us is a navigation beacon for orbiting starships. With a little luck, we can rig that to summon help from Spires."

"By *God* we can!" said Sun, looking cheerful for the first time since he'd found the radio was dead. His training to repair electromotive weapons as armorer gave him more hands-on skill with electronics than Daniel and Vesey had gotten at the Academy.

Daniel looked at the sky. The sun was midway to the western horizon. "Hogg," he said, "break up what we need for the march into loads we can carry. Food, water, tools. One tarp for shelter. We'll leave an arrow of rocks on the ground to indicate our direction of travel if anyone comes back for us."

"How about guns, sir?" Sun asked.

Daniel looked at Hogg and raised an eyebrow. Hogg rubbed his mouth with a knuckle, considering the spacers. "Two impellers," he said. "Sun, you carry one, I'll have the other. The officers . . . ?"

He looked at Daniel and raised an eyebrow in turn.

Daniel unsnapped his pistol, holster and all, and laid it on the rocks at his feet. "Quite right, Hogg," he said. "Our enemy now is weight, not anything we can shoot."

"For now it is," Hogg said in a musing, almost cheerful, tone. "But when we *have* got back, then I've got some ideas about the next thing we do."

From context, that had to be "camp," not "can't." Adele adjusted the character recognition parameters on her personal data unit, then used it to rescan the document's obverse. The machine whirred softly as it worked.

Adele stretched, wondering how long she'd been here in the attic of the Civil Government Building. The museum and library in the basement would have been a disappointment if she'd had any real expectations. She'd gotten a feeling she couldn't have explained when the museum's volunteer director, a retired ship chandler, mentioned the dead storage for items that weren't worth displaying, however.

Felt the thrill of the chase, Adele supposed. She visualized Hogg beside her in the dimness, waiting in perfect silence for prey to step into his sight picture. The thought made her smile, but there was truth in it nonetheless: every line of work has its tricks, and the people who know their craft very well always have an instinct that goes beyond the available evidence.

The data unit's display suddenly changed from opalescence to projected text. Moments before, about twenty percent of the document had been garbage; now less than half of that amount remained as a blur beyond analysis and reconstruction.

THE DAY AFTER THE DEATH OF CAPTAIN TYRFING, I LEFT THE CAMP AND PROCEEDED NORTH AS BEST I COULD JUDGE BY THE SUN. ANY NAVIGATIONAL MATERIALS FOR THIS GODFORSAKEN PLACE HAD PERISHED WITH THE SHIP'S COMPUTER DURING THE CRASH. . . .

The attic was musty, which was actually a good thing from the standpoint of this document's survival. It was written on leather, and now that she'd read much of it Adele had begun to wonder about the source of that leather. The ink came from the berries of what the writer called the Finger Bush. Adele couldn't match the writer's cursory description . . . THE HEIGHT OF MY FOREARM, WITH BRANCHES LIKE FINGERS AND FRUITS OF A SULLEN YELLOW ON THE TIPS THEREOF . . . with any plant in her database, but she knew she wasn't competent to direct the search for botanical answers.

The attic had a line of resistance lights in the ceiling, but the only two still working were on the far side of the big room. That didn't matter enough for Adele to get the bulbs replaced since she had a handlight and the data unit's display was self-illuminating. It did mean that when someone's body filled the square opening of the trapdoor, the dimming light attracted her attention as the squeaking of the ladder moments before had not.

Adele jerked suddenly alert, her left hand slipping down to the pistol in her pocket. *That wasn't a reflex I used to have. . . .*

"Yes?" she said in a carrying voice.

"Ma'am?" Dorst called. "Officer Mundy, I don't mean to bother you but Lieutenant Mon was wondering . . . ?"

"Yes, come on up, Dorst!" Adele said, knowing that she was being snappish because of the way she'd reacted to the surprise. "Wondered what?"

The midshipman climbed the last three steps and squatted down to face her. His head would clear the ceiling if he kept it between the rafters, but then he couldn't look at Adele.

"Ah, Lieutenant Mon was wondering if you'd heard anything from the captain, ah, Adele," Dorst said. "He hasn't reported in to the ship, and the guy who loaned him the car, da Lund I mean, he says he hasn't heard anything either."

"I've been here all day," Adele said, wondering how she felt at the news. Her normal reaction was to shut down all emotion so that it didn't get in the way of accurate analysis. That was still the correct reaction, but this time it felt . . . odd. "I don't care to be disturbed while I'm working."

"Yes ma'am," Dorst said, straightening abruptly and thumping his head into a beam of reinforced concrete. He winced and stumbled forward, then knelt on one knee so he could keep his spine stiff while facing Adele.

"Yes, sir," he said. "Lieutenant Mon didn't want to interrupt you, but just on the off chance . . . And I said I knew where you might be even if you weren't answering calls, so he told me I could come. Ah, Midshipman Vesey's with the expedition and . . . but it's probably nothing, they were just too busy to report when they landed."

Adele had already suspended the document analysis and was checking message traffic. Rather than looking at communications addressed to the *Princess Cecile*—the on-duty personnel were certainly capable of having done that—she coded her search for the time the comsats of Sexburga's low-orbit constellation were over South Land. It was just possible that a message had been received by a satellite which had failed to pass it on, or that—through some electronic hiccup between the local system and the corvette—the central communications node had swallowed the information.

The individual satellite logs showed no private messages coming out of South Land. The continuous broadcast from the navigation beacon on the northern headland was logged, providing Adele with proof that the satellites were working properly.

She paged Tovera through the transponder on the corvette—*Meet me at the ship ASAP*—then shut down her personal data unit and stood. The attic's contents were a shadowed jumble about her. Early on somebody had made an attempt to keep this overflow organized, but for the past several decades—judging by the dates of the documents Adele had unearthed—boxes had been piled on filing cabinets and into the aisles the initial planners had left.

She'd been working on a smooth-surfaced attaché case stacked on a packing crate of rubberized metal. She put away the data unit, then paused as she considered what to do with the document she'd found in a drawer of pre-Hiatus logbooks.

"What's that, ma'am?" Dorst asked, reaching forward as he spoke. "A piece of boot?"

"Don't touch that!" Adele said, then frowned at herself. Though he had to learn to ask before he put his hands on things . . .

"That is," she continued to the midshipman, ramrod straight

though still on his knee, "that's a diary of sorts from the initial settlement of the planet some fifteen hundred years ago. The writer was the only survivor of a wrecked starship who lived for nine years with the natives of South Land."

Adele frowned again. "He says he did," she added, because you could scarcely consider this unimpeachable evidence.

"That's writing?" Dorst said, leaning far over to bring his eyes closer to the document. He clasped his hands behind his back to show that there was no danger of him touching the leather. "What language . . . ?"

Adele smiled. "It's in Universal," she said, "but the writer had a very crabbed hand and he wrote on both sides of the sheet. *And—*"

"These are holes in the paper!" Dorst said as his mind finally realized that he was seeing the attaché case, not pale gray ink against the dark brown leather. He looked up at Adele in amazement.

"Yes," she said dryly. "The ink he used was mildly acid. It ate through the leather from both sides in the course of a millennium and a half. This makes transcription more difficult than it usually would be."

A document like this deserved care beyond anything available on Sexburga, but that couldn't be Adele's present priority. She opened the acetate folder she'd found it in and slipped one edge under the fragile wondrousness of the memoir. Closing the folder, she put the document back into the drawer where it had been.

It had survived there for decades or more. If matters worked out the way Adele hoped they would, she could return and preserve the account properly. If not, she didn't suppose it mattered very much.

She gestured Dorst to the opening. "Let's go," she said crisply.

"Ma'am," he said, rising to a stoop, "why don't you go down and I'll latch the trap behind us. It'll be easier for me, I think."

"Yes, all right," Adele said, squeezing past the midshipman. He'd spoken as though he'd been watching her sway as she worked the stiff bolt to open the attic. Well, you didn't have to be around Officer Mundy very long to imagine how clumsy she'd be on a ladder.

"Ma'am?" Dorst said, gripping her arm in a tactful but firm

fashion. "If you turn so you face the ladder, you'll be, ah, more comfortable."

"Safer," Adele said, supplying the correct word as she obediently turned and started down. Though falling fifteen feet onto her face—the Council Chamber was on this floor and the ceiling was high—would certainly be uncomfortable.

Dorst waited till she'd reached the hallway to follow. He slammed the trapdoor with no trouble: the sudden weight had almost swept Adele off the ladder when the bolt released it.

"I didn't know there were natives on Sexburga, ma'am," he said, dropping lightly onto the balls of his feet instead of climbing down the rungs.

He smiled in a hopeful, puppyish way. Adele realized that he was trying to change the unstated subject from her physical ineptitude. That was the sort of handicap that bothered people who *didn't* trip over themselves more than it did Adele herself, but she found the impulse engaging.

"There aren't any natives according to the printed data I've found," Adele said, striding briskly down the hallway. "That's what made this account so interesting. The writer says that he lived alone for months before they showed themselves to him. After that they fed him, and if I've followed the text correctly..."

Dorst glanced back at the tall step ladder, but Adele waved him on. The janitor had dragged the ladder out for her with bad grace despite the generous tip she'd given him; he could put it away or leave it in the middle of the corridor as he chose.

"If I've read the text correctly," she resumed as she started down the end stairs, "he claims to have formed a romantic alliance within the tribe. And to have fathered a child."

A group of Sexburgans chattering in accented Universal were coming up in a cluster around a woman so pale that Adele would have guessed she was an albino, except that her eyes were an icy gray-blue. The Sexburgans all watched the pale woman, but her eyes followed Dorst until she disappeared through the door onto the second floor.

"That can't be, ma'am," Dorst said. The outside door was stiff; it resisted Adele until the midshipman hit it, high and low with his palm and bootsole. "Species aren't interfertile, and for sure animals on two different planets can't breed."

"That was my understanding also," Adele said. Insufficient data could cause mistakes. Certainty about matters where the data were insufficient was a mistake on its face. "On the other hand, I wasn't there and the writer very possibly was."

The streets of Spires weren't lighted, and the sky was dark except for the stars. They were unfamiliar constellations in a manner of speaking, but Adele didn't know anything about the stars above Cinnabar either. She was a city dweller, and if she'd ever been interested in the night sky she'd have called up a computer projection of it.

"Ma'am?" Dorst said, falling abreast as they started up the street. "Lieutenant Mon's going to send our jeep south to find the captain and, and the others. It can't bring them back all at once if there's a problem, but it'll take another radio and some medical supplies. Are you going along?"

A ship took off from the harbor. Adele lowered her eyes, shielding them further with her hand as she waited for the plasma's artificial thunder to subside.

Dorst slipped his goggles into place, watching the liftoff as he strode along. "It's the *Achilles*, that's the yacht that made the fast run from Cinnabar," he shouted. "Of course, that was nothing to what we did under Captain Leary."

"I'm sure Lieutenant Mon can find more suitable personnel for a search party on South Land," Adele said, going back to the previous question. "I intend to learn what I can here about the Captal da Lund and his friends."

Percussion bands were playing at the upper and lower ends of the street, the tunes syncopating one another. Because Adele was unfamiliar with the local instrumentation, it took her a moment to realize that the counterpoint wasn't intended. The Strymonian yacht had shrunk to an unusually bright star in the heavens.

"And I think," she added, "that I'm going to see where the *Achilles* is off to."

Dorst looked at her. She shrugged and grinned. "Just a feeling," Adele said. "An instinct, if you like."

CHAPTER SEVENTEEN

The windblown grit didn't scratch the moissanite visors protecting the faces of the detachment, but bare skin—the backs of Daniel's hands and his throat above his collar—already felt as though it was sunburned. What was it going to be like a week from now?

Daniel grinned broadly. Well, that was something he could wait a week to learn. Any number of things could happen before then to render present concern empty. Some of the possibilities were even survivable.

"Unit," he said to key the general channel. "We'll camp here, down in the swale and out of the wind. Hogg, choose a site for the tent. Vesey, take Matahurd and see if there isn't water here too. Captain out."

Daniel took his knapsack off and waited as the crewmen slid over the crumbling bank. The region must get some rain for this dry riverbed and its contributory ravines to exist, but rain must be very infrequent. The hard-stemmed bushes growing to the level of the bank were at least several years old; a downpour as fierce as the ones that had excavated the riverbed would uproot any vegetation present at the time.

When Daniel himself stepped down, the sudden absence of wind was as great a relief as warm shelter after a blizzard. He hadn't appreciated just how enervating the wind's cutting pressure was until he'd escaped it—for a time.

Hogg was giving orders in a voice that remained clear despite obvious wear from the dust and dryness. They'd all been drinking their fill in expectation of replenishing their water supply, but the mucous membranes of noses and mouths still suffered in this *damnable* atmosphere.

"How far'd we get, sir?" Sun croaked. If the gunner had wanted information instead of a reason to speak to Daniel, he'd have read the figure off his helmet's navigation display. He was working his arms alternately to loosen them after the pull of his packstraps, switching the powerful impeller from hand to hand so that he wasn't flailing it around.

"Ten point three one miles, Sun," Daniel said. "A pretty decent hike for spacers on the first day, I'd say. We'll try to double that in the future."

"Umm . . ." Sun said, rubbing his mouth with the back of his free hand. He was a wiry man of middle height, and one of the solidest of the *Princess Cecile*'s crew—under normal circumstances. "I wonder, sir? If this gully was going in more or less the right direction—"

He'd obviously already looked at his map overlay. It would have showed him that the dry river entered the Middle Sea within ten miles of the cape where the beacon was set.

"—and we followed it, we could stay out of the wind."

"I wish we could do that, Sun," Daniel said truthfully, "but the vegetation down here is too thick for us to use ravines for passage."

He gestured, calling attention to the brush around them. Daniel could differentiate at least a dozen species, though they all had smooth trunks and small, oval leaves. Several varieties had foliage covered with fine spines, even though Sexburga had no large herbivores. Daniel had seen that sort of adaptation before in desert climates: the spines created a zone of still air so that constant wind didn't dry the plant out faster than the roots could replenish its fluids.

The armed leaves would nonetheless lacerate anybody moving through them quickly. Besides, the trunks of neighboring bushes twisted around one another in a slow-motion attempt to wrestle more of their valuable riverbed real estate.

Sun looked at the vegetation and sighed. "Yeah, I should've known that," he said. "I don't . . . I'm not used to the wind, I guess. Sorry, sir."

He turned and walked back to where his men had cleared a tent-sized area under Hogg's direction. The detachment had only one powered cutting bar, though Hogg had sharpened the two shovels on a rock slab at the landing site. They'd come here to view what might be foundations carved into bare rock, not to hack through the continent's rare stretches of vegetation.

Daniel didn't let the concern he felt for Sun reach his face. The constant wind was unpleasant to anybody, but the gunner's reaction was just short of phobia. It wasn't the sort of problem that would arise aboard a starship.

And there wasn't a thing to do about it now.

The fire's dense yellow flames crackled, throwing heat even to where Daniel stood twenty feet away. This South Land brushwood burned with an oily intensity, but Dasi and Pring had been unable to light it until Hogg feathered one of the chopped stems with his knife before touching the lighter to it.

Hogg sauntered over, smiling with satisfaction at a job well done—and also, if Daniel knew his servant, at his superiority to a bunch of city folk. "Want to take a little walk with me, master?" Hogg asked. "There's something you might want to look at."

"Certainly, Hogg," Daniel said, feeling a touch of excitement that took him back to his boyhood. That was the way Hogg always prefaced a chance to view a part of nature that almost no one ever saw. There'd been the day the crystal moths issued from every pore of a tree their grub forms had eaten hollow, mating in the sunlight they saw only once in thirty years; the cave under the sea cliff, always in the past empty, from which the scaly head of leviathan rose one evening to follow the line of Hogg's low-skimming aircar; the roc lifting as the sun woke updrafts from the hinterlands of Bantry...

Hogg picked up a shovel and handed the impeller to Barnes. "She's switched off right now," he said. "Which would be a pretty good way to leave her unless you want to blow somebody's ass off for fun."

"I'll be careful, mother," Barnes said with a grin. Hogg sniffed and gestured with his free hand for Daniel to follow him into the brush.

Hogg and the Sissies respected one another and had been through some tense times together. Both sides had a genial contempt for the group the other represented, however. Daniel had a foot in either camp. He found the mutual chauvinism amusing, since they'd shown that in a crisis they'd join ranks against a common enemy.

Hogg held the sharpened blade of the shovel out in front of him like a horseman's lance and duckwalked down a tunnel of branches growing from pedestals of dirt laced high by roots. The soil was so light and dry that even here in the riverbed the breezes carved it away except where something bound it.

Daniel's hands were empty, so he scrambled along on all fours. The knife on his equipment belt would make a satisfactory weapon at close quarters, but he saw no need to draw it now.

"There you go, master," Hogg said, making room for Daniel by squeezing against a bush whose tiny white berries grew from the underside of its leaves. He pointed with the shovel; its broad tip had a wicked sheen where he'd stroked the metal to an edge.

He indicated a bush whose stems swelled at intervals into fist-sized nodules. They weren't the result of disease as Daniel had thought when he first viewed them, but rather reservoirs in which the plant stored a white, starchy substance. Daniel had tasted a pinch and found it flavorless but not apparently harmful. He'd thought of using it to supplement their diet if necessary.

Half this bush had been stripped: the stems cut a foot or two above the ground, then cut again to excise the nodules. The undamaged stems looked forlorn, springing from a base meant for twice their number.

"It's not sawed," Hogg said, "and it's not hacked with a machete either. I'd say either teeth or a sharp little knife."

Daniel flicked on his handlight. The sky was still bright enough for normal vision, but he needed more intensity to judge how fresh the cuts were. Bark curled resiliently under the pressure of his fingertip. He said, "It didn't happen more than a day ago."

"Not even that, dry as this place is," Hogg said. "Less than an hour, I'd say. I'll bet he scampered when the thundering herd come down the bank."

"It could be a castaway," Daniel said. He didn't know what he believed, so he stated what seemed the most reasonable possibility. "Out of rations and living off the land."

"Could be," Hogg said. From his tone, *he* didn't know what he believed either. "That don't explain why he ran, though. *I* sure hell wouldn't want to be alone in this place if there was a choice."

He resumed waddling forward, along the trail rubbed in the friable soil. The markings were faint, but even Daniel could have followed them; Hogg had another generation's worth of experience in woodcraft.

Fifteen feet ahead, he gestured to one of the chopped-out nodules, dropped beside the track. Daniel nodded.

"*Captain, is things all right?*" Dasi asked through the helmet. The fact that it was a spacer checking rather than Sun, the petty officer in charge, was a bad sign. "*Over.*"

"Unit," Daniel said, "Hogg and I are scouting the perimeter. There's no problems, we're just making sure. Captain out."

The trail had led them back to the wall of the dry channel. A block of sandstone the diameter of a dinnerplate projected from the bank. It didn't look as though it belonged there. Hogg tested it with the heel of his left hand, leaning some, then all of his weight against it. "Stuck in from the other side and wedged, *I* say," he commented.

Daniel grimaced. "We need to keep moving," he said. "Much as I'd like to go after it, we can't take the time to do that now."

Hogg eyed the neighboring brush. He chose a plant, then notched its stem with his shovel and stripped a line of bark up from the cut. It was as tough and flexible as rawhide. "I'll tell you what, young master," he said. "You leave me here for an hour or so to set a snare. And then we'll see if something doesn't come to us."

Daniel chuckled. "Yes, all right, Hogg," he said. "Commodore Pettin ordered me to make a survey of constructions on South Land. This hole appears to be one of the more recent constructions . . . and I wouldn't want the commodore to think I'd disobeyed his orders."

Adele worked at the seven separate screens on her display while Tovera stood behind her chair, facing toward the bridge proper. The servant wore, unusually for her, an RCN commo helmet. She was echoing Adele's display on the visor.

"By God!" Lt. Mon said. He slammed his fist on the command

console and stood. "By God, I won't have them play games with the RCN! Officer Mundy, a word with you!"

Adele locked her display and set her wands on the flat surface. She rotated her seat to face Mon, but she was rubbing her eyes instead of meeting his furious gaze.

"Koop and Lamsoe just called in from South Land," Mon said. "They've reached the site and done everything but plow the ground up. Captain Leary isn't there, there's no sign that he ever was, *and* I can't get through to the Captal da Lund for an explanation! A message says he's not taking calls!"

A part of Adele wondered idly whether that was the sort of information that all RCN commanders thought they had to tell their signals officers. Whose console did Mon think the calls were routed through?

Aloud she said, "Yes, I'm sorry, Mon, I should've kept you better informed. I've been busy."

She gestured toward the command console. "Sit down again and I'll explain what's been going on."

Mon's face darkened for a moment; Adele realized that her brusqueness had tripped Mon's little-man belligerence. He nodded, remembering her civilian background, and sat down obediently.

"Sorry," Adele muttered, irritated with herself. If she'd been a man instead of a slender woman whose physical presence threatened no one, her error might have precipitated a scene in the current charged atmosphere.

She faced around and unlocked the display, saying, "No one's come out of the Captal's compound since his driver and aircar returned late yesterday evening."

Her wand highlighted a movement log, culled from the compound's own sensors.

"The car came back?" Mon said. "By—" He caught himself. "Go ahead, Officer Mundy," he said with the controlled tension of a gymnast balancing.

"Yes," said Adele, throwing up time-slugged imagery of the car landing in the courtyard. "And if you'll look here—"

She split the display to show two versions of the vehicle's left quarter panel recorded when it left the compound and on its return. The quality wasn't good enough to show detail, but the fist-sized dents in the latter image were sufficiently clear.

"It appears that shots hit the car between the time it left and when it came back," Adele said. "That implies that at least one member of the expedition was alive after Dorotige left them."

"Can you get me through to the Captal da Lund?" Mon said in a cold voice. "I'd like to discuss the matter with him."

For all the lieutenant's bubbling temper, he didn't bluster when there was a serious task in front of him. That was probably why Daniel liked having Mon as a subordinate.

"I can get you through his blocking program," Adele said. "I don't recommend that, however, since it would alert him to how open his systems are to intrusion. I have full access to his security system, for example. That's where this imagery is coming from."

Mon's mouth opened, then closed. "Christ," he said in a wondering voice, "you *are* a wizard, just like they told me after I got out of a cell on Kostroma. Do you have a plan?"

"I'm working toward one," Adele said carefully. Put as baldly as Mon had, she realized that she should've been discussing matters with the acting captain at every step of the way. "I have some ideas."

Mon touched the intercom key. When the attention call sounded, he said, "Officers to the bridge ASAP. Out."

Mon's words reached Adele through the helmet, through the air directly from his lips, and in a whispering echo from the ceiling speakers down the corridor. He gave her a smile as tight and sharp as the knots spun into a length of barbed wire.

"I'm supposed to handle your communications," Adele said apologetically. "I haven't been communicating very well."

"I'm more interested in people doing their jobs," Mon said, "than in them telling me about it. And right now I'm *damned* sure that Captain Leary feels the same way."

Woetjans and Taley dropped through the dorsal hatch, reaching the bridge a half step before Betts arrived from his sleeping compartment in the warrant officers' quarters. Pasternak had been in the Battle Direction Center for some reason. He came running down the corridor, the crash of his boots warning curious crewmen out of his path.

"Go ahead, Officer Mundy," Mon said. Betts sat at his console where he could import imagery from Adele's display, but the other officers would have to make do with their helmet visors.

"The Captal's dwelling is under Berengian exterritorial juris-
diction," Adele said, "just as the Cinnabar Commission is legally
Cinnabar territory. That means neither the Sexburgan local government nor Admiral Torgis can legally demand access to the
Captal's compound. Furthermore, the Captal is far too important a person on Sexburga for the authorities to be willing to
ignore the legalities."

Tovera had gathered much of the background on her own, even
before Daniel's disappearance created a need for it. She apparently liked to know the power structures wherever she was.

"I'm willing to ignore legalities," Mon said without raising his
voice. He was tapping the index and middle fingers of his right
hand into the opposite palm with the steady deliberation of a
bell-ringer. "I'm willing to hover the *Princess Cecile* on top of the
damned compound and let the exhaust burn it out if that's the
best way to get the captain back."

"Damn right," Woetjans said.

An instant later all the other officers nodded. They *must* know
as surely as Adele did that the Navy Office would have to treat
any such overt violation as piracy, to be punished by the conse-
quent hanging of the officers and crew of the offending vessel.

"That would not be helpful," Adele said in a tone of cold disgust. It wouldn't necessarily be possible, either: the Captal had
prepared defenses to meet just such an attack. Saying as much
would only inflame the officers around her into an attitude of
heroic self-sacrifice. "We need information which we won't be able
to get from a pile of slag and ashes. I—"

The code A501 flashed in red at the upper margin of Adele's
display. It wouldn't echo on the other displays and she'd toggled
off the audio cue; no one knew about it but the Signals Officer.
A502 would have meant the call was from squadron command;
A501 meant—

Adele locked her display and pointed a wand toward Lt. Mon.
"There's a call to the *Princess Cecile* from Commodore Pettin's
own console," she said. She'd lost track of who was on watch;
perhaps she herself was. "Shall I take it, or . . . ?"

Mon shook his head curtly and keyed his audio. "Acting captain," he said without inflection. "Go ahead."

"*This is Commodore Pettin,*" the speaker said. Adele might be reading irritation into Pettin's tone, but the man was certainly not above thundering angrily at any delay in getting the acting captain. Nor was he above regretting a chance to display that righteous indignation. "*I haven't been able to raise your Mr. Leary. Can you tell me what he thinks he's playing at?*"

"No sir," Lt. Mon said. His face, always angular, changed shape as the muscles tightened over his jaw and cheekbones. "Captain Leary proceeded to South Land via the civilian transportation which you had arranged for him, sir."

RCN communications were normally voice-only to minimize bandwidth. That was fortunate in this case, because Mon wasn't a good actor. His voice stayed almost flat, but the fury toward the commodore in his expression could scarcely have been more obvious.

"*I shouldn't be surprised to find insolence in Mr. Leary's subordinates, should I, Mon?*" Pettin said. "*Well, for now you may tell your captain that the squadron has been fully refitted and will lift in twelve hours, not the thirty-six I previously estimated. If Mr. Leary has not returned by then, the* Princess Cecile *will lift without him, under your temporary command. Is that understood?*"

"Yessir," Mon said through clenched teeth. "I understand you very well, Commodore Pettin."

"*By God,*" Pettin snarled, "*for half a piastre I'd slap you in custody and put my third lieutenant aboard that grubby little corvette. Half a piastre!*"

The transmission ended in an electronic click rather than the crash that Pettin obviously would have preferred if the technology permitted it. Adele smiled at the thought, then wiped her face blank lest Mon misunderstand her humor.

"If them buckets lift in twelve hours, they'll all three of 'em lose antennas before we make Strymon," Woetjans said. "They arrived here in crappy shape, and they don't have the crews to make things right even in the three days Pettin allowed at the start."

"He's playing games," Taley agreed, looking even more than usually as if she were following a coffin. "I wouldn't want to be the *Winckelmann*'s machinist, I can tell you that."

"Yeah, but how about us?" Pasternak said. "Can we find the captain in twelve hours? It's six just to fly to where he was supposed to be, right?"

"Officer Mundy has a plan to get information from the Captal da Lund," Mon said, his hands laced together so tightly that the fingertips raised white halos against the tanned backs. "We're going to do whatever it takes to execute that plan."

His face was savage. "*Whatever* it takes," he repeated, but his voice had sunk to a growl.

"All right," said Adele. Her wands twitched, expanding an image to full-display size. "Here's a set of the builders' plans for the Captal's dwelling. You'll note . . ."

The rattle of pebbles in empty ration cans wasn't loud thirty feet away from the tent, but it was so different from the wind's keening overhead that even before Hogg gripped his shoulder Daniel had awakened in a rush. He sat upright and slapped on the commo helmet, saying, "Unit, I'm going to look for an animal with Hogg. Nobody else leave the camp till summoned. Captain out."

"*Unit, don't get fucking trigger happy, it's me and the master out there in the woods!*" Hogg rasped. His helmet would continue to broadcast on the unit push because he hadn't closed the transmission. That was actually a good idea to keep the crew informed of what was going on. It was simply sloppy procedure on Hogg's part, of course.

Daniel had slept in his boots, but he paused to slide the closures tight before stepping out of the warmth of the tent behind Hogg. Barnes rose onto one elbow; he'd be outside as soon as Daniel's eyes were off him, joining his friend Dasi on guard.

It was the guards, Dasi and Sentino, that Daniel had been warning; the other spacers remained asleep. Spacers on a long voyage learned to sleep through any amount of racket and crowding, unless it was their name or their watch that had been called.

Daniel dialed his visor's light enhancement up to daylight normal as he crawled along after Hogg. Sentino squatted near the head of the track, her impeller pointed up at a 45-degree angle to show that it didn't threaten anybody. She lifted her left index finger to acknowledge Daniel; he nodded as he passed her.

The creature in the trap ahead of them was screaming. The sound was high-pitched and as loud as a saw cutting stone. It almost completely drowned the rattling of the cans tied to the snare.

The track curved around a bush whose branches dropped runners to the ground, completely blocking Daniel's view of the camp—and vice versa. When he was out of Sentino's sight, he drew his knife.

Hogg thrust the shovel into the base of a shrub with ghostly white stems, then lifted it with a twist of deceptively strong wrists. He flung the clump out of the way so that Daniel could squat beside him. Nobody whom Hogg had spanked would mistake him for a soft fellow beyond the curve of middle age.

Hogg had set his double noose snare over the mouth of the hole plugged by the sandstone block. The eighty-pound creature which had tripped the triggers now hung in the air, flailing in the grip of the pair of springy branches Hogg had used to tension the trap.

It was white and hairless except for bushes of red-gold hair in its armpits. It had four broad, stubby limbs and a neck so thick and powerfully muscled that the nooses which should have choked the creature unconscious by now merely served to suspend it. It gripped the right-hand tether with blunt claws, jangling the rattles Hogg had attached to the rig to warn him when he'd made a catch.

"By *God*," Hogg muttered, easing closer and cocking the shovel back for a thrust. Its broad blade would let the creature's life out faster than an explosive bullet. "That little bastard's *untying* the damn knots."

"Wait," said Daniel. He put his hand on Hogg's right shoulder, emphasizing the warning. "Don't. We don't need food."

The creature's screams had turned to mewls as Hogg and Daniel came into sight. Its eyes were large and round, set in circuits of bone. When it closed them in terror, sheets of muscle rather than thin skin covered the orbs.

The noose gave way: untied from the springy branch, just as Hogg had said. The remaining noose flicked the creature sideways like the popper of a whip. From behind it looked like a grub worm, ugly beyond easy description. Daniel might have underestimated its weight because there was no hair to bulk up its form.

Hogg swore softly. The creature squirmed both forepaws under the bark cord and tugged outward. Interrogatory chirps were coming from the burrow; Daniel could see fairy lights deep within the ground.

"*Master*," Hogg said, poising the shovel again.

"No!" said Daniel.

The tensioned branch sprang back. In a reciprocal motion, the creature leaped for the opening and vanished within as smoothly as water swirling down a hole.

Hogg was breathing hard. He kept the shovel pointed at the burrow even after the sandstone plug thudded into the opening and was wedged into place with a series of clacks muted by the surrounding bank.

"Did you see its face?" Hogg said. "When it jumped, it looked at us. Did you see?"

"Yes," said Daniel. "I did. Let's get some sleep. We've got a long way to walk tomorrow."

He turned and started back for the tent. He was panting too, though he hadn't been exerting himself.

"Christ, master, it looked *human*," Hogg said.

"Yes," said Daniel. "It did. Let's get some sleep."

CHAPTER EIGHTEEN

Hogg put his hand on Daniel's shoulder, pointed to the ravine ahead of them, and said, "Not a bad place to take a break, master."

Daniel glanced toward the back of the line where Sun, as senior petty officer, should be marching to chivy in stragglers. He was there, all right, but little Vesey was guiding him along. Barnes walked alongside, carrying Sun's pack as well as his own.

Which Hogg had already noticed. "Unit, fall out in the ravine!" Daniel ordered. "Ten minute break! Captain out."

The spacers were tired, but they broke into a jog and grinned as they passed Daniel and Hogg. Dasi took Sun's left arm and helped Vesey move the gunner's mate into a trot also. Sun's legs moved when prodded, but his eyes had no life in them.

"We're going to be carrying him by the end of the day," Hogg murmured. "Fuck me if we're not."

Daniel looked at his rotund servant. "Yes," he said. "Maybe we'd better look for suitable poles here, just in case. We can use the ground cloth for a bed."

He followed Hogg down the bank, which sloped because wind had recently undercut the lip and dumped it as a scree of pebbles and adobe clay onto the base of the ravine. Midway he paused to survey the bank to either side, then went the rest of the way down. The crew had already chopped a small clearing in the brush so that they didn't have to hunch under arched branches.

Sentino sloshed water from the last of their three jerricans into

233

a cup. The osmotic pump they'd set in the underground aquifer overnight had made up the seven or eight gallons they'd drunk from the original supply, but by mid-afternoon of this second day the spacers marching in dry air had absorbed ten gallons.

Sentino held the cup out to Daniel. "Here you go, sir," she said. "You get the cherry."

Rather than argue that he'd wait his turn—and besides, he was thirsty—Daniel took the cup and had it almost to his lips when the smell hit him. If he'd been out in the wind, he might have swallowed down most of the cup unawares, which would have been a great deal worse than going thirsty.

"Stop!" he said. "The water's contaminated. We'll have to discard the container, I'm afraid, because we don't have a means of cleaning it here."

Sun pushed Sentino aside and put his nose to the jerrican's wide mouth. He rose with a look of white rage. "God *damn* Pettin's shit-eating chicken-fucking whoreson excuses for spacers!" he shouted. His near stupor of moments before had passed. "And God damn me for accepting the cans without checking them!"

He picked up the jerrican by one of the paired handles on top and slung it a good twenty feet into the bushes. That was a remarkable throw for five gallons of water with the weight of the container.

"We got the jerricans from the *Winckelmann*, sir," Barnes explained softly. He and Dasi looked as miserable as Sun was angry. "The *Sissie* didn't have anything suitable, but the cruiser's outfitted for ground operations so we figured . . ."

"Traded them a bottle of brandy," Dasi said. Stolen from Delos Vaughn's baggage, no doubt. "It wasn't Mr. Sun's fault, sir, it was me and Barnes did it. And we didn't check the cans."

One of which had been used for some petroleum product, probably extra kerosine for the fuel cells of the *Winckelmann*'s big aircar; and hadn't been properly cleaned afterwards. Nobody on the *Princess Cecile* had noticed the smell before filling the container with water. They'd been in a hurry, of course.

"I think we can blame Commodore Pettin for the difficulty," Daniel said mildly. "Though such a trivial business doesn't seem worthy of an officer of the commodore's demonstrated ability. Vesey, take two men and get the pump working."

"Sir, the flow back where we camped was only a gallon an hour," the midshipman said. "And that was in the rivercourse proper."

"Yes," Daniel said, "but I'm hopeful that we can find a more bountiful source in the meantime. Hogg, what do you think of the block of limestone right over . . ."

As Daniel spoke, he pushed his way along the edge of the ravine, to the right of the collapsed bank. For the first twenty feet it was merely a matter of muscling through twigs as dry as old bones. Just this side of the sandstone inclusion he'd seen as he entered the ravine grew a plant the size and shape of a wicker hassock. Its body consisted of strands curving up from the base to a central stem. A few had released their upper attachment and lay like whips on the ground.

"Ah," said Daniel. "Bring me one of the empty jerricans soonest."

The one filled with contaminated water would be even better, but Daniel didn't blame Sun for letting out his anger. Besides, the thing was done.

Dasi tossed an empty plastic container to Hogg, who passed it in turn to Daniel. "Everybody get down," Daniel said.

He squatted, judged the distance, and threw himself flat as he lobbed the jerrican. It landed in the center of the plant. There was a *whap-pap-pap* as all the remaining strands released simultaneously. The seeds at the ends of each, glass-hard and the size of marbles, flew forty feet in all directions. The can spun into the air, then dropped onto the ruins of the plant.

"A much better idea than bumping into it," Daniel said; preening himself on his observation, but doing it in so quiet a voice that not even Hogg could have heard him. He stepped past the plant to the rock plug.

"I think it's another burrow," Daniel said to his servant. "And I think there must be water inside, don't you? The creatures dig, and it wouldn't be any great trick to trench down into the aquifer so they could lap it up at need."

"Speaking of things I never needed to see again," Hogg muttered. Over his shoulder he called, "Get the shovels up here. The master and me are going after water."

Jeshonyk, a power room technician, brought the shovels. He stepped gingerly over the discharged bush, carefully avoiding putting his foot on any of the now-flaccid strands.

Daniel had seen Jeshonyk tighten a fitting under the Tokamak, working in the full knowledge that a slip wouldn't leave his mates so much as a pinch of ash to bury. He'd been wholly unconcerned by that risk, but the notion of a plant that shot bullets bothered him. *It's all a matter of what you're used to. . . .*

Hogg handed Jeshonyk the impeller in exchange for shovels, then got to work with Daniel from opposite sides of the plug. Daniel could've passed the job off to one of the crewmen, but he probably had more experience with shovels than any of them did. It brought back memories of his boyhood, digging out Black-Scaled Rooters with Hogg.

You could lose your foot at the ankle from a rooter's teeth if you weren't quick. Daniel remembered *that* too.

He hit rock; he moved out a hand's breadth and put the blade in again, using all the strength of his upper body. This time it sank halfway and he stamped it fully in with the heel of his right boot.

He exchanged glances with Hogg, then both levered their shovels to the right and left in unison. A slab of dense clay fell away, baring a foot of the plug. It tapered to both ends and was wedged with smaller stones from within the burrow.

"I'll pull out the rock," Daniel said, thrusting the shovel into the ground beside him where it would be out of the way. "You be ready if anything decides to come out with it."

Hogg's lips pursed in consideration. "Right," he said. "Jeshonyk, I believe I'll take the gun back."

Daniel took the plug in both hands and wriggled it. The block weighed well over a hundred pounds, but nothing beyond its mass bound it into place from this side now that they'd dug the bank away.

Daniel drew back, gasping with controlled effort. Rotating his body he half lifted, half flung the plug into the brush behind him. As smoothly as if the same cam controlled him and his master, Hogg thrust the muzzle of the impeller into the hole—not to shoot, at least not instantly, but to physically prevent anything that tried to leap out.

Nothing did. The opening was lined with rock slabs. They weren't mortared into place, but they certainly weren't a natural occurrence. Distinct patches of light showed in the interior.

"Sir," said Sentino. She'd drawn her knife; with her left hand she unlatched her equipment belt and let it curl to the ground beside her. "I'll fit."

Daniel frowned. "Yes, all right," he said. He locked his visor down so that he could look into the burrow under light enhancement. "Barnes, Dasi. As soon as Sentino is clear, you'll start prying these blocks out so that a larger person—"

He patted his belly deliberately.

"—can get through the opening. And Sun, I'll take the other impeller, please."

"Sir," said the gunner's mate. He handed Daniel the weapon.

When Daniel used that tone, nobody argued—even if they fancied their own marksmanship beyond what they thought their captain was up to. Daniel had more real out-in-the-woods experience than any of the spacers, and he trusted himself *not* to shoot more than he did Sun or even Hogg.

He grinned at Sentino. "Go ahead," he said. "And Jeshonyk, you're probably the next thinnest. Take your gear off and get ready to pull Sentino back by the ankles if she gets stuck."

"Stuck!" Sentino sneered. She squirmed into the opening with as little difficulty as the creature from the night before had shown when it escaped. In truth, there wasn't much difference in weight, and the spacer had more of hers in her legs and arms.

Her boots disappeared down the tunnel. Barnes and Dasi lunged into their work, chopping the shovel blades into the bank and ripping away the dirt. They were used to working together. Even though this task wasn't a familiar one, they didn't get in each other's way.

One slab sagged, then the whole construct collapsed on itself. Barnes thrust his shovel in high, then lowered it and dragged out several feet of rock and dirt with the back edge.

Hogg looked at Daniel and raised an eyebrow in approval. They'd both dug enough holes to appreciate how much strength Barnes's action had required. Dasi leaned forward and cleaned much of the remainder.

"*Unit, I'm through,*" Sentino called over the intercom. "*Holy God, it's a real cavern in here! It opens up just a couple yards in and it's huge!*"

"I'm next," Sun said, stripping off his belt and flexing his shoulders. He grinned apologetically at Daniel. "Get some command authority in there."

Anger and a direct need for him had brought the gunner's mate back from a funk that seemed even more unreal now that it was past. Sun simply wasn't a man you could imagine that happening to.

"Right," said Daniel. "Take a shovel with you. I don't know how far I trust this tunnel now that we've widened it—"

He moved aside. Barnes and Dasi stepped back together with their shovel heads locked, making a final sweep of the debris.

"—and I want us to be able to grub it out from both sides if there's a cave-in."

Sun put his knife in his teeth and took the shovel from Barnes. He thrust it ahead of him as he followed Sentino.

"Barnes," Daniel said, nodding to the man. Anything Barnes's shoulders cleared would probably pass Hogg's belly, so it was a good test. "Miquelon, Jeshonyk, Dasi, Hogg, and me. Hogg, you take your impeller."

Nobody protested at the order of entry, not that a protest was going to change anything. There was a risk to splitting his small force, but Daniel was unwilling to let one or two of his personnel scout a burrow system that held scores or possibly hundreds of the creatures who'd dug it. A team of eight with an impeller could support itself.

"Vesey, you and your section will watch our gear and the entrance from outside," Daniel continued. Barnes had grunted his way into the tunnel and Miquelon was ready to follow; she held her equipment belt ahead of her rather than dropping it on the ground as the others had. "You'll have a shovel and the other impeller. Don't get frozen on the hole. There have to be other entrances, and we don't need whoever's inside—"

He'd meant to say "whatever," not "whoever."

"—to swarm around us from behind, all right? Over."

Vesey and Matahurd stood in sight at the corner of a bush whose tasseled crown fluttered occasionally like a stand of ultramarine flags. The midshipman trotted forward to take the weapon and shovel, speaking briskly. Daniel couldn't hear the words, so she was addressing the members of her section alone over the intercom.

Daniel nodded mentally, though his head didn't really move. She had the makings of a good officer.

"I don't expect you'll have any trouble," Daniel said as he gave Vesey the impeller. "But if I were sure of that, I wouldn't leave a guard to begin with."

Hogg, wheezing like a rooting sow, thrust himself into the burrow. Daniel waited a comfortable five seconds and followed. It was tight, but never so constricting that he wondered if he was going to be caught. At the far end of a tunnel no longer than the six feet Sentino had estimated was—

Well, was a paradise of pastel light and plants which swooped toward the twenty-foot ceiling like constructions of cast plastic. The spacers wandered among them in amazement. The air was noticeably more humid than that in the ravine outside.

"Don't get out of sight of one another!" Daniel said. Besides humidity, the air was perfumed. Gnatlike insects drifted through the mist of light, and—

"Where's the light coming from?" Daniel called, lifting his visor out of the way. He didn't need its enhancement nor protection from windblown grit. "Hogg, can you tell?"

"Sir, I think it's just blocks of quartz built into the ceiling for light guides," Jeshonyk said, pointing his arm as Daniel joined him under one of the bright patches. It was a good eight feet in diameter, made of quartz wedged into place with other bits of stone. The contruction was similar to that of the entranceway lining.

"Naw, it can't be," Dasi said, prodding one of the gorgeous plants with the point of his knife. "We'd have seen it from up above. Look, you can see a whole line of them down this tunnel. No way we could've missed all of that."

Daniel squinted. There were at least . . . ten bright patches in the ceiling, with more merging into the distance beyond just as Dasi said. The separation between pairs was about thirty feet, making Daniel's estimate of possibly hundreds of creatures in the burrow now seem absurdly low. Besides this central aisle of plantings, narrow passages led off to either side.

Daniel considered the pattern of light and shadow above him. The quartz blocks weren't uniformly translucent, and the faces refracted light so that the composite lens looked as though a giant spiderweb lay across it. Even so, Daniel could see that the western edge was brighter than the east.

"I believe Jeshonyk's right when he says light guides," Daniel said. "Given the depth of the floor here beneath the bottom of the ravine, there's about six feet of roof. If the inlets slant outward, they'll catch some light whenever the sun's up—but there won't be any huge mass of quartz on the surface like there is down here at the outlet."

"What kinda animal does that?" a spacer asked. Nobody replied, perhaps because the answer was too obvious when you thought about it.

Sun dug the shovel into the cavern wall, then withdrew it with a puzzled expression. Only a trickle of dirt followed the blade. "Hey, Captain?" he said. "There's plastic on the walls or something."

Daniel walked over to the petty officer, rounding a plant set into the floor in a stone-lined tub. All the cavern's vegetation was soft-bodied though it was more the size of trees than ordinary plants. The genera were unfamiliar to Daniel; certainly they weren't native to Sexburga's arid surface today.

"I know what it is," offered Dasi, holding up his left index finger. On it gleamed a drop of clear sap from the wound he'd pricked in the plant he was examining. "Hell, they gotta cover the walls with something or it'd all fall in, right?"

"How's chances we find some water and get the hell outa here?" Hogg muttered. He held the impeller across his chest, ready to spin in any direction and throw the weapon to his shoulder. He was perfectly poised, but he was also as uncomfortable as Daniel had ever seen him.

Daniel touched the wall with his bare hand. As Sun had said, there was a clear, slightly resilient, coating over the gritty clay. It felt warm to the touch.

"Yes, we'll do that," Daniel said, but his mind was more on the wonder of this *place* than it was on Hogg's question or the more general business of reaching the beacon to summon help. They wouldn't delay here—they had their duty, after all—but by heaven! what a report Commodore Pettin and the civilized universe would get. "This was perhaps the most scientifically useful piece of make-work and treachery that I've ever heard of."

"Hey, look!" Sentino cried. She darted into the passage.

Daniel heard a *spreek!* that might have been Sentino but probably wasn't. He stabbed his knife into the sidewall to free his hands and ducked to follow the crewman down the passage. He wasn't sure even Sentino would clear the low ceiling if she stood upright.

He supposed she was still carrying her knife in her hand. She almost had to be, since she'd left the sheath with the rest of her belt gear. Grabbing a creature with teeth like the one last night bare-handed was dangerous, but Daniel would just as soon Sentino not stab—

"I got—" she called. There was a tearing-paper sound. Sentino staggered back into Daniel's arms; the knife slipped from her flaccid right hand. Dropping the remains of a fist-sized puffball on the passage floor, the creature she'd grabbed with her left squirmed away. It began to dig furiously in the sidewall with spadelike forepaws.

There was a dry smell in the air, dizzying though not unpleasant. Daniel slapped his visor down with his left hand and felt the filters clamp his nostrils.

The hairless creature looked sideways at him through the spraying dirt and gave a wail of despair. Daniel grabbed Sentino under the arms and backed, pulling her with him. She was a dead weight, but he could feel her heart beating strongly through her coveralls.

Something came around the bend just beyond where the creature was digging into the sidewall. It completely filled the passage, brushing cascades of soil down where its shoulders rubbed. Daniel couldn't get a good look at it since his own body blocked most of the light coming from the main gallery, but he could tell that it was black and bigger than he was.

The smaller creature went "*Wheek! Wheek! Wheek!*" and vanished, apparently dropping into an adjacent passage. The newcomer paused, its eyes focused on Daniel and Sentino. Its four canines projected forward to crisscross like paired ice-tongs, perfect tools to take living prey. It hunched like a cat preparing to spring.

Daniel stepped over his crewman's body. "Unit, get Sentino out of here!" he shouted. "Somebody drag her—"

The predator flowed toward him like a snake striking. It pushed off with its spatulate forepaws but folded them back against its sides in the course of the motion.

Daniel caught it by the neck, shoulder-broad and covered with a ruff of bristles. The fangs clashed just in front of his visor. The impact was like that of a charging bull. Daniel had braced himself, but it threw him back anyway.

His right boot tramped something soft—Sentino's outflung hand, but he lifted his foot and felt her snatched back with no more ceremony than a case of rations would get. That was fine: dinner was just what she'd be if they didn't get her back quickly.

Daniel couldn't hold the creature, didn't *want* to hold it, but if he didn't continue fighting it would push him over backward. Then the only question was whether it'd tear his throat out or start by devouring his belly.

"Watch this bastard!" he wheezed. "I don't know how big . . ."

His toes skidded slowly backward down the passage. He felt his left knee start to buckle. He twisted that foot sideways in a desperate attempt to get more traction.

The jaws closed again. This time the tip of one lower fang hit Daniel's visor and slammed his helmet against the passage roof. Despite the shock-absorbant liner, Daniel's consciousness shattered into white light. As he felt himself going over, he kicked out blindly with both feet.

The predator made its first sound, a *whuff* of surprise as Daniel's bootheels hammered its muzzle. It flowed forward again.

Hogg, leaning over his master, socketed the impeller in the predator's right eye and squeezed the trigger. The *whack!* of the weapon's circuitry merged with the *CRASH!* of dense bone disintegrating at the impact of the hypersonic pellet.

The creature lurched into the central gallery and sprawled, its paddlelike hind legs covering Daniel's torso. Its body struck Hogg and sent him spinning away, though he still kept hold of the impeller. Sun drove the shovel into the creature's neck; it skidded off, gouging the floor and narrowly missing Daniel's hand. Other spacers were hacking with their knives.

"Get back!" Daniel shouted. "It's dead! Back away before you hurt somebody!"

He clutched his hands in to his chest, reminded by the comment that "somebody" might very well be him. The creature's head and feet twisted upward in a convulsion; Daniel used the respite to snatch his body clear of a weight that he hadn't been able to shift with his own strength.

He got shakily to his feet. Barnes put an arm around him and lifted him several steps back to where the creature's spastic movements couldn't knock him down again. Its limbs were modified for digging, but claws that cut through rocky clay would be just as destructive if they met human bone and muscle.

The creature flopped over on its spine and finished dying. Hogg's pellet had lifted the back off its skull, but the face wasn't seriously damaged save that one eyesocket was empty.

It weighed half a ton. It was as ugly as anything Daniel had ever seen. The foul breath that had blown from its mouth as it attacked now hung over the body like a miasma.

Apart from the crossed fangs, however, the face was undeniably human.

The *Princess Cecile*'s utility aircar was little more than a frame linking a quartet of fan nacelles to the open-topped cabin where Adele, Tovera, and two spacers sat on benches of metal webbing. Adele shifted. The seats weren't as uncomfortable as they looked, but they looked *very* uncomfortable.

Tavastierna landed with only a moderate bang and bounce. That was a creditable performance given the car's heavy load, but Adele scowled anyway. She knew it wasn't fair to expect professional competence from a rigger who hadn't driven an aircar in months, but "fair" didn't have much to do with the present situation. The operation had very little margin for error.

"Shut off the motors!" she said, shouting to be heard over the whine of the fans spinning at zero angle of attack. Tavastierna looked surprised since their helmet intercoms would easily damp that level of external noise, but he obeyed without question.

"I've cut off helmet communications from now until we execute the entry," Adele said as the blades wound down octave by octave. "They could be overheard. I doubt whether the Captal's staff is that alert, but I don't choose to take a chance with the lives of our shipmates."

And our own, come to think of it, though that isn't the first priority for me at the moment, she added internally.

Tavastierna had landed behind a ridge whose front side was a little over a thousand yards from the knoll on which the Captal da Lund had built his fortress. Even Adele could have climbed the slope on this side; Dorst and Tavastierna wouldn't raise a sweat. The weight of the guns the men carried—Dorst a stocked impeller, Tavastierna a submachine gun for the team's own protection—wasn't a significant factor either.

"Dorst, are you still comfortable with this?" Adele said. "Tovera can take over now if you have any concerns. Being unwilling to kill another human being is nothing to be ashamed of."

"No, ma'am," the midshipman agreed. "But you don't need to worry. I've trained for this."

When Adele checked the crew list for a sniper, she'd learned to her surprise that Dorst had been on the Academy marksmanship team and had won trophies in long-range competition. He'd assured her that his training involved hostage simulations rather than merely bull's-eye targets. He'd never done it for real—killed—but Adele well knew the effectiveness of training like what Dorst described.

A six-wheeled delivery van was trundling down the road from Spires; it would reach them in a few minutes. Adele and Tovera would join the spacers in the cargo box during the time the vehicle was out of sight of the Captal's residence, unless she decided to leave this job to Tovera after all.

Adele's servant looked at her and smiled. "He'll be all right, mistress," Tovera said. "If anything goes wrong, you or me can fix it then."

"Nothing's going to go wrong," Dorst said stolidly.

"No, I don't suppose it is," Adele said. She tried to smile. It doubtless looked forced, but her natural expression at times like these was something that only a sociopath like Tovera could find humor in. "Dorst, Tavastierna—you'd better get into position. Captain Leary is counting on you."

The spacers nodded and started up the slope at an amazingly fast pace. They moved like a rigger and a healthy young athlete, not a librarian with a tendency to trip over her own feet, of course.

It was odd what you remembered. The most vivid recollection Adele had of the duel she'd fought when she was sixteen wasn't the face of the boy when her bullet hit: it was instead the pink mist in the air behind him, a mush of blood and fresh brains. The simulators she'd used for hours in her parents' townhouse hadn't prepared her for that.

The van's suspension squealed and rattled as it approached. They—the Republic of Cinnabar, paying with funds which Mistress Sand had put at Adele's disposal—were renting the vehicle for a sum not much short of what it had cost new. Just in case, though, the vehicle's Sexburgan owner and its regular driver were aboard the *Princess Cecile* with all they wanted to drink. Half a dozen spacers were sitting with them to make sure that they didn't decide to leave and maybe call the Captal.

Tovera shifted her body, working muscle groups with a minimum of movement. She was perfectly cool, but after all she had no more emotion than the submachine gun in her hands. She looked at Adele and said, "I wouldn't be any better at long range than you would, mistress. Though I suppose either of us could manage if the need arose."

"I suppose," Adele agreed coldly. Why should it bother her that Tovera considered her mistress and herself merely a pair of killers at this moment? It was true, after all.

Unlike Adele, Tovera had no conscience. But that wouldn't make any difference. It never had before.

The van pulled up beside the aircar. Koop was driving, wearing a Sexburgan caftan and a soft cap. The rest of the team were in RCN utilities, comfortable and unobtrusively colored. If this event went wrong, there was no chance of hiding who was responsible for it, no matter what they wore.

Well, Adele didn't intend that it go wrong.

Woetjans lifted the roller gate and jerked Adele into the cargo box. Bemish offered Tovera a hand, but she'd already hopped aboard with her usual economy. Tovera didn't look graceful, but she moved without error. It was rather like watching a door open and close. The motion was without art, but it was always the same and always flawless.

"Go!" Woetjans shouted, and the van accelerated from its rolling stop. There were five spacers in the back; Koop drove with a submachine gun under a towel on the seat beside him. More personnel would have crowded the vehicle and wouldn't, in the opinion of Woetjans and Mon, have contributed to the success of the operation.

There were twenty-one people in the Captal's compound; the number hadn't changed since Dorotige had returned from South

Land. They were on alert, but that was different from really *being* alert. The van delivered food to the compound on a regular schedule. The guards would search the vehicle, but they wouldn't be surprised to see it arriving.

Adele smiled faintly. The surprise would come shortly after that arrival.

Adele looked at the faces around her, lighted through the opera window in one of the door's upper slats. "Is everyone ready for this?" she asked, more because the spacers seemed to expect something from her than out of real concern for the answer. "Ain't we just!" said Liebig, hugging his submachine gun to his chest. The others' guttural sounds of approval blended well with the groans of the van's suspension.

Adele put her visor down momentarily to check the distance to the Captal's front gate. She still wasn't comfortable with getting information from the helmet display; it made her resentful and more than a little angry not to be able to be able to use her personal data unit in normal fashion.

Normally she wouldn't be bouncing around in the back of a delivery van. Besides, the helmet display worked perfectly well as it read down the distance in yards: 831, 830, 829—a lurch as the vehicle rounded a switchback and its transmission shifted to a lower gear—827 . . .

Moronick began to sing under his breath: "*When I'm home you call me sugar honey, but when I'm gone . . .*" His thumb covered and uncovered the receiver switch that controlled his impeller's power. It was in the off, safe, position. He didn't turn it on, but the touch of the plastic fascinated him.

" . . . *you run around and play.*"

Adele was the only one of those present who didn't carry a shoulder weapon, either a submachine gun or a semiautomatic impeller throwing heavy slugs. There was a small pistol in her left side pocket. It was the weapon she knew, the weapon she pointed as if her eye and not her hand controlled it.

It would do. It had done many times in the past.

The van slowed gradually, then slewed shrieking to the right as a brake grabbed. 14, 13, 11 . . . Koop corrected with his steering wheel and brought them to a juddering halt.

Adele could hear the wind now, blowing the last of the grit

kicked up by the truck's wheels against the metal body. "Hey, where's Mariakakis?" an unfamiliar voice called.

"Mariakakis tells the boss he wants a raise," Koop said. The cab door opened, then slammed. "Boss tells Mariakakis fuck your raise, you're not worth what I pay you now. Mariakakis says fuck your job, then. And me, I get promoted when I just started work."

Adele blinked. Her impression of Koop was that he was rather more dense than the run of spacers. She'd told him to say, "Mariakakis is sick today," if asked. Koop's embellishment was wholly convincing, even though she *knew* it was nonsense.

"Yeah, well, get the back open and let's take a look," the gateman said, his voice moving along the side of the van as boots crunched on the road metal. Everyone in the cargo compartment squatted. Woetjans handed her impeller to Bemish and drew an arm's-length piece of high-pressure tubing from beneath her belt.

"Dorotige's got a wild hair up his ass and not letting us into town when we're off duty," the gateman continued. "There better be extra booze in this—"

The door rattled at Koop's touch, then shot upward as fast as Liebig and Gansevoort could raise it from the inside.

"—shipment—*hey*!!"

The gateman was a lanky fellow whose ginger whiskers tried to cover serious acne scars. Woetjans grabbed his throat with her left hand.

WHACK! sounded from the top of the stone guard tower.

Woetjans rang the tubing off the gateman's skull, knocking off his mauve beret and putting a welt across his forehead. He went limp in her grip. Adele grabbed the keypad chained to his belt and punched in 5154, the code that raised the gate today. She could have entered the compound's security system through its communications link, but this was faster and simpler.

The body of the guard who'd watched from the tower's walkway fell flat on the ground beside the vehicle. There was a hole precisely between her staring eyes; apart from that she looked perfectly normal. From the amount of matter oozing through the fan of her hair, the slug had removed the back of her skull like the top of a soft-boiled egg.

The gate's two leaves cammed open; the row of spikes beyond began to sink into concrete sheaths. Koop scrambled back into the cab, pausing to snatch up the hat he'd lost in the flurry of activity.

The door at the foot of the guard tower was open. Adele and Gansevoort jumped out of the cargo compartment as Woetjans slung the unconscious gateman behind her rather than leave him on the ground. The sprawled corpse couldn't be seen through the open gate.

"Go!" Adele said, but it was only her adrenaline-speeded senses that made it seem that Koop was delaying. The van jerked into motion, making those in the cargo compartment sway forward and back. Under cover of the vehicle, Adele and the spacer with her darted into the tower.

The van's back door was still open. Woetjans had retrieved her impeller from Liebig. The bosun's face had a detached expression, as though she were deciding who to assign to a mildly onerous duty.

Stairs led up from the anteroom of the guard tower. Through the other door was an office with a couch and refrigerator besides the control station. Adele sat at the control station while Gansevoort took the stairs two at a time, heading for the automatic impeller on top of the tower. He was Sun's striker, working toward a rating of gunner's mate.

The display was swirling pearly light. Adele brought up the main screen. A dozen keystrokes took her through the interlocks to first enter the security system, then to take complete control of all the compound's electronics. She displayed the courtyard imagery in a corner so that as she worked she could see the van driving past the barracks to the separated power room.

The power room door stood open, so she didn't have to bother unlocking it. Woetjans had a crate of explosives in the van against the possibility that the door would be closed with a manual bolt, but Adele was glad they could avoid noise for the moment.

Her control station had a touchplate. Adele's finger's danced across it, moving with precision if not what she would call verve. First she shut down communications to the other two guard towers, then switched their power off as well. The automatic impellers could still be fired, but without power traverse the guards would have to horse the weapons around manually to aim toward the courtyard. That would take minutes that they most certainly would not be allowed.

The van stopped in front of the power room. Woetjans led the four spacers with her into the squat building. The van, with Tovera now in the cab with Koop, made a U-turn and drove toward the Captal's residence.

Woetjans looked out of the power room and waved her free hand. "Ready, Gansevoort?" Adele called over the intercom.

"Ready!" Gansevoort answered, so loudly that his voice echoed down the stairwell. The building vibrated as his impeller turned inward.

Adele keyed the fire alarms for the barracks and the residence building. An electronic wail filled the compound.

Nothing happened for a moment. Adele disconnected the power to both buildings. A moment later a servant wearing puffed red-and-yellow garments ran from the residence and three half-dressed guards from the barracks. They looked around in a mixture of anger and confusion.

"Stay in the open!" Adele boomed over the public-address system. She turned off the siren. Woetjans and three of her team walked toward the barracks, their weapons aimed. "No one will be har—"

The house servant turned. His arms flailed and he sprawled across the threshold at the feet of two more liveried servants.

Tovera got out of the van, pointing her submachine gun one-handed in what might have looked a negligent fashion to anyone who hadn't just seen her shoot. She beckoned the two surviving servants toward her with her free hand. One remained transfixed; the other knelt, clasped his hands, and lowered his head in prayer.

"No one will be harmed if you cooperate!" Adele said. Her amplified voice rumbled through the open doorways, cold and hectoring. The guards who were already in the open didn't try to run in the face of the spacers' guns, but no more came from the barracks.

Adele's brain warned her of movement. Instinct slid the pistol from her pocket, but the threat showed on her panoramic display rather than in the room with her.

"Northeast tower!" she shouted. "He's—"

The tower guard braced himself on the catwalk rail, holding his pistol in both hands, and fired across the courtyard. Dust flew from the facade of the residence.

Tovera turned like mercury flowing. Even before she could fire, the top of the northeast tower erupted into dust, chunks of stone, and streaks of vivid color where osmium slugs struck the turret's metal fittings. Adele's control station vibrated with the violence of Gansevoort's long burst above her.

Gansevoort stopped firing. Woetjans' team and the guards in front of the barracks had thrown themselves on the ground. Bits continued to drop off the crumbled tower: the slugs had chewed away the west face of the railing and turret. The wind drifted dust from the compound like torn russet gauze. The only visible portion of the guard was his right arm lying among the debris in the courtyard, severed at the elbow by fifty grains of osmium moving at Mach 8.

"Everyone in the barracks," Adele said, "come out unarmed, *now!* In thirty seconds we'll begin raking the building until it falls in and crushes everyone who hasn't been killed by the projectiles."

Another man came from the barracks, doubled over as if he were walking into a storm. Liebig taped his arms behind him. Two more guards crept out, their hands high. A woman came from the south tower, stumbling in her haste.

Woetjans cupped her hands and shouted in the direction of the gate. Adele grimaced and switched the helmet intercoms live again. "Unit, your helmets work now," she said. "Signals out."

"*Signals, that's everybody from here,*" Woetjans voice said in synchrony with her lips on the other side of the courtyard. "*There's six servants and a guard in the residence with the boss, they say. Team One over.*"

"Team One, all right," Adele said, rising to her feet. "Leave a guard on the captives and join me at the residence. Ah, out."

She'd never get used to RCN communications protocols. Of course, communications had never interested her very much. Knowledge for its own sake had been her focus.

She was smiling as she walked from the gate tower toward the residence building. A great deal had changed since she met Lt. Daniel Leary.

For the most part the spacers were exhilarated from the operation's present success. Bemish was babbling that by *God* we're showing these wogs how it's done, but Adele didn't let her distaste for the vulgar chauvinism touch the surface of her mind.

Koop alone looked reserved. That was perhaps his normal reaction to things going well, but equally it might have had something to do with the bloodstains on his uniform where he'd knelt while securing the two living servants.

Tovera switched the ammunition tube under her weapon's barrel for a fully loaded one from the pouch on her left side. Her eyes darted in all directions, and her smile was as thin and cold as a streak of hoarfrost.

"Three servants are in the kitchen, hiding behind the central counter," Adele said. "They may as well stay there for now."

She shook her head at the silliness of anyone thinking they could hide in a building with a surveillance system as complete as the Captal's. Even his private suite was covered, though he probably believed he'd switched the cameras off when he realized that the compound was under attack.

"The owner is in his bedroom on the second floor," Adele continued. "One guard is in the main room of the suite with a gun trained on the door. That has a mechanical bar, so we'll have to blow it down."

"Right," Woetjans said. "That's you, Jiangsi."

The maintenance tech nodded. He was leaning against the doorjamb so that it supported some of the weight of his pack.

"Mistress?" Liebig asked. He'd looked hungrily at the Captal's big aircar when he trotted past it beside the bosun. "The guy inside isn't the one who flew the captain away, is he? Because if he is, he might know . . ."

"The driver, Dorotige, was the last one to come out of the barracks," Tovera said. Like Adele herself, she was using imagery from the compound's internal system to view their opponents.

The tip of Tovera's tongue touched her lips. "The man inside, preparing to die for his master, is named benYamani. There's no reason we shouldn't take him up on his offer."

"We'll give him another chance to surrender anyway," Adele said. She nodded to the open door. "Let's go."

In Adele's normal state of mind she would have been irritated by Tovera's enthusiasm for killing. At present—

She glanced down at the cratered back of the servant who'd tried to run. Blood was congealing in the holes where velocity had disintegrated the ten-grain pellets like tiny bombs when they struck.

If there is a God, may She forbid that I ever find this sort of business normal.

Woetjans left a man in the doorway and another in the foyer, then led the way up the staircase. Adele had locked the kitchen door and shut off the elevator, so there was no need of a guard down here. They wouldn't need another man upstairs either, though, so she didn't comment on the bosun's arrangements.

An ornate metal door stood in the center of the second floor's semicircular anteroom. It was finished to look like bronze, but Adele knew from the contractor's specifications that it was actually tungsten over a core of lime.

"System," Adele said as they faced the door. She'd set the compound's intercom to be cued by her helmet. "Mister ben-Yamani, unbolt the door and surrender. We won't harm you or your master. We've come here to get information, that's all."

There was no response. "Mistress?" Tovera said.

Adele grimaced. It was so unnecessary. "Yes, go ahead," she said.

"Officer Woetjans," Tovera said, holding out her submachine gun. "Let me trade weapons with you for a moment."

The bosun looked startled but handed over the stocked impeller when Adele nodded. Tovera, aiming by the image projected on her visor, pointed the weapon at the wall to the right of the armored door.

The *whack!* of the shot was startlingly loud in the enclosed space. The slug's driving band flashed as it ionized; it was a ghostly yellow glow remained in the air for several seconds. The wall was of thick structural plastic, intended to deaden sound but not to stop rounds from an impeller. Chips flew into the anteroom and a cavity the size of a soup dish spalled off the inside.

The slug continued straight and true. The waiting guard leaped up, rolled over a table, and fell prone across the hand-knotted carpet. His blood splashed a broad pattern around the hole the slug took through the wall of the Captal's bedroom.

Tovera gave the impeller back to Woetjans. "That should do," she said.

Adele squatted and took out her personal data unit; the helmet's inputs weren't sufficient for what she needed now. At a nod from the bosun, Jiangsi shrugged off his pack and began lifting out blocks of explosive with the blasting caps already in preformed sockets.

"Wait," said Adele, concentrating on her display. "We could do more damage than we intend with that."

"You want me to take down the wall instead of the door, mistress?" Jiangsi offered. "That won't be hard."

"*Wait*," Adele repeated.

She turned on the vision panel above the Captal's huge circular bed and routed to it the output of the security camera in the main room of suite; she focused the image closely on what was left of the guard's head. The slug must have been tumbling slightly when it came through the wall.

"Captal da Lund!" Adele said through the intercom. "We will let you and all your surviving personnel go free once you've answered our questions about what happened to Lieutenant Leary. Open the door to your suite. If we have to blow our way in, there's a possibility you'll be killed and a near certainty that you'll be badly injured."

"No 'near' about that," Woetjans muttered. Her big scarred hand patted the length of tubing in her belt. She'd wrapped tape around one end for a better grip.

"You've got thirty seconds," Adele continued. "I'm going to begin counting down. Thirty, twenty-nine—"

The man cowering in the bedroom suddenly snatched open his door. "Wait!" he cried. "For the love of God, wait!"

Adele rose to her feet and put her data unit back in its pocket. She lifted her visor; she didn't need to watch further. The spacers tensed, but Tovera merely shook her head in disappointment.

The bar scraped on the other side of the door. When Woetjans heard it click free of the staples, she kicked the panel open with the heel of her boot. It bloodied the Captal's nose as it knocked him down.

Adele had never seen the exiled dictator in the flesh. He would have looked distinguished under most circumstances, but blubbering so that tears streaked the blood on his cheeks was not his best moment. Woetjans and Jiangsi thrust their guns in his face.

"Please, please, I'll pay you more money than you ever dreamed!" the Captal cried. "I'll make you rich for life, only don't kill me!"

It was funny in its way. "Tovera," Adele said. "How much money would it take for you not to kill this gentleman if I told you to do it?"

"If you allowed me to do it, you mean, mistress," Tovera said. They were playing a game, she and her mistress, but every word of it was true. She shrugged. "I don't need money, mistress."

Adele was unable to keep to keep from sneering when she looked down at the sniveling exile, but perhaps that was the right expression for the purpose anyway. "When you've told us how to find Lieutenant Leary," she said evenly, "we'll release you and your personnel."

"They're all right, they're perfectly safe," the Captal said. He'd pulled his knees up to his chest and his fingers covered his face, pressing to either side of his nose. Was it broken, or was it simply fear that had so unmanned him? "It was nothing to do with me, really, I was just helping Vaughn out of friendship for his father. Getting your captain out of the way so that no one would give the alarm until Vaughn was safely back on Strymon."

Woetjans tapped the Captal's left wrist with her impeller muzzle. The heat shield was still hot from the recently fired slug; the prisoner jerked his hand down with a cry of terror.

"*Where?*" Woetjans said. "Or I'll tie your dick to the aircar and fly back to town. So help me God."

"At Site Two on South Land!" the Captal cried. "Dorotige took them there, he can find them again. Besides, it's in the car's navigation system!"

Adele frowned. "Is that true?" she asked the bosun.

Woetjans shrugged. "Likely enough," she said. "Liebig'll know."

She switched to intercom. Her lips continued to move, but the helmet's dampers smothered the words. A moment later she nodded and said, "Yeah, that's right unless they cleared the system. Liebig's going to check the car right now."

"We weren't going to do Leary any harm," the Captal said. "Just keep him out of the way till your fleet had gone. He had plenty of food with him and there's water at the site. And then Dorotige would have flown him and his servants back."

The Captal had brought his right hand to his face again but seemed generally to have relaxed. A good sign, Adele supposed. The heat shield hadn't even raised a blister. From the way he'd jumped, one might have thought his hand was being singed off.

"Mistress?" Woetjans said. "Liebig says that's right, the navigation record's still intact. If he can use that car, likely he can drive back himself to get the captain."

"We'll use the car," Adele said. "We'll take this gentleman and Mr. Dorotige with us as guides, however. Just in case."

The Captal slowly lowered his hands and let his legs extend slightly. "And then you'll let me go?" he said, his voice husky with fear.

"Yes, we will," Adele said. "And if Daniel and all his crew, his *servants* as you called them, are all right, we'll even leave you food."

Woetjans grinned, though she still had a worried expression. "Let's get going," she said. "I don't see any way in hell we're going to get the captain back before time the squadron's supposed to lift, but maybe the *Winckelmann*'ll lose all her thrusters when she lights 'em. There's a chance."

Jiangsi rolled the Captal over on his belly and taped his wrists. Woetjans looked sourly at the captive, then said to Adele, "Ah, mistress? How do you figure to go on from here?"

"Get all the prisoners out of the compound as planned," Adele said. "Dorst and Tavastierna will fly to the ship in their vehicle, the rest of us will go there in the Captal's. I suppose Koop should drive the van back; we said we'd return it."

"Mistress, time's *awful* short," the bosun said.

Adele nodded. "Yes," she said. "But I need to inform Lieutenant Mon about what I'm doing, which I'll do face-to-face rather than in any fashion that could be intercepted or recorded. He may request that Tovera and I carry on from here alone so that the ship can lift with as full a crew as possible."

"Right," said Woetjans. She bent and lifted the Captal by his bound wrists. He screamed until he got his feet under him to take the weight from his arms. "And the Senate may make me Speaker tomorrow—but the smart money bets that I'll be collecting bosun's pay for the next while."

She slung the Captal toward the stairwell. "Let's go tell Lieutenant Mon," she said, "that we'll be a while bringing the captain back to the *Sissie*."

CHAPTER NINETEEN

"We're about to land, ma'am," Jiangsi warned, looking out the side of the servants' compartment.

"All right," Adele said, but her mind was on entering the names and descriptions of the members of the conspiracy as the Captal Da Lund remembered them. He and Dorotige were curled on the compartment floor, their limbs taped. The Captal babbled while his guard chief remained as silent as a corpse except to answer direct questions.

Adele was making an audio recording of the information, but by entering key words manually on her personal data unit she put it in a far more accessible place: her current memory. She didn't know what she might need in the future, so she learned as much as she could.

Liebig rotated the aircar 180 degrees on its axis. They'd flown so smoothly that Adele had forgotten that she was in a vehicle; now she tilted forward out of the jump seat. Only Jiangsi's snatching arm kept her from toppling onto the prisoners.

"There you go, ma'am," Jiangsi said politely. "Liebig's putting us stern-on to the ship so that when the hatch opens—"

As he spoke, he unlocked and lifted the aircar's rear door. Liebig had put down on the quay just a few feet short of the *Princess Cecile*'s gangplank.

"—nobody who shouldn't gets to see our cargo here." He looked down at the prisoners with an expression of contempt. "Lieutenant Mon'll be waiting for you, ma'am."

More to the point, Woetjans was already outside the compartment with her arm crooked to keep Adele from tripping as she got out. Adele put her data unit away and grabbed the bosun's arm; she wasn't one to injure herself when she might be needed through a foolish overestimate of her abilities.

Adele started for the gangplank. Woetjans held her. "Mr. Mon's on his way, mistress," the bosun said; which was perfectly obvious, once Adele looked at her surroundings instead of focusing on her plans for the immediate future.

Tovera and Woetjans' team stood beside the aircar, their weapons less incongruous now than they would have seemed the day they landed. The *Princess Cecile*'s dorsal turret was not only raised but live: the plasma cannon slowly traversed the corniche above the harbor. Only two ventilation hatches were open. From them projected automatic impellers on mounts which Taley and her mate had welded from tube stock. The four guards at the entrance hatch were alert and completely sober.

Mon crossed the gangplank with the swift grace of a rigger. He wore his utilities and an equipment belt including a holstered pistol, something Adele had never seen an officer on shipboard do.

"Yes?" he said. Drunk, Mon became angrily morose, but he was always intense when sober. At the moment he looked as though you could etch glass with the angles of his face.

"Daniel and the others were marooned on South Land," Adele said, detailing the information in as bald and precise a manner as she could. "They're supposed to be unharmed. We have a pair of prisoners in the vehicle who don't seem unduly concerned about what'll happen to them when we locate our friends, so we can probably accept that as true."

She cleared her throat. "I'll be taking the Captal's aircar to pick up the expedition," she said, "but even if everything works out we can't possibly get back to Spires before the squadron's scheduled departure."

"The *Princess Cecile* will be here when the captain arrives to resume command," Mon said. Though his voice was emotionless, his scowl could have meant anything. "Choose what personnel you need. Oh—and will you want the *Sissie*'s jeep as well? Dorst and Tavastierna returned a few minutes be—"

The late-afternoon sky above the line of cliffs flashed amber, then faded to the pale grayish white of moments before. Adele felt the shockwave through her bootsoles. The water in the harbor rose in tight conical waves. All around the harbor, spacers looked up.

The airborne blast was measurable seconds later. It sounded more like a huge steam leak than an explosion.

"Right on time!" said Palaccios, the engineer's mate who'd wedged open the compound's power room before running to the aircar. He and Jiangsi clasped arms and pounded one another on the back.

"I don't think we'll need the jeep," Adele said.

"Anything I should know about?" Mon said, pointing a finger skyward. He sounded straightforward rather than sardonic. The flare had dissipated, but the western sky continued to sparkle as ions snatched free electrons and reverted to their normal state.

"Old gray-hair's fusion bottle blew," Jiangsi said, jerking his thumb toward the servants' compartment where the Captal lay bound. "If the safety doors'd all been shut, the building's roof'd have blowed off and that'd be the end of it. Since the doors *wasn't* shut, all that plasma vented out the front at the fancy house across the courtyard."

"Was anybody inside the compound?" Mon asked, interested but not concerned.

"Not unless somebody decided to be a hero after we shooed 'em all outa the front gate," Woetjans said. "There might've been some bodies from before then that nobody's going to be finding now. They won't find fuck-all since the plasma scoured out the inside of the compound."

Mon grinned broadly, the first time Adele had seen him wear a positive expression. "Good work, Officer Mundy," he said. "It's a pleasure to have you under my temporary command. Now, get off to South Land and return Captain Leary to where he belongs."

"If Commodore Pettin—" Adele said. If she'd been able to continue, she would—she *might*—have blurted the name of Mistress Sand.

"Mundy," Lt. Mon said, his face suddenly stark. "You have your orders. I'll thank you to leave my duties to me!"

It was odd to find out how much she had absorbed by being

in the RCN. Adele actually saluted before she turned to choose the three spacers who'd accompany her, Tovera, and the prisoners to South Land.

Daniel checked the sun and determined that it was five minutes short of local noon. His helmet would have given him the time correct to milliseconds, but for this purpose he preferred to use his eyes as he would have done in the forests of Bantry. He wouldn't always be wearing a helmet.

"*Forgot by the planet that bore us . . .*" sang the detachment behind him, Sun the loudest of all. He seemed to be all right— "seemed" being the operative word. The gunner's mate had done everything with enthusiasm since the spacers returned to the surface with full water cans and fruit from the cavern stuffed into the pockets of their utilities. He was an active man who deserved his rating, but his present demeanor smacked of a boy whistling in the dark.

"*Betrayed by the ones we hold dear . . .*"

That was perfectly all right with Daniel. All that mattered was that Sun had found a way to overcome his funk.

Vesey came up on Daniel's left side, opposite Hogg. They weren't trying to keep a formal order of march, though everyone knew to stay within a few paces of the next spacer ahead.

Daniel smiled at the midshipman and said, "I figured we'd take a break in a few minutes, Vesey. How does the unit appear to be holding up to you?"

"*The good, they have all gone before us . . .*"

"Quite well, sir," Vesey said. She meant her tone to be professional, but her dry throat tripped her into a squeak in the middle of the short phrase. "The fresh rations have made a great improvement, and finding an assured source of water also."

"I'd say half of 'em are high as kites!" Hogg commented, casting his eye back on the spacers. "Something more than juice in that stuff, I'd say, but it don't work on everybody."

"*And only the dull ones are here!*"

Hogg spat. "I wish t'hell it worked on me," he added.

"Sir, I wanted to ask about the fruit . . ." Vesey said. "And the caves and everything. The *animals*. Where do they come from?"

Daniel kept his expression blank as he considered both the

question and what was behind the question. The *Princess Cecile* was too small to rate a chaplain, so the crew's religious health was part of the captain's duties. That was pretty clearly the hat Vesey wanted him to wear now.

"There are cases of parallel evolution," Daniel said carefully. "On single planets and between species from planets a thousand light-years apart where there isn't the least genetic similarity. But I don't think that could be involved here."

There was a ravine close by to the left. Daniel had intended to declare a break and lead the expedition into it—and he would, but first he needed to deal with the midshipman's question in the privacy that the march provided.

"They're really human, aren't they?" Vesey said uncomfortably. "They're what colonists from the first settlement turned into, here on South Land."

"We have samples from the carnivore," Daniel said. Hair, skin, and a scrap of bone blown from the back of the creature's skull. The last contained marrow. "When we get back we'll be able to test them. Even the *Princess Cecile*'s medical computer should be able to make a genetic comparison. With human DNA."

The bushes growing to the lip of the nearby ravine made a brilliant contrast to everything around it. Though the small leaves were the dull red usual on Sexburga, they merely speckled the yellow and white striped bark of the trunks and branches. Daniel didn't recall anything so colorful from the natural-history database. The species might be new to science. Human science.

"The thing is, Vesey," he said, "we've had star travel for less than two thousand years, and to adapt ordinary humans into forms like those we saw underground would take either genetic engineering beyond what's possible today or a very great deal of time. It couldn't happen in less than fifty or sixty thousand years, and it might require as much as ten times as long."

"Then they're not human after all, sir?" Vesey said. She sighed with obvious relief. "I'm—well, it was just so creepy to think that they might be. What if my children—"

She stopped, flustered, then blurted onward, "If I ever had children, I mean, not that I . . ."

Daniel kept a straight face, suspecting that if he smiled it would delay the midshipman even more. Besides, he had more to say.

Vesey's misunderstanding was comforting to her, but Daniel couldn't in good conscience leave her in it.

"That's not quite what I meant, Vesey," he said. "None of the starfaring races we've met in the last two thousand years could live on human-habitable planets without full life-support systems. There's some evidence, though—*I've* found some evidence myself—that in the distant past there was another race living on planets we've colonized recently. The—seeming mammals we've found here on South Land, call them that . . . they're the only native verte-brates on Sexburga. If they're native."

Vesey raised her visor so that she could rub her eyes. "I see," she said. "Thank you, sir. That was very informative."

Which in the tone she used was equivalent to, "And next time, I'd prefer you give me a rectal exam with a shovel." Well, Vesey knew as surely as Daniel himself did that the RCN didn't train its officers to lie to their subordinates.

Daniel turned, his mouth open to order his people to fall out for a ten-minute break. "*Unit!*" said Jeshonyk over the intercom. "*There's an aircar coming from the south. Hear it? Over.*"

Daniel *did* hear the distant mixture of high and low tones now, though he hadn't until Jeshonyk called it to his attention. Power room crewmen had an almost mystical ability to pick up mechanical noises—and particularly variations in mechanical noises. When you were dealing with fusion bottles, quick diagnosis of strange sounds could be the difference between life and death for the whole ship.

"Everybody into the ravine under cover!" Daniel bellowed, lifting his visor so that the helmet wouldn't muffle his voice. He deliberately didn't trip the intercom. "Radio silence, but everybody echo images from my helmet so that you know what's going on."

The spacers scrambled over the edge of the ravine like children entering a swimming pool: in a variety of fashions, all of them clumsy. Hogg disappeared also, but without kicking up a sand grain or disturbing a leaf of the sheltered bushes. Hogg looked portly and seemed slow until he saw a need to move quickly.

"Sun, you're in command if there's a problem," Daniel continued. He faced the south and smiled for the oncoming vehicle which he couldn't see without magnifi—no, he could after all, there was a glint in the sky. "I suggest you be guided by Hogg till you reach an environment more familiar to you, however. God and the Republic be with you, spacers!"

Daniel lowered his visor again and increased the magnification. He sounded like quite the sanctimonious prig, now that his mind had leisure to review what he'd just said. At the time it had seemed like what was called for, though; and maybe it was.

The oncoming vehicle was an aircar, not an armored personnel carrier. It was large enough to carry quite a number of soldiers, but marksmen as good as Hogg and Sun could shoot it into a colander if that were required. Daniel's people wouldn't start the firefight, though, and Daniel himself made an easy target as well.

He grinned naturally at a further thought. He'd just made the sort of speech that would look well in a book like *Our Navy's Martyred Heroes*; which he'd read when he was eight, and which he might very possibly have stolen the words from. Well, the RCN put more of a premium on propriety than originality.

"*Leary Force, this is, ah, Mundy Force,*" Daniel's earphones announced in a crisp, familiar voice. It was like hearing his mother crooning when he woke screaming from an infant nightmare. "*Liebig tells me that we'll be landing beside you in approximately two minutes.*"

There was a pause which presumably included Adele getting some politely worded suggestions from within the aircar. "*Right, over,*" she said.

"Mundy Force, this is Leary," Daniel said. "We're very glad to see you. Break. Unit, you can come up to greet our friends now. Out."

The aircar was descending as it neared, keeping an even keel instead of dropping its nose in a dive. The driver—Liebig? Daniel doubled his magnification to 40x. Yes, Liebig. The driver was more able than Daniel had realized.

Daniel noticed who was with Liebig and Adele in the vehicle's cab. A slight frown wriggled his brows.

"*Hogg, this is Tovera,*" another voice said. "*I'd appreciate it if you not shoot Mr. Dorotige at least until after we've landed. I understand your feelings, but I didn't bring a change of clothes for my mistress. The impeller you're aiming is going to bathe her in brains if you fire now. Out.*"

Hogg stepped up beside Daniel, laughing like he hadn't done since one of Mistress Leary's city visitors had fallen into the Bantry cesspool. "I swear, master," he said between gulps of laughter. "Ain't she a pistol? Ain't she just!"

"Yes," said Daniel. "I believe Tovera is that indeed."

CHAPTER TWENTY

It was crowded with four on the cab's bench seat, but Woetjans had insisted in riding up front with Adele, Daniel and Liebig. The central driver's station was the problem: Adele was squeezed between Daniel and the right doorpanel, while Woetjans had the relative luxury of all the space to Liebig's left.

Woetjans didn't do things without a reason. Adele wouldn't have requested the bosun's presence, but her strength and experience had been a welcome addition when Mon ordered that she accompany Adele's party.

"Adele?" Daniel said. "Can you connect me with Spires? The squadron's scheduled liftoff is in ten minutes, so it's time for me to take my medicine from Commodore Pettin. The news will make his day, I'm sure."

"We told Captain Mon that you and the crew were fine, sir," Woetjans said. Adele felt her lips tighten at the bosun intercepting a request meant for her. "We called in as soon as we landed."

"Yes, I'm sure you did, Woetjans," Daniel said. There was a touch of reserve in his tone, an echo of what Adele herself was feeling. "But I need to report to the commodore directly and tell him that it'll be at least four hours before I reach the harbor. Adele, can you . . . ?"

"Of course," Adele said. She'd already wiggled out her personal data unit and brought it live. "Do you want the cruiser's communications center or a direct patch to Mr. Pettin?"

Adele had linked the aircar's satellite radio to her RCN helmet,

264

but she couldn't claim to be any more comfortable with the helmet than she was with the radio's own peculiar voice controller. She'd learned on the flight out from Spires that the aircar was as smooth as a library table, so she'd reprogrammed the unit in order to run it with her wands through the data unit.

She hadn't expected to be quite as cramped as she was at the moment, but the task was easy enough. She switched on the radio and brought up the RCN menu as she spoke.

"He'll send me a rocket whichever choice I make," Daniel said reflectively. He didn't sound depressed, but his voice wasn't as boyishly ebullient as usual. "I think the direct line, though."

He grinned. "I'd rather be accused of arrogantly calling my superior direct," he said, "than of being a coward and hoping that I could avoid his notice by dealing with his staff."

"Ma'am?" Woetjans said. "Officer Mundy? Don't make the call. Don't make any more calls out till we're back with the *Sissie*, all right?"

Daniel leaned forward to look at the bosun past Liebig. Obviously the driver had been warned to expect what was happening now, because he had a false smile and his eyes fixed front.

"Woetjans?" Daniel prompted gently. Adele froze her display and watched the tableau from her corner.

"I'm sorry, sir," Woetjans said. She did sound sorry. Though she faced Daniel, her eyes were focused a thousand miles away. "The captain's given me orders that you aren't to call anybody till you resume command of the *Princess Cecile*; Acting Captain Mon has, I mean."

Adele couldn't see Daniel's face from where she sat, but his silence itself was telling. Woetjans took a deep breath and continued in an anguished voice, "Sir, Mr. Mon gave me the job instead of, instead of somebody else—"

Adele dipped her chin in a nod of understanding.

"—because he knew I'd follow naval discipline. That I'd put this pipe through the radio—"

Woetjans tapped her length of tubing with a little finger. She'd brought it to encourage the Captal if that proved necessary. It wasn't. The prisoners hadn't even complained aloud at being marooned with the remnants of food Daniel's unit had brought to South Land.

"—if that was the only way to keep you from getting a signal out. Sir."

"I see," said Daniel. He leaned back in his seat and grinned. "Adele?" he added. "What would you have done if Captain Mon had given you the orders that he gave Woetjans?"

It was an honest question, so Adele paused a moment to form a complete and honest answer. "I like Mon well enough," she said. "It's clear that he has what he considers to be your best interests at heart. But I wouldn't thank anyone who tried to control me for my own good, and I wouldn't be a party to a plot to do that to you."

She grinned just enough to lift one corner of the knife blade line of her lips. "Of course," she went on, "I bow to *force majeure* in the form of Woetjans's bludgeon."

Daniel laughed merrily. "Well, Woetjans," he said, "I hope I understand naval discipline as clearly as you do. Captain Mon has given you a lawful order which I'll watch you obey, little though I care to do so."

He twisted to look through the window into the passenger compartment. Woetjans had brought a cask of Sexburgan beer for the rescued unit, saying that it wouldn't affect their ability to function when they reached the corvette. Adele wondered how Tovera was getting along with the festive spacers.

Daniel turned back with a satisfied expression. "I trust I'm allowed to listen to traffic between the squadron and the *Princess Cecile*, however?" he said. "Ah, assuming that's possible, Adele?"

"Of course it's possible," she said, frowning. Daniel didn't mean to be insulting, but how would he react if she said, "And can you walk through that open door, Daniel?"

"Yeah, sure," Woetjans said. "Sir, you know I didn't want to . . ."

"Part of being in the RCN is learning to carry out unpleasant orders, Woetjans," Daniel said without expression. He tried to smile but gave it up as a bad job after a moment.

Adele checked the machine-made transcripts of the past four and a half hours of commo traffic between squadron command and the *Princess Cecile*; for her, written text provided a quicker way to assess material than sound bites were. Each message in turn proved low-level and routine: duty rosters, liberty records, the current supply manifest, and similar matters.

While she was scrolling through the data, the display threw up a red sidebar: the *Princess Cecile* was receiving a communication for the captain and slugged Squadron Six—Commodore Pettin himself. Betts, the duty officer, had just passed the call on as directed.

Adele paused only a moment, then routed the message live through the speakers in both cab and passenger compartment.

"*Sir!*" Mon's voice said. "*Acting Captain Mon here, over.*"

"*Mon, if you're in charge, then Lieutenant Leary is still absent from duty,*" Commodore Pettin replied. Adele wasn't good at identifying voices, but no one else in the squadron would have shown such disregard for naval propriety. "*That's true, isn't it?*"

"*Sir,*" Mon said, "*I've failed to recall Captain Leary from the expedition on which you ordered him. I'll keep trying, and I'm confident that he'll have returned well before the liftoff time you originally set. Over.*"

Daniel's left hand clenched, released, and then clenched again. His expression remained calmly attentive, his head cocked slightly to the side.

"*Well, he won't find a ship to report to if he does,*" the commodore said, his tone suddenly cheerful. "*Lieutenant Mon, I'm making your appointment to command of the* Princess Cecile *permanent in the absence of Leary. A captain who can't keep in touch with his ship has no business in the RCN. Your command will lift in six minutes, according to the schedule of operations. Hold in orbit for the remainder of the squadron to join you. Squadron Six out.*"

"*Sir!*" said Lt. Mon. "*I'm very sorry, but the* Princess Cecile *is not ready to lift. While under my temporary command, the cooling system for her Tokamak went out of order. I haven't been able to repair the problem yet. Over.*"

"*By God, Mon,*" Pettin said. He didn't sound angry, just amazed. "*By God. I suggest you get your little problem solved in the next five minutes. Because if your foreign-built so-called corvette doesn't lift with the squadron, you will have no career at all. None!*"

The transmission ended in the hiss of an open line; Adele broke the contact. No one in the cab spoke for a moment.

Adele looked out the side window. The aircar was over land again; North Land, she supposed, but geography didn't greatly interest her. Most of the continent was as barren as its wholly uninhabited sister.

"I very much regret Lieutenant Mon's decision," Daniel said quietly. "But I'm not one to second-guess the man on the ground."

He gave first Woetjans, then Adele a smile with something of steel in it. "And a great deal can happen before Commodore Pettin returns to Cinnabar and files his report with the Navy Office. We'll see what we can do in the interim to change his mind."

As the aircar dropped in tight spirals into the harbor, Daniel noted that the *Princess Cecile* was ready to lift off as soon as the gangplank came in. The turret would have to be lowered and two hatches were for the moment being used as gunports, but in an emergency all that could be taken care of while the corvette was bound for orbit.

Daniel nodded in approval. That was what he'd expected, of course, from Mon or any competent RCN officer, but it was still a pleasure and relief to see that his confidence had been justified.

They landed just short of the gangplank. A curtain of spray flashed up from the quay: wheeled traffic had worn the stone enough that it filled when vessels maneuvering in nearby slips sloshed the harbor's surface. Liebig cursed because he hadn't noticed the puddle in the twilight, but Daniel wouldn't have cared if he'd been standing in the middle of the splash. He couldn't be much more bedraggled than the past few days marching in the desert had left him.

"Move it, move it!" Woetjans bellowed. The passenger compartment had double doors to ease the passage of the wealthy and corpulent. The spacers were neither, but they disembarked as hastily as they ran to action stations; the wide openings eased the process.

Woetjans was out before the car was fully at rest. Liebig followed an instant later after he'd shut off the power. Adele, on the other hand, was looking puzzled about what she should do next.

Rather than wait for her to open the door beside her, Daniel slid out past the steering yoke. "Woetjans, two men to help the signals officer!" he called as he trotted to the gangplank past the crewmen waiting tautly for their captain to lead them aboard.

Daniel felt thoroughly alive. The *Princess Cecile* had missed the squadron's liftoff, a difficult situation but not necessarily a career-ending one. He'd have to play his hand as well as ever an officer did to save himself, however.

"*Captain, I'm in the Battle Direction Center,*" said Mon's voice on the helmet earphones. "*I have a course to Strymon loaded, based on Commander Bergen's logs. I know you'll be able to refine it, but I thought we could get under weigh now and save a couple hours computation time over a cold start. Mon over.*"

Daniel went through the corvette's entryway at a brisk walk instead of the dead run that instinct urged him to. He didn't want to waste time, but in fact a few minutes here or there wouldn't make any difference. A hasty error would mean disaster—and if he spooked his crew into such an error, it could be just as bad as his own blunder.

"Thank you, Mon," Daniel said as he banged up the righthand—upward—companionway, taking the steps two at a time. That was normal practice, and a rigger's reflex kept his left hand gliding over the railing the whole time to catch him if he slipped. "Watch-standing officers report to the bridge and I'll brief you on our course. Out."

The ship's machinery was live, a symphony of whirrs, whines, and the occasional flurry of clanking like a drum riff. Spacers waited at their action stations. The bow dorsal section of riggers, both watches, stood suited in the corridor. They flattened themselves against either bulkhead as Daniel passed, nodding with a stern smile.

He threw himself into his seat and rotated the command console to face his officers. A year ago Daniel would've radioed his plans ahead to the *Princess Cecile,* trusting RCN encryption to limit his message to its intended hearers if he even bothered to think about security. A few months of contact with Adele Mundy had showed him that an information specialist with a powerful computer at her command could read *anything* she got in electronic form.

There might be eavesdropping devices on the *Princess Cecile's* bridge—and unlikely though that was, it was greater than the chance of there being another specialist of Adele's skill on Sexburga. Even so, Daniel had ceased to say anything over the air that he didn't want others to hear.

Mon and Pasternak—with a long cut on his forearm, covered

with a sprayed binder/antiseptic; the Chief Engineer didn't limit his duties to giving orders—came down the corridor behind Daniel. The other warrant officers (including Taley, who wasn't a watchstander but was understandably curious about what was going on) were already on the bridge.

Daniel beamed. He had a *great* crew, a crew that other captains would give an arm for, and they'd every one of them volunteered to serve with Lt. Daniel Leary. By God! they had.

"As everybody in this compartment knows," Daniel said, starting without preamble because he'd sound weak if he tried to articulate what he felt about the spacers he commanded, "we could better Commodore Pettin's time to Strymon with the crew on half watches and me sleeping for the whole run."

There was a general chorus of nods and murmurs. Woetjans slapped the bulkhead with her right hand and said, "Damned straight we will! They could sail the *Winckelmann*'s masts out and we'd still be waiting for 'em laughing when they finally staggered in."

Adele alone sat with the neutral expression Daniel knew by now was what her face wore when she was trying not to sneer. He was quite sure that Adele would make her opinion known if Daniel said he intended to humiliate his commanding officer in the most public fashion possible; but she wouldn't go out of her way to insult fellow officers simply because their understanding differed from that of noblemen like herself and Daniel—and senior officers like Commodore Pettin.

"We're going to do something much harder instead," Daniel said. "I'm counting on your skill and professionalism and that of the spacers under you to make it possible."

Faces grew shuttered; curious and, if not exactly concerned, then . . . Well, the crew of the *Princess Cecile* knew by now that if their captain said something would be difficult, they'd be sweating like pigs before they were through it.

"We're going to rendezvous with the squadron en route instead of meeting it at its destination," Daniel said. He thought about the ways his plan could go wrong and smiled. He'd worn a similar expression the day he made an offer to three women; and they whispered together, giggled, and all three followed him down the corridor.

It *could* go wrong, but it wouldn't. Not with this crew to back him and recover from any miscalculations he made.

Several of the warrant officers looked blank; Mon scowled, his mouth working as though he were trying to swallow something ghastly, while Woetjans merely scratched herself and grinned. "That'll teach him who's a spacer, won't it, sir?"

"But Captain . . . ?" said Pasternak. "The commodore didn't transmit his solutions to the *Sissie* when we said we weren't ready to lift. We don't know where the squadron'll be, except Strymon where they'll end up."

Pasternak was by the nature of his duties a highly educated man, though Daniel suspected that—besides Adele, of course—in raw intelligence the bosun may have been the smartest of the warrant officers. Working with a fusion bottle required a great deal of rote learning, but independent thought was a quick route to disaster. Pasternak could be depended on to know the accepted response to most standard shipboard problems, and to deny that any other response was possible.

"That may prove correct, Mr. Pasternak," Daniel said, "but I hope that by modeling solutions on our astrogation computer, we can determine which one the commodore will have chosen and then rendezvous with him. The computers are identical, after all, so the only question is which chain of intermediate exits from the Matrix Commodore Pettin chooses."

"He'll push," said Mon. "He'll want to prove he can make as fast a run as ever a junior lieutenant did."

"He'll *want* to push," Woetjans said, "but he'll know the *Winckelmann's* ready to pull her sticks out if he don't treat her tender. And if he *don't* know that, his bosun'll tell him."

Daniel said, "Commodore Pettin is an able officer and a careful—"

He'd swallowed the word "cautious" before it reached his tongue. Daniel had no desire to insult Pettin, and to this group of officers and the RCN more generally, "cautious" was indeed a word of insult.

"—one. I expect him to get the best out of his equipment, but he'll also know that his equipment is old and ill-maintained. I'll proceed according to those assumptions, with Mr. Mon's help and the help of my chiefs of rig and ship."

There were general nods and grins. Daniel's officers assumed that because he said the task was possible, then they'd accomplish it under him. Which, after all, was the assumption their captain made as well.

"We're going to need a great deal of luck," Daniel said, "and we'll be working through the whole run to tolerances as close as those of a battle which would be over quickly. It's going to be a strain on everybody, perhaps equal to the seventeen days that brought us here from Cinnabar."

Betts put his hands behind his neck and leaned back at his console. "I signed on with you, Captain," the missileer said, "because I thought that was the best road there was to getting a name for myself and enough prize money to buy a rose nursery whenever I chose to retire. I guess the same's true of every soul aboard the *Sissie* today, except maybe for the roses. You give us our orders. You don't have to worry about us carrying them out, whatever they are."

In the middle of the general approving chorus, Woetjans slammed her hand against the bulkhead again and bellowed, "*Damned* straight!"

That too was pretty much how Daniel felt.

Adele sat cross-legged in a cabinful of opened luggage while the *Princess Cecile* bustled about her. Liftoff wouldn't be for hours, or so she'd surmised when she left Vesey to handle routine traffic at the signals console while she spent her own time more productively.

The door—the hatch—opened abruptly. Adele's head came around quickly and her left hand spilled chips on the deck beside her as it dipped toward her pocket.

Lt. Mon stepped through and paused, looking as surprised to find someone else in the room as Adele had been an instant earlier.

"Sorry, mistress," he said. He looked taut but not particularly alert. "I forgot this was your cabin."

"Mine?" Adele said in surprise. The first lieutenant's uniform looked as though he'd slept in it; in truth, he probably hadn't slept at all.

"Yes, ma'am," Mon said, more patient now in his exhaustion than she'd seen him at times he was in better shape. "Yours and the Medic, now that our passenger's cut and run."

He gestured toward the ship's medical computer, a full-body

case which could diagnose and treat anybody who fit within its adaptive interior. "I came in to get my system flushed and another dose of Wideawake. But if you're unpacking . . ."

"For God's sake, use the, the—device," Adele snapped, angry with herself. Yes, of course this was the room originally assigned her, which she'd completely forgotten; and of *course* the medical computer would be in regular use throughout the voyage. Why in heaven had she decided to review Vaughn's documents here rather than in her half of the captain's suite?

Looking thankful, Mon stripped off the jacket he'd already unsealed in the corridor. "I'm just about gone," he said with a gray smile, gripping the pair of handholds and lifting himself feet-first into the cylinder with a grace that a professional acrobat might have envied. "Say, would you like somebody to help you with your gear?"

"This isn't my gear," Adele said. "Delos Vaughn abandoned his luggage when he left the ship. Presumably he felt that if he tried to retrieve it, even in Daniel's absence, someone would've taken alarm. I've had it moved to this room from the places where it was stowed during the voyage. I'm examining it for items of information."

On general principles she didn't care to go on with her business while Mon was in the room with her—not that she'd turned up anything he shouldn't know. Besides, a break to chat with another human being was probably a good idea.

The mesh and microtubing of the Medic's interior settled over Mon's body like fluid moving along a pipette; he gave a great sigh as the equipment began to sample his body chemistry through his bare skin. He hadn't sunk his head in the tube, so he was able to watch and talk to Adele.

"Is Captain Leary going to be in trouble for letting Vaughn escape?" Mon asked. Bitterly he added, "For *me* letting the bastard escape, I mean."

"No, I don't think so," Adele said. "Vaughn was using the *Princess Cecile*—and Daniel himself—to convince others that he had the support of Cinnabar for taking control of his home planet. That claim of support was probably false."

She'd already read far enough in Vaughn's secret correspondence to be sure that the Navy Office had no record of him boarding the *Princess Cecile*. Vaughn's organization had bribed the real courier with enough money to make even a Mundy blink. You could rent a senator for a year for far less.

Lt. Mon gasped as though he'd been dropped into cold water. The Medic was cleansing his system of fatigue poisons and the breakdown products of the drugs he'd taken to stay alert over the past several days.

Mon's face relaxed the way a wax mask would on low heat. Color—a healthier color than the previous sallow surface underlain by a metallic gray substrate—returned to his cheeks.

"Say, that's good to hear," he murmured, closing his eyes as his muscles luxuriated in chemical-induced relaxation. "What did you do with the bastard anyhow, the Captal I mean? I suppose you had him picked up so he doesn't just wander South Land for the rest of his life."

"As soon as the *Princess Cecile* lifts," Adele said, "a message will go to Admiral Torgis informing him where the Captal is and also providing information about the admiral's aide, Mr. Gerson. I expect the admiral will take care of both matters discreetly, for the sake of Cinnabar and more specifically the RCN. If it became public, it wouldn't be hard to make our rescue operation look like an act of piracy, after all."

Mon snorted. "It'd be damned hard to make it look any other way!" he said. "I sure wish I'd been along when you cleaned house on those bastards."

"Ah, Mr. Mon . . ." Adele said. It might not be her place to say it, but it was as much her place—because she was Daniel's personal friend—as it was anybody's, and she was quite sure that it ought to be said. "I'd like to thank you for your support when I used illegal methods to free Daniel."

She'd started to call them "improper methods," but nothing would have been improper to achieve that end. There were things that would have turned Adele's stomach even to consider, but Daniel Leary *would* have returned to the *Princess Cecile*, no matter what the result cost his friends.

"I'm well aware that in addition to the risk you ran in supporting us," she continued as Mon writhed in the ecstasy of not being in pain, "that there would have been personal advantages to you in obeying Commodore Pettin's orders."

Mon started to laugh. For a moment Adele thought the Medic was tickling him; then she realized that the lining had withdrawn against the body of the cylinder, freeing the patient from its ministrations.

Mon crawled out of the Medic, his bare chest ruddy as if from a vigorous toweling. He started to speak but broke into chuckling for a further moment while he donned his utility jacket.

"I guess you mean that I'd have a command of my own," he said at last. With a bitterness at shocking variance with his amusement of moments before, Mon added, "Quite a stroke of luck for a lieutenant who's learned to be thankful for bad luck because it was the only luck he was going to get, right?"

Adele said nothing. She looked up at Mon; her face calm, her gaze steady.

Mon patted the Medic's hood. "There's nothing like one of these for making you feel good," he said affectionately. "I tell you, if women were half so good, I wouldn't mind how much time I spend on the ground without a ship."

His face changed, though hardened wasn't quite the word to describe his new expression. He squatted so that he faced Adele with his eyes on the same level as hers. His elbows rested on his knees.

"Mistress Mundy," Mon said, "any religion I had to start out with, I lost before I was fifteen. I don't believe in any kind of afterlife and I *sure* don't believe in heaven. But Hell, that I believe in; only it doesn't happen after you're dead."

Mon straightened with a grin and stepped to the door. "I'm not going to put myself in Hell for the whole rest of my life," he added over his shoulder, "from remembering the way I sold out Lieutenant Leary after he gave me a break."

Adele watched the door close behind the lieutenant. It struck her that she'd just, for the first time, heard a religious philosophy with which she could agree.

CHAPTER TWENTY-ONE

As the Matrix rippled and pulsed beyond the tips of the *Princess Cecile*'s antennas, it struck Daniel that Adele's saving grace wasn't her immense competence at the things she did well. No, she survived because she didn't claim competence where she had none.

And as the good Lord knew, Adele was even clumsier outside a ship than she was within the hull.

Daniel touched helmets with her. "Look up along the tips of the forward dorsal masts," he said. "You see the ripples ahead of one, and between one and two; the patterns are the same."

"I'm looking," Adele said; obviously a placeholder to indicate she'd heard him rather than a claim of comprehension. She seemed to be looking in the right direction, at any rate. He'd learned by now not to take that for granted.

They stood at the first joint of Dorsal 4, a position Daniel had chosen because D4's top and mid sails were furled on the present heading. If he were alone he'd be conning the *Princess Cecile* from an upper yard or even the mast truck, but with Adele . . . well, Daniel didn't know of any case where a safety line had parted except when a whole antenna was breaking up; but riggers generally didn't use safety lines, and those who did weren't regularly snubbed up by theirs as they went drifting off toward some distant universe.

"Now look between two and three," Daniel said. He didn't point. All the crewmen in sight were watching him, and those on the peripheries were ready to relay his directions to their fellows stationed around the curve of the hull. "There's a feathering of the light, do you see? A herringbone. If you look very carefully, it's three separate patterns."

"I see the light," Adele said. That was along the lines of saying that she breathed air, but Daniel tried to keep from frowning. Adele was trying to understand, albeit trying to understand something that was obvious to him. "And I see what could be herringbones. But I don't see any difference from what it looks like between the other masts."

The cold, no-colored light surrounding the *Princess Cecile* was the human eye's response to the Casimir-Bohr Radiation that bathed the entire cosmos instead of being limited to individual bubble universes. The antennas and the sails of charged fabric they spread controlled the pressure of radiation on the vessel, driving it through and between universes whose physical constants differed from those of the sidereal universe.

Imbalances in Casimir radiation were the pragmatic reality of star travel. The light, pure as nothing in the human universe could be, was also beautiful beyond Daniel's ability to say.

"Stay here for a moment, Adele," Daniel said. "Ah, you might want to hold onto the mast with both hands. I won't be a moment."

He paused to make sure that she was taking hold of the mast— which she didn't do until she realized that Daniel was waiting and watching until she obeyed what he'd meant for an order though he hadn't been willing to phrase it that way to a Mundy of Chatsworth. Perhaps he was being overly cautious, but he'd twice caught Adele's feet as they missed rungs on her climb up the antenna.

Sure that his friend was safe, Daniel strode out to the tip of the main yard. The magnetic strips in his bootsoles gave him a positive grip on the steel yard; rigger style, he duckwalked so that his insteps followed the curve of the yard and maximized the surface-to-surface contact. The added square inches greatly increased the grip of a spacer who might unexpectedly have a spar or a length of heavy tackle catch him between his shoulder blades. That extra could be the difference between life and a slow death in some universe not meant for Mankind.

Daniel could see four riggers; there might be more, all but an eyeslit concealed by the hull and rig. Beneath him, the half-furled mainsail quivered minusculely to the rhythm of his step. An expert eye—his eye—could see a reflection in the Matrix of even that infinitely small variation in the corvette's balance of energy.

Daniel signaled, bending his arms in riggers' code. The first symbol was the antenna for which the command was intended; the rest of the string, shorter or longer as need required, described the operations which were to be carried out on the antenna.

For the most part the riggers were on the hull to execute commands transmitted from the bridge by mechanical semaphore. The astrogation computer could process more data than any number of human beings in a lifetime: the captain set a course, and the computer translated that human desire into a path through the Matrix.

But the Matrix was as variable as a cloud-wracked sky, so a computer had only approximations of the reality through which the vessel sailed. No sensors but the human eye were available outside the hull, but the eye was a tool of great subtlety when used in the right fashion.

Daniel's arms moved; swiftly, precisely. He was modifying the set of six antennas, two of them on the ventral row which was completely hidden from him. The spacers watching him would relay his commands around and along the hull to those who were in position to carry them out.

Daniel couldn't have navigated the *Princess Cecile* to Strymon or even across the Cinnabar system by himself. He could refine the choices made by the astrogation computer, however; and right now, viewing aberrations in the smooth whirls of Casimir radiation . . . and all right, perhaps they weren't herringbones, exactly, but they were patterns that didn't belong in the natural sequence of the Matrix . . . viewing *those* markings, Daniel knew he'd found three ships travelling in close company.

Only naval forces did that. Well, naval forces and pirates coming to grips with their merchant prey. From the course and location, so close to what Daniel had plotted for the commodore, he was sure that he'd found the RCN squadron.

He grinned, seeing a faint reflection of himself in the faceplate of his rigging suit. Of course if it *did* turn out to be a pair of pirates homing in on an argosy, that would be all right as well. Much as Daniel wanted to join Commodore Pettin and mend fences on his own behalf and that of Lt. Mon, a chance to see off a pair of pirates on the way would be more than welcome.

Daniel finished his series of commands; the sails of Port and Starboard Two already beginning to ripple. Whistling a tune he'd learned as "Pity the Poor Poacher"—in the RCN it was sung as "Pity the Poor Rigger"—he returned to the mast with his arms crossed before his chest.

Adele stood like an awkward piece of equipment clamped to the mast, watching Daniel with a stony face. She'd obviously felt insulted by the degree of his concern that she'd do something fatally foolish.

Touching helmets with her, Daniel said, "I appreciate your going along with my whim, Adele. There's a risk to walking out along the yard—"

There was a risk the reprocessing latrine would explode when he used it too, but in neither case was it one that he'd bother to mention except as a way of soothing a friend's ruffled feathers.

"—and having any other concern on my mind, however unlikely, would have added to my danger."

Adele deliberately took one hand away from the mast and said, "Yes, it looked very dangerous to me. What were you doing?"

Daniel could feel the corvette start to rotate beneath him. The change was minute, a degree or two. The light of the cosmos flared in great banners from the *Princess Cecile*'s mast trucks, highlighting the maneuver for those to whom the motion of the vessel was too subtle a cue.

"On our calculated heading, we would have returned to the sidereal universe within optical range of the squadron," Daniel explained, "but too far out for communication since they won't be expecting our arrival. I've made some small refinements so that when we drop from the Matrix three hours from now, we'll be within hailing range of the *Winckelmann*."

He grinned more broadly than he might have done if there'd been anybody to see his face. Since he was leaned sideways into contact with Adele's helmet, not even she could tell his expression. "In fact," he added, "I believe that we'll be within the regulation twenty thousand miles, which is considerably closer than either of the destroyers is going to manage on their present headings."

"And you can see all that from streaks in the sky," Adele said. He could visualize her wry smile. "Well, every profession has its unique language."

Daniel cleared his throat. "I can't identify individual ships from their wakes," he said. "That's an assumption based on probabilities, so in case I'm wrong the *Princess Cecile* will exit with the crew at action stations. Pirates have the same problem, of course: they risk dropping into sidereal space with a warship instead of the freighter they thought they were tracking. Rather than fight a battle, they're always prepared to slip at once back into the Matrix and hope their opponent can't follow them there."

"Ah," said Adele. Daniel waited for her to decide how to raise the topic that had brought her onto the hull with him in the first place. "Daniel, I've been reading Delos Vaughn's files, as you know. One thing that appears from them is that his niece Pleyna— or at any rate the regent, Friderik Nunes—really is intriguing with the Alliance. That wasn't simply a story to gain Cinnabar support for Vaughn's return."

"I see," Daniel said. It struck him that his words were a perfect echo of Adele's when he was trying to point out wakes in the Matrix to her. He'd heard what Adele said, but as for understanding what she meant, she could've been trying to communicate by eyeblinks. "Ah, do you mean that the *Princess Cecile* has a political mission, Adele? That is . . . ?"

He simply didn't know how to go on. Did she expect him to aid Delos Vaughn openly? And if Daniel did, how in heaven's name was he going to explain his actions to Commodore Pettin, let alone the board of the court-martial which would surely be convoked on his return to Cinnabar?

"I don't see that there's anything we could do directly," Adele said, probably unaware of the relief her words gave Daniel. "I do think that we ought to warn Commodore Pettin, however. If you can think of a discreet way to do that, which I'll admit I cannot."

"Ah," said Daniel. "Yes, I can see that. Well, perhaps I can find a way, though getting the commodore to listen to me is another matter. Even assuming he doesn't order me removed from command at our first interview."

Daniel found himself smiling faintly. There was a real risk of Pettin reacting with explosive anger as soon as the *Princess Cecile* joined the squadron, but for all that Daniel didn't find himself particularly concerned. This voyage, even more than the record run from Cinnabar to Sexburga, was a piece of astrogation that Uncle Stacey and his friends would discuss for hours over mulled rum in the office of Bergen and Associates. Whatever happened to his career, Lt. Daniel Leary had a name that real spacers would always mention with honor.

Thinking of the coming interview with Commodore Pettin raised another question in Daniel's mind. "Adele?" he said. "I gave you some tissue samples collected on South Land to run through the Medic's analysis when an opportunity presented itself. Have you . . . ?"

"Yes," Adele said. "Yes, of course. I did that before we lifted, but it slipped my mind to give you the information with the bustle since then. And my own researches, of course. Both were healthy at present, though Sample A showed signs of a recent viral illness."

"I beg your pardon?" Daniel said. "The samples I gave you were for DNA matching to human beings. A portion of skull from the carnivore that attacked us, and some skin cells that Sun found under his fingernails after struggling with a, an herbivore in the cave we found."

"Oh?" said Adele. "I misunderstood, then. I simply checked them for disease. They must have been human to five decimal places or the Medic wouldn't have been able to proceed on the normal setting."

"Good God," Daniel said. People couldn't have reached Sexburga under their own power back the forty, sixty, perhaps one hundred thousand years ago. It would've taken that long to modify humans into the creatures the expedition had found in the burrows under South Land.

Chickens hadn't reached Sexburga under their own power either; but there were chickens there now.

"What do you think it means, Adele?" Daniel asked.

She laughed, the sound made metallic by being transmitted through the sides of their helmets. "I'm a librarian, Daniel," she said. "I organize and retrieve information. As for what it means, I'm afraid you'll have to go to some other kind of specialist."

Daniel thought for a moment, then clapped her on the shoulder. "Let's go in," he said. "I need to make sure my 1st Class uniform is wearable, because I'm quite sure the commodore is going to expect me to make a formal appearance on the flagship."

Daniel had never served on an Archaeologist-class cruiser, and this visit aboard one—even more than his first in harbor on Sexburga—made him thankful of the fact. The *Winckelmann* had been designed during a period when compartmentalization was the fad among naval constructors. The result was a squat cylinder divided into quadrants longitudinally as well as by decks on her vertical axis.

In theory the *Winckelmann* could continue to fight with at least a quarter of its strength after a direct hit by a missile anywhere except on the power room. In practice the class was inefficient in action even when undamaged, required larger crew complements than ships of comparable force, and broke down approximately four times as often as less complicated designs.

As usually happens, reality trampled a brilliant theory into the dust. Again as usual, the theory left behind detritus of which the *Winckelmann* was one of the more prominent clods.

Daniel grinned as a signalman guided him up a third armored companionway, this like the others half-lit and dank with condensate which sometimes formed rust-bright pools along the welded seams. He didn't imagine he'd enjoy this visit to the *Winckelmann* if she were outfitted and maintained like Corder Leary's townhouse.

"Here you go, sir," said the signalman, stepping aside so that Daniel could enter the H Level rotunda serving the squadron commander. The armored hatch was locked open and showed rust on the hinges. Daniel didn't need a micrometer to tell that the jamb was warped beyond any possibility of sealing the hatch in event of disaster.

Four offices opened off the rotunda; the hatches of three were closed. A senior lieutenant in his late thirties sat at the central console, looking at Daniel with no expression whatever. He spoke into the intercom, his words smothered by the console's active muting feature.

Daniel struck a brace before the console. "Sir!" he said. "Lieutenant Leary reporting to the commodore!"

"Cabin One, Leary," the lieutenant said. He nodded minutely in the direction of the open office. "The commodore requests you to close the hatch behind you."

Daniel stepped into the anteroom of the squadron commander's office, closing the hatch as he'd been directed. Commodore Pettin watched him silently from across the console in the inner office beyond.

Pettin was wearing Dress Whites, just as Daniel was. Daniel didn't know precisely how to take that, but he supposed he'd call it a good sign. Optimism didn't cost anything, after all.

Daniel strode through and stopped two paces from Pettin's console. The room was as bare as a cell. He drew a deep breath and was a heartbeat short of announcing himself.

"Sit down, Leary," the commodore said. He didn't sound in the least friendly, but neither was he snarling. "I'm going to proceed informally."

Daniel hesitated. There were two chairs on his side of the console, to his right and left, and he didn't know which would be the better choice. The less bad choice. Besides, the paranoid part of his mind was in control at the moment, and it had no difficulty in imagining Pettin having him court-martialled for sitting down before saluting and announcing himself.

"Sit down, dammit!" the commodore said. "Don't you understand Universal?"

Daniel plopped into the chair to his right. His 1st Class trousers didn't strain the way they usually did; marching across South Land on cold rations had been good for his waistline.

There was a moment's silence. Knowing the risk he was taking, Daniel said, "Sir, I regret I didn't inform you before I gave Lieutenant Mon orders to dismantle our fusion bottle for servicing while I was absent. The *Princess Cecile*'s inability to lift with the rest of the squadron was my own sole responsibility."

"Bullshit, Lieutenant," Pettin said, not unpleasantly. "But that's not what I've summoned you here to discuss."

Daniel folded his hands over the saucer hat in his lap. "Yes, sir," he said.

"I suppose I've got to decide you're either the finest astrogator alive," Pettin said, "or the luckiest son of a bitch ever born. Or both, of course. Do you have anything to say on the subject, Lieutenant?"

Daniel's mind mulled the response, "No, sir," but he didn't let the words reach his tongue. This wasn't the time to play safe by keeping a low profile; if there was ever such a time.

"Sir," Daniel said, "my Uncle Stacey is the finest astrogator alive. I don't know of anyone who can match his abilities."

The commodore laughed: briefly, high-pitched, and as bitter as wormwood. "Commander Bergen, yes," he said. "I think of his career often when I'm contemplating my own. Whatever you got from your uncle, Leary, you didn't get his luck—because he never had any."

Pettin formed his right hand into a fist but he didn't slam it against the top of his silent console as Daniel thought he might. He looked old and very weary.

"You were lucky, *damned* lucky, to join the squadron on our first exit from the Matrix," Pettin said. He relaxed his fist. "You know that, don't you?"

"Yes, sir," Daniel said. "The variables fortunately cancelled one another out. We were *very* lucky."

Pettin nodded. "But you were going to join before we reached Strymon," he said. "That wouldn't have been luck. We have six intermediate exits, and you were going to keep refining your data at each one until you were in communication range of the *Winckelmann*, weren't you?"

Daniel nodded. "That was my intention, sir," he said. *This is as good a time as any will be. . . .* "Admiral Torgis asked me to join you before you entered the Strymon system if it was humanly possible. He'd received some intelligence data just too late to provide it to you directly before liftoff."

"Torgis?" the commodore said, showing for the first time during this interview the petulance that had been so characteristic a part of his personality during Daniel's past meetings with him. "What does he have to say?"

"There's very credible information that the Regent of Strymon is intriguing with Alliance representatives," Daniel said truthfully, though the statement would be news to the admiral who was its implied source. "There's a risk of active hostilities directed against the squadron."

Pettin snorted dismissively. "Torgis still likes to pretend he's part of the RCN," he said. "Passing on harbor gossip as if it came from

Guarantor Porra's private chamber is his way of forgetting he's in a job that a dancing bear could do with clothes and the right barber."

Daniel sucked his cheeks in. Nothing he could say would have a desirable effect on the commodore.

Pettin saw and understood the expression. "When you're next having a drink with your good friend the admiral, Leary," he said with more analysis than rancor, "you can tell him that you delivered his warning, and that the squadron spent its time on Strymon as it would on a recently conquered planet. I don't need drunken rumors to know that there's no lack of people on Strymon who hate and resent the Republic."

Pettin's face twisted into what Daniel with difficulty identified as a smile. "I might add that I understand Mr. Torgis' wish to be something more than a wall hanging as well," he said. "I suppose it would be unreasonable to expect him to be thankful that the Republic found *some* duties for him after he retired from the RCN. Many of us will not be so fortunate."

Daniel dipped his head to show that he'd been listening, but he said nothing. He'd had his share of stupid urges in life, but none that would be as insane as encouraging the commodore to open his heart about the way his career had proceeded.

Pettin grimaced and drew himself up straighter. "It won't surprise you to learn, Lieutenant," he said briskly, "that in the time since you unexpectedly rejoined my command I've been considering what I ought to do with an officer of your varied capacities. I think I've found a mutually desirable solution."

He smiled at Daniel. It hadn't been a question in so many words, but Daniel knew better than to ignore it. "Yes, sir?" he said.

"The *Winckelmann* and her original consorts will land on Strymon as planned," Pettin said, obviously relishing the situation. "Your *Princess Cecile*, however, will proceed to the naval base on Tanais. You're familiar with Tanais?"

"I've reviewed the *Sailing Directions* for the entire Strymon system, sir," Daniel said carefully.

As though Daniel hadn't spoken, Pettin continued, "It's the satellite of Getica, the giant planet on the rim of the system. The *Princess Cecile* will spend the next two weeks in the naval dockyard there, having her fusion bottle removed and refitted by trained staff so that we can be sure it's no longer a source of problems. And of course the officers and crew will remain with the vessel out of security concerns. Do you understand?"

"Yes, sir," Daniel said. "I understand perfectly."

"According to my understanding," Petting said, "the night life on Tanais tends to be of the basic sort. It's an ice ball, after all. Crib girls and industrial alcohol to drink. I sincerely hope this won't cramp the style of a socialite like yourself, Lieutenant."

Daniel smiled faintly. "I expect I'm going to be too busy with the power room refit to be concerned about socializing, Commodore," he said. "Ah—may I ask if the squadron's astrogation plan has been transmitted to the *Princess Cecile*?"

"Yes, yes," Pettin said. He waved toward the hatch. "We'll enter the Matrix in an hour and a half, so you'd better get moving. I fear that your ship's company wouldn't be able to function without you to lead them."

Daniel froze. "Sir," he said in a voice he hadn't meant to use, "the officers and crew under my command are the equal of any in the RCN. Sir."

Pettin grimaced. "No doubt they are," he snapped. "Now get the *hell* back to your own ship. After you've had two weeks freezing your feet on Tanais, I'll see if your deportment has improved to the point that I won't feel required to mention it on your next fitness report. Dismissed!"

Daniel stood, saluted, and walked out of the cabin as quickly as he could without running. He reclosed the hatch behind him; he'd had no orders on the subject, and it certainly made him feel better to know that there was a steel panel between his back and the commodore.

He threw a smile toward the startled lieutenant at the console. Daniel regretted being sent to Tanais for the crew's sake, but to be perfectly honest the recreation available there was about what most of them would have chosen on Strymon proper.

Adele might miss the lack of museums to tour, but Daniel was pretty sure that her real work was expected to begin after she reached the Strymon system. She'd be very busy, and the heart of a naval base was at least as suitable a site from which to send out electronic tendrils as the capital would be.

As for Daniel himself, even two weeks on Tanais would be a vacation compared to the run from Cinnabar to Sexburga. He could take it easily.

And it was a great improvement over the career-ending efficiency report that Pettin had probably planned to issue at the time the squadron lifted from Sexburga.

CHAPTER TWENTY-TWO

Adele echoed the right half of Daniel's display—a schematic of the Strymon system rather than the astrogation data on the left portion—as a sidebar on her own screen. Frankly, the icons on ghostly orbital tracks didn't mean a great deal more to her than the abstruse mathematics of Matrix navigation, but she knew Daniel would want to walk her through the display when he had a moment.

Her communications board was as silent as a snake waiting for prey. Within the Matrix, there was nothing to hear but static; so the experts said. Though sometimes the static formed patterns that almost mimicked communication.

Once Adele imagined that she heard her sister calling, "*Adele . . .*" After that she no longer listened to her equipment until the *Princess Cecile* reentered normal space.

"Going to put her right in the slip when we exit, sir?" Betts called from the attack console. His display was a mass of overlying curves in many colors.

Adele checked for curiosity's sake and found that the missileer had set up twelve separate attacks for each of his pair of launchers. The first factor in each equation was blank. The actual courses would be determined when the *Princess Cecile* exited the Matrix and thus had a location in the sidereal universe.

"No, we're going to be very discreet and not offend our hosts," Daniel said. He leaned back in his chair, watching his display but obviously not called on to act at the moment. "They deal with pirates who enter normal space adjacent to their target and use plasma cannon to strip the sails. A ship exiting near Tanais the way a pirate would is likely to be hailed by eight-inch cannon instead of a microwave dish."

There was general laughter on the bridge. The corvette was noisy with preparations for its return to sidereal space, but the spacers were talking normally instead of using the helmet intercom. Adele found communication systems interesting, though she felt a mild surprise whenever she remembered that she was no longer merely an observer.

"*Eight minutes to exit,*" rumbled the PA system in Lt. Mon's voice.

"Adele?" called Daniel. "Are you—yes, of course you are. Do you want a rundown of the Tanais control area?"

"Yes, Daniel," Adele said, careful to speak loudly so that she'd be heard. She was vaguely curious about the place they'd be spending the next two weeks, but not nearly as interested as Daniel was in informing her. The layout of the Strymonian naval base was a matter of record. What Adele had been sent to the system to learn was of a subtle and immaterial nature, not concrete and tunnels.

"*The base has three orbital forts, you see,*" Daniel said, now switching to intercom to keep private a conversation of no general interest. Carets of red light stabbed into the display. "*Because of tidal forces from the primary, that's Getica, they can't use an automatic defense array—*"

A constellation of nuclear mines in orbit, each ready to punch a light-speed rod of charged particles through a hostile vessel.

"*—unless they were willing to renew it every week. The orbital forts are powered, of course.*"

"I see," said Adele to indicate her presence. As she listened, her wands called up a catalog of the frequencies and codes on which the Tanais forts had operated in the past. The information had been gathered by visiting RCN vessels over six decades.

The Strymon fleet didn't pay nearly as much attention to communications security as it should: when a code changed, it generally reverted to one that had already been used in the past. The pirates who were the main threat to Strymon apparently didn't concern themselves with signals intelligence.

"*The* Sailing Directions *give a hailing point sixty thousand miles short of Tanais and in a direct line between the satellite and her primary,*" Daniel continued. His highlight this time formed a tiny sphere in the blankness, trundling slowly across the screen in concert with the large, peach-colored Getica and the smaller, bluish ball that was Tanais. "*We're going to exit a little farther out than that just to be safe. We're not expected, and I don't want to startle some sleepy watch officer into thinking he's being attacked.*"

Adele created a probability rota for codes and frequencies. There was no reason to hunt for a solution if one were already at hand. With the algorithms Mistress Sand provided, the *Princess Cecile's* main computer could turn any intercepted transmission into plain speech within minutes if not seconds, but even short delays could be significant.

A quarter second was enough time for Adele Mundy to draw her pistol and fire a pellet into the brain of another human being, for example; even less on a good day.

"*Two minutes to exit,*" Mon announced.

"*Ah—it appears that Getica is on the other side of the sun from Strymon,*" Daniel went on in sudden concern. "*When we arrive and during the whole period we'll be docked there. Will that be a problem for you, Adele?*"

"There's arrangements for message traffic between the base and Strymon, surely?" Adele said. Her wands quivered, putting her question into electronic form almost without her conscious volition. Data sprang to life on her display. "Yes, of course. A trio of transponder stations at three hundred million miles. There'll be delays, of course, and probably some corruption, but nothing that will prevent me from carrying out my tasks."

"*As if anything could, short of death,*" Daniel said. The intercom didn't transmit his chuckle, but she heard it faintly from across the bridge.

"I like to think so," Adele said. She allowed herself a smile, though there wasn't a great deal of humor in it.

Her work for Mistress Sand would be mostly archival. Conspirators—competent ones, at any rate—would shut down their operations while a Cinnabar squadron was in port, but there would remain vestiges of past activities that they couldn't remove even if they realized the need to do so.

Tanais would have a supposedly secure link to all government databases on Strymon proper. Adele would tap it within a few hours of the *Princess Cecile*'s arrival. Sorting for evidence of treachery would take time, but she was confident that before the squadron was ready to leave the system, the only thing that would prevent her from finding what she was looking for was total innocence on the part of Pleyna Vaughn and her government.

Adele's smile grew minutely broader without gaining much in the way of humor. She didn't believe in innocence as a concept, save perhaps in children like her late sister, Agatha.

Any responsible government in Strymon would have opened lines of communication to the Alliance. But if the present one had done so, its members would go the way . . . Agatha, say, had gone. Damned if you do, damned if you don't.

"*One minute to exit,*" Mon said. Tones echoed themselves up and down the *Princess Cecile*'s corridors.

"*Good, good, I was sure you'd manage,*" Daniel said. In his official voice he continued, "*Captain to ship. Prepare to enter normal space. Captain out.*"

The starship shuddered in a pattern that had by now become as familiar as Adele's nightmares and very nearly as unpleasant to experience. Colors inverted to their visual reciprocals. For an instant Adele saw not one compartment but an infinite series of compartments, each identical—almost—to the others.

She kept her eyes open. She'd tried closing them the first few times, and the result was even worse.

Another shudder. It was as disconcerting as the previous series even though Adele's conscious mind knew that when she was growing up *this* was the only universe she'd ever expected to know.

"*Hallelujah!*" a spacer shouted. Over the intercom, Lt. Mon bellowed, "*By God! I don't think we're the ship's length out of our calculated exit. Three cheers for Captain Leary!*"

Adele heard the cheering with a distant part of her mind. The rest of her, body and soul, was busy with the glut of information the *Princess Cecile*'s communications suite was gathering.

Signals Officer Mundy was at work.

"RCN corvette *Princess Cecile* requests landing clearance for Tanais Base," Daniel said, feeling expansive. "We'll need dockyard assistance in removing and refitting our fusion bottle, but the ship will be able to lift to another berth after initial touchdown if necessary. *Sissie* over."

Daniel was glad that Lt. Mon had told the crew about how precisely they'd exited the Matrix, because otherwise he might have said something himself. Daniel didn't like boastfulness, in himself or in others, but there were some things so uniquely wonderful that they shouldn't pass without comment.

"*Tanais control to RCN vessel,*" an agitated voice said after more than the normal lag for communications over a 70,000 mile separation. "*We have no information regarding your arrival here. You are not approved for landing. I repeat, you are not approved for landing! You must land on Strymon and get authorization from the Fleet Office before you can land here. Tanais control over.*"

Daniel frowned, the expression of an RCN officer and Cinnabar nobleman who'd just been told what to do by wogs. He glanced at the course schematic which had replaced the astrogation display when the corvette entered sidereal space. The *Princess Cecile* retained considerable velocity from the bubble universe from which it had exited. The High Drive was braking at .5 gee, the hardest a reasonable captain would stress a vessel with its sails set.

Lt. Mon had laid out a complex powered orbit that would bring the *Princess Cecile* around Tanais alone instead of looping the primary. He'd calculated it to give them time to scrub off momentum during the expected bureaucratic delays an unannounced vessel could expect before being assigned a berth.

The present business was not at all to be expected.

"Tanais control, this is RCN, I repeat, *RCN*, vessel *Princess Cecile*," Daniel said. He was handling the communications chores himself, both because he was more familiar with procedures than Adele and because her specialized skills could be put to better use at this moment than routine. "Your response is not satisfactory. Be advised that I intend to dock my vessel at Tanais Base in accordance with Strymon's treaty obligations to the Republic of Cinnabar. Over!"

His hand reached for a red button set into the material of the console; not a holographic construct. Before he touched it, General Quarters chimed through the corvette: Lt. Mon in the Battle Direction Center had been a hair quicker than his captain.

"*RCN vessel, wait please,*" said the controller. He sounded as though he was on the verge of a coronary or a nervous breakdown. "*Please wait. Tanais out . . . ah, over.*"

The bridge whispered with the motions of officers focusing on their individual domains. In the corridor the riggers who'd come in during exit—it was possible to make the transition with crewmen on the hull, but physical and psychological disorientation made it very dangerous for them—were locking their helmets shut in obedience to Woetjans' order over the intercom.

Daniel switched the left half of his display to a real-time image of Tanais. The corvette's course had already brought her within the forts' interlocking orbits. The whine of the High Drive gained in volume as it maintained balance between the conflicting pulls of Getica and of the smaller but closer satellite. Tanais Base was a scrawl within the ice sheet, visible from diffracted light. Thermal imaging would make the tunnels even more evident.

"*RCS Princess Cecile, this is Tanais Control,*" said a new voice: male, forceful, and very determined. "*Return to the challenge point immediately and stay there until you have authorization to close. You are in a restricted area at a time of national emergency. Return to the challenge point or we will fire! Tanais over!*"

Good God, there was a heavy battle squadron down there! Not in the base proper but on the ice on the side of Tanais which eternally faced Getica.

"Tanais Base, we're withdrawing immediately!" Daniel said as his fingers typed preset emergency codes. The first of them returned control to the command console from the Battle Direction Center. Lt. Mon might be able to handle this as ably as Daniel could, but it was God's truth that they couldn't both be responsible at the same time.

If Daniel had had time, he'd have prayed that he didn't miskey . . . but if he'd had time, he'd have been able to check his work. "I repeat, RCS *Princess Cecile* is withdrawing immedia—"

"*Daniel,*" said Adele's voice over the intercom. She didn't sound nervous but her tone was as joyless as a slaughterhouse. "*Base Command has just ordered the forts to open fire on us.*"

With the command console locked down the way it was, no one should have been able to break in. No one but Adele could have.

"Shit!" Daniel shouted. That probably startled Tanais Control, but a lot of people were getting surprises today. Daniel's left hand chopped the High Drive while his right engaged the sequence that would return the *Princess Cecile* to the Matrix.

"Ship!" Daniel said. "Spacers, we're under attack by Tanais Base. I'm inserting us into—"

The forts each mounted eight-inch plasma cannon in turrets on the north and south axes. The *Princess Cecile's* course had carried her planetward between two of the forts. Their guns fired as pairs within microseconds of one another. The bolts—dense, thigh-thick gouts of charged particles—tore through vacuum a hundred yards behind the corvette. They made their own light, like sections ripped from a star's corona.

"—the Matrix where—"

Daniel could feel the *Princess Cecile* start to shift out of sidereal space. The hair on his neck tingled and a trembling in his gut mimicked the onset of panic.

"—we'll be able—"

The forts missed because Daniel had shut off braking thrust as he prepared to reenter the Matrix. The gunnery computers calculated lead based on the rate of change in the corvette's progress—and therefore fired short. The delay between discharges for heavy cannon was fifteen to twenty seconds; otherwise heat buildup in the chamber would cause a catastrophic failure when lasers compressed and detonated the second tritium pellet. The *Princess Cecile* was safe from the guns that had already engaged her.

The third fort came around the curve of the satellite on a combination of the corvette's momentum and the fort's own orbital velocity. The *Princess Cecile's* vector above the surface of Tanais carried her directly toward the fort, giving the guns a zero-deflection shot.

Sun couldn't fire his own pairs of four-inch cannon because of the *Princess Cecile's* sails. When set they draped the hull like shrouds and would absorb the vessel's own discharges in fiery cataclysms.

"For what we are about to receive . . ." the gunner said, shouting because words were the only response he could make to a situation he appreciated even more clearly than his captain. "The Lord make us thankful!"

Two eight-inch plasma bolts ripped through the portion of the *Princess Cecile* which hadn't yet trembled out of sidereal space. Their scouring impact flared across Daniel's display.

CHAPTER TWENTY-THREE

"Well, things could be a great deal worse," said Daniel in a pleased tone, leaning back in his console.

The words and tone were perfectly predictable, Adele thought as she looked across the crowded bridge at the captain. Daniel would say the same thing—and mean it—if he'd just had both legs amputated. If Daniel Leary had a motto, it would be *While there's life, there's hope.*

On duty, at any rate. Off duty his motto would probably involve the age of suitability for girls.

Adele smiled faintly. Her own motto would be more along the lines of *While Daniel's alive, there's hope.* The *Princess Cecile*'s crew was a normal assemblage of human beings, some more sanguine than others; but not a soul of them would disagree with Adele there.

Woetjans and Pasternak stood in the center of the bridge. Even without Betts and Sun at their consoles—they were on the hull, checking the launcher hatches and gun turrets respectively for external damage—the chiefs of rig and ship filled the compartment. Condensate dripping from metal fittings of their rigging suits shrouded them in a clammy reminder of the environment from which they'd just returned.

"It's bloody well bad enough!" Woetjans said. "The sails, all right, we can patch and pair so that with the spares we've got pretty much a full set. They'll be the devil to furl where we've double-hung a yard to get full coverage out of rags, but we'll cope. The masts, though, the masts are fucked good."

296

"The hull's as solid as the day she came from the builders, though," said Pasternak. "The bolts pretty much dissipated on the sails—"

He glanced at the lowering Woetjans.

"—which is hard lines for the bosun here. I'm not saying I'm happy about what happened to her sails, but we're all better for not having taken an eight-inch bolt square on the hull, right?"

Woetjans grimaced, but she nodded agreement.

The corvette was full of noise. She was double hulled, and the cavities held spare rigging along with other stores which cold and vacuum wouldn't affect. The sound of hollow steel spars being withdrawn through the outside hatches rang within the hull like a tocsin.

Adele's screen quivered with pairs of conversations, sometimes a dozen at the same time, as spacers assessed the damage and started repairs. The *Princess Cecile* hung in normal space. Sun and Gansevoort had inserted intercoms from the internal helmets into prepared sockets in the riggers' suits, though Adele as Signals Officer had to activate each unit before it could be used.

A low-power radio signal on the hull of a starship in the Matrix would distort navigation by many light-years and in theory could rip antennas out of their steps. The *Princess Cecile* wouldn't be returning to the Matrix any time soon, however, so Daniel had approved his chiefs' request for quicker communications on the hull.

Lt. Mon entered the bridge, slipping between Woetjans and Pasternak without touching either of them. "All the spars are out of storage or will be," he announced. "Unless the bosun salvaged some pieces I don't know about, though, we're short six masts *and* four more of 'em are going to hang shorter yards than the standard."

He glared at Woetjans. Mon always looked angry, on the verge of a snarling explosion. From what Adele had seen of the man, his normal expression accurately described the personality beneath.

Despite that—because of it?—Mon's bubbling anger in a crisis was just as bracing as Daniel's cheerful insouciance. No one seeing either man could imagine they thought there was anything to be afraid of in the present situation.

"Naw, we're screwed," Woetjans agreed. "It was just bad luck that so many masts were burned through or near through, but because it happened when we were entering the Matrix . . ."

She shrugged. "The pieces're scattered through three, maybe four bubbles. We'd do better to carve new poles from asteroids than we would to go searching for the ones we lost."

"If we hadn't been entering the Matrix, there wouldn't 've been enough left of the *Sissie* to make you sneeze," Mon snapped. "The captain saved our *butts* by shunting us out so fast."

He rotated his glance around the room in search of anyone to deny his statement. Adele met the look with a cool frown; Mon's attitude affronted her, foolish though she understood her reaction to be.

"I think we can count ourselves lucky," Daniel said with a reminiscent smile. "I don't believe many corvettes have survived a pair of eight-inch bolts from such short range."

"We're safe enough," Woetjans said, "but it'll take us a month to limp back to Sexburga with the rig we've got left. Unless—"

Her voice changed, growing noticeably brighter.

"—you're planning to punch us straight back to Strymon, sir?"

"No, I'm not planning to do that," Daniel said without losing his smile. "But I assure you, Woetjans, the next time I need volunteers for a suicide mission I'll keep you in mind."

He looked at his officers, his face quite different from that of the man with whom Adele shared a two-room suite and who chatted about natural history and girls. His hand touched a key. In the air between him and the standing officers—Mon and Woetjans stepped back—appeared a holographic image of six starships against the icy surface of Tanais.

"The battleship is *Der Grosser Karl*," Daniel said. "She must be on her shakedown cruise."

"The bloody *Winckelmann* hasn't been in first-line service for twenty years," Mon muttered, "and the *Winckelmann*'s no bloody battleship."

"Yes, that's so," Daniel said. His tone was neutral, but Mon heard the reproach in it and colored. His lips formed a silent apology.

"The heavy cruiser is of the Marshal class," Daniel continued, "but she isn't any of the previously described members of that class. Presumably she's also a newly built vessel on her first commission, so we can hope that she's crewed largely by green personnel and hasn't been properly worked up as yet."

Everybody nodded. Adele didn't need Mon's editorializing to realize that the same could be said about the crews of Commodore Pettin's three vessels.

"The destroyers are R class, and they appear to have made a hard voyage to reach Strymon," Daniel said. "Two are missing masts, and a third has hull damage that may have been caused by thruster failures during landing. My guess is that the Alliance commander plans to refit his squadron on Tanais before proceeding to Strymon proper. The anti-Cinnabar faction in the government can seal off a naval base, but as soon as an Alliance squadron appears above Strymon, there's a certainty of word getting out."

"If Pettin catches the Alliance ships on the ground, he can handle them with even what he's got," Woetjans said. "It's suicide to lift when the other guy's shooting down a gravity well into your throat. Even a bloody battleship."

"There's the Tanais forts," Mon said. "Go back on the hull and look around if you've forgotten about them."

"More to the point," Daniel said, "there're normally four Strymonian frigates in orbit over Strymon. Because of the orbital positions of Strymon and Tanais I can't be sure, but we have to assume that the conspirators are being at least normally careful at this time."

"One moment," Adele said. Her wands called up the data she'd swept from the electromagnetic spectrum during the corvette's minutes in the Strymon system, then sorted it according to times and naval slugs. Among the officers behind her swirled a discussion of the danger even to a cruiser if she tried to lift with hostile frigates in orbit above her.

Tanais was 712 million miles from Strymon—somewhat closer to their common sun—when the *Princess Cecile* had approached the base. Rather than using the relay satellites, routine information was passed by courier vessels which shuttled back and forth through the Matrix, using microwave to cross the final 100,000 to 250,000 mile leg instead of landing at either end. Adele's data included the latest pair of transmissions.

It struck Adele that the crews of the courier vessels probably found the duty very boring; though her realization was based on what the spacers she served with would feel rather than any personal distaste for such duty. So long as Adele had a sufficient database to occupy her, she really didn't care whether she was on the ground or in a ship moving in a repetitive circuit.

Adele pulsed an amber caret across the top of Daniel's cabin-center display. She didn't want to break into the discussion, but she *did* have information the spacers might need.

"Yes, Adele?" Daniel said, interrupting Mon's gloomy assessment of Pettin's chances if he met the Alliance squadron on equal terms.

"Here are the four vessels on picket duty above Strymon," Adele said, replacing the Tanais display with her own. "Here are their officers and crew lists."

Amber sidebars hung beneath the holograms of four vessels— *101, 122, 124,* and *203.* Each was the shape of the *Princess Cecile* and approximately nine-tenths the size.

"Here are the armament inventories for the vessels," Adele continued. She frowned. "They appear to be complete, but I don't see any listing for missiles."

"Almighty God, I wish *I* didn't," Pasternak said. "I forgot those bastards were optimized to hunt pirates."

Daniel touched a key, highlighting in red a line in all four tables. "Strymonian frigates don't carry missiles the way you're used to thinking of them, Adele," he said.

He smiled, perhaps thinking as she was of the concept of Adele being used to anything naval. "What they have instead are chemical rockets that actually accelerate faster over the short ranges required than missiles powered by the High Drive. They carry a great number of them because the rockets are so much smaller."

"Ah," said Adele in understanding. Three hundred and twelve rockets apiece, launched in clusters of twenty-four at a time. "Yes, well I'm glad that my data were accurate."

Mon looked as though he were going to blow steam out of his ears, but Woetjans guffawed and said, "By *God* you're something else, mistress!"

"Yes, she is," Daniel said through his own laughter. "And she's pointed out why I'm not going to go orbit Strymon to warn the rest of the squadron. We can't do that safely until we're able to clear the picket vessels at the same time as we give Commodore

Pettin the alarm. I have the greatest confidence in the fighting ability of my ship and crew—"

His voice trembled a little. Emotion was never far from the surface of Daniel's mind. Sometimes like a porpoise it broke into plain sight when he clearly would rather keep it hidden. Adele smiled with sudden affection.

"—but I don't believe we'd succeed if we alone engaged four frigates as well-crewed and maintained as Officer Mundy shows us these are."

"Back to bloody Sexburga, then," Woetjans said. She turned her head, looking for something harmless to slap with her gloved hand. There was nothing in arm's reach of where she stood; Pasternak watched the movement with more than idle interest.

"If that was the only other choice, Woetjans," Daniel said, his voice almost musical with his effort to keep it calm, "then we'd try the odds on Strymon. I'm not leaving Commodore Pettin to be massacred by an Alliance squadron during the time we limp to Sexburga. Fortunately, there are other options."

He switched the image to a navigational display. It probably meant as little to Woetjans and Pasternak as it did to Adele, but Mon nodded and slipped his visor down over his eyes.

"The navigational computer has located us, I'm happy to say," Daniel said, keying a red highlight in the middle of the projected starfield. "You'll appreciate—"

He grinned at Adele, who hadn't really given the matter thought.

"—that my concern at Tanais was to go away rather than to go somewhere in particular. The damage to our sails during entry would have thrown us off course anyway."

"Seven light-years from Strymon?" Mon said, showing that he hadn't just been making a show of understanding.

"Yes, and just over twenty-four light-years from Dalbriggan," Daniel said. "That's the seat of government of the Selma Cluster. I make it approximately ninety minutes to Dalbriggan in the Matrix with our present rig. Once repairs are complete, of course."

"Dalbriggan?" said Pasternak. "The *Pirate* Cluster, sir?"

"Now, five years ago the Selma Cluster became a client state of the Republic," Daniel said, smiling like a little boy given the gift of his dreams. "The treaty's quite clear. They've sworn to eschew piracy and devote themselves to trade and other whole-some pursuits."

"Right," said Mon. "And my little girl was an immaculate con-ception, being born just before I got back from a two-year cruise."

"I'm aware that there may be quite a difference between what treaty signatories agree to and what they'll actually do," Daniel said. He pressed his palms together and seemed on the verge of rubbing them in the pleasure of his thoughts. "But it also seems to me that not-quite-reformed pirates might make willing allies against a pirate-hunting world like Strymon. Especially if the pirates are told they have the weight of the RCN on their side."

Daniel sobered slightly. "Not the full weight, I'll admit," he said, "but they'll have the *Princess Cecile*."

"By God!" Woetjans said. She stepped sideways—Pasternak, prepared, gave her room—and slammed the bulkhead between the missile and gunnery consoles with her hand. Spacers pass-ing along the corridor glanced into the bridge in concern.

"By God, who wouldn't that be enough for?" Woetjans said. "And by God, before we're done it'll be enough for those sneak-ing bastards that shot at us too!"

"I certainly hope so," Daniel said, his face beaming with anti-cipation. "I certainly do."

The riggers came inside with the thumps and crashing of even greater haste than their usual. Before the inner lock was closed, Woetjans unlatched her visor and shouted, "Sir! We're battle-rigged and ready to roll!"

Daniel looked at his display—he'd trust his bosun over what-ever the electronics said, but spacers become old spacers by double-checking everything—and saw that the schematic too believed the corvette was rigged for immediate action. The sixteen antennas on the rings nearest the bow and stern—A, B, E, and F—were folded along the hull. That gave free traverse to the gun turrets and permitted missile launches without the risk of losing sails to the antimatter exhausts.

The *Princess Cecile* would handle like a pig on entry and exit from the Matrix, but this was a hop of short duration: S1, the sun about which Dalbriggan rotated, was noticeably brighter than other stars in a hullside view of the corvette's surroundings. Daniel had entered the system to within 200 million miles of Dalbriggan, then paused to rerig.

"Preparing to enter the Matrix . . ." Daniel announced over the warning chimes. He felt forces shifting, finding a balance that wasn't of the human universe. "*Now!*"

The *Princess Cecile* and her crew entered the Matrix. To Daniel it was the motion of a coin flipping in some fourth dimension, *obverse/reverse/obverse/reverse*, though he knew others described the experience in very different fashions. The reality was beyond human understanding, so no analogy could be more than partial.

Almost as the *Princess Cecile* entered, the clock began counting down seconds to exit. The intermediate appearance within the S1 system didn't constitute a risk of detection: the *Princess Cecile* would be arriving above Dalbriggan before the light of her previous exit had reached observers on the planet.

"Action stations!" Daniel ordered, but of course the crew had been at action stations for most of the past hour. Betts and Sun were intent on their displays; Adele alone was watching Daniel. The tension at the corners of her eyes was due to the Matrix, not because of fear of what they would meet when they returned to sidereal space. "Prepare to exit the Matrix!"

Vibration at his nerve cores, the feeling of wires drawn to the point of rupture—

Exit!

Gasping, suddenly aware that he'd been holding his breath for the past minute or more, Daniel keyed his transmitter. It was set to 15kH, the hailing frequency here in the Sack in contrast to the 10kH push used generally on the worlds outside.

"RCS *Princess Cecile* to Dalbriggan Control," he announced. "We're scrubbing velocity with a circuit of your planet, then we'll land at Council Field. Wake your chief up. This is his lucky day, whether he knows it or not. RCN over."

They were a hundred thousand miles out from Dalbriggan. They'd returned to sidereal space squarely over Council Field, which the *Sailing Directions* said served as a capital for as much of the cluster as was under unified control at the moment. It was a dry-land site. Daniel counted thirty-seven ships on the ground, though some of them were probably hulks as incapable of star travel as his own left boot.

None of the vessels was the size of the *Princess Cecile*, and few were more than half her size. They bristled with light plasma cannon, sometimes in fixed mountings of four and eight tubes like a bank of organ pipes. At close range a rack like that could strip a merchantman's sails in a matter of seconds without endangering the hull and valuable cargo.

"*RCN ship, this is Dalbriggan,*" responded a voice promptly. "*You want to wake up the Astrogator, you go right ahead. Maybe if he's feeling kindly, he'll cut your throat before he stuffs your balls in your mouth.*"

There was a pause before the voice continued, "*There's a ship lifting whenever Hesseltine gets her thumbs outa her ass, but I don't guess that'll happen before you're on the ground. If you don't set down on the first go-round, though, you better check back with me. Out.*"

"Riggers topside!" Daniel ordered. The bosun had already opened the inner hatch of Bow Dorsal airlock. The High Drive keened, slowing the vessel. Working in a haze of not-quite-complete matter-antimatter cancellation was unpleasant for the riggers, but the quicker Daniel was on the ground confronting the Astrogator, the better. Surprise and the name of the RCN were the best weapons Daniel had at the moment.

Course vectors for landing filled the right half of Daniel's console, set by Lt. Mon from the Battle Direction Center. Daniel switched the real-time display on the left to a Plot Position Indicator. Three vessels were in eccentric orbit around the planet. There was no certainty that they were guardships rather than hulks, but Dalbriggan Control seemed quite competent, albeit eccentric by the standards of more settled worlds.

"*Captain, I've got set-ups on the three pickets,*" Betts said as he concentrated on his attack console. The missileer's fingers continued to type in coordinates, though his words had claimed the courses were already planned. "*If we don't watch out, they'll be all over us like stink on shit! Over.*"

Daniel smiled faintly. Obviously Betts shared his belief that the pirates were keeping a proper guard. Instead of replying, however, he said, "Dalbriggan Control, we'll land after one circuit."

The schematic showed all the sails were furled and most of the masts had been unlocked. Woetjans would have her riggers back aboard well before the corvette had completed its forty minute orbit.

"Have you assigned us a particular berth? RCN over."

Daniel was emphasizing his association, the Republic of Cinnabar Navy, rather than the name of his vessel. The folk who ran the Selma Cluster didn't care about ship names, but by God! they knew to care about the RCN.

"*RCN, you can land any bloody place you want,*" the controller said. "*Just remember we don't run to limousine service here, so if you don't have your own ground transport you're going to do a lot of walking.*"

Daniel thought the controller had finished without signing off, but a moment later the voice added, "*The Astrogator says he'll meet you in the Hall and that you better not keep him waiting. Out.*"

The riggers were thundering back aboard. Daniel checked the landing vectors and nodded appreciatively. A red-outlined overlay at the top of his screen showed the ground plan of the Council Field with the large building along the north side careted. Trust Adele to have information waiting before he needed it.

"Dalbriggan Control," Daniel said, "this is Lieutenant Daniel Leary of the *Princess Cecile*. Assure the Astrogator that I understand him very well, and I'm pleased to see that he understands me as well. RCN out!"

The whine of the High Drive gave way to the roaring pulse of plasma thrusters as the *Princess Cecile* braked hard on its way into the atmosphere. Daniel was smiling. He had a good feeling about this one.

Though he didn't suppose he could explain why in words that didn't leave everybody else thinking he was out of his mind.

CHAPTER TWENTY-FOUR

The *Princess Cecile* came down on the patch of dirt between two Dalbriggan cutters, a hundred yards from the Hall. This was a normal landing place: already blast-scarred and separated by a berm from the Hall which faced it.

"Normal" meant a berth for a 300-ton cutter, however, not a corvette four times as heavy. The *Princess Cecile*'s plasma thrusters slammed the vessels to either side of her, flinging rocks and clods of baked clay against their hulls.

When the *Princess Cecile* finally came to rest, Daniel rose to his feet feeling shaken. "Almighty God!" he said to Adele because she stood facing him. "I almost let reflected thrust flip her over on her back. On water . . ."

He let his voice trail off because he feared he was making excuses. When a starship landed on water, as Daniel had on every previous occasion, a tilted thruster raised a plume of steam which righted the imbalance gently. From a hard surface, the plasma reflected in a violent shock wave. The *Princess Cecile* had pogoed from outrigger to outrigger in the half-second it took Daniel to cut thrust by three-quarters.

"The boarding party's waiting at the main hatch, sir," Woetjans said. The bosun held a stocked impeller and wore a bandolier of reloads besides her equipment belt. She didn't look any more concerned about the landing than Adele did.

"*Not* before the master puts on his pretty white suit," Hogg announced. He held the jacket and trousers of Daniel's 1st Class uniform; Tovera, smiling faintly, stood behind him with the shoes and hat. "You're going to see the high muckymuck of the whole cluster, after all."

Adele looked at Hogg curiously. "The Astrogator is a pirate, Hogg," she said, an observation rather than an argument.

"All the more reason, mistress," Hogg said firmly. "You've got to put on side with wogs or they don't respect you."

Adele grimaced—Daniel knew she didn't like the ethnic pejoratives that were universal with Hogg and most of the Cinnabar spacers. She turned up her palm and let the subject drop.

Daniel changed clothes, which mostly meant moving his limbs as directed while Hogg and Tovera stripped off his garments and put on fancier ones. "Adele?" Daniel said. "Will you be needed at your console, or . . . ?"

"Certainly not," Adele said tartly. "I'll be with you in case the Astrogator requires detailed information."

Daniel smiled. "Yes," he said. "That too."

Adele looked suddenly worried. "I don't have to change clothes, do I? I don't have a white uniform."

"Just the master dresses up, mistress," Hogg said with assurance. "The rest of us look like a buncha scruffs, but we carry enough hardware to blow a hole in the landscape. Not that I expect shooting, but we gotta blend in t' talk to these types."

Daniel heard the main hatch undogging in a metallic chorus. The bolts withdrew with quick hammerblows that rang through the fabric of the ship. He keyed the PA system and said, "Mr. Mon, you're in command until I return from a chat with the Astrogator," he said.

Starting for the companionway, Daniel added, "Woetjans, I think an escort of ten crewmen under a petty officer will be sufficient."

"You've got twenty and I'm in charge of them," the bosun said as she preceded him. "Besides your own party. Sir."

Which amounted to—Daniel looked over his shoulder to see who was following—Adele with Hogg and Tovera both. The pale spider whom Adele used for a servant carried the attaché case which contained her submachine gun. Hogg had slung a knapsack over his left shoulder; on his right hung a submachine gun muzzle-forward in a patrol sling.

"We're not going to fight a whole planetful of pirates, Hogg,"

Daniel said, knowing he sounded peevish. If there was fighting at all, it meant that his plan had gone wrong.

"If we look like we're ready to, young master," Hogg said, wheezing down the companionway behind him, "then maybe we won't have to. And anyway, I'm not as sure as you are just what's going to happen in that warehouse you're taking us into."

Daniel grimaced but said nothing further. In all truth, a gunfight in the pirate's council hall would be a lot less surprising than the recent attack by the Tanais defenses.

The guards in the entryway were alert, which wasn't entirely a good thing. Daniel had been raised in the country and had handled guns from before he could write in cursive. Most of the spacers were as ignorant of firearms as they were of formal etiquette. There was a real possibility that a tense guard was going to blow a hole the size of a dinner plate through Daniel as he walked down the gangplank.

"Hogg, remind me to institute a program of small-arms training as soon as we've sorted out this business with Strymon, will you?" he said.

"That's if none of our good friends have shot holes in our backs in the meantime, you mean," Hogg muttered.

"Yes, indeed," said Adele, and even Tovera was nodding with her serpentine smile. It seemed to be a general concern among all members of the community who really knew which end of the gun the slug came out of.

The crewmen of the escort waited in the B Level corridors to either side of the entryway, keeping out of the way until it was time to leave. They jostled as they fell in behind Daniel.

All were volunteers, but virtually every spacer on the *Princess Cecile* would have joined the party if Daniel had been willing to strip the ship. Those Woetjans had chosen were those she wanted to have at her back in a brawl: mostly big, invariably aggressive, and for this mission armed to the teeth.

The ground reradiated the heat of its recent bath in plasma. The local time was just after dawn, and the blue-white intensity of S1 cast sharp shadows across the Council Field.

"They've got some defenses here and no mistake," Woetjans muttered, nodding in the direction of a circular wall like a well coping, one of six such ranged in a diagonal line across the field.

Each was a cluster of hypervelocity rockets which could skewer a starship in orbit.

"I've taken over the central controller," Adele said primly, "but each installation has an optical sight and manual controls that I can't touch. Well, from outside the installation itself, I mean."

"I don't believe we'll need to assault the harbor defenses," Daniel said, wondering if Adele had been seriously considering that. Council Field was nearly a mile square, though the ships were mostly at this end, near the Hall. Houses were scattered throughout in the neighboring forest. Running over bare baked earth to attack the most distant rocket pit didn't strike him as a practical proposition.

He smiled. Woetjans saw the expression and said, "Sir?"

"I was just thinking," Daniel explained. "Needs must when the Devil drives. But I really doubt he's going to drive us hard today."

The sky rumbled with the arrival of another starship. The flickering plasma threw faint highlights into the long morning shadows.

"*Ship to boarders,*" explained the intercom in a female voice— Vesey, for a fact. "*One of the pickets is coming down. Seven cutters have lifted from outlying locations and are proceeding toward the Council Field within the atmosphere. Ship out.*"

Aircars were approaching the Hall also. As Woetjans led the dismounted party into the opening through the berm—built out in an elbow to block blasts from landings and liftoffs—a big vehicle overflew them at low level. It had started life as a truck, but the addition of armor and pintle-mounted weapons turned it into an assault vehicle of sorts. The Selma pirates attacked settlements on the ground as well as preying on merchant vessels.

The powerful fans buffeted the spacers beneath, knocking some to their knees. It was like being caught in a millrace. Daniel glanced back. Hogg, his feet braced wide apart, held Adele like scaffolding about a slender pole. Grit and larger pebbles bit as they spun about the narrow passage.

"Boarders, don't shoot!" Daniel said, using the intercom to make sure of being heard over the aircar's roar. "We knew they'd be playing games, so just keep your tempers! Over."

"It scarce can keep in the air!" shouted Barnes, who'd driven aircars both as a civilian and under Daniel's command. "They're a load of bloody fools to load the bitch that way!"

The aircar dropped below the berm and landed noisily just out of sight. Other vehicles, similar but not quite so extensively modified, came from all directions to join the assembly. Daniel wondered if the car that had hammered them did so not as hazing but because the entranceway was the only place the driver felt confident of getting his overweight vehicle over the berm.

"Boarders, they're for scaring civilians, not for real fighting," Daniel said. He used the intercom again so that all his crew could hear the calm in his voice. "They know we're here to bargain and they're just starting the haggling early. Over."

"They come down on Bantry in them clown cars and they'll learn what real fighting is," Hogg said. He was genuinely angry, a very different thing from the loud bluster he used to cow people who were frightened by open emotion. "Me and half a dozen of the boys'd take care of the business without having to reload."

Hogg had a cut on his cheek from some jagged bit of debris, though he seemed to be more concerned about Adele . . . who was fine, as her quick nod assured Daniel.

"For the moment my priority is with the people who fired plasma cannon at us, Hogg," Daniel said, coloring his voice with the hint of superciliousness which never failed to remind Hogg that Daniel was his master in fact. "There may be a chance to discuss matters with the folks who blew dust on us later, but I can't say it concerns me a great deal."

"Sorry," Hogg muttered. "Won't happen again."

"Carry on," said Daniel mildly. Nothing had really happened, of course, but Daniel knew his servant too well—and Hogg knew himself—for either of them to take the matter lightly.

The Hall was the size of a maintenance hangar, built of wood on pilings that raised it three steps above the ground. A sounder of lean gray pigs, Terran stock but feral, trotted along the side of the building in the direction of the garbage dump to the rear. In the lead was a boar who clashed his tusks at the strangers coming through the berm. The pigs ignored the garishly dressed locals swaggering toward the Hall.

Three aircars landed in quick succession. Each driver tried to put his vehicle closer to the Hall's entrance than the other two. What would've been a shoving match in humans meant screaming metal, then a crash like a sack of anvils falling.

"They're saving us effort, Mister Hogg," Tovera called in a clear voice. "Perhaps we should be thankful."

Hogg guffawed loudly. Daniel leaned close to Adele and said into her ear, "I didn't know your servant had a sense of humor, Adele."

"I'm not sure she does," Adele replied with cool amusement.

The Hall's roof had a high central peak and flaring eaves. Though the air was dry at present and dust blew along the ground, the structure gave every evidence of being built for downpours. Which raised the question of refilling the *Princess Cecile*'s reaction mass tanks on a dry field, but that could wait for a more suitable time.

Instead of a door, the whole end of the Hall was open. Daniel looked upward and saw, furled beneath the eaves, curtains of bark fiber to shield the interior in event of rain.

On the broad porch fronting the entranceway stood Dalbriggans in flowing, garish dress. Weapons—knives, guns, and the occasional rocket launcher—were the universal accessory items. More locals joined those already present, not overtly hostile but showing no sign of opening a passage for the approaching Cinnabars.

"Barnes, Dasi, Hogg, front of the line *now*," Woetjans ordered. Barnes and Dasi were the biggest men on the ship, nearly as tall as the bosun and with the male animal's greater muscle mass.

Hogg, short and pudgy, was on the end opposite Woetjans for reasons other than size. He reached into his knapsack, came out with three fist-sized bundles, and began juggling them. That was an impressive trick while walking forward with gear strapped over both shoulders.

The Cinnabars started up the building-wide steps toward the jeering mass of pirates. Daniel saw the locals brace themselves shoulder to shoulder to resist the spacers' impact. Behind them, their fellows leaned forward to add their weight to the line.

Daniel grinned faintly. He wondered when it would be that a pirate noticed that Hogg was juggling—

"Ganesh bugger me!" a Dalbriggan shouted over the catcalls of her fellows. "That's metallic hydrogen he's tossing around!"

Hogg neatly reversed the flow of his juggling from clockwise to counterclockwise. Three identical items were nothing for a juggler as accomplished as he was. He'd kept the young Daniel amused for hours with up to seven objects—eggs, stones, or the cook's knives, it was all the same to Hogg—in the air at one time.

Now it was blasting charges of metallic hydrogen in zero-zero insulation. Metallic hydrogen had greater energy density than any other explosive, and more shattering power—greater propagation speed—than anything but capacitor-discharge units.

The charges had no fragmentation effect, of course: the explosive's violence would rupture any casing into its constituent atoms. The blast alone would puree everybody on the porch and deafen their neighbors half a mile away.

"Hey, make way, you ratfuckers!" called a front-rank pirate over his shoulder. "These guys juggle bombs!"

"Hold up!" Daniel called, though the veterans around him didn't need to be warned. They'd already paused on the second step for the message to spread over the noise of the crowd.

A corridor opened through the crowd, caused in part by Dalbriggans going into the Hall ahead of the strangers. The game was over. The locals had pushed, the Cinnabars had pushed back; there was no longer any point in standing out on the porch when the real business would take place inside.

Adele stepped close and said, "They aren't frightened."

Daniel nodded. "Well, no more than we are," he said with a grin. "I assure you, tossing around hydrogen charges scares all thought of sin right out of me. . . . "

He felt his grin broaden into a sunny smile. "Well, perhaps not *all* thought," he added. "Did you see the little blonde in leather dyed the color of her hair?"

"The one with the right side of her scalp shaved and the hair on the left side down to her waist?" Adele said. "Yes, as a matter of fact I did notice her. Though I obviously lack the eye of a connoisseur."

"Let's go!" Woetjans ordered, starting the party forward again. Hogg had stopped juggling. He slipped two of the bombs into his pockets and held the third in his left hand with his thumb though the safety ring. His grin showed he'd gotten over his ill-temper of a few minutes before.

The Hall had a cathedral ceiling forty feet high at the ridge-pole. Clear panels set in the roof lighted the interior during day-time, but Daniel noted that a system of cold-discharge illumination ran along the roofbeams. Though the Hall appeared rustic, its fittings were as advanced as those of the Senate House in Xenos . . . which also held to the appearance of past times for tradition's sake.

The Hall's only furnishings were a curving, five-step dais at the end opposite the opening and a lectern at one side of it. A score of Dalbriggans stood at various levels of the dais, a hierarchy that both Daniel's interests in natural history and his experience in the RCN fitted him to understand. The man alone in the center of the top row was tall, thin, gray-haired, and as surely in charge as Speaker Leary at the height of his power a decade before.

"Astrogator Kelburney," Adele said, speaking into Daniel's ear. She avoided using the intercom except when there was no other choice.

With the spreading nonchalance of water poured from an overturned bucket, locals entered the Hall around and behind the Cinnabars. Occasionally a Dalbriggan would join the leaders on the dais, but for the most part they stood in self-defined groupings on the open floor. At a quick glance Daniel judged about a third of those present were women, though their numbers on the dais formed a lower percentage.

A middle-aged woman in severe black, the only person Daniel saw who wasn't armed, stood at the lectern. She spoke, her voice filling the vast room from scores of speakers hidden in the roofbeams. "Captains and officers to the front, common crew in the body of the Hall! No exceptions!"

Daniel turned his head with a smile. "Boarders," he said. The Hall was alive with sound. "Officer Mundy goes with me, the rest of you take your places in the front of the crowd. Over."

"Sir, I'm an officer!" Woetjans said, her face screwed tight with concern. She held the length of alloy tubing that was her weapon of choice in any circumstances that permitted it.

"Yes," Daniel said. "And I'm your captain. Carry out your orders, Officer Woetjans."

Those closest could hear them, but this discussion wasn't over the intercom. Woetjans wasn't concerned about status. She simply wanted to be beside Daniel if trouble started.

Halfway up the pillar which supported the roof at the open

end was a platform holding a life-sized statue of the man at the top of the dais. It was of gold; not a significant cost increment to a spacefaring nation which could gather metals in any volume in asteroid belts, but nonetheless an untarnishable assertion. Its blue-glinting eyes were faceted sapphires.

Daniel smiled. His father hadn't gone to quite that length, but he would certainly have appreciated Astrogator Kelburney's gesture.

Hogg nudged Woetjans in the ribs. "Hey," he said. "Stick by me, cutie, and I'll let you hold one of my bombs."

The bosun looked down at him, then barked a laugh. "Right!" she said, smacking the tubing into her left palm with a sound like a whiplash. "Boarders with me. We're going to get a good spot to see Cinnabar's best make monkeys out of a bunch of wogs!"

"Come on, Adele," Daniel said. Loud enough to be sure that everyone in his party could hear, he added, "We'll get a good view of the room from the top step, don't you think?"

Most of the smells peculiar to this part of Dalbriggan were unfamiliar to Adele, but they were pleasant enough. She particularly liked the spicy sweetness that seemed to come from the wood of the Hall itself.

The hog-scavenged dump was downwind, a considerable improvement on her apartment in Xenos where the street was cleaned primarily by the heavy spring rainfalls. It wasn't a matter of great concern to Adele, but she noticed it as she noticed many things.

She walked forward with Daniel. Their escort had stopped a pace back, but there was no longer a crush that Woetjans and her henchmen had to muscle through. The Dalbriggans had left room for the escort at the front of the gathering; the space was tight, but the Cinnabars were no worse crowded than the locals themselves.

"As the local representatives of the Republic of Cinnabar," Daniel declared at the foot of the dais, "my companion and I will take our places beside the Astrogator!"

He'd started out speaking at maximum volume. A hidden directional microphone picked up his words and amplified them around the Hall without need for human effort. Daniel let his voice drop and found that the public address system compensated with no more than a stutter.

He glanced at Adele and winked; she kept a straight face, concerned about what she was to do. This was worse than a formal dinner in the *Princess Cecile's* wardroom. There at least it was unlikely that she could make a mistake which would lead to the massacre of all her companions.

She smiled, a reflection of the amusement she knew Daniel would express if she'd been able to speak the last chain of thoughts aloud. That wasn't practical, so she had to laugh on her friend's behalf.

"Captain Leary stands by me," said the Astrogator. His voice had a resonance that could have filled the vast building unaided. "His officer stands on the bottom row where she belongs."

Daniel took the first step and the second at a measured pace, gesturing Adele along with a minuscule crook of his index finger. "When you come to Cinnabar," he said ringingly, "you follow Cinnabar custom. When Cinnabar comes to you, Astrogator Kelburney, you still follow Cinnabar custom. We represent the Republic!"

Daniel took the third step, then the fourth; none of the captains already on the dais moved to bar his way. Adele followed, watching her feet. The treads were deeper than she was used to, and it wouldn't help the mission if she were to fall on her face.

Kelburney laughed; it was impossible to tell how much of the humor was real. "Come up, then, Captain," he said. "And bring your bitch as well if you're so devoted to her."

They took their places on the top level, Daniel to the Astrogator's right and Adele beside Daniel. She turned and looked back the way she'd come. The Hall had very nearly filled during the time it took the Cinnabar contingent to walk its length. There were several thousand people present, more than Adele would've imagined possible from the Hall's forested environs.

"Silence for the cup!" said the woman at the lectern. So many people in a single room couldn't be really silent—their breathing alone was a deep susurrus like that of a sleeping dragon—but the voices stilled. A pair of servants came forward.

They were old, and both were crippled: the man stomped along on one leg and a peg, while the blast that scarred the left side of the woman's face had also burned off her arm. She carried a wineskin on a strap over her good shoulder. The man had a gold-mounted cup in his hands.

Adele's face hardened. The cup was made from the brainbox of a human skull. For a moment Adele had permitted herself to imagine that the able use of technology made Dalbriggan a sophisticated planet.

The woman filled the cup, lifting the strap with her shoulder and squeezing the wineskin between her elbow and torso. The man handed the cup to the Dalbriggan on the end of the bottom row. He drank, an honest swallow, and passed the cup to the officer beside him. She drank as well and passed the cup in turn.

Four more had drunk before the last handed the cup to the servants to be refilled. The ceremony continued.

Adele didn't let her mind wander; rather she slipped into a world where no one could touch her. It was a cold place and utterly colorless, but it was familiar to her. She'd spent a great deal of time in grayness since the day she learned that her family had been massacred, leaving Adele Mundy a destitute orphan.

She could function in this place but she couldn't feel a thing; which was generally for the best.

There was a sound in front of Adele. Her eyes locked into focus with those of the cripple offering her the refilled cup. "No, thank you," Adele said in a clear voice.

Daniel reached past her and took the cup. The bone was old; yellow on the outside, dark as the wine itself on the inside from generations of use.

"No!" said Kelburney. He stepped in front of Daniel on the broad tread and put his hand over the cup before Daniel could lift it. The Astrogator was taller than he'd seemed when the Cinnabars first entered the Hall, and his powerful wrists belied his slender appearance.

Kelburney wore a cloth-of-gold tunic over pantaloons of the same material. His wide belt and crossed bandoliers were scaly leather, sagging with the weight of ammunition, knives, and pistols in open-topped holsters. The weapons showed signs of hard use.

"She'll drink from the cup, *Captain* Leary," the Astrogator said, "or she leaves the Hall. That I swear, though a Cinnabar fleet orbits above us!"

Adele stared calmly at the tall Dalbriggan; her mind analyzed the situation as coldly as it would if she were not directly involved. Kelburney's boast that he'd defy a Cinnabar fleet was just that, a boast. The *Princess Cecile* was the only RCN vessel present, however—and it was quite clear from Kelburney's expression that his anger and determination were real. Tendons stood out on his neck.

Adele smiled. It appeared that the ceremony of the cup was a major aspect of Dalbriggan faith. Well, faith or not, it was equally important to Adele that she not sup with utensils made from human bodies.

"You misunderstand me, sir," she said. The hidden director controlling the parabolic microphone picked up her voice and amplified it so the whole room could hear. "My religion forbids me to drink—"

As Adele spoke, her eyes holding the Astrogator's, her left hand reached out and slid the pistol from the cross-draw holster at his left hip. She didn't know the weapon, but the range was too great for the light projectiles of the pistol in her own pocket.

"—and requires that if I do—"

Kelburney felt the weight of the pistol withdrawing. He tried to grab Adele's hand. Daniel caught his wrist. The two men remained locked together motionless. Kelburney's expression changed to amazement; Daniel only appeared soft.

"—I must kill the person who compelled me," Adele said.

She turned side-on to the far end of the Hall, the pistol extended in line with her left arm. She'd been trained as a duelist, not a pistolero.

The audience was shouting, but Adele doubted anyone was going to shoot at her so long as she was standing close to the Astrogator. The captains nearby on the dais were more of a threat, but they seemed willing to let matters take their course. Anyway, Adele couldn't control what other people did.

She could only control the pistol in her hand.

The weapon was stone-axe simple, with only a post and ring for sighting. At this range, a little over a hundred yards, Adele wouldn't have minded holographic magnification; but she'd make do.

The power was already switched to the coils. Kelburney wasn't the sort to let his last act in life be fumbling to take his pistol off safe.

Adele squeezed the trigger as she exhaled, both eyes open. The sound of the room departed like water vanishing down a drain. The front post was sharply focused; her target was a blue glint in a gray-gold blur.

WHACK!

The snapping discharge through the impeller rings was a surprise as usual, accelerating the heavy slug to several times the speed of sound. The pistol recoiled in Adele's hand, the muzzle lifting. It was well balanced, settling back on target as naturally as Adele's own familiar weapon would have done.

The head of Kelburney's statue twisted awry. Whether she'd hit the right eye or not, she'd certainly torn the casting enough that the sapphire flew out of its socket.

WHACK/WHANG!

In her concentration Adele hadn't heard the sound of the first slug's hammerblow on the metal, but she did the second as gold ripped apart. Long splinters, reddish against the age-blackened surface wood, stood out from the post like a halo where the shots had penetrated after striking the metal.

The top of the statue's head tumbled ringingly to the floor. Dalbriggans in the back of the Hall scrambled to get out of the way.

"I believe you have a second cup now, Astrogator Kelburney," Daniel said, releasing the older man and stepping back. "If you'll have somebody bring it up to us, perhaps you and I can use it to drink to a new understanding between your people and mine."

He smiled toward Adele. "At any rate," he added, "I believe you understand Officer Mundy better now."

Adele took the pistol by the receiver with her right fingertips and offered the butt to Kelburney. The flux had heated the barrel to yellow heat in only two shots. It was a powerful weapon, meant to punch through body armor.

"Thank you for the loan, sir," Adele said.

The only noise in the Hall was the continuing echo from the commotion moments before. The Dalbriggan officers on the dais drew back with sharp expressions, more tense than they'd been while Adele was aiming the weapon.

Kelburney took the pistol expressionlessly. He looked at the truncated statue, obviously judging the likelihood that he could duplicate Adele's feat—and correctly deciding that there wasn't a snowball's chance in Hell of it.

"Here, woman," he said, handing the pistol back to Adele. "Anybody who can shoot the way you can ought to have a gun of her own."

And what in heaven's name am I supposed to do with a cannon like this? Adele thought; but she took the weapon with a tight smile. That was the politic thing to do, after all, and it was a *very* nice piece of workmanship.

Kelburney turned to face the assembly and placed his hands on his hips. "Siblings of the stars!" he said. "Free citizens of Dalbriggan and the universe! Is it your will that I and your council examine these strangers and make policy based on what we learn?"

The shout built from a dozen throats to a hundred; finally the whole assembly shook the walls with its bellowed response. At first there were a few cries of, "No!" among the general assent, but as the volume built so did the agreement.

Kelburney raised his arms skyward. The shouting stopped, though the Hall still rumbled with shuffling feet and indrawn breaths.

"Siblings!" Kelburney said. "Will you be bound by our decision?"

This time there was no opposition. The assembly's decision was implicit in its first response; and this would not, Adele suspected, be a good environment for people who recalcitrantly espoused a minority view.

Kelburney gestured Adele and Daniel both close. He shouted into their ears, "The Council Chamber's through the door behind us. I'm glad to learn the RCN has a proposition for me, because as it chances I have a proposition for the RCN."

He gestured them ahead. Others from the dais were already going into the room beyond, though the Hall proper still reverberated with the enthusiasm of the full assembly.

I wonder, Adele thought, *if I should ask for a holster and belt while I'm at it?*

CHAPTER TWENTY-FIVE

The *Sailing Directions* said the Selma pirates took slaves along with their other loot, so Daniel was surprised to see that the only servants in the semicircular council chamber were a half-dozen adolescents and the two aged cripples who'd brought the cup around at the assembly. From the freedom with which they bantered with the officers, all were freeborn Dalbriggans.

Adele walked beside him, holding the heavy service pistol as gingerly as a spinster with a baby. She could put it in a cargo pocket since the barrel had cooled by now, or she could lay it on the scarred table. Daniel didn't say either of those things because Adele was as able to see the possibilities as he was; and as with the spinster, there was more than a little pride in her expression.

She leaned close and said, "Interesting. They don't allow slaves to be present during governmental deliberations. That shows better judgment than most slaveholders display."

The Astrogator pointed to a seat in the middle of the table and said, "I'd like you there, Leary, facing me. Unless you're scared to have your back to the door?"

Daniel chuckled. He gestured Adele to the chair beside the one indicated and said, "I doubt I have as many enemies on Dalbriggan as you do, Kelburney. Now that you've raised the question, though, I'll try to control my fear that somebody'll shoot through me to get you."

The Astrogator snorted. He lowered himself into the chair across from Daniel—handsawn wood of simple design like the others, but the only one in the room with arms—and said without preamble over the sound of the others scraping into their seats, "I saw your ship when you landed. Looks to me like you didn't show the best judgment in who you mixed it with."

"The fight wasn't our choice," Daniel said calmly, "and it's not over yet. On my honor! it's not. But yes, the *Sissie* needs some work. My crew will handle the labor, but I'll be purchasing supplies from your stores."

"We run to small craft here," Kelburney said. "There's no masts on Dalbriggan to fit a corvette like yours."

He turned his right palm out to forestall anything Daniel might try to interject. For the moment at least it appeared the form "I and your council" meant "I, the Astrogator." The ships' officers ranged up and down the long table watched carefully as they drank from the mugs servants were handing out, but they held their peace.

"We can help you get what you need, though," Kelburney said. He smiled like a hungry cat. "If you've got the balls."

Daniel spread his fingers on the tabletop as he considered the Astrogator. A boy put a goblet carved from rock crystal on the wood beside him; the mahogany-colored fluid foamed slightly.

Taley and the *Princess Cecile*'s riggers could fish and weld spars meant for Dalbriggan cutters into a working set of masts for the corvette; everybody in the room—with the possible exception of Adele—knew that. Kelburney was offering a plausible excuse as a bargaining ploy.

That was fine: Daniel was here to bargain. He smiled back and said, "I think you'll find the RCN always has the courage to do its duty, Astrogator Kelburney; whatever the circumstances. Why don't you describe your plan so that I can decide where my duty lies?"

"Bring in the prisoners," Kelburney called. A door hidden behind hangings at the side of the room opened. Six concerned-looking spacers entered behind the black-clad woman who'd presided at the lectern during the assembly.

Daniel watched the newcomers with no expression. There were things he couldn't permit. If this pirate chief so overstepped himself as to offer Cinnabar slaves in return for RCN help—

"Not our prisoners, Captain," Kelburney said. The wariness in his voice showed that he'd picked up on Daniel's change of expression. "Distressed spacers, put off in a lifeboat in the Dalbriggan system by pirates from Falassa."

He gestured to the cripples filling mugs from a tapped keg on the serving table behind him. "Kephis, Bradley—give our guests some beer while they explain to Captain Leary how well we've cared for them after their misfortune."

The young servants offered the next batch of refilled tumblers to the newcomers. Daniel sipped from his own goblet. The beer was dark and more bitter than he was used to, but an RCN officer didn't look alcoholic gift horses in the mouth.

Falassa was the habitable planet of star S2. The Selma pirates had generally operated as a loose sodality which chose its leader in common, with the Council Hall here on Dalbriggan as the seat of government. As the *Sailing Directions* made clear, there was nothing new about a ship, a squadron, or one of the three planets going its own way for a time, however.

Massacre rather than reconciliation was the preferred method of repairing divisions. Daniel smiled faintly. The *Princess Cecile* had other important business before it, but he'd hoped when he received his orders that his mission might involve fighting pirates. He could scarcely complain about having his wishes granted, could he?

"My name's Slayter," said the balding forty-year-old leader of the spacers brought in for display. "I'm captain and owner of the *Pretty Mary* out of Rohaska."

Several of the *Sissie*'s crew had been born on Rohaska. It was a Cinnabar protectorate with a long spacefaring tradition.

Slayter took a deep draft of his beer. He and his fellows were starting to relax at the sight of Daniel in his RCN dress uniform. Though the spacers seemed to have been fed well enough, Daniel could imagine that the chance of being shot on a pirate's whim must have been a matter of realistic concern to them.

"*Was* captain and owner," Slayter said. "We were on route to Strymon with a cargo of fuel cells when three cutters hit us when we came out of the Matrix."

He tried to drink again, but his hands had started trembling. "They shot my mate," he said into the trembling cup. "He was trying to hide his private cargo in a mast, not that it would've mattered. They took the *Mary*."

Slayter pressed his arms to his chest and seemed to get control of himself again. "I thought they were going to kill us all, shoot us or just space us, but they put us on our lighter and dumped us here. They said to tell all the siblings on Dalbriggan that unless they want to starve on the scraps Kelburney lets them have, it's time for a new Astrogator."

Kelburney waved Slayter to silence. He said to Daniel, "Captain Aretine doesn't think our treaty with Cinnabar was a good idea, Leary. She calls herself Overlord of Falassa and she's got most of the captains based there agreeing with her. They were always a flighty, foolish lot."

An officer midway down the table spat ringingly into a spittoon against the back wall. He appeared to be underscoring his Astrogator's judgment of the Falassans.

"Now, I don't know what there may be available in ship chandleries on Falassa," Kelburney continued, "but I figure a twenty-three hundred ton freighter like the *Mary*—"

He cocked an eyebrow toward Slayter. The Rohaska captain jumped as though he'd been jabbed with a cattle prod. "Yes, yes," he said. "Twenty-three hundred tons and as clean—"

Kelburney waved his hand; Slayter fell instantly silent. Daniel kept his face still, but he didn't like to see a man being trained like a dog.

"The masts from a freighter of that size ought to be just the ticket to put your corvette in apple pie order," Kelburney said. "And Slayter here would be more than happy to offer them to his savior."

"Oh, yes," said Slayter. "Oh, if you'll just get my ship back, sir, *anything*."

"You know where the *Pretty Mary* is held, then?" Daniel asked. He lifted his goblet and swirled it, watching patterns in the remaining bubbles while his mind spun skeins of action.

"Aye," said Kelburney, "she'd be at Homeland on Falassa along with Aretine and the crews who back her. Aretine's gathering ships from Horn—"

Horn was the planet orbiting S3. The three stars of the Selma Cluster were within four light-years of one another and followed a common trajectory.

"—besides those from Falassa, and I shouldn't wonder if she had some Dalbriggan captains wondering if she didn't have the right idea."

The officer who'd spat before did so again. This time, as the bucket quivered with the hollow peevishness of titanium, the fellow said, "Bugger 'em!"

Others nodded. Not all did.

"There'll be vessels on guard above Falassa as there were here, I presume?" Daniel said. Beside him, Adele had her personal data unit on the table beside her new pistol. The display was a pastel blur above the little box.

"Cutters on picket," the Astrogator said. "That's no problem—we'll take care of them for you. It's the *Hammer* that you'll have to handle yourself. She's a hulked cruiser, no masts but she has her High Drive and a full weapons suite. *And* her crew'll be awake. With the noises Aretine's making, they'll figure that unless somebody here blows *my* head off, something's going to happen on Falassa."

He looked around the room, smiling grimly. "Nobody's tried it here," he said. "Yet."

Daniel nodded twice while his mind finished its series of considerations. He exchanged glances with Adele; she nodded crisply. He didn't know precisely what she meant by the gesture, but it was clearly positive.

"Very well," Daniel said. "Astrogator Kelburney, as an officer of the RCN it's my duty to eliminate a band of pirates operating against citizens of the Republic. I direct you under the terms of your treaty to aid me in this endeavor."

"I said we'll take out the pickets," Kelburney said. "And you won't have to worry about a thing on the ground. We'll take care of that too."

The spittoon rang again.

"That's well and good," Daniel said, sounding—deliberately sounding—like his father addressing clients who'd gotten in over their heads and begged his help. "There'll be a few other items as well. First, you'll have to embargo movement from Dalbriggan until it's time to launch the operation. That may be several days."

Kelburney's brow furrowed momentarily at Daniel's tone; then it cleared and he slapped the table. "Of course!" he said. "Do you think we're children? We'll party till it's time to leave. Anybody who tries to get off-planet before then winds up in space without a suit. Is that all?"

"Not quite," said Daniel, letting his own smile widen. He'd been concerned by the Dalbriggans'—by the pirates'—loose discipline, but that clearly didn't extend to operational matters. "Officer Mundy here must have full access to any logs or other records that have information regarding the movements of the *Hammer* over the period she's been in orbit. That would be several years?"

"Ten," said Kelburney. "The Falassans bought her off of Umbro at scrap prices."

"That should be a satisfactory sample," Daniel said brightly. "We'll get to work immediately, then."

"She *is* a bloody cruiser," said the officer who'd been spitting.

"Yes, and we *are* a corvette of the RCN," said Daniel, rising to his feet. "I consider that a fair match."

He beamed at the gathered pirates. He was boasting, of course; but if he hadn't meant the words, he wouldn't have spoken them.

The armored hatch of the Battle Direction Center squealed as it opened outward into Corridor C. Without taking her eyes from her console Adele said, "Are you blind or are you simply too stupid to read the sign on the door? Keep out!"

The hatch started to cycle closed again. Midshipman Vesey looked up big-eyed from the console to Adele's left and said, "But mistress, that was the captain!"

Oh.

"Daniel!" Adele called to the slight opening which remained—a warship's battle doors open and close with enthusiasm. "I'm sorry, I—"

She got up, bumped the edge of the console, and promptly fell on her face because both her legs were numb. She'd sat too long without moving. Dorst and Vesey were helping her to her feet when Daniel stuck his head into the compartment again.

"Adele?" he said. "I didn't mean to disturb you, but . . ."

"Yes, I asked for your input," Adele said, "and then snapped at you when you came to the door. I suppose I thought you'd reply through the display. Well, I *didn't* think. I'm obviously not thinking clearly at all. I apologize."

Her throat hadn't been so dry since she'd fought her way out of an Alliance prison, breathing dust and air burned to ozone by electromotive weapons. She sounded terrible and probably looked worse. Dorst handed her a drinking bulb. She sucked deeply on it.

Not until the third swallow did she identify the contents as milk—the perfect choice once she thought about it. As Dorst had obviously already done.

"I'm very sorry," Adele said, irritated by the concern in the eyes of her three companions, and even more irritated because she couldn't deny she gave them reason for it. "Daniel, we, ah, have provided some alternative courses for the guardship and . . ."

Her knees were wobbling now. Great heavens, what was wrong with her?

"Mistress," said Vesey, "you haven't had a thing to eat or drink in eighteen hours. Please won't you sit and let us bring you some food?"

Dorst guided Adele back into the seat where she'd been working. She was accessing the ship's computer through the familiar pathway of her personal data unit. The battle computer's great holographic display showed what looked like a twisted circle of ribbon: the track of the guardship *Hammer* as it orbited Falassa. Date variations were color coded from violet to the deep red of the most recent.

Dorst put another bulb of milk in Adele's hand. Vesey said earnestly, "Sir, she's done it all herself. The only help we've given is to calculate the orbits from the data she's found in the logs."

Daniel nodded. "You asked me to look over your plots, Adele," he said. "I did, and I found them quite satisfactory. I'm amazed that the orbit's been so consistent over a ten-year period."

He gestured; obediently Adele drank more of the milk. For a moment her stomach threatened to rebel; then the combination of texture and food value went to work and she began to feel better.

She managed a smile. Of course she still had quite a lot better to feel.

"I thought it was rather like a moon," Adele said. "The orbit stays the same, that is. Doesn't it?"

"It's a low orbit, mistress," Dorst said. "They have to burn the

High Drive every few days to keep atmospheric friction from dragging them back to the surface. But they want to overfly Homeland every orbit, so they porpoise up and down without any lateral motion to speak of."

"Yes," said Daniel, "and very useful that is to us, I must say. I'll have the course plotted to three decimal places, though we'll have to exit, say, five light-seconds out for the final refinements. I just wanted to know if you felt that additional computation might lead to significant changes?"

"What?" said Adele. "No, no. We had a perfectly adequate data sample. And anyway, there *isn't* any more data. Not that I've been able to find here on, on wherever this place is. Dalbriggan."

She scowled to hear her own words. Her mind wasn't working any better than her body seemed to be. She'd been lost within the problem, and now that it was solved—her task was complete, at any rate—she couldn't get back to normal.

Adele giggled. "Mistress?" Vesey said.

"I thought, 'normal,'" Adele explained. "But of course I meant 'what passes for normal with me.'"

The midshipmen looked aghast, but Daniel grinned at her. "Very good," he said. "I'll have Lieutenant Mon draft a movement order for the fleet while I develop the actual attack. Ah, will you have further need of the Direction Center?"

"Oh, heavens no," Adele said. She heaved herself to her feet again and managed to keep upright this time. "I had to have Vesey and Dorst with me—somebody who understood navigation, at any rate—so I couldn't block off the people around me as I usually would. But I did need privacy."

Daniel offered Adele his arm. "I was about to get something to eat in the galley," he said, probably a lie. "Will you join me, then?"

"Yes, I'd better, I suppose," Adele said. The milk had awakened a raging hunger that she'd suppressed while she copied and collated data.

The pirate cutters operated on unique internal clocks, determined either by the whim of the captain or as an accident because the astrogation computer had been shut down and reset to zero following repairs. Though Adele didn't suppose that had added much to the complexity of the operation. Even if they'd all been

RCN warships, she would've felt constrained to check each time slug against reported star positions. There was no such thing as acceptable error in *her* universe.

The galley was on B Level opposite the entryway. Between mealtimes when the *Princess Cecile* was under weigh it served as a lounge, but usually when the corvette was on the ground the personnel spent their free time in facilities ashore.

Not here on Dalbriggan. When Daniel entered with Adele— the two midshipmen trailed behind like nervous pets—thirty-odd spacers rose to their feet in greeting. Most of them were armed: many with weapons from the arms locker and bandoliers of ammunition, but the others displayed less formal clubs, knives, and in one case a wire garotte.

"Sir, can you tell us what they're planning to do?" asked Liebig with a nod of greeting to Adele as well. "These bloody pirates, I mean. Are we going to attack?"

"A Number Four breakfast for Officer Mundy, if you please, Wharnock!" Daniel called to the spacer who was getting a mug of hot cacao from the mess dispenser. He settled Adele into a table vacated for them and said, "The free citizens of Dalbriggan are our friends and allies, Liebig. They're going to help us find necessary supplies to repair the *Sissie*. And just incidentally we'll clean out a nest of *real* pirates at the same time."

Wharnock brought over the meal packet. He stripped the top off with a gush of steam as he set it on the table before Adele. She stared in sudden horror at the bacon, eggs, and grits—and as suddenly felt another rush of hunger. She picked up the spoon attached to the container and began eating.

"Sir, d'ye trust these bastards?" a spacer asked. Adele didn't notice who spoke; she was balancing the spoonful of egg at the edge of her lips, blowing softly to cool the contents.

"Trust 'em to cut our throats if we turn our backs," another said. "They say they only go after Alliance shipping now, but you *know* they don't want us nosing around to see what loot they really got hidden away here."

Through the chorus of "Yeah," and "That's God's truth," Daniel—who wasn't eating, as Adele had suspected—said, "As a matter of fact, I do trust the Dalbriggans to help us, Swade. The leaders, that's most of the captains, not just Kelburney, don't want to be ruled from Falassa, but they know that's what's going to happen unless they do something fast. Our coming here gives them a chance to strike before so much support drains away to the Falassans that one of Kelburney's friends will have to shoot him."

Adele started on the grits; to the best of her knowledge she'd never eaten bacon, so she was leaving that for last, if at all.

Daniel's outline of politics in the Selma Cluster mirrored Adele's reading of the cluster's history. She smiled wryly. There was a great deal of similarity between Selma and Cinnabar, if it came to that. Her parents would certainly have agreed with that at the end.

"Officer Mundy?" Daniel asked. "How do you assess the situation from your specialist viewpoint?"

Daniel wasn't asking for a real analysis. At another time, in private, he'd certainly be interested in what Adele in all her different guises thought, but what the two of them were doing now was an exercise in theater to keep the crew's morale high. Though—Adele's private opinion would be precisely the same as the one she offered now.

"Speaking as a scholar who's studied politics and the history of the Selma Cluster," she said, "I agree with your outline. And speaking as a Mundy of Chatsworth—"

She tried to scoop up a strip of bacon but decided it must be finger food instead.

"—I must say that I'm pleased to have Speaker Leary's son on *my* side this time."

There was general laughter, some of it amazed. Every member of the crew knew who Daniel's father was, and by now rumor at least must have identified Adele with the leaders of the Three Circles Conspiracy. In this case by rare exception, rumor was perfectly correct.

Vesey put a steaming mug of cacao beside Adele's meal packet. Adele sipped. She'd have preferred water, but this bitter, stimulant-rich drink was the RCN's on-duty staple; she supposed she'd have to get used to it.

"I've kept you aboard the *Sissie* to avoid accidental problems," Daniel said, glancing around the room. "Astrogator Kelburney's giving a party to keep his crews occupied while we—"

He nodded.

"While Officer Mundy and the midshipmen assisting her, that is, provided me with the information I needed to plan the operation. You all know the trouble drunken spacers can get into."

He grinned broadly. The crewmen broke into appreciative hoots and laughter. More spacers were entering the galley, summoned by word—and how delivered?—that the captain was holding an informal ship's meeting and giving everyone the scoop.

"On the other hand, I thought it would be good to make sure nothing untoward was going on," Daniel continued, "so I sent Hogg to make purchases for my private stores. He'll report back with anything he finds interesting. And I believe Officer Mundy's servant went out also. With my blessing."

"With or without," a spacer muttered. He was far enough back in the room that Adele couldn't have seen him if she'd tried. "*That* one'd squirm through a cable port like a snake."

"Yeah," said Liebig, who'd watched Tovera in action at the Captal da Lund's fortress. "But she's *our* snake, Smokey."

Adele munched the last of her bacon. Tovera would be amused.

"All right, sir," said Matahurd. "We'll follow you anywhere, you know that. But what *is* it we're going to be doing?"

The cacao had cooled enough for Adele to finish the mug, though she didn't know that doing so was any better an idea than the bacon appeared to have been. It was staying down for now, but the long-term prognosis was no more than even. She stood, needing to stretch her legs.

"Falassa depends on a dismasted heavy cruiser for its defense," Daniel said, rising beside her. "It mounts sixteen four-inch plasma cannon in quadruple turrets and carries a quantity both of missiles and of multilaunch rockets for use against pirate cutters. We'll eliminate her to permit the Dalbriggan forces to assault the planet proper. I'm going out in a minute to inform Astrogator Kelburney that we're ready to lift at his convenience."

There was silence in the galley. Sun, standing near the doorway where he'd just entered with Woetjans, said, "Yeah, all right, we can do that. But when're we going to pay back them bastards back on Strymon, sir?"

"That'll be our next concern, Sun," Daniel said cheerfully. "*After* we've shown these pirates that going into battle at the side of the RCN is the shortest route to loot and victory!"

He gestured Adele to the doorway with a lift of his eyebrows. They exited together, followed by the cheers of the assembled crew.

CHAPTER TWENTY-SIX

A dele clumped down the companionway between two spacers of the escort who'd been equipping from the arms locker. They looked wary, but Daniel was pleased to see that Adele was getting the hang of walking on the boot-polished steel surfaces of a warship's interior.

He was also glad to see Lott and Tavastierna were looking after her.

"Ah, if you'd rather get some sleep, Officer Mundy," he said, "that's quite all right. I thought it best to see the Astrogator in person, but the meeting shouldn't require your special expertise. Any of them."

Adele gave him a smile that could have passed for a nervous tic. "I find it hard to predict the future," she said. "Accurately, at any rate. I just went back to my room to dress for the occasion."

She patted the butt of the service pistol belted over her utility uniform in an open-topped holster. Adele wore the weapon in the middle of her abdomen instead of hanging by her hip. There the holster, canted for right-hand draw, would have interfered with her personal data unit in its pocket.

"Hogg found me the holster and belt," Adele added. "Ah, do you think it's appropriate?"

"Indeed I do," said Daniel. "I'm sure Kelburney will appreciate the gesture. Shall we go, then?"

Kelburney, having seen Adele shoot, would also appreciate that the pistol was more than a gesture when she carried it. Daniel had said that there shouldn't be any difficulty, and there shouldn't; but he agreed with Adele about the difficulties of predicting the future. He nodded to Woetjans.

"Listen up!" the bosun said, sweeping her fierce glare over the ten spacers of the escort detail. "We're here for show, period. Keep your guns switched off till you're told, and remember—nobody shoots till Officer Mundy shoots! Do you all hear?"

"And what's going to be left to shoot at when she's done?" Bemish said to general laughter.

Daniel grinned also, but he saw that Adele's expression had tightened. The change was minuscule, something that only a friend would have noticed.

"Let's go!" he said, louder than he'd intended. The main hatch cycled open.

Hogg got up from where he'd been waiting beside the berm. He was wearing a broadly conical straw hat, obviously local though not a garment Daniel had noticed the day before.

"Tovera said you were coming out to find the Astrogator," Hogg said as the heavily armed spacers approached him. "She sent me to guide you in."

He looked at Adele with an unfathomable expression. "You got a good one there, mistress," he said. "Though I guess I could teach her a few things in open country."

In Adele's ear Daniel said, "I gather from Hogg's comment that Tovera has listening devices aboard the ship?"

Adele shrugged. "That's what I assume also," she said. "Tovera likes to gather data even more than I like to arrange it. Both activities are beneficial so long as we serve an executive who isn't incapacitated by the mass of information."

Daniel's grin was delayed by a moment, but when it came it melted all the concern out of his mind. The RCN's way was to use the tools at hand to achieve victory, and he couldn't complain about the past usefulness of Adele's odd servant. "Yes, I'd agree with that," he said.

In a loud voice he said, "Now, let's go find Astrogator Kelburney so we can get on to the real business of the RCN."

He looked around the escort. "Which is *not*," he continued, "despite what you might have assumed from watching your captain, a matter of screwing as many different locals as possible on liberty."

The bellowing laughter from every throat but Adele's broke the tension. Daniel grinned at his crew. There were good officers who were too proud to make a joke at their own expense, but that wasn't Daniel's style. He kept his pride for other things than his sense of self-importance.

Perhaps because of the laughter, Woetjans permitted Daniel to walk at the head of the party alongside Hogg instead of being surrounded by hefty crewmen like glassware wrapped for shipping. When he saw that the scene on the occupied side of the berm was one of repletion, not riot, Daniel beckoned Adele up beside him also.

"See the fun we missed by staying cooped up in the *Sissie* all day?" he murmured in her ear.

"Yes," Adele agreed with the dry amusement he'd learned to expect from her. "I dare say I regret the loss even more than you do."

Dalbriggans in various stages of undress sprawled in the doorways of buildings and on crushed-rock pavements which connected them more like the passages of a maze than a street grid. Some held bottles, some twined with or stacked upon one another, and not a few lay crumpled like the dead of a battle.

Other citizens were upright, more of them sitting than standing; the few who walked did so with the awkward deliberation of the aged. Some distance into the forest several voices sang in good harmony about the "Bouncing Boys of Lyme." They sounded cheerful, though their tempo was slower than normal for that standard of spaceports across the human universe.

Servants—well, slaves, to give a thing its right name—puttered about ministering to fallen citizens. The slaves were easily identified by not carrying weapons and the fact they were moving at all. Even so, most of them looked the worse for wear following the debauch.

"Hogg?" Daniel said. "Is it safe for the, ah, citizens to party like this when they have so many slaves?"

"They ain't in quite such bad shape as they look, master," Hogg said as he stepped over a Dalbriggan with a beatific smile, no trousers, and her fist around a broad-bladed knife. "I mean, they are, but I've knowed this sort. They can get up if they have to."

Hogg was leading them toward a squat cylindrical building some

distance behind the Hall. Uniquely, this structure was of stone
rather than wood. Differences in masonry techniques and the aging
of the material used indicated that there were weapons which could
blast through thick rock walls—and that they'd done so here in
the past.

"The several slave revolts of past centuries," Adele said, "have
all been put down with great cruelty."

She gave Daniel a tight smile. *As the Three Circles Conspiracy
was.* "There's never been a unified rising on all three worlds of
the cluster, but Hogg is correct that the siblings on the affected
planet have generally reacted promptly enough to handle matters by themselves."

They skirted a youth cradling the head of a bearded Dalbriggan
in his lap, offering sips from a chased metal tankard. The youth's
large, liquid eyes followed the Cinnabars warily.

"Another aspect of the situation," Adele continued drily, "is that
captives can become citizens of the cluster easily enough if they
desire to. As a result, slaves with the sort of drive and ruthless-
ness required for successful rebellion are coopted into the ruling
elite."

She smiled at Daniel again, with as little humor as before. "One
could describe the result," she said, "as a democracy not so very
different from our own."

Daniel looked over his shoulder. The youth was still staring
after the Cinnabars. There was hunger in his expression, but Daniel
wouldn't have cared to guess what the hunger was for.

"Yes, I see that now," he said aloud. "And this is our destination, Hogg?"

"Yeah, but we want to knock careful," Hogg said. "Though it
wasn't the party here like what it was everywhere else around,
you know?"

Daniel stepped into the recessed entrance of the Astrogator's
dwelling. Beyond question there were sophisticated sensors and
weapons pointed at him, but stains indicated the slit in the roof
arch had been used to pour blazing fluids.

Electronics were well and good in their place, but an enemy
of Adele's skill could turn them against the original user. A gallon of pitch or napalm, lighted and tipped into the opening, had
its uses in the most modern setting.

The door chime was a section of osmium tubing from the barrel of a projectile weapon. Centuries of use had given it a surface like hammered glass. Daniel struck it with the piston rod hanging alongside for the purpose.

"Astrogator Kelburney!" he called. "The RCN has a proposal for you!"

The door opened in two halves before he'd finished speaking; Daniel had to step back quickly. Not surprisingly, the Dalbriggan leader used the hatch from a starship's airlock for his portal.

Kelburney was dressed in a spacer's jumpsuit; he wore only a single holstered pistol instead of being a walking arms locker as he had during the assembly the day before. *Informal garb for a private gathering*, Daniel thought with a smile.

A dozen members of the Council got to their feet in the room beyond. Several held drinks, and the girl who went scampering out of the field of view wasn't dressed for a policy discussion. Nonetheless, the Astrogator and his paramount chiefs hadn't been involved in anything that would've gotten one thrown out of a society party in Xenos.

"You took your time, Captain!" Kelburney said. "You'd have to calculate courses faster than that to make the grade with our squadrons."

"If your squadrons were capable of doing the job you require, Astrogator," Daniel said with a pleasant smile, "I don't suppose we'd be having this conversation. In the RCN we prefer to do a job right; as I believe we're prepared to do."

Kelburney looked at him sharply. "You're ready to take out the *Hammer*?" he demanded. Those members of the Council who were present watched the principals narrow-eyed, even when they drank their liquor.

"Yes, indeed," Daniel said. He felt a tingling all over his body. *This is happening, it's* really *going to happen!* "In fact I'd bet my life on it."

The burly captain who'd been spitting for emphasis during the Council meeting made a gagging sound. Daniel blanked his face for an instant, uncertain of what was going on. Beer sprayed out of the Dalbriggan's nostrils and he slapped his thigh with his free hand.

"Damn your bones, Kelburney!" he bellowed through his hacking laughter. "If you won't have him in *your* bloody crew, I'll take him in mine!"

Kelburney smiled as his subordinates laughed. "You might do after all, Leary," he said.

His expression hardened. In this mood the tall pirate had the look of a saint or an inquisitor. "You have the course plot in a form you can transmit?" he demanded.

"Yes," Daniel said, professionally curt. "When will your fleet be ready to accept it?"

"We're bloody ready now," said Kelburney. Over his shoulder he boomed, "Mineo, send out the call. Liftoff in half an hour!"

The burly captain grimaced, then walked through a side door with a gait between a waddle and a saunter. Other members of the Council tossed off the last of their drinks and prepared to leave as soon as Kelburney got out of the doorway.

"You going to be ready to lift, RCN?" the Astrogator said with a cant of his eyebrows.

Adele gave Daniel a tiny nod, indicating that the *Princess Cecile* had already been alerted. "Yes," he said.

He turned and said, "Let's go, Sissies!"

"Hey, RCN?" a Dalbriggan called. Daniel looked back over his shoulder but didn't speak. The speaker was Mineo, who'd returned to the main room.

"Good hunting!" he said.

"You got that right!" said Woetjans, lengthening her stride on the way back to the corvette and the shadow of battle.

"Prepare to exit in one minute!" Dorst announced from the Battle Direction Center, his powerful baritone deepened and blurred by the ship's PA system. The lights pulsed their version of the warning.

Adele turned from her blank display. The spacers all around her were motionless but as tense as wires stretched to within a feather's weight of breaking. The riggers prepared to go topside, while the gunner and missileer poised to fight the *Princess Cecile* out of an ambush by Alliance forces or by the Falassans, or indeed by their self-styled Dalbriggan allies.

Daniel was running reentry scenarios in sequence, changing the parameters according to this or that assumed degree of damage from the enemy attack. Similar preparation had saved the *Princess Cecile* at Tanais when her armament could not have done so.

"*Exit!*" and yet again Adele realized, with perfect clarity, that if she put her pistol in her mouth and pulled the trigger she would never, *ever* have to feel that nausea again. The fit passed as quickly as it came. She returned to being Officer Mundy, with things to live for and responsibilities to others.

She smiled faintly, remembering a snatch of ancient dialogue called "The Arkansas Traveller." "I can't fix the roof when it's raining, and when the sun comes out the roof don't leak no more."

The commo display was alive with conversations among starships which had emerged within a hundred thousand miles of one another. A dozen ships had arrived already, and more popped into the sidereal universe every few seconds following the *Princess Cecile.*

Whether the vessels spoke through microwaves or modulated laser, the hull of the receiving ship reflected part of the energy in secondary radiation. The *Princess Cecile*'s sensors and correction algorithms were sensitive enough to turn the leakage into coherent speech.

The splendid RCN communications suite isolated and recorded pairs of conversations. Adele checked each one, finding they were uniformly the chatter of captains seeing which of their fellows hung in space around them. When she'd heard enough to allow the software to review the remainder—there was a new burst of empty small talk every time a ship appeared—she leaned back in her chair and sighed.

"Adele?" Daniel said over a two-party intercom link. "*I gather everything's under control from your viewpoint?*"

Adele smiled. She'd have liked to turn and call her answer across the bridge, but she respected Daniel's desire to keep the discussion private.

"Nobody's saying, 'Now let's cut the throats of those dogs from Cinnabar,' at any rate," she said, letting the intercom direct her words to most recent sender in lieu of a specific recipient. "It's more along the lines of, 'What, hasn't that wreck you're sailing fallen apart yet?' "

There were more than thirty ships on her display now. They continued to appear, but the rate had slowed considerably.

"*They're certainly astrogators,*" Daniel said musingly. "*They know their own region, of course, but even so, to manage such precision both in time and place on short notice is remarkable. An RCN squadron so well handled would be highly commended.*"

"Daniel?" Adele said, uncomfortable in speaking but unwilling not to say something about a matter of such importance. "I suspect that some of the captains accompanying us may be in league with the Falassan rebels. If I'm correct—"

"*Good heavens, of course you're correct,*" Daniel said in breezy amazement. "*There'll be several captains in a fleet like this who've pledged themselves to Aretine but stayed on Dalbriggan as spies, and I'd guess there's a dozen others who'd go over on half an excuse. Kelburney's writ may run beyond the length of his arm—but not a lot beyond, I'd judge, not at a time like this.*"

"But if the Falassans are warned . . . ?" Adele said, trying to make sense of what she'd just been told. If this was a head-on attack against a heavy cruiser without surprise . . .

"*I said some of the Dalbriggans support Aretine,*" Daniel explained. "*I'm confident that no ship left the planet after Kelburney embargoed liftoffs, though. You probably noticed that one of the cutters in orbit was replaced just before the assembly.*"

Adele wondered if that was simply a kindly exaggeration or whether Daniel really did think the movement of starships to and from a planet meant something to her. She sighed. It saddened her to realize that she would never glimpse more than the surface of many subjects which the knowledgable found of great internal beauty.

"*The captains left on guard would be Kelburney's closest associates,*" Daniel said. "*And there were three, you notice, just in case.*"

He chuckled and went on, "*We should shortly be able to identify the would-be traitors. They'll be the ones attacking with the greatest enthusiasm to prove their loyalty.*"

"Opposition to the current ruler doesn't make one a traitor to the state," Adele said quietly. On that at least her parents and Speaker Leary could have agreed.

The matter of Alliance backing for the Three Circles Conspiracy remained, as did Agatha's childish features staring over Pentacrest Vale from the bloody stump of her neck. But that was a long time ago. It was no business of RCN officers Leary and Mundy today.

Adele heard the shudder and clang of hatches closing. The rigging crews had come back within the hull, but they remained crowded into the airlocks in case they were needed instantly. They must have gone topside as soon as the *Princess Cecile* reentered sidereal space, but Adele's own signals concerns had stifled any awareness of other people's activities.

"*There's forty-three ships out of forty-five,*" Daniel said abruptly. His words were light but his tone was as professional as an organization chart. "*Time to get back to work. Have you IDed Kelburney's ship?*"

"Yes," said Adele, trying not to sound hurt. Daniel in his professional persona was no colder than she herself was at all times. Daniel switched from one guise to the other with the suddenness of an axe falling, however, and the experience always took Adele aback.

Her wands highlighted the numbered icon on the display that represented the Astrogator's flagship, a 300-ton cutter like the rest of the Dalbriggan fleet. Identification transponders returned only an alphanumeric without personal information, and the pirates hadn't bothered to supply the codes to their new Cinnabar allies.

Adele didn't need the codes, though she wondered whether they'd been withheld or if the question had been ignored. A matching program combined each alphanumeric with data gathered from eavesdropping on intership conversations.

"*RCN to Selma Command,*" Daniel said. He'd deliberately keyed the transmission to include Adele, though she would of course have listened regardless. "*We're ready to execute the second and third portions of our task as soon as you inform me that your force is also ready. RCN over.*"

The Astrogator's cutter was a half light-second distant, enough to create noticeable lags in conversation. There was no additional delay, however, before Kelburney's sneering tenor voice replied, "*Selma to RCN. Give us a time hack and execute in thirty seconds. You won't have to wait for us the way you would for people who think a fancy uniform makes a spacer. Out!*"

On a whim, Adele inset a head-and-shoulders view of Daniel in a corner of her display. He was smiling faintly, perhaps remembering as Adele did that the Astrogator's cloth-of-gold costume at the Assembly was even more ornate than Daniel's Dress Whites.

He touched a key and said over the PA system, "Prepare for entry, exit, and reentry to the Matrix in one minute."

The chimes and lights echoed his words. "Prepare for immediate action," Daniel went on. "Captain out."

His eyes in the little inset seemed to meet Adele's. Did he know that she was using the broad bandwidth required for visuals in this completely needless and un-naval fashion? He must, because he winked.

"*RCN to Selma Control,*" Daniel said. "*We'll go into action in thirty seconds from . . . now! RCN out.*"

Adele's display whirred; the Astrogator's flagship was relaying the synchronization data to his whole fleet in a single multirecipient burst. Two more icons had joined the forty-three of a moment before, meaning that every ship which lifted from Dalbriggan had arrived within minutes of schedule at a point two light-years distant.

"*If they can fight the way they sail,*" Daniel said on his secure link to Adele, "*then this should go very well. Of course, their Falassan kin may be equally able. That'll mean a real battle.*"

He sounded quite cheerful at the prospect.

CHAPTER TWENTY-SEVEN

Normally entry and exit from the Matrix made Daniel as queasy as they did any other spacer, no matter how experienced. This time he was aware of the sensations but couldn't really be said to feel them. His body had become no more than the apparatus his mind used to effect his plans.

"—*reenter normal space!*" Lt. Mon's voice was saying as the lights pulsed.

The *Princess Cecile* dropped into consensus reality, then fluttered back into the Matrix like a butterfly with a damaged wing. They'd appeared five light-seconds from Falassa, close enough to determine the guardship's exact location.

The attack console held a hundred preset launch patterns; the final choice depended on where the *Hammer* really was. Adele's data showed a consistent pattern, but a pattern wasn't a bull's-eye—and nothing short of a bull's-eye would suffice when the *Princess Cecile* was on the wrong end of such a disparity of force.

Betts was running solutions, one for each of the two ready-launch missiles. Daniel did the same at his command console, not quite so quickly but with an assurance that surprised a dispassionate part of his mind.

Daniel was no longer the *Princess Cecile*'s captain, giving orders to the crew and controlling the machinery which would execute his will. He'd become part of the vessel. His awareness of the rig, of the output from the fusion bottle—even of the hums and clings and whines of the parts working in concert—was subconscious.

He no more thought about the commands his fingers typed than he thought about breathing. It was all one, and it was all Daniel Leary.

The display plotted a missile track in red, another track in blue, and between them a streak of purple merging the solution which Daniel and the Chief Missileer had both picked. The attack computer would execute the chosen pair when the *Princess Cecile* next exited the Matrix. Daniel didn't trust humans disoriented by the transition to launch missiles with the split-second timing this attack required.

Without hesitation, Daniel entered his solutions instead of Betts's.

Betts turned from his console to look at his captain. Daniel was aware of the missileer as a portion of the composition Ship and Crew, but Betts no longer had a separate existence in which his thoughts and fears could have meaning.

Mon had already set up the slight necessary adjustments to the sail plan. He and Daniel together had planned the *Princess Cecile*'s course from Dalbriggan to this point within the S2 system with the attack in mind. Modifications of the charge levels rather than the area and angle of the sails would take the corvette the final stage to her target.

The external electrics of a well-maintained starship operated properly ninety-five times in a hundred. The hydromechanical gears and pumps that moved the masts and sails failed—froze, broke, or simply dragged—ten times as often. On an ordinary voyage the riggers would fix the trouble and the astrogator would compensate for the divergence during the next leg.

Having riggers topside on this hop would condemn most of them to death, although that was a relatively minor concern. After all, an error in the location and vector of the corvette's return to sidereal space this time was probably a death sentence for the whole crew.

Daniel looked at Mon's plan, then raised the charge on both sails of the starboard row by a few milliamps. That would give the *Princess Cecile* a slight axial torque as she exited the Matrix, spreading her missiles as they left their tubes. The dispassionate part of Daniel's mind realized that this adjustment was why his launch solution had differed slightly from the missileer's. For these few moments, the *Princess Cecile* was a creature of soul and body, not an object crewed by men.

Daniel engaged the exit sequence on the astrogation computer. "Ship, prepare to exit the Matrix in thirty seconds," he announced. "Reentry will follow immediately. S-s-s *captain* out."

His tongue had wanted to identify him as the Ship. The small part of Daniel's brain that remained objective wouldn't permit his muscles and subconscious to confuse his crew that way. He smiled, amused at himself and trembling with anticipation.

The *Princess Cecile* began to shiver. Casimir energy squeezed the starship in three mutually exclusive directions, forcing it out of the interstices between bubble universes and back into the universe of men.

Still smiling, Daniel switched from the navigational and attack screens to a simple real-time display. The other data were attempts to predict and modify the future. If he hadn't done his job correctly, there *was* no future for the *Princess Cecile*.

Entry into the sidereal universe: gut-wrenching, mind-wrenching. Adele looked across the bridge at him. Her face was that of a crucified saint.

The *Hammer* filled Daniel's display.

The Umbrans had the reputation of building handsome vessels, but the guardship in its present form looked like a pair of hulks progressing through the breakers yard. The *Hammer* had been dismasted or nearly so: the lower sections of three forward antennas remained to support the communications gear, and those of the final ring sternward—when a heavy cruiser, the *Hammer* was an eight-row vessel—were stubbed out to attach a bladder holding additional reaction mass.

As an Umbran heavy cruiser the *Hammer* had weighed 12,000 tons, but the cylindrical bladder the Falassans had added was nearly half the volume of the original hull. The parts were connected by eight tensioning cables around the rim as well as by fifty feet of rigid tubing, giving the whole the form of an unbalanced dumbbell.

The *Hammer* was elevating the plasma cannon in her quadruple turrets; the shutters were sliding back from her rocket and missile tubes. Daniel had hoped the *Princess Cecile*'s initial in-and-out appearance would have passed unnoticed, but the Falassan crew was definitely alert.

The corvette's hull rang as jets of superheated steam ejected one and then the other loaded missile from her tubes. The missiles were thirty-foot spaceships containing an antimatter converter, reaction mass and twin High Drive units; exhaust would devour the launchers if they were lighted within the vessel itself.

There was no warhead, though at burnout the missile would separate into four segments to increase the coverage area. When a missile exhausted its reaction mass, it was travelling at a significant fraction of light speed; a warhead, even a thermonuclear device, would add nothing to the effectiveness of a kinetic energy weapon.

The guardship was less than ten miles away from where the *Princess Cecile* reentered sidereal space. *Uncle Stacey would be proud of me.*

"Prepare to reenter!" Daniel said, shouting in an unconscious attempt to speed a process that would take its own time regardless. A matter of seconds, no more, but lives end in a fraction of that. . . .

The corvette had risen into sidereal space, launched her missiles, and now was dropping back into the Matrix like a fish straining to hide again below the surface. The *Hammer's* turrets couldn't slew on target in the moments available, but her rockets course-corrected by angling their thrusters in accordance with data supplied by the targeting computer. Gas puffed from ports all along the guardship's flank as she fired a desperate salvo.

The *Princess Cecile's* missiles hit: one grazing the *Hammer's* stern and then rupturing the tank of reaction mass into a gush of steam the size of a planetoid, the other taking the guardship squarely in the bow. The missiles weren't anywhere close to their potential velocity when they struck the *Hammer,* but the impact of thirty tons accelerating at twelve gees was enough to smash through the cruiser's hull and out the other side.

The second missile's exit plume was brightly coruscant. Particles of uncombined antimatter from the exhaust raged merrily in the *Hammer's* interior. The ship's bow canted at an angle to the remainder of the hull, on the verge of separating.

Reentry, and never was the wrenching disorientation more welcome. The guardship's rockets had become a flurry of sparks swelling in the final image on Daniel's display as the corvette departed sidereal space.

Spacers cheered. Betts blubbered with joy; beside him Sun pounded the gunnery console with both hands. Daniel hadn't allowed the gunner's mate to rake the target with his plasma cannon for fear the bolts would interfere with the *Princess Cecile*'s missiles, so he was wild with a combination of frustration and triumph.

Daniel checked his status screen. Dorst was already shouting hoarsely over the intercom, "*All green! All green! No damage!*"

"That," said Daniel aloud, "was very close; but then, it had to be."

He wasn't speaking to anyone except the part of his mind that analyzed his actions after the fact. It was with surprise that Daniel realized Adele was watching him through the curtain of his holographic display, and that she was nodding in agreement.

He grinned and keyed the PA system. "Prepare to enter normal space in one minute," he ordered, hearing the electronic echo of his voice filling the whole of the vessel. "Prepare for action. Captain out."

Daniel engaged the reentry sequence, set up like the previous two before the *Princess Cecile* left Dalbriggan. Their exit after launching missiles should have moved them ten thousand miles out from Falassa with zero motion proper to the planet. If they'd sustained damage during the attack, he and Mon would have had to modify the plan; but there'd been no damage.

While the PA system chimed and the crew continued cheering, Daniel allowed himself for the first time to think about the maneuvers he'd just directed. He'd learned the art of precise astrogation from his Uncle Stacey, true enough, but it hadn't been Stacey Bergen who'd showed Daniel how to pick an opponent's weak point and then to press home his attack regardless of consequences.

It was possible that Corder Leary would also be proud of what his son had just achieved.

Adele grimaced as the *Princess Cecile*'s thunderous plasma thrusters cut in. The High Drive's keening vibration was even more unpleasant in its way, but Adele had found that while working she could tune it out the way she did hunger pangs. The thrusters' thumping bass and the atmospheric buffeting which inevitably accompanied the pulses were impossible to ignore.

Besides, when the ions of the exhaust changed state and recombined, they created omniband interference. Even the commo suite's sophisticated software couldn't sharpen more than a fraction of the transmissions into intelligible form.

Adele continued listening to intership signals, of course; it was just harder.

The last of the riggers were stripping their suits off with cheerful animation. Twenty feet farther down the corridor, their quicker fellows were catching the impellers and submachine guns which Gansevoort tossed them from the arms room.

Woetjans, with an impeller in her hand *and* a submachine gun slung across her chest, pushed her way onto the bridge and stood behind Adele's console. "Mistress?" the bosun said. "Can you transmit the show of the cruiser getting it in the neck to the starboard watch's helmets? We were in the airlock and couldn't see squat."

Adele looked up, ready to snarl that she was busy. She looked at Woetjans, who'd spent the critical moments of the attack in a steel box tighter than a coffin—and a coffin indeed if anything had gone wrong. Woetjans, whose present concern was that her riggers get a taste of the *Princess Cecile*'s victory before they went out with small arms to further risk their lives.

"Yes, of course," Adele said. She blanked her display, then searched the current imagery files for the set in question. "Signals to Vesey!" she said as her wands flashed. "Take over communications duties immediately. Signals ov—no, signals *out.*"

Either midshipman could handle the commo chores; in fact the suite's routing software could probably manage unaided, little though Adele cared to admit the fact. She'd picked Vesey rather than Dorst for the duty because a marksman of Dorst's ability had other uses during a battle on the ground.

Hogg, wearing RCN utilities and a knapsack of munitions, stood close to the command console where Daniel continued to make course corrections and talk with his division chiefs. Hogg carried his own weapon, a stocked impeller. He held his master's equipment belt, which included a holstered pistol, but nobody took Daniel's job to be that of gunman.

Which reminds me. . . . "Tovera," Adele said, keying the intercom, "bring me my belt equipment now. Including the new pistol, if you please."

She'd forgotten to sign off, but with Tovera that wouldn't—

Woetjans crooked her finger in a tiny gesture. Adele jerked her head around. *Wouldn't matter,* she'd been thinking, but in fact Tovera already stood behind the console, smiling faintly. Adele's equipment belt was in her left hand.

Tovera wore a smoke gray jumpsuit with crossed bandoliers of ammunition and grenades. She didn't have the attaché case because today she carried her submachine gun openly. The weapon was subtly different from those being issued from the arms room: it was of Alliance manufacture, a relic—like the sociopath's training—of the time she served a Fifth Bureau spymaster.

Adele transmitted the guardship's final moments, then called up the series showing the Dalbriggan assault on Homeland as recorded during the *Princess Cecile*'s run back to Falassa in sidereal space. The riggers were topside at the time, taking down the antennas, but they wouldn't have been doing any sightseeing. Apart from informing her shipmates, the bosun might be able to explain details that puzzled Adele.

The second sequence began to run on the display. The imagery had been gathered under high magnification and blown up further by the computer. Adele pointed with her index and middle fingers together at cutters looking like six bright sparks as they appeared from the Matrix in the upper reaches of Falassa's atmosphere.

"Here," she said. "They came too close and tore themselves apart—but Daniel says the Dalbriggans are very able. What . . . ?"

Woetjans bent to get the best viewing angle. "Bugger me!" she said. "The bastards *are* good!"

Adele winced at the thought of somebody trying to sodomize the bosun. Just a figure of speech, but an unfortunate mental image nonetheless.

The six Dalbriggan cutters had entered sidereal space with considerable motion relative to Falassa. The rigging that propelled them through the Matrix ripped away in long trails of fire: even the attenuated atmosphere forty miles above the surface was too dense for antennas and sails to withstand at transorbital velocities.

"They're hitting the port defenses, mistress," Woetjans said. "If they came in normal they'd be sitting ducks, but—"

When Adele first saw the puffs of half-burned gases envelop

the Dalbriggan cutters, she'd thought all six of them had exploded. Now she realized that they'd instead launched their full magazines of chemical rockets. She was seeing the exhausts, not the debris of an explosion.

"They're trading their rigs for real surprise, you see?" Woetjans said. Adele *did* see, now that it was explained to her. "They can step new antennas after the fight, but if they don't knock out the missile pits on the ground—"

"The missiles, not the enemy ships?" Adele asked, her eyes narrowing.

Woetjans sneered. "Not with this lot, mistress," she said. "They *ain't* enemies, they're all on the same side—once they sort out who's the top dog, you see? It's not like it is with us."

Adele said nothing aloud. *Actually, it's quite a lot like the Three Circles Conspiracy and its aftermath. But of course Woetjans meant "not like the RCN."*

The cutters which had attacked in the stratosphere skipped up from the denser layers of atmosphere instead of trying to land. One disintegrated in a fireball which continued on its previous course like a brief comet.

"Ground defenses," Woetjans explained; she wriggled her finger momentarily in the hologram, disrupting the five silvery streaks which slashed up and past the vanished cutter. "One of the missile crews was quick enough and lucky enough to get home."

She chuckled. "Not lucky enough to be home in bed when about a dozen rockets landed on their pit, though, I'll wager," she added.

The remainder of the Dalbriggan fleet appeared in orbit with the suddenness of raindrops spattering a dry surface. Unlike the initial attackers, these cutters had used the Matrix to greatly reduce their relative motion. Plasma thrusters flared, braking them down to Falassa's surface.

"See the antennas come down already?" Woetjans demanded in a mixture of envy and delight. "They had their riggers topside when they transitioned. There'll be a empty few berths tonight or I'm a virgin."

The bosun shook her head and added, "But God love me, mistress, what spacers these bastards are!"

The guardship, wrecked beyond repair but still mostly complete, passed through the image area. Several of the gun turrets were intact. The plasma cannon had been elevating at the moment of the *Princess Cecile*'s attack; Adele noted with surprise that now the weapons were lowered and realigned with the guardship's axis. That meant that portions of the *Hammer*'s crew and armaments were in full working order.

Adele highlighted the guardship in red, using a flick of her wands instead of poking her finger through the image. "Isn't it dangerous to leave the Falassans that way?" she asked. "Couldn't they shoot?"

The bosun's eyes narrowed. "Damn if I'd want an Alliance cruiser where the *Hammer* is," she said, "but I'd guess it's a matter of local rules. They could make themself unpleasant, but they couldn't change anything much—not with their central fire control screwed for sure. They're being quiet so somebody'll take them off the wreck before they run outa air. Which won't be long, not the way they been hit."

"On the ground in three minutes!" the PA system blared in Daniel's voice. "Boarding party to the entryway!"

Woetjans straightened. "That's us, mistress," she said. She patted the length of tubing under her belt.

"Yes," said Adele, rising and taking her own equipment rather than permitting Tovera to buckle it about her. The bosun's cudgel seemed superfluous, given that the stocked impeller would make a satisfactory club if one were required; but more than logic determines the choices one makes when setting out to kill or be killed.

Adele checked the little pistol in her side pocket, making sure that it was still easily accessible. It was.

"Ready, Adele?" Daniel asked, adjusting his helmet slightly. He wore his visor down as a matter of course, a practical technique that made Adele feel caged.

"Yes, of course," Adele said. Sandwiched between Woetjans and Daniel, she trotted toward the companionway. Tovera and Hogg had gone ahead. The corridor was clear: all crewmen who weren't necessary to the immediate needs of the vessel stood on B Level, armed and ready for ground combat.

"We're landing at the north side of the Homeland community," Daniel explained cheerfully. "The Dalbriggans came down at the spaceport to the south and secured the ships there. They'll be pushing what resistance there is toward us, I suspect."

"Make way for the captain!" Woetjans bellowed. The entryway was crowded. If there'd been an attempt to leave an aisle, spacers equipped for ground deployment had filled it like sand in a mold.

In the delay before shoving wider the crack the crewmen tried to form, Woetjans said over her shoulder, "You don't think the fighting'll be over by the time we're on the ground, sir?"

If Daniel answered, his words were lost in the blast of the thrusters doubled by reflection from the surface. The corvette bucked violently. Adele would have fallen and then been bounced like a ball except for Daniel's firm hand on her shoulder.

She smiled, an expression she knew by now would have frightened anyone who saw it. In this crush, nobody would.

Even as a child, Adele Mundy had known the fighting would never be over. If there wasn't a battle raging at this place *now*, there were battles going on elsewhere and would always be battles until there was no longer a species called Man in the universe.

As a child, though, Adele hadn't imagined that she would be one of those who fought.

CHAPTER TWENTY-EIGHT

As soon as the main hatch tilted forward enough to break the seal along the upper edge, smoke and ashes swirled into the *Princess Cecile*. The automatic impeller fixed to the wardroom hatch on the level above cut loose with a long burst, making the hull ring as it recoiled. An incoming projectile whanged off the corvette's bow.

"Boarders, spread out and form along the road on this side!" Daniel shouted. "Over!"

The hatch thumped down in soft soil, rolling up sparks from the weeds and brush ignited by the *Princess Cecile*'s exhaust. A ridge of slightly higher ground supported a grove of trees, but the river a hundred yards north of the corvette flooded often enough to rot the roots of large vegetation on the flats. The road just beyond was built on a levee and made a good blocking position.

Daniel started for the grove, well behind the riggers in his fifty-strong party. They'd jumped while the end of the ramp was still ten feet in the air. The thrusters had baked the ground solid. The mud was more organic than mineral, so the stench was worse than that of a fire in a charnel house.

There was a bright white flash in the direction of the distant spaceport. Almost immediately the ground shuddered, but the crash of rending metal was many seconds delayed. The bow of a pirate cutter tilted up, then toppled again below the line of the causeway. There was no way to tell which side had been responsible for the destruction.

"*Boarders, gunmen are taking position on the other side of the—*" Tovera said. Her cold voice was little changed by the compression of the helmet radio link.

A stocked impeller began to fire behind Daniel, the slugs passing close overhead. He stumbled on a root that remained tough despite the charring. Righting himself he glanced backward. Hogg was seated cross-legged on the top of the ramp. His arms were braced on his knees and the impeller's sling, locking the weapon on target.

Every time Hogg fired, a head slipped out of sight behind the causeway. Sometimes there was a splash in the air behind where the head had been.

Midway between the road and the corvette, the ground was still soggy. Daniel's right boot sank ankle deep, throwing him forward. Spurts of mud and pulped foliage leaped high, drawing a diagonal across the line of advancing spacers. The man to Daniel's right crumpled, holding his belly and screaming. His equipment belt twisted away from him as he fell, severed by the slug.

The *Princess Cecile*'s upper turret roared, raking the causeway with pulses of plasma. The bolts were hammerblows of pure heat on the back of Daniel's neck and bare hands. Several of the spacers fell—unharmed, or he hoped so, but thrown to the ground by the crashing discharges.

Daniel's visor blacked out the flashes that would otherwise have destroyed his retinas. What he saw as he continued to stagger forward was an invisible giant chewing hunks out of the roadway. Wet silt exploded in steam and the dark red flames of carbon; rock ballast blew to glassy shards or white, searing calcium flames.

The Falassan gunfire ceased. "Boarders, form along the roadway!" Daniel wheezed. "Over!"

Sun ceased fire after his twin cannon had devoured three hundred yards of roadway. Through the smoke of the new fires, Daniel saw people running back toward the town to the south or standing with their hands in the air.

Several of the spacers were shooting wildly as they advanced. They weren't going to hit anything—well, they weren't going to hit any Falassans, though their fellows were at risk—and the locals seemed to have stopped fighting anyway.

"Boarders, cease fire!" Daniel ordered. He thought again about his notion of small-arms training for the crew. There'd have been time for it during refit on Tanais. The Sissies would've been excited to have something real to be doing on a barren iceball. Instead—

Another explosion shook Homeland. An orange fireball lifted a metal roof and a human body. The figure was pinwheeling; the arms and legs had separated from the torso before it all dropped out of sight.

This causeway would make a good target backstop, but this probably isn't the time.

Daniel reached the causeway and stepped carefully into a smoldering divot gouged by the plasma cannon before pausing to take stock. A figure in coveralls sprawled on the road to the right. The only thing moving was the row of ribbons sewn along his seams, fluttering in the breeze.

Adele sat beside Daniel on a chunk of rock fill. Thermal shock had crazed the surface, but either it had cooled or this was another example of Adele's unconcern for her physical comfort. She took out her personal data unit.

Daniel eyed the straggling mixture of woods, wire-fenced gardens, and stone houses to the south. The terrain was rolling, and the houses were generally built in clumps on the higher ground. Earthen mounds raised the two warehouses near the road ten feet above the surface.

Vehicles full of armed personnel moved on the paths between buildings. Even with his visor magnification at 160x Daniel couldn't see any current fighting. Two houses burned sullenly, and occasionally sparks gouted from the spaceport well to the south.

"I can get you imagery from Kelburney's command car if you like, Daniel," Adele said. Her voice broke in mid-sentence for a cough, but she didn't sound winded. "The turret has an electronic sight. Which I've tapped."

How in heaven's name . . . ? But the method didn't matter, and the information certainly did. "Yes, please!" Daniel said. "Ah, Quadrant One."

He didn't want somebody else's field of view covering his own completely. A compressed image on the upper left corner of his visor would give Daniel the information he required without preventing him from doing whatever might suddenly be required.

Shooting an unexpected enemy, for example; though with Adele and Tovera both in the hole with him, that was of vanishingly low probability.

Several hundred people were coming toward the causeway on foot. Were they attacking, or—

"Boarders, don't shoot!" Daniel said in sudden horror. Much of the crowd was children, and many of the adults carried infants or toddlers as well. His first thought was that all of them were unarmed, but that wasn't technically true. A number of the figures wore holstered pistols, and one female carried a submachine gun slung across her back. She'd presumably forgotten about it; her arms were stretched out to hold the hands of a pair of three-year-old twins.

"Boarders, don't shoot," Daniel repeated. "They're surrendering to us instead of taking their chances with Kelburney's lot. On your honor, don't shoot!"

The Dalbriggan image echoed onto the corner of Daniel's visor provided a travelogue through the streets of Homeland. It was so smooth that he thought for a moment that Kelburney was in an aircar or at least an air cushion vehicle, but the forehull bobbled repeatedly into the bottom of the frame.

The gun was stabilized both in azimuth and deflection. It was mounted in the turret of a car armored so heavily that only a firm connection with the ground could support it. Daniel had briefly confused the smoothness of the sight picture with that of the vehicle itself.

The fighting was over; Daniel wanted to catch the Astrogator at the moment of triumph to have the best chance of succeeding with the next stage of his plan. "Lieutenant Mon," he ordered. "Have someone bring the jeep to me immediately. I need to speak to Astrogator Kelburney. Out."

"I can reach him, Daniel," Adele said, looking up with a frown of concern. She must wonder if he believed she was incompetent.

Daniel laughed at the absurdity of the unspoken thought. "I believe face-to-face would be the better choice, Adele," he said. "I'm going to have a hard sell, I'm afraid."

The ringing whine of the fans lifting the little vehicle out of the *Princess Cecile*'s stern hold followed Daniel's request by only moments. Vesey's voice said, "*Captain Leary, the jeep's on the way to your position, out,*" but the driver must have been not only prepared but cued into the command net.

Mon had cut corners to save time his commander might need. "A very good officer," Daniel said aloud. To Adele's raised eyebrow he added, "Lieutenant Mon, that is."

Kelburney's gunsight steadied on a low circular structure whose stone walls had a pronounced slope. Immediately slugs from an automatic impeller rang from the car's armor. The heavy-metal projectiles ricochetted with green, purple and magenta sparks, vivid even in full daylight. One round must have struck the turret because the sight picture jolted skyward even as the car backed to safety behind a residence.

Daniel switched away from the remote image and overlaid his visor with a sixty-percent mask showing Homeland's topography. The circular building was nearly in the center of town; it wasn't simply *a* building but a thick ring surrounding a central citadel.

"The Falassan chiefs depend more on physical protection than the Astrogator and his predecessors on Dalbriggan do," Daniel said with a grim smile. "That's a confession of weakness, of course. It appears that we've picked the right side."

Woetjans had come over to report. "Whichever we pick is the right side," she said. Her tone made the pronouncement sound rather like a comment on the weather. "We're securing the prisoners, sir. That all right?"

The corvette's small utility aircar landed at the back of Daniel's position. Gramercy, one of the power-room techs, was driving. He showed a gentler touch on the controls than Daniel had come to expect of RCN drivers; but then, perhaps he'd gotten lucky.

"Yes, carry on, bosun," Daniel said. "Signals and I are going to discuss the next stage with the Astrogator."

He walked toward the idling vehicle. Ash from the recent bath of plasma spiraled in the wash from the drive fans.

"Sir, I'll come with you!" Woetjans said. She *knew* she had to remain here to command the ground party, but her request was as certain as sunrise.

"There isn't room for you, mistress," Tovera said as she stepped between Woetjans and the aircar. "But if you like, I'll kill one of the locals for you?"

Daniel got into the front seat beside the driver. He'd never thought he'd see Woetjans with a shocked expression; but he knew exactly how she felt.

The Dalbriggans didn't have a command channel: they had seven separate frequencies on which subchiefs and their followers gabbled orders and nonsense in their excitement.

"Don't fire at the RCN aircar approaching from the north!" Adele said. She used her personal data unit to cue the corvette's powerful transmitters for a multiband rebroadcast, hoping—another person would have thought "praying"—the message would reach every one of Kelburney's gunmen.

She'd *found* seven frequencies. What if there was an eighth that she'd missed, that of a guntruck whose weapons were even now swinging on the jeep?

Adele's mouth quirked in slight humor as she repeated, "Don't fire at the RCN aircar approaching from the north!" In that case she was unlikely to live long enough to be tortured by failure. The universe had a kindly side after all.

Daniel switched on the jeep's klaxon as the driver took them low through the streets of Homeland. When the vehicle swooped up on edge to slice between a building and a car with an automatic impeller welded to each of its four corners, Adele wished angrily that they'd lift high enough to hold a steady course across the community.

The thought didn't reach her tongue, fortunately. It had scarcely formed when she realized that would mean a straight course down the throat of the Falassan holdouts. She had her duties and areas of competence; which were different, fortunately, from those of the spacer who was driving.

Adele could hear the sound of gunfire over the klaxon and the howl of the drive fans. A red spark shrieking like a banshee curved out of the sky and banged the car's bow, just ahead of the open cockpit. The driver shouted and jerked his control yoke. Daniel reached past and steadied the vehicle before they wobbled into the building to the left.

"A ricochet," he explained—to everyone in the car, but Adele was the only one who might not have known without being told. "Wars are dangerous places, aren't they? But of course, you can slip in the bath and break your neck."

Adele supposed he was only acting the part of a good commander in calming his troops, but on reflection she couldn't be sure. Nothing seemed to faze Daniel.

Adele didn't care about her own life to speak of, but she found the notion of being snuffed out at random was oddly disquieting. Logically it shouldn't matter whether she was killed by a sniper's deliberation or instead by a few ounces of impact-heated osmium plunging from the sky. She obviously wasn't as much a creature of logic as she preferred to believe.

The jeep rounded a knoll on which stood several houses, one of them afire. The swale beyond was a plaza of sorts with a triumphal arch and a number of plinths from which the statues had been recently shot away. Five armed vehicles parked on the pavement, with a group of heavily armed Dalbriggans hunched behind them.

One of the Dalbriggans saw the jeep out of the corner of his eye. He shouted and leveled a stocked impeller.

Tovera lifted slightly to aim: the light pellets of her submachine gun wouldn't penetrate the windscreen of the open car. Before she could fire, Daniel rose to his feet and raised his hands high.

"Quite all right!" Daniel shouted, keeping his balance even though the driver reacted to the threat by landing in what was virtually a controlled crash. "Captain Leary here to speak with the Astrogator!"

Kelburney stepped forward, holding a drawn pistol. The man with the impeller looked hesitant and didn't lower his weapon. Kelburney backhanded him with the pistol butt from behind, knocking him face-down to the ground.

"Leary!" he shouted, advancing to give Daniel a bear hug. "Bloody good work with the guardship! There aren't six captains in my squadron who'd have been able to equal that!"

In the assembly, Kelburney had been a monarch; in the council meeting later he was the canny man of business. Here on this field of smoke and blood, Adele saw a much more primal figure that she suspected was the stuff from which the Astrogator had molded his other personas.

Automatic impellers opened fire from somewhere out of sight. Projectiles bounced skyward like a neon fountain. *And where are they going to come down?* Adele wondered, but with detached curiosity. The near miss had inoculated her against fear of death from that sort of randomness.

A white flash lit the sky to the west. There was a sharp explosion and the firing stopped.

"I gather Captain Aretine has gone to ground in the circular fortress just over the hill?" Daniel said, pointing in the direction of the shooting. The air stank of ozone and smoke from burning fuels, plastics, and flesh.

"We'll get'er out, never fear!" said a hulking gunman. The folk around Kelburney now were bodyguards, not the officers of his inner circle. Those folk would be directing their own contingents of fighters, here in town and back at the spaceport.

"No doubt you will," Daniel said in a cool tone and a glance that meant, "Don't interrupt when your betters are speaking, dog!" He cleared his throat and continued to Kelburney, "I think I might speed the process a good deal, Astrogator. That is, if you don't care what happens to the defenders with the exception of Captain Aretine herself?"

Several automatic impellers opened fire simultaneously. Orange flame mushroomed over the houses, lifting a gunshield from one of the makeshift fighting vehicles. The firing stopped.

"Care?" Kelburney said, his brow furrowing. "God rot my bones, boy, I don't care what happens to her either! You can burn her . . ."

His expression changed into a cat's smile. "Ah, I see," he said. "You mean, do I mind letting them live afterwards?"

"Yes, that's right," Daniel said. "I realize that they're pirates, but regardless, I wouldn't care to talk them out of their position and have them massacred as a result."

Ah! Adele understood now. She sat on a cracked marble paver and began setting up the link. She'd use the transmitter in the Astrogator's command vehicle rather than going through the *Princess Cecile*'s communications suite. The personal data unit was close to the limit of its unboosted range for reaching the ship from here in the middle of Homeland.

Kelburney laughed. "I could say you were a soft bastard," he said, "but the truth is I don't see reason to kill a lot of good people if I don't have to. Go ahead. I've got a loudspeaker on the car. Or are you going to chance your uniform to keep them from blowing your head off?"

Daniel dusted the breast of his tunic with his fingertips. "Thank you, Astrogator," he said, "but I believe Officer Mundy has patched me—"

Adele nodded, her wands flickering. There were three separate nodes connecting displays in the Falassan strongpoint. She wanted to be sure Daniel's address would blanket all of them.

"—through to the communications network within the fortress. I think that will be the most effective way of proceeding."

"*In*side?" Kelburney said. "There's no bloody way she can do that—it's all shielded."

"Officer Mundy doesn't give me advice on sailing a starship, Captain," Daniel said, every inch a Cinnabar aristocrat again. "And I allow her the same freedom in dealing with communications tasks. It works out quite well."

"Do you want the feed through your helmet, Daniel?" Adele asked. "Or would you prefer a larger display? There's quite a modern one in the command vehicle."

She nodded.

"The helmet will be fine, Adele," Daniel said. He squared his shoulders unconsciously and faced westward, although there was a hill and a building between him and the Falassan headquarters.

Adele made a final adjustment. She'd opened the circuit by aping the power management commands of the Falassans' standby batteries. That portion of the system had no safeguards whatever in place, but it was connected through the transmitter to every computer inside the stone walls.

"I've put you through," she said. Tovera was looking at Kelburney with much the same smile as if she watched him over a gunsight. "Go ahead."

Adele's display gave her the image of the operator seated at each of the seventeen separate units within the fortress. Six were gunnery displays controlling the weapon emplacements in wall turrets, and five consoles were unused at the moment.

At one of the six remaining sat a woman in her mid thirties. A scar ran from her chin into her scalp, skirting her left eye by very little. Her hair was a bright, artificial red except for where it grew over the scar; there the dye didn't take.

"Wartung!" she screamed to someone out of the image area. "Wartung, you bastard, they've entered the system!"

Even without the scar, no one would have called Aretine attractive. Her features were too sharp, and her eyes glinted like the points of icepicks.

"Siblings of the Selma Cluster!" Daniel said. "I'm Lieutenant Daniel Leary of the RCN with a proposition that will save your lives."

He'd instinctively raised his voice, though of course Adele was controlling the volume of the output speakers. She'd turned the command circuitry to her own purposes. Short of shooting the units to pieces, the Falassans couldn't affect their own equipment.

"My corvette, the RCS *Princess Cecile*, mounts four-inch plasma cannon," Daniel continued. "If I have to, I'll hover over Homeland and use them to burn your little fort into a pool of lava. I believe that will take about a minute and a half, but perhaps less."

Aretine and a muscular young male with a metal pincer in place of his left hand were trying to block the electronic intrusion from separate consoles. They had as little success as they'd have had gnawing through rock. The Falassans at the other consoles, including three which had been unused until Daniel began to speak, listened intently to the proposal.

"I've arranged for your lives to be spared," Daniel said. "On my honor as an RCN officer and a Leary of Bantry."

He turned his head toward the Astrogator. Daniel's expression left no doubt in Adele's mind that he meant his words in the most direct sense possible. If Kelburney went back on his word, there would be Hell to pay. A Cinnabar gentleman had promised as much.

Kelburney probably understood the terms being offered and the price that would be exacted for noncompliance on his part. Tovera certainly did. She smiled like a statue of ice as her eyes counted the Dalbriggans nearby; the targets, it might be, that she would kill in a few minutes. For the moment, her submachine gun slanted up at an angle that threatened no one.

"The condition is that you arrest Captain Aretine and hand her over to the authorities for trial on treason charges before Astrogator Kelburney," Daniel said. "The Republic of Cinnabar doesn't presume to dictate legal procedures and penalties to the governments of allies like the Selma Cluster, so I specifically except Mistress Aretine from my guarantee of safety."

Aretine had left her console. As Daniel spoke she reappeared at one of the gunnery displays, wrenching the man there aside and sitting down in his place. The unit was supposed to control three of the automatic impellers in unmanned barbettes on the outer wall. It was as dead as a pile of gravel now; the Falassan commander jerked at the joystick uselessly in frothing fury.

Adele frowned, realizing that she could have shut down the fort's active defenses much sooner than she did, thus saving lives among the Dalbriggan attackers. Though . . . looking at the thugs guarding Kelburney, that wasn't a prospect for which she could summon much enthusiasm.

"I realize you'll need to discuss this among yourselves," Daniel continued. He sounded utterly sincere, but he winked to those watching him from the interior of the fortress. They'd have thought he was simple-minded if he hadn't. "You have five minutes to accept or reject my offer; and if the latter, a trifle longer to make your peace with God. RCN out."

The Astrogator looked down at Adele. "You, Mundy?" he said. "Can you make all my people hear me the way you warned about you Cinnabars driving up in the car?"

"Yes, I can do that," Adele said, keeping her tone neutral. If another Cinnabar aristocrat had spoken to her in so brusk a fashion, she would have called him out; but Kelburney was clearly being polite in his own fashion. *The custom of the country. . . .*

"Do it, then," Kelburney said, "and I'll warn 'em about the prisoners. We don't want any slipups."

He nodded toward Tovera with a grim smile. Truly, the Astrogator wasn't a man who missed much.

Adele pulled off her RCN helmet and tossed it underhanded to Kelburney. "Use this," she said.

"Would to God I had you on *my* ship," Kelburney muttered as he settled the helmet on his head. The lining adjusted automatically to his larger skull. He nodded toward Daniel, engrossed in the interplay visible through the fort's seventeen displays. "I thought he was blind to pick a girlfriend like you."

"I prefer not to be called a girl at all, Master Kelburney," Adele said. "You can address your personnel now."

On the range of miniature screens monitored through the personal data unit, the one-handed Falassan turned with a snarl and grabbed the bell-muzzled weapon beside him. Three splashing holes in his chest flung him back into the console. It went dead when a second burst ripped through the man's body and the box itself.

"This is the Astrogator!" Kelburney said. "Listen up! The bastards who holed up in the HQ are gonna surrender in a minute or two. We're gonna let 'em. Hear me! You're gonna treat 'em all like they was your long-lost sister, you hear? Anybody shoots a prisoner, he goes out an airlock without a suit, I don't care who you are!"

Aretine was no longer visible. The Falassans weren't looking at their displays; some of them remained at their consoles, but they'd rotated the seats outward and held weapons ready. Sparks crackled from the wall in front of an unused display, submachine gun projectiles disintegrating on concrete.

Kelburney gave Adele a lopsided grin. "Figure that'll do the job?" he said.

She shrugged. "You know your people better than I do," she said. "It seemed clear enough to me, certainly."

Kelburney squatted beside her, his eyes on Daniel who appeared oblivious. "Takes a lot on him for a young fellow, doesn't he?" Kelburney said.

Three Falassans carrying pistols ran through the image field of the console at which Aretine had sat when Daniel began his speech. One of them threw his hands in the air and toppled forward.

"He's acted as his father's envoy since he turned sixteen," Adele lied in a conversational tone. "This is a relatively minor matter compared to some he's undertaken."

"What?" Kelburney said in amazement.

Daniel walked a little apart as though he were completely lost in the events within the fort. He and Adele hadn't had a chance to plan this, but from their first meeting they'd shown an aptitude for counterpointing one another. *Now, if only Aretine will hold out for a few minutes longer.*

"Why yes, Daniel is Speaker Leary's son," Adele said. "Your opposite number in the Republic, one might say; though we too have our factions."

She nodded in the direction of the fighting with what she hoped was a good-natured smile. Good nature wasn't a subject on which Adele Mundy had a great deal of experience.

"I hope that you didn't think that Daniel's come to you as a junior naval lieutenant?" she said. "The RCN is completely apolitical, I assure you. You'll be negotiating with a Leary of Bantry, sir."

A Falassan inside the fort began shouting into what had been Aretine's display. His bearded face was contorted with emotion. Adele had shut off the sound pickup along with all the unit's other functions.

"I see," said Kelburney without inflexion. "That's interesting, Officer Mundy. I'm glad you told me."

The Falassan gave up trying to speak into the console. He and a fellow reached down and together lifted Aretine by the hair into the image field. The rebel leader's eyes bulged and dribbles of blood ran from her ears. She'd probably been shot in the back of the head, but it was impossible to tell from this angle.

"Cue me," the Astrogator said with a curt nod to Adele. "All right, siblings, the fighting's over! Remember what I told you about the prisoners. Now it's time to party!"

He took off the RCN helmet and returned it to Adele as Daniel came sauntering back. Several of the bodyguards started shooting gleefully at the sky.

"Astrogator Kelburney," Daniel said, "now that the business here has been taken care of, I want to discuss a matter that will greatly increase the influence of your cluster in the Cinnabar Senate."

"They're coming out!" shouted a Dalbriggan who had a direct view of the fortress.

"Not just yet, Leary," the Astrogator said. "We'll talk tomorrow after you've got your ship rerigged, and you won't be sorry for the result. But not just now."

Adele sighed, gathering her strength to stand up again. She and Daniel had saved quite a number of lives by ending the battle in this fashion. She supposed she should feel cheerful.

But the air stank of blood and destruction, and Adele felt only disgust—at herself and at the species of which she was a part.

CHAPTER TWENTY-NINE

"You appear to be getting the *Pretty Mary* nicely back in shape, Captain Slayter," Daniel said as the glum-faced merchant captain walked up as he surveyed the *Princess Cecile*. "Have you made headway in locating your missing fuel cells?"

Daniel judged that the corvette was about three hours short of being able to lift with her rig in inspection order, but Woetjans had surprised him in the past with the speed her crews could work. Of course the readiness of the *Princess Cecile* wasn't the question that most concerned him at the moment.

"Oh, we found most of them," Slayter said. "There was a pile off-loaded right beside her, left right out in the weather, the lazy bastards. Your lot of pirates say they won't stop us, but they don't help us reload the ship either. We're a merchant ship with an economic crew, not an army of folks sitting around in case there's a cargo to be shifted without stevedores."

"Indeed," said Daniel, sauntering toward the corvette's stern. It hadn't escaped his notice that Slayter referred to the Dalbriggans as "your lot of pirates," implying Daniel was responsible for their actions or inaction, nor had he missed the swipe at RCN crews paid by taxes and tribute.

The Homeland spaceport was a plain blasted to purplish ceramic by thousands of starship movements. Canals fed by the river to the north crisscrossed the land and provided reaction mass, but the Selma pirates didn't favor water harbors the way most starfarers did.

Their cutters didn't sink deeply into bare soil as heavier ves-sels would, but there was another practical reason why the pirates weren't fussy about where they landed. Besides capturing ships as they exited the Matrix, the Selma cutters raided outlying settle-ments where starships didn't normally land. They were used to the tricky business of landing on hard ground, and the practice they received at home made them less prone to error when repeating the process under fire.

"Your crew took away all my masts," Slayter said, following Daniel. Well, there hadn't been much chance the Rohaskan would take the hint of a turned back and leave. "Not just a couple to replace your damage."

Other people—though not many RCN officers, come to think—might have apologized to Slayter or defensively brought up the civilian's promises during the council meeting. Daniel turned like a gun training and said, "We've replaced the six antennas that were lost at Tanais, Captain Slayter, and in addition we've replaced the spares we used to make good as much of the damage as we could at the time."

An aircar overloaded with hogsheads of liquor flew across the field from the south. Its four fans were lugging in synchrony, so the vehicle's progress toward Homeland was a bass *thrum . . . thrum . . . thrum . . .* A naked man danced on the cargo.

"My understanding was that the *Pretty Mary* was being refit-ted with spars from the stocks available on Falassa," Daniel said. "They won't be full length, but they'll get you home. Slower, perhaps, but you're short-handed so the lesser sail area is an advantage."

Slayter had started to speak, but Daniel continued raising his voice to keep the floor. He took a step toward the civilian. Slayter held his ground momentarily, then stepped back.

"That's my understanding, as I said," Daniel continued, "but my only concern at this moment is to prepare my warship in the most expedient fashion for action against the enemies of the Republic. The loyal citizens protected by Cinnabar are obligated to help in any way possible to achieve that end. Now—"

Daniel placed his hands on his hips and glared at the civilian.

"—is there any aspect of your duties to the Republic that you fail to understand, Captain Slayter? Or is it your loyalty that's in doubt?"

"I'm loyal!" said Slayter, who'd shrunk six inches during Daniel's polemic. He knew the penalties for treason to the Republic, and he must have suspected that Daniel was willing to execute them—and him—out of hand. "Look, I'm just a loyal captain trying to have a friendly conversation with a fellow citizen!"

Daniel beamed. "I'm very glad to hear that, Captain," he said, again a picture of friendliness. "It helps those of us in the fighting forces to know as we ready for battle that the civilians we leave behind in safety understand and appreciate us."

Slayter quivered between relief and resentful anger. Above on the hull Woetjans bellowed, "Another inch, another inch—put your backs into it, you buggering women!"

Daniel glanced up. A team was stepping a new mast, the last of the six being mounted. They'd used the hydraulic winch to get the heavy tubing roughly into position, but the final adjustment had to be made by hand. Five riggers were hauling on a six-block tackle, while the bosun herself knelt holding the pivot pin in place with her left hand and a heavy maul short-gripped in her right.

"One—hold it!" The maul crashed down like the impact of a slug.

Woetjans stood. She saw Daniel watching and waved her maul in triumph. "Twenty more minutes, sir!" she called. "You can lift any time after that!"

Daniel waved back. That was only true, he suspected, if he lifted with crewmen on the hull reeving the last of the cables and mounting the sails. But if he gave those orders, neither Woetjans nor any of her riggers would complain about the danger.

Slayter had used the distraction to head for his freighter in the berth across the canal to the east. When Daniel moved the *Princess Cecile* from her blocking position by the river, he'd landed next to the *Pretty Mary* so that his crew wouldn't have far to transport the masts and spars they were commandeering.

Daniel preened himself mentally. He was learning how to set down on dry land without bobbling dangerously on reflected thrust. It wasn't a skill an RCN commander often needed, but someday it might be the difference between life and death.

Tovera stepped out of the main hatch. She looked oddly nondescript, even when carrying a submachine gun slung so that the butt was in her hand beside her right hip.

Tovera saw Daniel and nodded minutely. Two spacers coming back from town carrying a rolled carpet between them stepped sharply to the opposite side of the ramp, careful never to make contact with the servant.

Daniel's face became still. The nod meant that Tovera was bringing him a message that Adele didn't choose to send over the air.

He'd have walked toward the ramp to meet the servant halfway except that the howl of a two-stroke engine racing from the town drew his attention. Hogg had liberated an air-cushion scooter for the duration of his stay on Falassa. It bounced across a canal. Hogg was driving in a beeline toward the *Princess Cecile* with the little engine punched out. Daniel suspected he'd make better time if he crossed at the culverts instead of driving over the canals simply because he could, but Hogg had a fondness for the direct approach.

A fondness that had rubbed off on his charge, Young Master Daniel. Subtlety had its place, but there were worse tendencies in an RCN officer than the willingness to go straight for the throat of a problem.

Daniel stood where he was, flipping a coin mentally as to which messenger would reach him first. Tovera did, a few seconds before Hogg tried to stop the way he would in a truck and learned that redirected fans don't give nearly the braking effort that tires against a solid surface do. The scooter slid twenty feet past Daniel on a chorus of curses from its driver.

"Mistress Mundy wishes to tell you that the Astrogator has called an assembly of all siblings in half an hour," Tovera said with her usual look of cool amusement. "Twenty-seven minutes, now. He's told everyone to gather in front of the Cinnabar corvette."

"Ah," said Daniel. He touched the switch on his helmet, cuing it manually rather than using an oral command to engage the intercom. "Lieutenant Mon, please recall all personnel to the ship without delay. Captain out."

"Master, the whole load of pirates's coming here for a meeting!" Hogg cried as he leaped off his vehicle. "That's the Falassans, the ones still alive, besides all the lot we come with and any odds and sods from the third bloody planet besides, whatever the bloody name is! It don't sound like anybody's pissed off, but there's going to be a shitload of 'em swarming out here!"

"The third planet of the cluster is Horn," said Tovera without expression.

Daniel looked up at the riggers. "Woetjans?" he called, using his lungs instead of technology. "Don't be concerned about the visitors who'll be arriving shortly. Just keep working till you're done, because I very much want to be able to lift from here on a moment's notice."

Adele felt Daniel's presence behind her and turned. To her surprise, he'd changed into his Dress Whites since she last noticed him. She'd been busy, of course.

"Adele?" Daniel said. "I don't like to bother you, but could you make sure the external speakers are cued to my helmet? The simple way to learn would be to test the link, but I don't want to look uncertain in front of our visitors."

"Yes, I've connected you," Adele said. She got to her feet, feeling a trifle wobbly. She hadn't actually been at her console so very long, but she'd been *very* focused for the last half hour. "Would you like me to run the Astrogator's words through our system also?"

The ship was restive though quiet save for the sounds of machinery. The crew was at action stations. Along with all the normal assignments, Dorst had a squad of marksmen in the wardroom ready to join their fire to that of the automatic impeller at the open hatch. If things went wrong.

"Kelburney has speakers on his armored car," Daniel said. "I assume he intends to use them ... but if you can disconnect those and switch his voice through ours, yes, please do it. The symbolism would be useful."

Adele turned and entered a preset command, using the console's virtual keyboard instead of taking her personal data unit out of its pocket. If *she could do it, indeed!*

"Two minutes to go," Daniel said. "I believe I should be punctual even though the Astrogator hasn't directly informed me of the assembly. Although—"

He smiled broadly as Adele fell in beside him on their way from the bridge. Tovera waited at the hatch with Adele's gunbelt; Hogg had gone to join the squad of marksmen.

"—I don't imagine that he believes that I won't hear whatever he says that pertains to the RCN."

"There's been nothing to suggest an attack," Adele said. "But there's been no reason at all given for the assembly, just the order decreeing it. I'm truly sorry, Daniel. I've listened to conversations between Kelburney and his closest associates, and there was no hint of this till it happened. The only person whose opinion matters in an autocracy is the autocrat."

"Speaking as the captain of a warship, I wouldn't have it any other way," Daniel said, stretching with the care that his uniform's strait limits required. He grinned.

Adele walked down the companionway behind Daniel and with Tovera following her. He glanced back and said, "Adele, if you would, please arrange that the Astrogator doesn't speak until I have."

"Yes, I took care of that," Adele said in the dry tone she used when someone told her to do something obvious. *When a Cinnabar aristocrat attends a gathering of barbarians, of course he takes precedence.*

She shook her head in self-amusement. She'd thought of herself as an egalitarian when she worked in the Academic Collections on Blythe. There, of course, she'd been surrounded by other well-born intellectuals.

A boarding party with submachine guns and grenades filled Corridor B in both directions from the entryway. Woetjans and Barnes headed the sections.

"You show 'em, sir!" a spacer called.

Woetjans snarled vainly for silence, but the whole party was cheering as Daniel and his companions walked into the sunlight. And perhaps that wasn't such a bad accompaniment after all.

The corvette and the captured freighter were at a corner of the port distant from other vessels. The plain before the *Princess Cecile*'s main hatch had filled with pirates and the vehicles that had brought them to the assembly. There were several thousand of them, a staggering number in comparison to the empty purple wasteland Adele had seen a few hours before.

She sat on the deck, her back against the jamb of the main hatch, and brought her data unit live. At the top of the display Adele put a panorama of the crowd, but her own concerns were with matters that might not take place openly.

Tovera was across the hatchway, scanning the thousands of faces on the ground below. She too had specialized concerns.

Kelburney had parked his armored car at the bottom of the ramp. He stood with his back to the vehicle, behind a line of his bodyguards. On seeing Daniel appear, he started his oration.

The noise of the crowd, most of it drunk or still drinking, completely covered Kelburney's unaided voice. A technician with a desperate expression stuck his head out the rear hatch of the vehicle.

Daniel raised his hands in greeting. "Siblings of the Selma Cluster," his voice boomed. "I greet you in the name of Cinnabar and the RCN. Astrogator Kelburney, I'm particularly glad to see you."

He beckoned Kelburney forward with his left hand. "Come, join me and address your people from the deck of a Cinnabar warship."

It struck Adele that if the Astrogator hadn't been so determined to avoid informing Daniel of his plans, Daniel wouldn't have chosen to embarrass him in this fashion. The fact that only Kelburney and a few of his closest aides knew what was happening now made the insult bearable but all the deeper.

Kelburney's face went white, then red. Finally he rocked forward in a gust of laughter. Pushing through the line of his startled bodyguards, he strode up the ramp and took his place beside Daniel.

"I wished for a while that you were one of my captains, Leary," he said in a low voice. "Now I'm glad you're not, because I see I'd have to shoot you and your tech officer there—"

He nodded toward Adele.

"—before the month was out."

Adele looked at him. Kelburney wasn't a stupid man, but living in this milieu of drunken pirates had led him to the habit of making stupid boasts.

"And I'm not sure I could," Kelburney added, in the same whimsical tone.

Daniel clasped him, forearm to forearm. "Astrogator Kelburney," his amplified voice said. "Together we've put down a rebellion against your authority and an affront to the Republic of Cinnabar. I now request that you and your siblings join the RCN in teaching a lesson to those on Strymon who think to revolt against Cinnabar sovereignty!"

Where Adele sat, shielded by the curve of the corvette's hull, Daniel's voice through the speakers on the dorsal ridge was merely loud. In the front rank of the assembly it would be painful, though of course most of those listening had numbed themselves with ethanol.

"God's *blood* you're a clever bastard," Kelburney whispered. He faced the assembly, raising his hands as Daniel had done a moment before. Adele nodded to him.

"Siblings of the stars!" Kelburney thundered. "We've lived with the libels of the sanctimonious merchants of Strymon for as many generations as we've gone into space. Their lies, their treachery, these are well known to you."

He held out his left arm toward Daniel as though demonstrating a prized possession. "I've discussed these matters with Admiral Leary here, the son of Speaker Leary, the Emperor of Cinnabar. He has agreed to put the resources of the RCN at our disposal, to chastise the hypocrites of Strymon once and for all. Are you with me, siblings?"

Daniel glanced aside toward Adele and mouthed, "Does shit stink?"

He could have shouted his joke through the corvette's speakers and still not been heard. The assembly's cheers of agreement had a savage undertone, like the growls of great carnivores expecting to be fed momentarily.

The Astrogator faced Daniel. "Admiral Leary," he said, "how long will it take you to prepare for this great joint enterprise?"

"Astrogator Kelburney," Daniel said. "My ship and crew are ready to lift immediately, but I'll need twenty minutes to transmit the course and attack instructions to your vessels. I await your readiness."

He and Kelburney were playacting for a group of adults with the simplicity and cruelty of children, but there was nothing in it to raise a smile. Except perhaps a rictus like that which lifted Aretine's lips the last time Adele had seen her. . . .

"To your ships, siblings!" Kelburney said, shaking his right fist. "We lift in half an hour!"

The cheers of the dispersing pirates were lost in the snarl and whine of their vehicles' engines. They were in motion, swarming toward their cutters, before the last echoes of the Astrogator's voice had died away.

Kelburney looked at Daniel with an expression compounded of admiration and pique. "You've really got a battle plan?" he asked.

"I had to do something while you were planning your charade, Astrogator," Daniel said. "I think you'll find it satisfactory, but frankly I'd have preferred to have gotten your input before I imposed it on you. Another time, perhaps you won't choose to keep yourself incommunicado when there's work to be done."

"Another time!" Kelburney said. Then he grinned at first Daniel, then Adele, and added, "But you do make life interesting, RCN."

CHAPTER THIRTY

The sixty-seven Selma cutters plotted on Daniel's display vanished and reappeared, moving toward Strymon in short hops through the Matrix. It was like watching a swarm of locusts leapfrogging one another as they advanced. Though there seemed no organization, the motion was as inexorable as the rising tide.

The four Strymonian frigates orbiting the planet shook out their sails, then slipped into the Matrix themselves rather than contest with a force ten times superior to them. The *Princess Cecile* was already above the planet, broadcasting her warning to Commodore Pettin's ships below.

"*A very pretty play,*" said Lt. Mon, who was viewing the same simulation from the Battle Direction Center. "*Now, if we can only get the other actors to follow the script. And if the next scene isn't the Alliance squadron thundering down on us because our new allies didn't destroy the relay satellites before the guardships got a message off to Tanais. That's going to take some tricky astrogation.*"

Daniel scratched the hair over his left temple where the rim of his cap rode when he was wearing one. For no obvious reason, he tended to itch there when he was in the Matrix.

"The satellites are on a schedule," Daniel said, "and the Selmans *are* excellent astrogators. Woetjans believes they're capable of the necessary precision, at any rate."

"*Screw that!*" Mon said. "*I believe they can do it too; but I'll be a damned sight happier when I can say they* did *do it.*"

"Yes, I wouldn't look forward to facing an Alliance battleship

374

either," Daniel said. "Still, even if a warning makes it through we can hope an RCN squadron can get under weigh faster than anything wearing Alliance colors. Commodore Pettin and I may not be soulmates, but my experience of him bears out his reputation as an able man."

"Five minutes to exit from the Matrix!" Dorst's voice noted. The midshipman was speaking louder than necessary, a sign of his tension.

"Mon out, sir," Mon said, returning to his immediate duties.

Daniel wasn't a dreamer, not really, but he had his reveries. For a moment he let his mind wander to the inevitable RCN punitive expedition that would retake Strymon and put paid to the Alliance interlopers. Would the *Princess Cecile* be a part of it? And would, for that matter, Lt. Daniel Leary still be in command of the *Princess Cecile?*

Daniel chuckled, calling up the sail plan, power output, consumption, and all the scores of other displays that were the same as they'd been before he and Mon discussed the attack. With near certainty they'd remain the same until the *Princess Cecile* returned to sidereal space. Daniel was still better off looking them over once more than he'd be building castles in the fairyland of the future.

Adele had rotated her seat away from the opalescence of her empty screen and was looking across the bridge. She nodded minusculy when Daniel caught her eye; but she hadn't been, he realized, looking at him or at anything else within the starship's limited confines.

Adele was uncomfortable in the Matrix. From the little she'd said, she disliked transitions even more than most of the humans who had to undergo them. She didn't have work to occupy her so she was sending her mind into another place entirely.

Daniel stood and walked over to his friend. He didn't have any duties for the moment either, so using his time to raise the morale of a valuable member of his crew was clearly called for.

"I hope Commodore Pettin can get his whole squadron into orbit within an hour of our warning," Daniel said conversationally. "I'd expect him to lift the *Winckelmann* immediately on her anchor watch and ferry the remainder of the crew up aboard the destroyers, but it's possible that he'll do it the other way around. In any case, we shouldn't be alone above Strymon for very long."

"Two minutes to exit from the Matrix," the PA system announced, this time in Mon's voice. The atmosphere of the ship didn't change, but someone on B Level began singing, *"'I walk in the garden alone...'"* in a wheezy bass.

Adele focused on Daniel. Her face would never look soft, but some of the edge of tension over her cheekbones eased. "Will we be fighting other ships?" she asked; a polite question rather than a matter of personal concern.

"The guardships ought to run instead of fighting," Daniel said. "If they do fight, Kelburney's fleet will sweep them away without needing our help. There's no guarantees, of course, but I don't anticipate that sort of trouble."

He grinned. "Which is not to say that Betts and I haven't prepared firing solutions for up to twelve targets, just in case Pleyna Vaughn increased the number of picket vessels. We don't know what's been happening on Strymon."

Adele smiled the way a cat does before biting. "I hope that we *will* know after we've been in orbit for a few minutes," she said. "I'll be—we'll be, that is—entering the databases of the Ministry of the Navy and the Presidential Palace both. I've programmed the computer to sort for recent information bearing on the *Princess Cecile* in particular and the RCN more generally. I'll be reviewing the data as it comes in. That should give us an idea of the government's intentions very quickly."

"One minute to exit from the Matrix," Mon announced.

Daniel felt a surge of anticipation. There was nothing in the world like it. The moment that a girl drops her pretense of modesty and coos, "Well, maybe *one* kiss," wasn't in the same league.

"Showtime," Daniel said with a grin. He squeezed Adele's shoulder and strode back to his console with the economy of a captain who knows every inch and ounce of his ship.

Betts continued obsessively running missile solutions, but Sun turned from the gunnery display and gave Daniel a thumbs-up. Adele had her personal data unit where the console's virtual keyboard would normally be projected. She raised her wands; a ripple ran across the pastel blankness of the display.

"Entering normal—"

Images flipped in Daniel's mind. He saw himself from four angles; a trail of future selves stretched to infinity from each possible existence.

"—space," Mon closing in a gasp rather than the intended shout, as though he'd been punched in the stomach while the word was still in his throat.

Strymon, a blue ball with more land than water, hung 13,000 miles below the *Princess Cecile.* Three frigates were in geosynchronous orbits at 24,000 miles; the calculated position of the fourth put it on the other side of the planet from the corvette.

Daniel shrank the real-time view of Strymon to a sidebar and expanded the Plot Position Indicator from the right half to his whole display. He'd set the PPI's field for 300,000 miles above the planetary center. That was an unusually large volume for the purpose, but it allowed him to view the pirate cutters as they entered sidereal space.

"Strymonian vessels!" Daniel ordered, using modulated laser beams directed at the three visible ships. "Surrender at once to the forces of the Republic of Cinnabar. If you attempt resistance, the sixty-eight ships of my fleet will respond with overwhelming force!"

The *Princess Cecile* had exited directly above the capital, Palia, and the harbor serving it. Lt. Mon had the job of contacting the ships of Commodore Pettin's squadron on high-power microwave while Daniel warned off the guardships. Under the circumstances, Daniel didn't think the commodore would object to being left to an underling, though you could never be sure.

The PPI glowed, the pattern shifting like tinsel drifting in still air. Several, then a score, of the pirate cutters had vanished into the Matrix only moments from their first appearance in sidereal space. Now they reappeared, less than half their previous distance from Strymon.

"Strymonian frigates!" Daniel said. The fourth vessel had edged up from the planet's shadow; the *Princess Cecile*'s commo suite directed a laser emitter at the Strymonian without further input from Daniel or Adele. "We have no quarrel with the loyal citizens of Strymon, but the traitors who've intrigued with the so-called Alliance of the tyrant Porra will be rooted out and punished if they don't give up immediately. Surrender to the Republic of Cinnabar to save your lives and your honor!!"

Precisely how surrender was an honorable option for the picket vessels was a question beyond Daniel's ability to answer, but it seemed a useful phrase to throw in at the moment. His father would've nodded with understanding.

The High Drive whined at maximum output to hold the *Princess Cecile* in position above Palia. Because the corvette was well below geosynchrony, that meant braking against its initial orbital velocity. Pray heaven that Mon had a clear link to the squadron!

Only a handful of the pirate cutters remained where they'd originally appeared, well out from Strymon. A gaggle of thirty trembled from the Matrix within 40,000 miles of the planet. Though there was nothing seemingly organized about the pirate formation, Daniel noted with delight and amazement that the ships were in precisely the same relative alignment as they had been before they entered the Matrix a few minutes before.

Woetjans and both rigging watches were on the hull, despite the danger and the fact they had no job to do at the moment. Daniel wasn't going to land so there was no need to take the antennas down, but he didn't know—couldn't know—what the corvette's next course might be. The riggers waited in case an emergency required an immediate adjustment to the sails.

Not, after all, an unlikely occurrence under the present circumstances.

"Strymonian vessels!" Daniel repeated. "Surrender to the RCN or die!"

He'd inset real-time imagery of the frigates across the bottom of his display. The Strymonians orbited with eight antennas partially extended, permitting them to shift into the Matrix on short notice but also able to maneuver in normal space. For the most part they expected to deal with smugglers or merchantmen lifting without paying their port duties, not actual warfare above their homeworld.

Several Selma cutters came out of the Matrix within Strymon's gravity well. None were particularly close to the guardships, though their varying altitudes and orbits meant that the parties could have volleyed rockets at one another if they'd chosen to do so.

Another score of pirates appeared in near space. Daniel shrank the scale of his PPI to a normal hundred thousand miles; if he'd halved the radius again, he'd still contain the entire Selma fleet.

Most of Kelburney's captains could have exited within pistol range of the frigates if they'd chosen to do so. The Strymonians would have fired rockets out of reflex before there was time to parley; and then would have died in salvos from the remaining scores of pirate cutters.

Few captains, no matter how brave, would throw their lives and ships away uselessly against overwhelming force—and those few would be restrained or shot by their own crews if they attempted such general suicide. By showing the Strymonians that resistance was pointless, Daniel was letting them save their lives.

Kelburney had accepted the plan with laughing agreement. Daniel didn't doubt that the pirates would slug it out at knife distance if forced to, but theirs was a business rather than a crusade. Death meant the end of the party and was therefore to be avoided.

"*RCN vessel, this is Frigate One-Two-Seven,*" said a high-pitched female voice which came to Daniel on a direct link. "*We have declared for President Delos Vaughn. Welcome, allies! I repeat, we are allies of the RCN in suppressing the tyranny of the pretender Pleyna Vaughn. What are your requests? One-Two-Seven over.*"

President Delos Vaughn? Good God, what had been happening on Strymon during the past few days?

Two of the four frigates vanished, their icons from the PPI and the real-time images from the sidebar as well. They'd shaken out sails on their partial rigs and were escaping into the Matrix rather than trust the mercy of the swarming pirate fleet.

Daniel had expected and intended all four of the pickets to flee during the opportunity he'd given them. 127's—surrender? claim of alliance?—was a pleasant surprise, leaving only the fourth—

"*RCN vessel, this is Two-Oh-Four!*" a male voice buzzed through a poorly modulated laser link. "*Long live President Delos Vaughn! Long live the Cinnabar Navy!*"

Daniel cued his console to respond to both of the surrendering patrol vessels and also to the Astrogator's flagship. The *Princess Cecile* wasn't equipped to contact all sixty-seven ships of the pirate armada in a single transmission; he could only hope that Kelburney was.

"Strymonian vessels One-Two-Seven and Two-Oh-Four," Daniel said. "This is RCS *Princess Cecile*, Admiral Leary commanding. Make all your weapons safe, withdraw your gun turrets into your hulls, and hold your orbits. You will not be harmed if you obey these orders to the letter. RCN out."

There was always a risk that some pirate would settle an old grudge by rocketing sitting ducks like the Strymonian frigates, but that wasn't Daniel's major concern at the moment. What happened, happened.

The PPI was alive with cutters circling Strymon, in as many orbits as there were ships. The patterns had the chaotic complexity of a kaleidoscope, seemingly random motion which was nonetheless as precise as a sword dance. Serving alongside the pirates provided memories any captain would cherish. And other memories as well, of course.

Kelburney's own vessel was in the same orbit as the *Princess Cecile*, braking hard to hold position ten miles astern. Like the rest of the Selma cutters, it stepped a full set of antennas despite the stresses of maneuvering in normal space. The pirates favored shorter, thicker masts than the starships of more traditional states; even so, the Astrogator must be risking his rig in his desire to be able to race off through the Matrix without delay.

"*Sir, Commodore Pettin requests to speak with you,*" Lt. Mon said. "*Do you wish me to take the conn? Mon over.*"

As the *Princess Cecile* struggled to hold position over Palia, it was dropping toward the surface of Strymon. Eventually Daniel was going to have to gain altitude or enter the atmosphere—and he certainly wasn't going to enter the atmosphere. Still, he didn't have to make that decision quite yet.

"Right, hold position as long as you can, Mon," Daniel said. "And Mon? Warn me if our allies do something I need to know about, even if that means breaking in on the commodore. Out."

Adele's body was rigid. Her hands danced like a pair of balletomimes, and her display was a mass of data. It meant no more to Daniel than his astrogation vectors would have meant to her, but so long as Adele was at the signals console he knew he'd have all the warning there could be from that source.

He switched to the squadron command frequency that Mon had used to alert the ships on the ground. "Sir!" he said. "Lieutenant Leary reporting, over!"

Pettin wouldn't have heard Daniel claim to be an admiral to overawe the guardships. With luck—and a Signals Officer who was preternaturally adept at wiping records—he never would learn about that.

"*Leary, what the hell is going on, over?*" Pettin said, his voice beginning to break up in the higher registers.

"Sir, you've got to—" wrong word, junior lieutenants don't tell commodores what they've got to do "—get your personnel aboard and lift ship soonest!" Daniel said. "I'll explain as soon as—"

The command link was dual frequency, with the emitting and receiving antennas at bow and stern respectively. The separation wasn't enough on a vessel as small as a corvette to send and receive simultaneously through an atmosphere without interference, but it did allow Pettin to manifest his fury in a roar of static that silenced Daniel.

"*—the* Winckelmann *will be in orbit in ten minutes, Lieutenant,*" the commodore was saying in the enforced silence. "*I'm asking you now, what the hell is going on? Over!*"

Daniel let out his breath in a sigh of relief. Regardless of what happened to the career of Lt. Daniel Oliver Leary afterwards, the *Winckelmann* and her consorts would be safely out of the Strymon system within the hour. It might be months or even years before circumstances allowed the RCN to reenter the Sack with a force sufficient to deal with the powerful Alliance squadron now based on Tanais, but at least the Cinnabar ships and a thousand trained spacers had avoided massacre.

"Sir," he said, "we were attacked when we discovered an Alliance battleship, heavy cruiser, and four destroyers on Tanais. We repaired our battle damage on Dalbriggan and returned immediately to warn you of the danger. Ah, we're accompanied by a squadron of allies from the Selma Cluster. Over."

"*God help me,*" Commodore Pettin said. The words sounded heartfelt. "*Leary, we'll discuss this at a time of greater leisure, and I don't have to tell you what will happen to you if you're lying. Right now I've got my hands full gathering up the seventy percent of my crews who're on detached duty thanks to the rebellion you started. Squadron out!"*

"*And if you want to know about that rebellion, Daniel,*" said Adele over the intercom, "*I have some information for you here.*"

Strymon was a developed world with a highly organized information infrastructure. It occurred to Adele as she viewed clips of the chaos below that she could probably find similar records of the Proscriptions following the Three Circles Conspiracy.

She'd heard her parents had been shot against the wall of the garden behind their townhouse. Adele hadn't been an outdoors child, but her room was at the back of the house. She had familiar memories of ivy growing against the sun-bleached red bricks.

"Ten days ago . . ." said Adele, using a two-party link to the command console. "Rumors were circulating that Cinnabar had decided to support Delos Vaughn. The secret police couldn't determine precisely who was starting the rumors. Nunes, that's the Guardian, Friderik Nunes, had his agents stir up a mob to attack the Cinnabar Observer's residence. He thought Observer Mariette was behind the rumors and hoped the threat would make him stop."

Adele brought up imagery of citizens wearing bright Strymonian costumes marching up three avenues to the square on which the Cinnabar Residence stood, one of several ornate buildings behind walled forecourts. The pavement was plasticized clay, seamless and unable to provide missiles, but the leaders of the mob had thoughtfully provided themselves with sacks of fist-sized stones.

"*Why would they imagine Cinnabar was behind rumors like that?*" Daniel wondered aloud. "*That's scarcely our style. Thinking we were about to send a plenipotentiary to order a change in the government, now, that might have happened.*"

Two uniformed police at the entrance ambled away as the mob approached. One of them even tipped his cap to a woman in the front rank.

"The secret police provided the leaders and hired a number of additional thugs," Adele said. "There was quite a lot of spontaneous response, though. A large element of the civilian population hates Cinnabar almost as much as they fear us."

"*They'll have reason to fear one day soon,*" Daniel said quietly.

Four chattering women came out a side door of the residence and started down the street. They were members of the housekeeping staff, Adele knew from the records of the incident. All were born on Strymon, though they came from country districts rather than Palia itself.

They saw the oncoming mob, hesitated, and tried to get back through the door by which they'd left the building. It had locked behind them. The women started running in the opposite direction, only to meet another limb of the mob.

Stones flew from both directions. The women hunched, trying to protect their heads with their arms. Members of the mob knocked them down with clubs, then finished the job with boots.

"No Cinnabar citizens were injured," Adele said without expression. "All the windows on the ground and second floors of the Residency were broken, but the leaders of the mob didn't permit invasion of the grounds. It was meant as a warning."

Daniel sighed audibly. "*It takes a particular sort of person to kick an old woman to death,*" he said. "*Well, politics is no proper business of an RCN officer.*"

"The next day," Adele said, "Delos Vaughn appeared at one of his family's estates three hundred miles south of Palia. With him was a force of eight hundred off-planet mercenaries, paid for by a consortium of shippers and landholders. You met many of the conspirators at the Captal da Lund's dwelling on Sexburga."

She called up a montage of images, some from news media and others gathered from the conspirators' own files. Though the mercenaries had been hired as individuals on a dozen different worlds, they were outfitted with battledress of a standard pattern bearing the badge and shoulder patches of the Land Forces of the Republic, Cinnabar's army. They carried stocked impellers and submachine guns of Cinnabar manufacture, with a limited number of crew-served weapons.

One of the images showed Delos Vaughn addressing a crowd of civilians. The sound bite attached to the clip rang, "*My people, the Republic of Cinnabar has sent me to regain my rightful position as President of Strymon and to free you from the tyranny of Friderik Nunes and his puppets!*"

"The secret police believed the troops really were from

Cinnabar," Adele said. She shook her head in disgust and amazement. "They also believed there were six thousand of them."

The *Princess Cecile* was maneuvering constantly to optimize its position above Strymon. Neither the changing vectors nor the whine of the antimatter engines disturbed Adele now that she had real work to do.

"What was the position of the army?" Daniel asked. *"Or does Strymon even have an army, come to think?"*

"There's a Presidential Police Reserve," Adele said. She'd searched for army deployments, found none, and finally worked back from clips of the fighting to learn what the government troops were called so that she could determine their strength. "It's about twenty thousand personnel at full strength, but there was quite a lot of desertion as soon as word got out that Delos Vaughn had returned with Cinnabar backing."

"I see why the commodore blames me for the trouble," Daniel said. *"And I greatly fear that he's more right than not."*

Adele selected an image: government troops with violet collar flashes arriving in twenty-place aircars on the outskirts of a village. They began to advance down the main street, still mounted on the vehicles which flew low, using ground effect for support.

A podium with a dozen chairs, many of them knocked over when the speakers hastily fled, had been erected in the town square. As the lead vehicle approached, a man in the clock tower opened fire with an impeller. Slugs punched through the aircar's aluminum body and sparkled off the cobblestone pavement.

More guns fired from basement windows; the houses were frame with wooden shingles, but they had stone foundations. Troops on the vehicles returned fire wildly, occasionally dropping their fellows with ricochets. Civilians flung roof tiles to shatter on vehicles and the pavement.

The aircars turned and raced back the way they'd come, still hugging the ground. One of the buildings was beginning to burn. A civilian's body lay in the street, and half the troops in the back of the last vehicle out were sprawled or writhing in smears of blood.

"There was a good deal of skirmishing like that," Adele said. "Nunes was afraid to strike with his full strength because he couldn't trust even the troops which hadn't deserted. He called for assistance from the Alliance squadron that had just arrived at Tanais. Admiral Chastelaine, the Alliance commander, refused. He didn't say why."

"*His ships must have been without port facilities for at least thirty days, perhaps twice that,*" Daniel said. "*I don't imagine many squadron commanders under those circumstances would delay their refit because some wog was worried about riots.*"

Adele's lips tightened, but that was a precise description of Chastelaine's probable attitude. That it was also very likely Daniel's own attitude was inconsequential for the time being.

"Our friend Delos was continuing to gather support on the basis of his Cinnabar backing," she resumed, "so he didn't have any reason to push for a quick conclusion. Then Commodore Pettin arrived."

The *Winckelmann* dropped majestically toward the bay around which Palia was built. A merchant ship was lifting at the same time. Many of the vessels which had been in the harbor at the start of the riots had already left.

"*I am surprised that Nunes permitted our ships to land, though,*" Daniel said. It must have been going through his mind as it was Adele's that while the remainder of the squadron was settling peacefully onto Strymon, the *Princess Cecile* had been raked by the Tanais defenses.

"Observer Mariette contacted the commodore in orbit and demanded he land immediately to provide protection for Cinnabar property during the riots," Adele said. "As the trouble appeared to be an internal Strymonian matter, the commodore brushed aside objections from the harbor controller and landed as requested."

"*Another officer might at least have left a destroyer in orbit,*" Daniel mused. "*I suppose he wanted all the available personnel to bolster his guard detachments.*"

"Observer Mariette was very insistent," Adele said, though part of her wondered why she was bothering to make excuses for the commodore. She wasn't the one to judge the military reasons that had put the whole Cinnabar force on the surface, but it wouldn't have taken information-gathering skills nearly as sophisticated as her own to warn Pettin that more was going on than the Observer realized.

"*Then Vaughn would have claimed the squadron had arrived to support him,*" Daniel said. "*Which a reasonable Strymonian citizen would find easy to believe.*"

He was stating his analysis rather than asking a question. Adele said, "The whole planet except for Palia and a few regions where Nunes had family connections declared for Delos. Palia is less pro-Pleyna than simply full of rioters looting anything they can. For the most part they haven't attacked properties guarded by RCN detachments, but there've been sniping incidents every day since the squadron landed."

Adele pursed her lips, then said, "Daniel, Nunes asked for help again when Pettin arrived, but Admiral Chastelaine still refused. Surely he isn't going to simply ignore an RCN squadron?"

"*Ah,*" said Daniel. "*No, he wouldn't ignore us, but by the same token he won't venture out of his fortified base before he's certain his ships are fully repaired. Fully* prepared."

"But Daniel," Adele said, struggling to understand a situation devoid of logic. "Their ships are bigger and newer and there's more of them. Surely Admiral Chastelaine knows that?"

"*Yes, Adele,*" Daniel said. "*But he also knows that we're the RCN. No Alliance commander ever forgets that.*"

"Ah," Adele said. "Yes, I understand."

"*Sir, there's a ship rising from the surface,*" Lt. Mon said. "*It's a private yacht, the* Achilles, *and President Delos Vaughn's aboard. He says he's coming up to meet with you. Over.*"

He'd broken in on a dedicated link from the Battle Direction Center to Daniel's command console. It didn't pass through the signals console, but Adele had set the system to echo everything to her unit regardless of provenance. There was no information that she *might* not need, some time, some where.

"*Does it indeed, Mon?*" Daniel said. "*I can't imagine what Master Vaughn wants of me, but I certainly have some matters I'd like to raise with him. I suppose we'd better bring him aboard. Make the necessary arrangements. Captain out.*"

Adele had called up the message and was running the speech attributed to Vaughn through voice recognition software when Daniel said, "*What do you think about this development, Adele?*"

"I don't have the faintest notion," she said. "Except that it really is Vaughn; and the heads of Friderik Nunes and Pleyna Vaughn have been stuck on poles in front of Delos's headquarters in the suburbs of Palia, so I suppose he's President of Strymon as well."

CHAPTER THIRTY-ONE

The *Achilles* looked to be a dumpy little vessel at present because her rig was stowed. Even when fully telescoped, the masts of the first and last of her four rings stuck out beyond the yacht's short hull. Extended and wearing a full suit of sails, those masts would give her an area-to-mass ratio equalled by few if any other ships of Daniel's acquaintance. To him, that was a mark of great beauty.

The scale of the image was too small to show the boarding line connecting the yacht to the *Princess Cecile*, though Daniel could have directed the console to emphasize it if he'd had any reason to. Vaughn had asked to board via a tube and to bring several of his aides with him. Daniel had granted neither request.

The outer airlock dogged home; a moment later the inner valve opened. Woetjans, her faceshield flung open, half dragged, half guided, Delos Vaughn into Corridor C. Vaughn's expression through the synthetic sapphire of his visor was both irritated and frightened.

Daniel glanced again at the image of the *Achilles*. To Adele across the bridge he said, "That yacht's far too fine a vessel to be used for an orbital ferryboat the way our guest just did. They could've found a cargo lighter easily enough."

Adele shrugged. "You can't hold a landsman to a spacer's standards, Daniel," she said. With the bosun's help, Vaughn was struggling out of a rigging suit meant for someone a size larger, shooting frustrated looks toward her and Daniel but for the moment unable to join them. There was too much ambient noise for him to overhear. "I doubt whether he could, let alone does, understand that he's done anything questionable."

"Yes," said Daniel, "but that's rather a picture of his life, don't you think? The ability to do whatever's expedient without knowing or caring about anyone else's viewpoint?"

Vaughn kicked out of the suit's right leg and stepped to the hatchway. "Permission to enter the bridge, Captain Leary?" he said in a clear voice.

"You may enter the bridge, Mr. Vaughn," Daniel said. Then, because he didn't want to seem petty, he corrected himself: "President Vaughn, that is."

"'Mister' is quite sufficient between old shipmates," Vaughn said with his familiar engaging smile as he strode forward. "And present allies, I'm pleased to say."

Sun looked over his shoulder, then went back to his display; Betts never paused in obsessively computing missile courses. Adele continued to listen to the snips of intership and surface communications which her software culled out for her, but her eyes and her primary attention were on Delos Vaughn.

"I didn't expect to see you again, sir," Daniel said. "Not after the way you left us on Sexburga."

Facing Vaughn, he found it hard to be sure of how he felt about the man. Not hatred, certainly, nor even anger. There was a sort of admiration, Daniel had to admit, for a person who was so pure an example of the thing he was; and disgust as well, at what that thing was.

"I won't bother to apologize for the way I tricked you, Captain," Vaughn said, bluffly disarming. "Nothing I could say would be enough, and you wouldn't accept it anyway. I'll make up for the trouble in every way possible, however. One of the estates Nunes confiscated has been put in your name already. You may well want to spread the largess among those of your servants who were left on South Land with you. You'll be able to make them very happy without noticing the cost, I assure you."

Tovera watched from just inside the captain's suite; her right hand rested lightly on the grip of her submachine gun. Hogg was in the bridge hatchway, toying with a loop of fishing line and grinning.

"I'm a Leary of Bantry, sir," Daniel said quietly. "We understand cost very well, but the term rarely has anything to do with money when we use it."

"I take your point, Captain," said Vaughn; and he did, the tightness around his nostrils showed that clearly. "I've come for help clearing up the final patches of resistance to my assumption of the presidency. The two sons of the usurper Nunes are forted up in the family residence in the Tatrig Mountains. They'll require heavy weapons to blast them out, and—"

"President Vaughn," Daniel said. "I'm aware of your claims that the Republic backed your rebellion. You and I both know there's no truth to that. I won't become involved in what is clearly an internal Strymonian matter."

Vaughn's smile was crystal hard. "Well, Lieutenant, so far as Strymon knows, your Observer Mariette included," he said, "you're already involved. Pleyna Vaughn came out of Palia to discuss settlement terms because my military liaison, Lieutenant Daniel Leary of the RCN, guaranteed her safety. Of course I'll be able to correct this misapprehension as soon as you—"

Sun rose from his console in a fluid movement. His face was red. Adele grabbed his wrist. Sun jerked loose, but Hogg now stood between the spacer and Vaughn, and Tovera was behind him with her gun's muzzle a millimeter from his spine.

Everyone was looking at Daniel. "I'm not concerned with the lies of foreign rabble, Officer Sun," he said mildly. "Return to your duties, please. The *Winckelmann*'s lighted her thrusters, so we can expect further orders shortly."

Vaughn was a brave man to have boarded the *Princess Cecile* now. Despite that, he wasn't a fool, so he must need Daniel's help very badly.

"A combination of those who oppose the new president . . ." Adele said. Her left hand came out of her pocket; Sun was at his console again and the two servants had backed off the bridge.

" . . . and the large percentage of the population who resent their president being chosen by Cinnabar," she continued, her eyes on something far distant in time, "will make it difficult for the regime to stay in power if there's a center of armed resistance."

She looked at Daniel, then at Vaughn. She added, "We on Cinnabar know something of conspiracies also, Mister President."

Vaughn swallowed. He said, "All I want from you, Captain, is a word to the frigates who've surrendered to you. The Fleet was thoroughly in Nunes's camp—and intriguing with the Alliance as well, *that's* no fable. If those ships enter the atmosphere and use their rockets against the Nunes positions, my mercenaries will have no difficulty in mopping up what remains. I don't trust the captains to obey me, however, and there're no other Fleet elements on Strymon. They all lifted for Tanais when your commodore landed."

Adele looked at Daniel sharply. He nodded. Vaughn knew his rivals had plotted with the Alliance, but he didn't realize that Admiral Chastelaine had reached the Strymon system.

"President Vaughn," he said, "you've entered a realm of politics that's properly the business of the Cinnabar Observer. If you prefer to raise the matter with Commodore Pettin, my superior, feel free to do so—his flagship will be in orbit shortly. For my part, I must request you return to your own vessel immediately, because I have—"

"Daniel!" Adele said. She'd rotated her seat to face her console again. "I'm cuing this to you!"

Vaughn's mouth opened, probably to protest. He was suddenly between Hogg and Tovera, backing quickly to the hatchway. Woetjans and the riggers with her in the corridor watched in amusement, but they didn't get involved where they would so clearly be superfluous.

"*RCN, this is Kelburney,*" said the Astrogator's voice. "*I left the cutters where the relay satellites used to be, just in case something came through that I'd like to know about. Ten minutes back, Strete outside Tanais Base picked up a transmission saying that Admiral Chastelaine was lifting for Strymon with his whole squadron. I guess you know more about what that means than we do, but we know it means we're headed back home soonest. If you're smart, boy, you'll do the same. Kelburney out.*"

Daniel glanced at the Plot Position Indicator. The pirate cutters were beginning to vanish like dewdrops in the sunlight. Captain Strete had brought word through the Matrix to his fellows, then fled only moments ahead of them. Daniel really couldn't blame the Selmans; not that it would have mattered if he had.

He hit the alarm button. "Ship, general quarters," he ordered.

"All riggers topside. Riggers will remain on the hull during transitions until recalled. Captain out."

The *Winckelmann*'s plasma thrusters covered the RF frequency with thunderous white noise, but the laser communicator should punch through the exhaust iridescence clearly enough to get the point across. Another hour would have been enough; but the RCN didn't depend on luck or prayer, either one.

"Adele," Daniel said. "Give me maximum emitter output and a tight focus to the flagship."

He cleared his throat and continued, "*Princess Cecile* to Squadron. We have an emergency. . . ."

Somewhere behind Adele, Delos Vaughn squealed briefly. She'd guess that Hogg was trussing and gagging the president rather than cutting his throat. Hogg being Hogg, you couldn't be sure; nor was it a question about which she could raise much concern.

Both Strymonian frigates were sending increasingly shrill questions toward the *Princess Cecile* as they watched the pirate cutters disappear into the Matrix. The *Achilles*'s captain sounded querulous also, but since the yacht was unarmed—Adele had looked up the registry description—that wasn't a matter for present concern.

The patrol vessels were. Daniel and the officers in the Battle Direction Center were concerned with the ship and Commodore Pettin; but Adele was the signals officer, after all.

"Strymonian vessels Two-Oh-Four and One-Twenty-Seven," she said, using microwave because Daniel was on the modulated laser. "This is RCN Flagship *Princess Cecile*. You have your orders. If you violate them, we will destroy you without compunction! Ah, *out!*"

Were you supposed to say "flagship" if you were claiming to be a flagship? She'd ask when there was leisure, so she'd know the next time the question arose. For now, the terrified babbling of the Strymonian officers was sufficient.

"—*the* Princess Cecile *will therefore proceed to the neighborhood of Tanais,*" Daniel was saying, "*and screen the remainder of the squadron while your crews board. Leary over.*"

The corvette shivered as hydraulic jacks extended the antennas and spread the sails. For a moment Adele heard *clang-clang, clang-clang.* Riggers on the hull were freeing a jammed tube with their mauls.

"*Leary, this is Pettin,*" a voice replied on a laser beam from the *Winckelmann.* Despite the initial tight focus and the voice sharpening provided by the *Princess Cecile*'s communications suite, static roared through the commodore's words. "*You are not, I repeat, not to engage the enemy. You will proceed with utmost dispatch to Cinnabar and warn the authorities there of the situation in the Sack.*"

Adele glanced at the image of Daniel inset at the top of her screen. His fingers hammered at his virtual keyboard while his eyes flicked back and forth at the data appearing on the display before him. Daniel was a sure and reasonably fast typist, but he put as much effort into his keystrokes as he would in splitting logs.

"*Leary, there's nothing a corvette can do to affect a squadron of that weight,*" Pettin continued. "*You've shown how fast you can push your* Princess Cecile. *Get home, get help, and tell Anston to get back here before the Alliance has the Sack sewed up. Acknowledge and get moving! Pettin over.*"

"One minute to entering the Matrix," Midshipman Vesey's voice warned over the PA system. The signal lights pulsed.

"*Princess Cecile to squadron,*" Daniel said. His fingers and eyes continued to move as though controlled by an entity outside the person who responded to Commodore Pettin. "*Sir, your transmission is breaking up. I'm therefore maneuvering as previously described.* Princess Cecile *out.*"

He broke the connection. The eyes of his image met Adele's.

"Daniel?" she said. "I've downloaded a report on the Strymon system into both our message cells. If you set them for Sexburga, there's a sixty percent chance one will arrive. The authorities there can send a courier vessel to Cinnabar."

"Thank you, Adele," Daniel said, calling across the noisy bridge so that the other officers could hear as well. "But that'd mean shifting the ready-use missiles out of their tubes. I believe we're going to have more use for them than Cinnabar has for a message."

"*Entering the—*" Vesey said, and Adele's world everted itself in what was becoming a familiar fashion.

✧ ✧ ✧

"Lieutenant Mon," Danieas well l said, "I'm going topside. Please take the conn. Out."

He stood, feeling the *Princess Cecile* heel through the soles of his feet. The ship was a living apex of the infinite directions and forces of the Matrix. Adele turned from her console and said in a tone of inward-directed anger, "There's nothing to add to the bare message! If Captain Strete had any imagery of the Alliance fleet, he didn't transmit it to the Astrogator; and now he's gone."

"Come up on deck with me if you would, Adele," Daniel said. "We have twenty minutes before the next exit, and the *Sissie's* wearing almost her full suit of sails. It's not something you'll often have a chance to see."

"For a variety of reasons, perhaps," he added. He tried to sound solemn, but he didn't manage very well. "Regardless, it's a lovely sight."

"Captain?" Betts said, looking over his shoulder as Daniel followed Adele toward the suit locker. "You'll be taking down Four Dorsal and Four Ventral to clear the tubes, right?"

"I won't know till we have a plot of the enemy formation, Betts," Daniel said. Tovera and Hogg were in the corridor, readying Adele's rigging suit. Hogg's face was a thundercloud; Tovera seemed, as usual, mildly amused. "I will say that I'll launch through a sail if necessary, though. Make your solutions regardless of the rig."

"You've got *no* business going out right now!" Hogg snarled to Daniel, his face turned aside as he lifted Adele without ceremony for Tovera to pull on the legs of the suit. "That's Woetjans's job. You're just full of yourself 'cause you spit in Pettin's face, you know. You're going to take a chance too many one of these days, young master!"

"I'm checking the rig, Hogg," Daniel said quietly as he donned his suit in a practiced reflex: legs, arms, and then close the plastron; three simple movements that he could do in the dark or so hungover that he could scarcely stand. "Which *is* my business."

He cleared his throat and added, "You'll recall that I stopped telling you where we should place our snares before I turned six."

"You didn't stop being a smart aleck then, though," Hogg said. He squeezed the rigid shoulder of Daniel's suit before turning away again. He muttered, "Wish there was *some* fucking thing I could do."

"You've already done it, Hogg," Daniel said. "You raised me to be a man."

He gestured Adele into the airlock, then stepped through and dogged the hatch.

Daniel started to clamp Adele's helmet for her. She raised her hand. "Daniel?" she said. "Why aren't you plotting missile courses now? And don't tell me because that's Betts's job, competent though I'm sure he is."

Daniel shrugged and pursed his lips. There was no reason she shouldn't know, after all.

"We're going to be too close for the missiles to course-correct after they're launched," he said. "The ship's vector and attitude are going to determine whether the rounds hit or miss, not whatever we program into the attack console. But Betts *is* very good at his job, and he'll be more comfortable if he's able to focus on it."

Adele gave him an odd smile. "Yes," she said. "And I dare say I'll be more comfortable trying not to fall off the hull than I would staring at the fact I completely failed to gather useful information."

Daniel chuckled. He closed her helmet, closed his—ordinarily a pair of spacers going topside would check each other's fittings, but that wasn't going to work here—and opened the outer hatch onto the hull.

Daniel paused a step from the coaming. As always, the beauty of the Matrix brought a lump to his throat.

The *Princess Cecile* trembled through veils of light more delicate than spiderweb, bathed in colors that had no name in the world of landsmen, and formed patterns that reproduced themselves all the way to an infinity not of one universe but all universes. Daniel Oliver Leary was a part of this splendor!

He handed Adele onto the hull and touched helmets with her. He said, "What do you see when you look out, Adele?"

Daniel felt her suit stir against his; she'd probably shrugged. "The light, you mean?" she said. "It seems gray where I look, but at the corners of my eyes it seems . . . pastel? I couldn't put it more clearly than that."

Ah, well; she found an excitement in databases that seemed likely to continue eluding him.

Daniel hooked Adele's safety line to a staple, then closed the hatch behind them. The *Princess Cecile*'s twenty-four masts were at their full extension; topsails shimmered on all of them, and the huge lower courses were set on the dorsals as well.

He and Adele stood silent—he entranced, she . . . well, polite and docile might be the correct description of her feelings, but in the shrouded anonymity of the suits he could at least imagine that some of the wonder reached her below the level of awareness. The riggers were scarcely noticeable even when they were in direct view. The sails were huge and alive with the energy of the cosmos pressing them, while the humans who walked the yards to make final adjustments in the spread and lay were mere shadows against the effulgence.

The mainsails on rings C and D shifted clockwise. The *Princess Cecile* trembled, then sank from one bubble universe to another. The astrogation computer had chosen the latter's physical constants as most suitable for this stage of the voyage. To Daniel it was as if the heart of a sun had opened momentarily, blinding in its beauty.

Whatever Adele felt or saw caused her to snatch at him so violently that her boots lost their magnetic grip on the hull. Daniel's arm encircled her and guided her back to firm footing.

"We'll make three more shifts before we exit for a look at our colleagues from the Alliance," Daniel said. "We'll be three light-seconds sunward of Tanais; a quick in-and-out, the way we set up for the Falassan guardship."

Daniel cleared his throat, lifting his helmet away from Adele's momentarily so that the sound wouldn't pass. "I want to get the feel of the region we're sailing in before I set up the attack," he went on. "The most precise calculations in the world will leave you fifty miles out if the Matrix is slow. . . ."

He frowned, thinking about the way Adele had tried to describe the sensation of Casimir radiation on human retinas as gray or pastel. "Slow" was a word whose normal meaning had nothing to do with the interplay of forces between the universes; but Daniel had no better word, so he used what there was to give false meaning to a concept that even many astrogators wouldn't have understood. There were things that you could only explain to someone who already knew.

"Fifty miles isn't important if you're making planetfall," Daniel went on with a sigh. "You start your braking effort a little sooner, a little later. But for our present purposes..."

The topsails of E Ring furled forty percent. On Dorsal, the sail fluttered but jammed well short of the programmed amount. Daniel took a step forward—and caught himself, feeling silly, because with both watches on duty there was someone at the antenna already.

He watched the rigger climb stays hand over hand, throw a leg over the yard, and then kick the parrel with his other foot. The sail's taut fabric fluttered loose, then drew tight again as the jack hauled it into position.

"Beautiful," Daniel whispered. "Just beautiful. Any captain would give an arm to have a crew like mine."

"Daniel," Adele said, all expression squeezed out of her voice by the helmet-to-helmet contact. "Thank you for making me a part of your crew, part of your family. Regardless of what happens next."

By reflex Daniel opened his mouth to say, "Now, don't count us out yet..." but that wasn't the right response for a friend.

"Yes, well," he said. "I expect the *Sissie* to give a good account of herself. Beyond that, the future's rather in the lap of the Gods. There's some reason to hope that Chastelaine's crews won't be in the best condition after what must have been an unusually difficult voyage."

He stepped slightly apart to stare at the Matrix between the sails of the corvette's A and B rings. All time and space danced in that shimmering wonder.

Helmet to helmet again with Adele but speaking as much to himself, Daniel said, "I suppose I came out here for a...for *another*, let's not say last, look at the Matrix before I set up the next series of maneuvers. Quite wonderful, don't you think?"

"I too think my present situation is wonderful, Daniel," Adele said with the understated precision that was even more a part of her than the personal data unit.

Daniel laughed and hugged her through the rigid bracing of their suits. "Let's go below," he said. "We'll have business with the Alliance very shortly. And by *God*, the Alliance has business with us!"

✧　　　✧　　　✧

Lt. Mon came up Corridor C from the Battle Direction Center, moving like an angry boxer. Somebody called to him from a compartment—Hoagland, the technician who was going over the Medic again before it might have to be used. Mon ignored him and glared at Adele when she looked up to watch his approach.

"Permission to enter the bridge!" Mon said loudly. He didn't use his knuckles but slapped the hatch flange twice with his fingertips to make it ring.

"Granted, Lieutenant," Daniel said, muting his holographic display to only a shimmer like dust motes between him and Mon. Daniel's face showed very little, but to Adele he appeared as puzzled about what Mon was doing here as she was herself.

"Captain," Mon said. Even Betts turned briefly from his console before going back to his fantasy of missile tracks. "We won't have much time after we exit for observations so I thought I'd say this now. Goddam little in my life went the way I'd have liked it to, not till I met you. I guess on average I've come out ahead."

Mon thrust his hand through the display area of the command console. Daniel leaned forward and lifted slightly from his seat to clasp arms with his second in command.

"It's a mutual pleasure, Mon," he said. A familiar smile lit his eyes and made the right corner of his mouth quirk upward. "I hope, however, that the association won't continue on the atomic level after today."

Mon looked blank, then guffawed. He slapped his left hand over Daniel's right, sandwiching it against his biceps muscle, then unclasped and stepped away.

"Sun, all of you?" Mon said. "I always figured I'd die in bed with my wife. Thanks to God and the RCN, I may be spared that. Good luck to all of you!"

He turned and strode back the way he'd come; an angry little man who always saw the worst in a situation and who never did less than his duty. Adele felt a surge of, well, friendship for him.

Daniel started to bring up his display, then grinned more broadly at Adele and activated the PA system instead. "*Fellow spacers!*" he said. "*We've shown the RCN how to sail and the Selma pirates how to navigate the Matrix. Now we're going to show the*

Alliance how to fight. Three cheers for the Princess Cecile! *Hip-hip—"*

"*Hooray!*" the ship answered. Unaided voices, several shouting on the intercom, and Midshipman Dorst using the PA system itself from the Battle Direction Center.

"*Hip-hip—*"

"*Hooray!*"

"*Hip-hip—*"

Everyone aboard the *Princess Cecile* was cheering. Illiterate engine-wipers, women whose families had been RCN for every generation in living memory, men whose idea of patriotism was that anyone not from Cinnabar was a wog with no honor and no rights.

All those people cheered; and so did Mistress Adele Mundy, the scion of Chatsworth, a woman whose culture was as broad and deep as all human history.

"*Hooray!*"

Lt. Mon, returned to the Battle Direction Center, announced, "*One minute to reentry to normal space!*"

CHAPTER THIRTY-TWO

Transition. Daniel's display came live with imagery; he adjusted the scale so that the edge of the frame encompassed without waste volume the Alliance squadron forming above the huge disk of Getica. In Daniel's present state, the discomfort of being slowly disemboweled wouldn't have prevented him from functioning.

"Reentering the Matrix!" he said, personally decreasing the charge levels of the *Princess Cecile*'s current set of thirty-six sails. In Daniel's mind, negative images of the bridge and his companions were projected in infinite series "up" and "down" through a nongeometric dimension.

Mon, the midshipmen, and an artificial intelligence within the astrogation computer were all working on an attack solution. If Daniel dropped dead in the next ten minutes or so, perhaps one of those courses would be chosen. Otherwise, Lt. Daniel Leary would be trusting his own instincts with only the barest regard for other opinions. A warship wasn't a democracy, and a captain who didn't lead was a fool and a disaster for those whom he commanded.

A red-lit sidebar appeared at the top of his display. He glanced at it in furious annoyance, thinking, *What a bloody time for the screen to malfunction—*

And noticed to his amazement that the six tiny images there were the ships of the Alliance squadron, rotating to show what appeared to be their current sail plans rather than the maximum theoretical rig. Optical data gathered at three light-seconds distance wasn't good enough to provide such detail.

Daniel enlarged the images, looking through the haze of coherent light toward Adele. Through the intercom her voice said, "*Admiral Chastelaine believes in keeping tight control of his formation. The flagship,* Der Grosser Karl, *microwaved full rigging instructions to the other vessels, and I've copied them to you. Do they help?*"

"Well, dear one, they may just save our lives," Daniel said. He felt an odd elation. He'd expected to die in the next few minutes . . . and it might still happen, of course; there were no guarantees in life. But now that Daniel knew the angles from which the battleship's secondary batteries would be screened by the expanse of her sails, he would give his command opportunities for survival that couldn't be expected from pure chance.

Oh, yes. The sail plans helped.

"Attack officers," Daniel said, cuing the message to Betts, Sun, and the Battle Direction Center; and Adele of course, but not by *his* determination. "The attachment is the rig the Alliance squadron will be wearing. Adjust your solutions accordingly. Our desired reentry to sidereal space continues to be one mile, plus or minus one half mile, from the Alliance battleship. Out."

Betts nodded without looking away from his console and continued working. Sun looked around in amazement, however. Sun had been a rigger in the merchant service before enlisting in the RCN and finding a new focus in gunnery. He knew, though not as well as Daniel himself, how difficult it was to navigate through the Matrix with that degree of precision.

The *Princess Cecile* shifted again between universes. A vessel couldn't remain at rest within the Matrix, so to hold position it moved from one bubble to another, balancing flow against time to return to its original position.

The Alliance squadron had almost certainly noticed the *Princess Cecile*'s brief return to normal space. A merchant vessel wouldn't have been able to transition so quickly, so even though Daniel had turned off the corvette's identification transponder Admiral Chastelaine would know that a warship had spotted his ships.

Whose warship remained an open question: Strymonian frigate,

Selma pirate, or just possibly an RCN ship like the one which the Tanais defenses had mauled or destroyed a week previous? Chastelaine would pause to make sure his ships were in full fighting trim before he set off for Strymon to put down the rebellion there.

Daniel grinned as he started a new set of course calculations. The Alliance admiral wasn't the only one wondering about the future.

Tovera stood at the wardroom hatch, looking in all directions without appearing either nervous or furtive. She and Hogg must have moved Delos Vaughn from the suit locker to there. Knowing Hogg, Vaughn was trussed to the clamps that held the table legs during meals.

Daniel smiled as he calculated potentials—on the astrogation display, not the attack screen. If he'd had time, he'd have had to order a more polite form of confinement for their guest and ally. Fortunately, Daniel was very busy.

Maroon a Leary of Bantry in the desert, would he?

The attack involved three aspects of the *Princess Cecile*'s course: velocity, vector, and location in sidereal space. Velocity was a mere mathematical conversion of force applied through the physical constants of the universes which the corvette had traversed after entry to the Matrix. Vector was more difficult, the real business of astrogation; but there were thousands of astrogators who could achieve an approximation that would be adequate to the needs of the present attack.

Absolute location, though . . . that went beyond science, perhaps beyond art. It required that the astrogator—that Daniel—read the Matrix from topside and keep it in the back of his mind as he viewed the gauges on his display.

The weight of Casimir radiation affected the potential of the sails resisting it to thrust the *Princess Cecile* through the Matrix. There were ongoing efforts to develop software which could chart deviations from the calculated mean and adjust the sails to take maximum benefit from the actual conditions. All the programs to date had failed: they overcorrected, inducing a pyramid of errors into the system until the computer had to shut down for reprogramming.

A human being who'd seen the flow of universes beyond the

sails and who felt each stress, each charge, of the ship he captained could hope to do what no electronic mind could encompass. It was no more than a hope, of course; but for the crew of a corvette preparing to attack a battleship, hope was an unusual boon.

"Battle Direction Center," Daniel ordered. "Bring forward your solutions."

"*Sir, I've not complet—*" Dorst began to say.

"Now, *spacer!*" Mon said before Daniel could offer his equivalent of the same thought. Knowing Mon, if Dorst was within reach at the time he started his excuse there'd been a slap as punctuation.

If that'd happened, Daniel hoped Dorst would have better sense than to resent it. The midshipman was big, young, and healthy, but Mon was too experienced a veteran to fight fair. He'd literally mop the deck with Dorst's face after kicking him in the balls a few times to induce the proper frame of mind.

There were things you learned in the Academy, and there were things you learned from the Mons and Woetjans and Hoggs of this world. You needed both to be a credit to the RCN.

Lt. Daniel Leary wore a smile as he viewed the solutions of Mon, Vesey, the computer, and Dorst's own partial. The last was a good start, but the boy had to learn that sometimes having the answer right was less important than having the answer *now*.

The computer's course would require fourteen hours in the Matrix and two intermediate returns to normal space to fix the corvette's location. No other procedure could achieve the required accuracy parameters.

Vesey had done something quite original, plotting back from the target. It wouldn't work in the real world because the small change in the *Princess Cecile*'s course during the plotting couldn't be factored in; the whole solution had to be recalculated. Despite that, it was an intelligent attempt to deal with requirements that one of the most advanced computers in the human universe found beyond practical resolution.

Mon's solution was practical and practically suicidal: wham, bam! Thank you, Admiral Chastelaine. Following exit, the *Princess Cecile* would have to reenter the Matrix within thirty-one seconds to avoid plunging into Getica's upper atmosphere. Daniel wasn't sure so quick a transition was possible, and he *knew* it wasn't possible if they received battle damage during the run-in.

Which left Daniel's own solution, the one he'd probably have chosen even if he'd had Admiral bloody Anston as well as Commander Foulkes, the Academy's instructor in tactics, in the BDC sweating over their alternatives. Lt. Daniel Leary commanded *this* vessel.

Daniel chuckled as he entered the chosen course into the active file. The schematic of the corvette's sails changed; potentials fluttered, spiking before dropping to zero as the *Princess Cecile* slid dimensionally *sideways* into another universe. The set of the sails immediately began to change for the second of the three legs of the approach.

"Ship, this is the captain!" Daniel said. His voice sounded vaguely bored when he heard it over the PA system. "We will reenter normal space in three minutes thirty . . . five seconds. Prepare for action. All personnel don emergency suits."

He and Adele—she under protest—were still wearing their rigging suits. Sun had slipped on his emergency suit of thin fabric while Daniel was topside. Betts, looking at his display with anguish for the perfect solution he still couldn't find, stood. He jerked open the drawer in the chair seat and pulled out his.

Tovera had disappeared into the wardroom. There were emergency suits there, so she and Hogg—

Almighty God, what about Delos Vaughn?

"Wardroom!" Daniel said. The servants and their prisoner were probably the only ones present in the compartment, but Daniel needed to get the message to anyone who could possibly help. "Get President Vaughn into a suit soonest! Hogg, do you hear me? Cut him loose and suit him up!"

The *Princess Cecile* made another transition, this the one that brought her onto the long final approach. On Daniel's display the sail schematic changed again.

The topsail of Ventral 6 rotated to 238 degrees instead of the programmed 257 degrees; abruptly it leaped another five degrees, then warped around the remainder of the way in tiny jerks. Daniel thought of riggers ignoring the transition and hauling around by main force the frozen tackle.

The rig was aligned. Daniel checked the schematic again, then fed to the sails the charges that would cause them to react against the pressure of Casimir radiation. The *Princess Cecile* canted in space-time.

Daniel pressed a dedicated signal button on his console: ALL PERSONNEL WITHIN THE HULL. The six arms of every semaphore station on the hull now stuck out like the petals of a daisy, a clear sign to the riggers that they were to come in immediately. Those who couldn't see a station themselves would be warned by hand-signals from their fellows, but veterans like the *Princess Cecile*'s crew knew without being told that the corvette was making her attack run.

"*Two minutes to reentry into normal space!*" Dorst announced in a firm, normal-sounding voice. Daniel would be able to praise the lad to his grandfather without hesitation. Both midshipmen were assets to the *Princess Cecile*'s crew.

The riggers weren't coming in.

Daniel cleared the semaphore control, then hammered it with his fist. That was waste effort, he knew, but he had to do it anyway.

"Adele?" he said desperately. "Is there anything wrong with the topside signal apparatus?"

If there was, he could send a man out—could go himself, he was wearing a rigging suit—and bring the crew down with hand-signals.

Adele brought up a display, checked it, and quickly checked it against three columns of similar data—the recorded values from past occasions when the semaphores were known to be working properly. He'd known there wouldn't be anything wrong.

"*No, Daniel,*" she said without inflexion. "*The equipment's in order. Is there a problem?*"

"*One minute to reentry into normal space!*"

"Woetjans's keeping her crew topside," Daniel said. He felt a sudden despair, though he knew he'd have done the same thing if he'd been the *Sissie*'s bosun. "She wants them ready to clear battle damage immediately so that we can maneuver as quickly as possible."

The survivors would be ready.

"*Thirty seconds to reentry!*" said Lt. Mon. "*God bless the RCN!*" Transition.

The first missile released with a *thump* so quick that Adele thought it was part of the buffeting of the corvette's return to sidereal space. The second, launched five seconds later so that it wouldn't be damaged by the exhaust trail of the first, corrected her misapprehension.

Not that Adele cared. She was in the sea of information which flooded from the ships of the Alliance squadron and Tanais Base. Admiral Chastelaine was organizing his force and simultaneously trying to learn what the Strymonian base personnel knew about the recently sighted warship.

Reading between the lines of the queries, Chastelaine didn't trust his new allies even though he'd left a force of Alliance personnel both on Tanais and in the orbital forts defending the base. She smiled grimly. The only certainty with traitors was that they'd stab you in the back also if they found it expedient.

"*God the mother of us all!*" somebody screamed over the PA system.

Adele flicked her left wand, a hair's breadth from cutting access to the idiot who'd misused the system for babble at a time of crisis. She saw for the first time the image echoed from Daniel's screen to the top of her display.

It was still a misuse of the PA system, but this time she'd let it pass. She stared transfixed at the image.

Der Grosser Karl's mass hid all but an edge of Tanais because the corvette viewed her at such close vantage. Adele had seen the *Aristotle* from closer yet, but that had been in dry dock with the *Aristotle*'s sails removed and her antennas folded against the hull. The bulk of *Der Grosser Karl*'s seventy thousand deadweight tonnes was increased by fully extended eighty-meter antennas and enough hectares of electroconductive sails that a small city could hide beneath them.

"*Entering the Matrix in—*" Dorst was announcing.

Working forward along the battleship's hull, a topsail, a midsail, and last the mainsail of three successive antennas bulged against their original stress and tore. Sparks of antimatter exhaust danced through them, devouring more of the fabric. The missile had grazed *Der Grosser Karl*, but without seriously affecting the target's ability to sail and fight.

"*—thirty seconds,*" Dorst said.

The maincourse of an antenna near the battleship's stern vanished in a rainbow fireball. *The second missile,* Adele thought, but then two more sails, amidships to port and starboard, ruptured. The battleship's plasma cannon were clearing their own fields of fire, blasting away rigging that had been in the way. The *Princess Cecile* jolted sideways in a bath of flame.

A deep, three-hundred-foot-long gouge opened along *Der Grosser Karl's* bow in a roostertail of coruscance. Red, yellow, and white sparks erupted into vacuum. Metal burned where sufficient air escaped to support combustion; otherwise it merely radiated away the frictional heat that had ripped it apart.

Alliance ships were signaling wildly. Adele noticed with a grim smile that two destroyers were sending in clear and that the heavy cruiser's messages were encrypted according to two separate systems—apparently depending on whether they originated on the bridge or in the Battle Direction Center. She was quite certain that the Alliance vessels were having more trouble understanding their own communications than she was.

"Entering the Matrix in fourteen seconds!" a voice said, Daniel's. Adele cut in an image of his face, set and a little redder than usual. The recalculation to adjust for loss of sail area to the battleship's plasma bolt must have been a strain both mental and—as Adele well knew—physical in the need for absolute precision in typing in the commands that alone could save the corvette.

"Entering—"

Der Grosser Karl fired another rippling volley, but the missile's grazing impact and damage to several High Drive nozzles caused the great ship to slew. The bolts missed the *Princess Cecile*. An antenna in the battleship's sternmost ring exploded, the uppermost ten meters shooting off as a projectile driven on a shockwave of the portion vaporized by plasma.

Transition.

People were shouting, perhaps everyone aboard the corvette except Adele herself. She sorted the data her equipment had gathered during the *Princess Cecile's* seconds within normal space.

Most were ordinary communications, the ash and trash of the Alliance squadron leaving port for the first time after a difficult voyage, but there was also the series of messages dealing with the briefly spotted unknown warship. Then, like shouts of "Fire!" in a crowded theater, came the disbelieving reactions to the corvette's reappearance in the middle of the squadron—

And nothing, because the *Princess Cecile* was again within the Matrix, safe from attack and probably beyond pursuit by those aboard the Alliance ships. They weren't Selma pirates.

Adele gave a snort of laughter. They weren't Daniel Leary, either.

The alarm that had been pulsing cut off. Lt. Mon said on a dedicated channel between the Battle Direction Center and the bridge, "*No hull penetration, I repeat, no penetration. Damage on Dorsal Three-Four-Five, the mainsails fucked and masts severed below the topsails. Minor damage on Starboard Two but the topsail is still eighty percent. Shall we start repairs immediately? Over.*"

"*Negative,*" Daniel said as he typed, his strokes as hard and exact as a hammer driving nails. "*We'll make our second run with the present rig. Mon, I want you to go out on the hull and tell Woetjans this time she's to bring her crew in when I give the order. Break. Hogg?*"

"Standing at your side, master," Hogg said, not shouting but speaking loudly enough to be heard over the sounds of a ship at war. Missiles rumbled on their loading tracks, making the whole vessel vibrate. The remaining rounds in the magazine added their thunder as well, each rolling into the space vacated by the one ahead of it.

"Go with Mon, he won't let you drift away," Daniel said. His voice sounded like wind roaring through a long tube. "Go out with a pistol in your hand. Tell Woetjans that you'll shoot her if she disobeys my order. I won't ask that of Mon; but I will of you, Hogg, and Ellie knows that you'll obey."

"Yeah, all right," Hogg said. He turned to watch Mon coming up Corridor C, dressed in a rigging suit. "But I tell you, he better *not* let me float away."

Sun stared without expression at the servant's back as he went to join the lieutenant. He felt Adele's glance, nodded, and forced a smile to her. "She'll bring 'em in," he said. "She knows the captain means business."

Adele looked at her friend. She didn't remember ever having seen Daniel so bleak. It was as though she were again staring up the bores of the *Aristotle*'s great plasma cannon in Harbor Three.

She hand-cued the intercom and said, "Daniel?"

Daniel's face changed in a way she couldn't have described even though she watched as it happened. The planes of muscle over bone fractured into minuscule slivers, then reformed into the smiling young man she'd known—for months only, but the most important months of her life.

"*We'll be making four shifts on this approach,*" he said. "*The last 'll be a long one, four minutes twelve seconds; we'll be building velocity for our return to normal space. After we exit at the end of the run, we won't need riggers topside, and I won't throw them away.*"

As he spoke, the *Princess Cecile* trembled between universes. Within the bubble of space-time formed by the ship's electric charge, nothing palpable changed; but the pressure of the universe beyond was different.

"Daniel?" Adele asked. "I, I'm glad that you're bringing the riggers in, I don't mean that. But are you sure that you won't need them on the hull?"

They shifted again. The first three stages must be intended simply to align the corvette with its target. Adele no longer noticed the feeling of her body falling into four separate infinities.

Daniel smiled again, though there was a rueful quality to it this time. "*Chastelaine will be ready for us this time,*" he said. "*We won't need riggers topside because after those eight-inch cannon hit us, we won't have any sails left.*"

CHAPTER THIRTY-THREE

Daniel whistled "Been on the Job Too Long" as he computed tracks for the eighteen missiles remaining aboard the *Princess Cecile*. It was quite a cheerful tune, though the words were another matter. That was true of a lot of catchy songs, come to think.

When the women all heard that King Brady was dead—

The *Princess Cecile* would pass through the Alliance squadron at high velocity. That wouldn't affect the plasma cannon, of course, except to minimize the corvette's exposure to the bolts, but it did mean that Alliance missiles would have a long time catching up even at twelve-gee accelerations.

They went back home and they dressed in red.

The converse was that the *Sissie*'s own missiles, save for the pair already loaded in the tubes, would be fighting a great deal of negative inertia as they struggled back toward their target. *Der Grosser Karl* would be able to avoid them easily.

All Daniel's missiles were aimed at the battleship: if *Der Grosser Karl* were damaged, the powerful remainder of the squadron would be more concerned with defending the cripple than in chasing down Commodore Pettin's force. A big "if," of course.

They come slippin' and aslidin' up and down the street—

Light flickered as the *Princess Cecile* shifted onto the final leg of her approach. Daniel's course calculation had taken fifteen minutes, three times as long as so short a voyage would require, because he'd added a fourth parameter to the mix.

Usually an attack was made with a minimum of rig aloft so

that the vessel could maneuver on High Drive without damaging its antennas. This time Daniel wanted every possible—every surviving—mast raised to its full height and all sails spread. That was a strikingly inefficient way to navigate the Matrix; but in a portion of normal space bathed with the point-blank output of eight-inch plasma cannon, it was the corvette's only hope of survival.

In their old Mother Hubbards and their stocking feet!

Daniel paused in his calculations—for rounds fifteen and sixteen, and if the *Sissie* survived to launch them she and her crew would be very fortunate indeed—to watch the sail schematic change to reflect the new rig. Starboard Three and Four didn't budge at the thrust of the jacks. Though undamaged at the quick glance which alone was possible after the initial attack, a splash of plasma had welded their base hinges.

Woetjans must have expected that, because at least six mauls slammed rhythmically into the masts within seconds of the jam. Both began to lift. S3 continued normally, but the pump pressure driving S4 flatlined when the antenna had only elevated a few degrees. A hydraulic line—scored by plasma, fractured by an injudicious hammerblow, or simply filled with the cussed determination of machines to fail—had broken.

Brady, Brady, Brady, don't you know you done wrong?

The mast resumed its rise, again within seconds of the initial failure. The bosun must already have rigged tackle to blocks at the head of adjacent, previously extended, masts.

Daniel felt a rush of affection. By God! he wasn't going to let Woetjans throw her life away. Not even if saving her required a sincerely offered threat to blow her head off if she didn't obey.

Antenna Starboard 4 locked into place and, without further hesitation, unfurled its suit of sails. The *Princess Cecile* was wearing nearly eighty percent of her rig, an unusual event made more remarkable by the battle damage that alone prevented the figure being even higher.

Atoms stripped of electrons and accelerated by repulsion up the bore of a plasma cannon had velocities little short of light speed, but negligible mass. Their ravening touch would destroy the first layer of any matter they collided with, but they wouldn't

penetrate. Damage beyond the target's outer layer was a result
of transmitted impact—which in the case of sail fabric was almost
zero.

After the battleship's initial volley had removed the sails, further bolts would scour the hull. At point-blank range, fluxes
intended to change the course of missiles approaching at .6 C
would make short work of a corvette.

You bust into my bar when the game was on . . .

The astrogation computer changed the sails' potentials as programmed; Daniel checked the results against the plan and his
instinct. All was well.

He grinned. If that was the phrase to use under the circumstances.

"Three minutes to reentry to normal space!" Dorst said.

The riggers, their job completed, were clanging back within the
Sissie's hull. The inner airlock opened outside the bridge. One
figure stepped through, Lt. Mon lifting off the helmet of his rigging
suit. He closed the hatch behind him.

You sprung my latch and you broke my door . . .

Catching Daniel's eye, Mon shouted, "Hogg's staying in the lock
with Woetjans. Says it's as good a place as the next, he figures."

Daniel thought of his short, dumpy servant and the rangy
bosun. Under the circumstances the two were an ideal pair: they
understood one another perfectly. Missed communications had
killed more people than ever malice dreamed of doing.

"Daniel?" Adele said. She'd waited until she saw his attention
drawn away from the calculations on his display. *"When we return
to normal space, I intend to direct the other ships, the escort ships?
Direct them to return to Tanais in the name of Admiral Chastelaine.
I doubt they'll obey, but I thought it might confuse them. Is that
all right?"*

Daniel opened a window in his holographic display so that he
could meet Adele's eyes without a fog of light between them. She
looked worried, concerned about having overstepped her proper
authority.

"Great heavens, yes!" Daniel said. "But won't they—oh, I see.
You *will* be sending it in the proper Alliance code."

Adele smiled faintly. *"Yes, that's my greatest question,"* she said.
*"Less than half the flagship's communications are encrypted prop-
erly, so it might be more believable if I introduced errors in my*

transmissions. Doing that offended my sense of rightness, however, so unless you require me to . . . ?

"Quite all right," Daniel said. "I'd hate for your last act in this life to be one you found to smack of impropriety."

"*One minute to reentry to normal space,*" announced Mon. "*Prepare for action.*"

"What do you mean, prepare for action?" shouted someone— shouted Delos Vaughn coming up the corridor toward the bridge. The helmet of his emergency suit was hinged open, bouncing on his chest. "We've escaped, I saw us escape! We're safe now!"

There was a display in the wardroom. Tovera must have set it to receive real-time data during the attack. She'd have known how, after all.

Daniel frowned. He'd ordered Hogg to release the president, but it hadn't occurred to him that Vaughn would then choose to interfere with the business of war.

He noted with further irritation that Tovera walked just behind Vaughn. Her smile could easily be described as mocking, though one had to admit that Tovera's expressions were pretty much a blank slate for the viewer to color with emotion.

"Mister Vaughn—" Daniel began.

Vaughn strode onto the bridge, either oblivious of Daniel's orders or in defiance of them. He said, "I won't let you kill us all!"

"Secure the civilian!" Daniel said.

He actually didn't see Tovera's hand move, gripping Vaughn by the left ear and twisting. Vaughn screamed, then stopped as he, turning his head to reduce the pain of his ear, brought his right eye into contact with the muzzle of Tovera's submachine gun.

They backed off the bridge. Adele nodded to Daniel and put her pistol away.

"*Reentry into—*"

Der Grosser Karl, broadside and apparently huge as a planet, filled the real-time display. Her sails were ragged, torn both by the missiles and by gouts of plasma from her own cannon. She was of the latest Alliance design, mounting thirty-two 21CM plasma cannon in quadruple turrets.

Thump! First missile away.

Hellfire vaporized the *Princess Cecile*'s sails and antennas, dressing her in a glowing ball of her own rig. Plasma continued to rip from at least eight yawning muzzles, but the vapor of destruction protected the corvette from worse.

Thump!

The *Princess Cecile* yawed with a world-filling crash. Her hull whipped, frames warping and plates in the double hull gaping apart. Cabin pressure dropped and Daniel reflexively closed his faceshield.

There hadn't been enough time for the battleship to plot trajectories for her own missiles, but at such short range the heavy cannon had virtually the impact of solid projectiles. As the corvette punched clear of the expanding cloud, one bolt or possibly two had struck her well forward on the underside.

The first missile entered *Der Grosser Karl* amidships, like a pin through the thorax of a fat-bodied butterfly with tattered wings. Gas puffed from the point of impact; sparkling fire exploded where the remains of the missile, liquescent from friction, tore its exit. A gun turret, almost complete, lifted from the hull. Three of the heavy iridium gun-tubes spun away on separate trajectories.

Daniel's display flared, but the volley that overloaded the hull sensors didn't actually strike the corvette. Close doesn't count—

The *Princess Cecile*'s second missile clipped the battleship's stern and converted itself and a thousand tonnes of its target into white fire. The corvette had exited the Matrix at .1 C; her missiles added that to the kinetic energy of their own acceleration when they struck.

The *Princess Cecile* was through the squadron, dismasted and with half her High Drive nozzles unserviceable. She was going nearly directly away from *Der Grosser Karl* and should have been an easy, low-deflection, target for the battleship's cannon.

Der Grosser Karl had stopped firing.

And now you're lyin' dead on my barroom floor!

Daniel switched his display to the Plot Position Indicator. The *Princess Cecile* was already off her programmed course. A glance at the systems sidebar showed why: red dots for nine of the sixteen High Drive nozzles, red circles for three more. The four nozzles which the sleet of ions had spared weren't sufficient to warp the corvette around the curve of Getica and out of line with *Der Grosser Karl.*

The rumbling of missiles within the corvette's belly had stopped. Daniel knew unconsciously there was something wrong. His own mind hadn't put a cause to it till a heartbeat later when Betts leaped up from his console and shouted over the general channel, "*The fucking outer doors are fucking welded shut! All fucking missile personnel to the fucking tubes! We'll draw the fucking ready rounds and blow the fucking doors open!*"

The Chief Missileer disappeared down the forward companionway. His lips were still moving, but his words no longer filled the general channel. Either he'd switched his helmet to his unit push or—more likely—Adele had switched it for him.

Either way, both Missiles and Signals were in good shape; at any rate, as good as human effort could make them. As for the rig . . .

The battleship hadn't resumed firing, and the remainder of the Alliance squadron was too distant for plasma weapons to be a serious threat. There was still risk; but then, there was always risk.

"Riggers topside!" Daniel ordered. "Woetjans, do what you can— I'm not expecting much. Break. Engineering, send as many techs topside as you can spare. I want the three nozzles with minor damage repaired soonest, and if it's possible to replace any of the others, that too. Captain out!"

Daniel doubted replacement would be possible. The rosette of nozzles must have taken a direct hit. Pasternak had shown himself to be a good man in milder conditions; now he'd have a chance to test his mettle against battle damage.

Sun was twisted around in his chair, staring at Daniel in anguish. He said on the command channel, "*Sir, I could've raped her sails, raped them! I can still hurt her bad, sir.*"

Daniel looked at his gunner. "Could you have done *Der Grosser Karl* a tenth the harm she did herself trying to claw us? You know you couldn't. And I know that if we need your cannon, I won't want their bores shot out from playing games."

More gently Daniel added, "We've *almost* got maneuvering way, Sun. Luck and your guns are the only things that're going to keep us alive for the next hour."

Sun bit his lip and nodded. "*Sir*," he muttered, turning back to his console.

There was nothing fatal about *Der Grosser Karl*'s injuries, though she'd be a year in dock repairing them or Daniel hadn't learned anything in the time he'd spent hanging around the premises of Bergen and Associates. He understood why the battleship's crew was wholly concerned with its own problems instead of acting to finish off the crippled corvette. What he didn't understand was why Chastelaine—or the acting squadron commander if Chastelaine was a casualty—hadn't detailed a pair of destroyers to that task.

Unless—

Daniel shrank the scale of his PPI to encompass a sphere nearly a million miles in diameter. There should have been six ships in that volume besides the central pip of the *Princess Cecile* herself. Instead there were nine: the Alliance squadron, and three vessels more at the outer edge of the coverage area. They had their identification transponders switched off, but Daniel knew who they were as surely as the Alliance commander must.

Commodore Pettin hadn't fled in the breathing space the *Princess Cecile* had provided him. In the best tradition of the RCN, he was coming to fight.

Adele kept her face expressionless as she viewed the corvette's outer hull through imagery provided by Woetjans's suit. If she hadn't known better she'd have guessed she was looking at a nickel-iron asteroid, pitted and half-melted by a pass through the upper reaches of an atmosphere.

The internal air pressure was beginning to rise. Damage crews filled spaces with quick-setting foam, blocking leaks through torn plates and ruptured seams. It wasn't up to eight pounds yet, and Adele had been repeatedly warned during drills that there could still be catastrophic hull failure at this stage of the proceedings.

She unlatched her helmet anyway. It constricted her mind, and that was far more worrisome than the chance of death.

"They're launching!" Sun said. He'd opened his helmet also; his voice was squeaky but clear to Adele in the next station. "*Look* at those bastards! Well, we didn't get their fire control, that's for sure!"

The Alliance ships exchanged course data on what they assumed were secure links. Adele intercepted and decrypted the signals, then forwarded them to Daniel. Presumably he was doing whatever could be done with it, his face intent as he typed furiously.

Voice communications within the Alliance squadron were properly Adele's own area of responsibility. They passed through her ears and she filtered them for content. Occasionally she summarized them for Daniel and the Battle Direction Center.

Admiral Chastelaine hadn't panicked, but he was in a fury—an equally disruptive state of affairs in respect to the good governance of his squadron. He'd announced he was proceeding by gig to the *Yorck*, the heavy cruiser, to transfer his flag; had cancelled that order and summoned a destroyer to carry him from the damaged battleship to the *Yorck*; and had finally, at least for now, determined to direct the battle from aboard *Der Grosser Karl*. Adele had no idea of what was going on inside the Alliance vessels, but she very much doubted that the moral atmosphere resembled the ordered enthusiasm aboard the *Princess Cecile*.

Adele's ears were given over to duty, but her eyes were her own. She echoed Sun's display in a corner of hers, replacing the wasteland of the corvette's hull.

At once she felt her spirits lift—not for what she saw, but because she no longer viewed the *Princess Cecile*'s mutilated exterior. Adele wasn't the sort of sentimentalist—the sort of fool!—who imagined machines have life, let alone personalities. Even so, there are tools which serve their users so well that it could be reasonable to feel regret when they break.

Sun's attack screen looked similar to Daniel's PPI, save that it showed missiles as colored tracks rather than points. The computed courses were orange, with the portions already traversed in scarlet.

Adele understood the gunner's amazement. *Der Grosser Karl* had launched twenty-four missiles, more than the corvette's capacity at full load; and as Adele watched, another dozen rippled from the battleship's tubes.

"*Adele!*" Daniel snapped as his eyes and hands continued their separate work. "*Can you transmit the Alliance courses to Commodore Pettin. Soonest!*"

"Yes, Daniel," Adele said mildly. "I've been doing that."

She didn't add, "Of course." This was no time to play foolish games.

There *were* proper times for punctilio, of course. She was a Mundy of Chatsworth and had no intention of brooking a deliberate insult; but she'd have been equally curt with Daniel if she needed something from him and failure would be the price of delay.

Daniel opened his helmet. Adele suspected the delay had been because he was busy, not that thin air or the risk concerned him. Internal pressure had risen to over ten psi, enough that Adele's lungs no longer felt as though they couldn't fill.

"Admiral Chastelaine knows he's not very maneuverable," Daniel said. He spoke conversationally, but Adele noticed that his eyes were on the data, not her face. "He's using his magazines to do what his High Drive can't, keep our ships away from *Der Grosser Karl* while the rest of his squadron destroys them."

He smiled brilliantly and met Adele's eyes for an instant. "And as your intercepts show, he's mad enough to chew rocks."

The three Cinnabar vessels—points undifferentiated in size at this range—vanished from the display a few seconds apart. Instead of lowering their antennas to maneuver in normal space, they'd reentered the Matrix.

The *Princess Cecile*'s missiles began to move on their trackways. A metallic screech quivered through the ship, bringing a violent curse from Sun. Adele had no idea of whether or not the sound had anything to do with the missiles.

Daniel brought up real-time imagery of the Alliance ships. Adele hesitated a moment, then echoed the vessels in a line across the top of her display.

When the *Princess Cecile* appeared, Admiral Chastelaine had been preparing to enter the Matrix on a short voyage from Getica to Strymon. Now the *Yorck* and two of the destroyers were taking down all their antennas to ready themselves for battle, and the remaining pair of destroyers were lowering all but the rings at their far bow and stern.

"R Class destroyers," Daniel said in a tone of professional approval. "Quite good ships. Their ordinary magazine capacity's sixty rounds."

"They're the *Ihn* and *Steinbrinck*," Adele said, expanding a sidebar to check the names. "The other two are the *Koellner* and *Giese*; and yes, they reported magazines full at sixty missiles each."

The Alliance ships were reforming in a hollow globe thirty thousand miles in diameter. Each vessel was under power at a constant one-gee acceleration. The course schematic made it look as though they were in orbit, but in fact they circled a point in empty space. Tanais's orbital motion was carrying the moon slowly away from the squadron, though the ships were already beyond range of support by the base defenses when the *Princess Cecile* attacked.

"Chastelaine's marking time, waiting to see what the RCN's going to do," Daniel said. "He'll react then—you see that he's ready to respond either to an attack or to dog us with two destroyers until the rest of the squadron can rejoin if Pettin tries to run. Though . . ."

He pursed his lips judiciously, peering at the flagship's image.

"I don't think the admiral would either leave his battleship without escort or engage with his force divided," he said. "With *Der Grosser Karl* in its present condition, his squadron would have a very long chase to run down even a crock like the *Winckelmann*. But I really doubt that question's going to arise, because Commodore Pettin will—"

Three ships coalesced out of the Matrix, again within seconds of one another. They were driving toward the Alliance squadron, perpendicular to the plane of the Strymon system. Daniel had programmed his display to include them without further input: the *Winckelmann*, *Active*, and *Petty*, broadside to their axis of movement so that their missile tubes amidships were clear. They began lowering their antennas at the moment they reappeared in normal space.

The ships were glossy with false precision. The *Princess Cecile*'s software was integrating real-time images with archival files to refine views of vessels which were more than 200,000 miles from the corvette.

Slivers separated from first the *Winckelmann*, then the two destroyers. They were launching missiles.

"Look what he's done!" Daniel said. "Look, look where the *Yorck* is, Adele! That's your doing, letting the commodore plan his attack like this!"

Adele stared at the display. She didn't understand. She wasn't used to thinking spatially, so the fact that the Alliance heavy cruiser was near the axis of the Cinnabar squadron's motion didn't mean anything to her. Some vessel was bound to be, after all.

Alliance ships were launching missiles also; some seconds behind the attackers but in greater numbers regardless. *Der Grosser Karl* alone spasmed a dozen, then a second dozen from her dorsal and ventral batteries respectively. Adele knew from the transmitted manifest that there were hundreds more rounds available behind a first salvo that by itself outdid the total output of Commodore Pettin's force.

Beside Adele, Sun shrieked in delight; both Mon and Vesey were crowing happily over the command channel. "Daniel, I don't *see!*" she said.

The ships were maneuvering, though their initial velocities—particularly those of the RCN vessels—were much higher than the increments added or subtracted by their High Drives. Missile tracks spread across the display like wisps of colored hair, the orange predictions changing to red as the seconds passed.

Daniel hammered keys, adding the ships' projected courses to the display. "Oh," said Adele in sudden understanding. "Oh!"

The *Yorck* was sailing into the junction of not only the RCN missiles but those from *Der Grosser Karl*'s capacious magazines. Commodore Pettin had maneuvered the Alliance heavy cruiser into an inferno of friendly fire.

The *Princess Cecile*'s hull rang, a sound as sharp as that of the riggers' mauls but much louder. Moments later a second blow made the frames clang.

"*Bridge, that's Tube Alpha clear!*" Betts's breathless voice announced. The low-frequency grumble of missiles moving started again. "*She'll be reloaded in a minute thirty, and by the Lord we'll have Beta ready in five minutes more! Missiles out!*"

Daniel's jubilant face suddenly shed all expression. He began again to type with grim determination.

"Captain!" Lt. Mon reported from the Battle Direction Center. "The battleship just launched a round at us. Over."

Adele frowned. *What does one missile matter against the scores they've already fired?*

She looked at the display and found it suddenly clear. The

geometry was simple enough that even she could see the relationships.

The *Princess Cecile* was heading directly away from the battleship it had slashed at point-blank range. By now the distance was very great due to the velocity the corvette had built up in the Matrix, but the two ships' proper motion was nearly zero. The computed track of the missile and the corvette's projected course were identical.

And, with the damage to her High Drive, there was virtually nothing the *Princess Cecile* could do to change that relationship.

Pasternak was topside. Many chief engineers would have denied that it was their duty to clamber about the hull of a ship while it was under weigh; they weren't riggers. If the thrusters or High Drive nozzles needed looking after, why then there were technicians to take the risk of drifting toward infinity while the ship accelerated away from them.

If Pasternak had felt that way, he'd have been looking for a different berth at the end of this voyage, and he *wouldn't* much like the character Daniel offered when discussing him with other captains.

Daniel looked again at his course calculations. Mind, the *Princess Cecile*'s present voyage might end very abruptly and under such conditions that none of her crew need worry about the future. Still, there was hope.

"Mister Pasternak?" Daniel said. Had the Chief Engineer thought to fit his suit with a radio before he went topside? Pray God he had, though needs must Daniel would use Hogg or a rigger to relay his message. "What's the status of the damaged nozzles? Captain over."

"*Sir, we're just finishing Number Five,*" Pasternak came back instantly. "*The sheathing—*" the electromagnetic tape that kept the stream of antimatter centered until it reached the nozzle to interact with the spray of normal matter "*—burned through but the tube and nozzle were all right. The feeds to Ten and Twelve are fine, but they shouldn't be run till the nozzles 're replaced. Fifteen minutes apiece if we're lucky, but if the ion stream welded the fittings we'll have to cut them loose. I can't promise much then. Over.*"

Daniel looked at his calculations. With three more nozzles on line, just possibly . . .

Aloud he said, "Pasternak, finish up on Five soonest and bring your crew aboard. Break. Woetjans, we'll be increasing thrust to one point six gee as soon as engineering has Nozzle Five ready. Nozzles Ten and Twelve may fail at any moment, so watch yourself around Frame Sixty."

Daniel stared at his display for a moment, then added, "Woetjans? I recommend you bring your crews aboard now, unless you're convinced their work over the next five minutes is crucial. It's possible that we'll be maneuvering violently. Over."

"*Roger*," Woetjans said. There was physical strain in her voice. Daniel suspected the bosun was bracing herself with the grip of one hand and using the other to put as much force on the end of a come-along as three ordinary crewmen could've managed. "*You handle the bloody course, we'll handle the bloody rig. Out!*"

"*Task accomplished, coming aboard,*" Pasternak said crisply. "*Engineering out.*"

Daniel cut in the additional High Drive nozzles. The icons for Ten and Twelve went solid green under dint of Daniel's overriding command, but they pulsed to show the computer's displeasure.

Daniel smiled faintly. They'd never build a computer that could fight battles successfully: to win, sometimes you had to do things that made no logical sense. You had to be willing to die as well, but an RCN officer was just as willing to die as any machine was.

On the attack screen, three Alliance missile tracks intersected that of the *Petty*. The destroyer was braking at three gravities, thrust that was certain to ripple plates and start seams. The scale was too small for certainty: to the last Daniel was able to hope that what looked like a hit was in fact a narrow miss.

The *Petty's* image deformed. A ball of gas puffed around the destroyer like blood pooling beneath a corpse. The fusion bottle failed then, devouring everything astern of the blast wall in a white flash. Debris from the bow section shotgunned away. Some of the fragments might be suited crewmen, but there was no possibility of them being rescued.

"*Sir!*" Mon said urgently. "*We're accelerating on our previous course. I've figured thrust to produce the greatest possible tangent. Shall I take the conn?*"

"Negative, negative!" Daniel said. "Mr. Mon, I'll determine the *Sissie*'s course!"

He checked his display to make sure that he hadn't handed off control to the BDC at some past moment and failed to retrieve it. It was absolutely critical that the course remain *exactly* as he'd set it.

Even if he'd guessed wrong. A ship could have only one captain, and Daniel Leary was the *Princess Cecile*'s at present.

One of the stern airlocks cycled with a hesitation noticeable to a spacer experienced in the *Princess Cecile*'s patterns. The inner valve had warped, though it must still be sealing adequately or Pasternak's crew wouldn't have been able to use the lock without authorization from the command console.

An RCN missile hit the *Yorck* forward. Three seconds later, a missile from *Der Grosser Karl* spitted the Alliance heavy cruiser at virtually the same frame but from starboard instead of the port side.

The *Yorck* continued on its previous course. A bubble of atmosphere surrounded the vessel, expanding slowly. That the cruiser stayed centered in the ball of gas showed that its High Drive had shut down: until the double impact, the *Yorck* had been braking hard in a desperate attempt to avoid the kill zone.

The *Winckelmann* was so distant from the Alliance battleship that missiles the ships launched at one another burned all their fuel, then continued on ballistic courses. At burnout the missile separated into four segments, closely spaced but nonetheless increasing the coverage area considerably. Though the difference didn't show at the scale of Daniel's display, he knew that the missiles about to intersect both flagships were more likely to achieve hits than those launched at closer targets.

"*Tube Alpha ready!*" Betts shouted. Daniel's finger was already stroking the firing switch. The *thump!* of the missile launching was simultaneous with the *whang!* of Bett's team breaking free the outer door of Tube Beta with a charge of explosive.

"Sir, permission to fire?" Sun begged. He was poised over the key that would trigger the four plasma cannon.

Der Grosser Karl's Parthian shot continued its track toward the *Sissie*. It was very close to burnout now, but its twelve-gee acceleration had given it more than sufficient residual velocity to overhaul the corvette in another ninety seconds.

"Negative!" Daniel said. "I'll give the order. Not till I give the order!"

Der Grosser Karl ran through the path of the *Winckelmann's* first salvo. There were seven missiles; the eighth had ruptured the *Yorck.* Either Pettin or his Chief Missileer had done a brilliant job of targeting. It wouldn't have been possible without Adele's intercepted course data, but not every officer would have thought to aim so as to threaten two enemy ships at a considerable distance from one another.

A segment struck the battleship's port outrigger, retracted since lifting from its berth on Tanais. There was a bright flash: metal blasted to vapor by kinetic energy. The secondary shock wave—the ball of glowing gas exploding from the impact at a significant fraction of light speed—hammered *Der Grosser Karl's* hull, whipping the vessel despite its enormous mass.

Though the battleship's targeting had been both hastier and less skillful than the *Winckelmann's,* her multiple tubes made up the difference. The *Winckelmann's* acceleration allowed her to pass well wide of all but three of the twenty-four missiles of the initial launch; regardless, a segment caught her squarely amidships. The flash had an electrical quality to it, high in the ultraviolet.

The missile aimed at the *Princess Cecile* reached burnout and separated. Daniel plotted the four tracks, then careted one and ordered, "Now, Sun! Everything you've got!"

The corvette's plasma cannon rang from both turrets. Surges of ionized nuclei spurted at light speed through the sole opening in the laser array and down the iridium bores.

Inevitably there was some leakage which the refractory gun-tube had to contain. Sun had the weapons on high rate, the four tubes cycling at a combined rate of six pulses per second. That couldn't be sustained for long periods because it didn't leave the guns long enough to cool between discharges.

It was the only chance the *Princess Cecile* had of surviving for a long period, however.

Despite the guns' enormous energy output, they couldn't hope to destroy tons of solid metal thousands of miles away. What they could do, if skillfully directed, was to nudge missiles aside by subliming material off one side as reaction mass.

Tube Alpha showed ready. Daniel launched another missile at

Der Grosser Karl. With luck, Alpha would be reloaded again in time for another round, a last round if luck or the Gods decreed. The *Sissie*'s crew might never know if these missiles too had struck—but they had three certain hits on a battleship, not a bad record to take to a spacers' heaven.

The *Winckelmann* swung into a slow tumble through the void. Her High Drive shut down momentarily, then restarted as Pettin or his replacement aligned the nozzles to counteract the thrust from the missile impact.

The crippled cruiser launched two missiles, then two more. By *God* she did!

"Daniel, the enemy's going to enter the Matrix!" Adele said. Had he ever heard Adele shout before? "Chastelaine's signaled 'All units shape course for Sonderfell immediately.' Daniel, they're running!"

Tube Alpha *was* loaded. Betts must have set the transport rollers to overspeed.

Daniel launched again, feeling the missiles in B magazine also starting to move. With Tube Beta in operation, the *Princess Cecile* was in fighting trim—except for mobility.

Segments of the incoming missile arrived. Vapor glowing with the fury of Sun's cannon bathed the corvette for an instant, a flash like lightning across Daniel's real-time display. There was a *click* like a distant whiplash; a few gauges jumped.

The *Princess Cecile* was end-on to the missile, showing minimal cross-sectional area to the threat. Daniel had aligned her with the center of the pattern formed when the missile separated. Three of the segments missed of their own, and Sun's plasma cannon thrust the last enough to the side that only thin-spread gas expanding from the flank of the projectile touched the ship.

Der Grosser Karl blurred off the display. Moments later the destroyers *Ihn* and *Steinbrinck* vanished also. They'd rerig in the Matrix before they started the long voyage to Sonderfell.

Daniel shook his head. Sonderfell! That route to the Sack was four months of sailing for well-found vessels. No wonder Chastelaine's squadron had managed to avoid being spotted en route! But how friendly the Khans of Sonderfell would be to a force so obviously defeated...?

Daniel smiled. He had a degree of sympathy for Chastelaine

as a fellow captain and spacer; but he couldn't say he was sorry about the result, no.

The admiral's decision made perfect sense. *Der Grosser Karl* was a new battleship, many times more valuable than the entire RCN squadron. She'd been badly damaged already and could with further bad luck—Chastelaine would think it was luck—be destroyed. It was his duty as a prudent commander to avoid further losses by withdrawing.

A computer would have agreed to the depths of its electronic soul.

The order to flee caught the *Koellner* and *Giese* with their antennas stowed. Both destroyers cut their thrust to zero to make the riggers' job easier, proceeding on a ballistic course. The *Giese* slipped into the Matrix within three minutes, a very creditable time, but her sister ship barely struggled out ahead of the missiles that the *Winckelmann* and *Active* launched at them for want of a better target.

Daniel shut down the High Drive, then let out his breath and felt all the strength drain from his body. Goodness, he'd merely been sitting at his console for the past hour. It felt like he'd been breaking rocks!

He switched the intercom manually. "Lieutenant Mon," he said. "Take the conn if you please. Coordinate with Engineering as to the best way to proceed toward the flagship while refitting our High Drive and plasma thrusters. Break. Mr. Pasternak, you may resume repairs. Coordinate with Lieutenant Mon."

The *Princess Cecile* was still streaking toward the rim of the Strymon system and the void beyond. The velocity at which she'd entered sidereal space would take days to brake with the High Drive, even if all the nozzles were operating. If Woetjans couldn't get some sort of rig operable with the corvette's own spares, Daniel would have to beg help from the *Active*.

"Daniel?" said Adele. "The *Yorck* is signalling that it surrenders. Commodore Pettin's ships are much closer than we are, but I'm not sure they're monitoring the open channels at the moment. Would you like me to retransmit on the squadron's command link?"

"What?" said Daniel. "Yes, if you would please, Adele. There's no point in having hundreds more of the poor devils die when there's no reason for it."

"*Captain?*" Woetjans said. The bosun was breathing hard. "*We're getting three antennas on each of the aft rings rigged. Forward we're fucked, maybe even in a shipyard we're fucked, but you'll be able to crawl into the Matrix inside of ten. Over.*"

Daniel beamed. "Woetjans, I'd marry you if I thought I were worthy!" he said. "Break. Lieutenant Mon, the Chief of Rig says we'll have partial sails available in ten minutes. Plot a course toward the flagship, if you please; and also a course back to Strymon, where I expect we'll be directed as soon as the commodore learns who our passenger is. Captain out."

Daniel stood carefully, using the back of his chair as a support until he was sure that his legs weren't going to fail him. When he sat at the console he locked one leg under the chairpost. During the battle just over, he'd clamped it firmly enough that he'd cut off circulation.

"Adele?" he said. "Would you care to come with me to the wardroom? I think it's time to release President Vaughn and offer our apologies. I'd like some company."

Offering Adele his hand, Daniel added—smiling but truthful nonetheless, "In addition, I prefer to have you beside me when I talk to Tovera."

Daniel had left a short imagery loop running on the command console. *Der Grosser Karl* hung in a black field, gouting plasma from its turrets—

Then spewing gas and flame from both flanks as the *Princess Cecile*'s fourth missile struck.

Cinnabar forever!

EPILOGUE:
XENOS

Barnes and Dasi, hired to bring Adele's personal gear from Harbor Three, walked ahead of her like a noble's retainers. They were joking with one another and whistling, either man able to carry both duffle bags without noticing the weight. Civilians watched them curiously: this wasn't a district that saw many of their sort.

Woetjans and Pasternak both had offered Adele a real escort, as many spacers as she wanted from the crew of Frigate *204*—renamed *Little Sis* while in RCN service. She'd refused. Adele had an increasing disdain for empty state, and to appear with forty or more servants would be making a boast to her neighbors that the reality of her purse couldn't live up to.

"I was a fool to ask for this house back," Adele said to Tovera beside her. "I can't afford basic maintenance, let alone the kind of staff it requires to be run properly."

Tovera shrugged noncommittally. She might not have responded even if she'd been asked a real question. Money simply wasn't something that Tovera cared about.

Adele smiled faintly. Tovera was quiet, self-effacing, and abstemious. Viewed from the correct angle, she was a saint.

"The one with the guy in blue out front, ma'am?" Dasi asked. He gestured with his free hand, an underhanded motion as though he were lobbing a ball.

Adele leaned to look past the two burly spacers. There shouldn't be—

But there was, a well-set-up man in a tunic of blue with silver piping. Adele hadn't hired servants to replace those who'd left with the Rolfes. The deed to Chatsworth Minor had been waiting for Adele in a message locker at Harbor Three, along with the—expected and unnecessary—summons to see Mistress Sand at her earliest convenience, day or night.

"Yes, that's the house," Adele said.

The doorman, seeing Adele coming up the street, stepped back and rapped on the panel. "The mistress has arrived!" he said in a voice that could be heard from one end of the block to the other. Doormen who'd sneeringly ignored the passing entourage now focused on the RCN warrant officer and her companions.

The door panel was now plain beewood, sandblasted to emphasize the distinctive grain. It opened from the inside; a blue-liveried footman bowed Deirdre Leary out.

"Perhaps it's not my place to welcome you to your own home, Mistress Mundy," Deirdre said with a sweep of her hand. "But welcome anyway. I'm delighted to be here when you arrive; I'd been held up by business and was afraid I wouldn't be able to greet you."

"I also had business to take care of," Adele said without emphasis. Chances were that Corder Leary's daughter knew Adele was connected with Mistress Sand, but if so that was an even better reason not to discuss it. "With that out of the way, I decided to visit the house; though I wasn't sure what I'd find when I arrived."

"Ma'am?" Barnes said, bouncing the laden duffle bag in the palm of his hand to call attention to it.

"Hoskins, show Mistress Mundy's servants where to put her things, if you will," Deirdre said. The words and even the tone were polite, but Deirdre's manner brooked no more discussion than her brother would when snapping out orders in a crisis.

Smiling, another person as Barnes and Dasi followed the footman into the townhouse, Deirdre went on, "May we be Adele and Deirdre, mistress? I prefer terms of friendship with those for whom I act."

Adele stopped on the threshold. The hideous mosaic was gone

and the ancient flooring shone with a high gloss. She didn't even want to think about what that must have cost.

But she didn't grudge the expense, not even if it meant she had to miss meals again. A Mundy stood again in Chatsworth Minor. What did money matter in comparison with that?

"I'm not used to informality," Adele said. "Still, your brother's been training me into an appreciation of it, and I dare say I'll be able to extend the process to you. Deirdre."

Adele was finding it hard to speak through the lump in her throat. *Things don't matter!* But at one time not so far in the past, she'd thought people didn't matter either, only knowledge. People *did* matter. And it seemed that Chatsworth Minor mattered as well, at least to Adele Mundy.

She stood in the entrance hall, entranced by the rich familiarity of the beewood underfoot. It wasn't home any more, but it was as surely a part of her as the skills and knowledge she'd gained in the years she'd lived here.

That thought led to another. Adele said, "Ah, I don't know how much you've heard—" how much Deirdre understood was the real question; she certainly had access to the bare facts "—about your brother's situation. The ship he commands, the *Princess Cecile*, was seriously damaged in action and is being repaired by the Tanais shipyards. Daniel accepted a temporary appointment to bring Commodore Pettin's dispatches to Cinnabar aboard a Strymonian vessel commandeered for the purpose."

Adele could see furniture through the doors opening off the hallway; not the Rolfes' furnishings. These were tastefully chosen antiques and *extremely* expensive. She cleared her throat and added, "The dispatches credit Lieutenant Leary with a major part of the victory our forces won over an Alliance squadron. Well-deserved credit, I'm happy to say."

"His father will be pleased," Deirdre said. "As am I."

She too cleared her throat before she continued, "I've prepared accounts for you—"

Deirdre made a slight gesture toward the upper floors. A lifetime ago Adele had sat in one of the rooms up there and scribbled a note to Deirdre Leary.

"You'll want to review them at leisure, of course," Deirdre said.

"But if you wouldn't mind, I'd like to take a moment now to go over the main heads of my actions as your agent."

"Yes," said Adele crisply. She hadn't intended to hand over general control over her assets, but she didn't doubt that Deirdre's lawyers would be able to show that she had. Did she have any money at all left? "I think that would be best."

Deirdre paused for a moment, perhaps wondering if Adele wanted to adjourn to one of the drawing rooms. All Adele wanted was to learn her present financial condition in the quickest, baldest fashion possible.

"Realizing that your present household doesn't require all the available space," Deirdre said, "I leased the second floor to a bank. It will use the rooms for confidential meetings and may sometimes house clients who desire complete privacy while staying in Xenos."

She gestured around her, then continued, "Under terms of the lease, the bank is responsible for renovating the building. It also provides both ordinary staff and security."

At the word "security," Tovera's mouth bent in what Adele had learned to call a smile. There was humor of a sort in the expression.

Deirdre started minutely, as though she'd touched something that gave her a static spark. Her voice remained firm as she resumed, "If you object to the bank's choice of decor—"

"I do not," Adele said. The words came out like the wards of a lock falling.

"Very good," said Deirdre. "You retain power of veto, however, whether or not you choose to exercise it."

"When you say 'bank,'" Adele said, "you mean the Shippers' and Merchants' Treasury, do you not? Your bank."

"I'm an officer of the Shippers' and Merchants', yes," Deirdre said with a cool smile. "In the present case, however, I was acting solely as your agent when I dealt with the president and majority shareholder."

"That would be Corder Leary," Adele said. She hadn't thought to look up the bank's ownership, but realistically she had no need to do so. "Your father."

"Yes," said Deirdre. "It would."

Men were coming down the street. One of them bawled out

the house numbers as they passed in a voice better suited to calling cattle home.

"The bank's use of the premises will be infrequent," Deirdre said. "I understand they've employed a blind agent to sublet their portion to a young naval officer who needs rooms while he's in Xenos. Most of the time he'll be away on naval business. RCN business, I believe you'd call it?"

"Yes," said Adele. "That's what we call it. And if I'm not mistaken, Deirdre, here comes that young naval officer right now."

She turned to look down the street.

"Why look, Hogg!" cried Daniel Leary. "There's Adele! What are you doing here, Adele? And by heaven, isn't that my sister Deirdre?"